THE HUMAN LEGION
FREEDOM CAN BE WON

RENEGADE LEGION

Also by Tim C. Taylor
Marine Cadet (The Human Legion Book 1)
Indigo Squad (The Human Legion Book 2)
Renegade Legion (The Human Legion Book 3)
Human Empire (The Human Legion Book 4)
War Against the White Knights (The Human Legion Book 5)
The Battle of Earth Part1: Endgame (The Human Legion Book 6)
The Battle of Earth Part2: Restart (The Human Legion Book 7)
After War (Revenge Squad prequel)
Hurt U Back (Revenge Squad Book 1)
Second Strike (Revenge Squad Book 2)
The Midnight Sun (A Four Horsemen Universe novel)
The Reality War #1: The Slough of Despond
The Reality War #2: The City of Destruction

Writing as Crustias Scattermush (YA science-fantasy)
Treasure of the Last Dragon
The Ultimate Green Energy

Also in the Human Legion Universe by JR Handley
The Demons of Kor-Lir (Sleeping Legion prequel novella)
The Legion Awakes (Sleeping Legion book1)
Fortress Beta City (Sleeping Legion book2)
Operation Breakout (Sleeping Legion book3)
Insurgency: Spartika (Sleeping Legion book4)

though
THE HUMAN LEGION
«« FREEDOM CAN BE WON »»

RENEGADE LEGION
TIM C. TAYLOR

Human Legion Annals
—Book 3—

HumanLegion.com

Renegade Legion

Copyright © Tim C. Taylor 2015
Cover art by Vincent Sammy

Published by Human Legion Publications
All Rights Reserved

HumanLegion.com

ISBN: 978-1512006711
Also available in
eBook and audiobook editions.

The author wishes to thank all those who work-shopped, proof read, or otherwise supported the making of this book. In particular, Paul Melhuish for allowing me to raid his vault of filthy Skyfirean vernacular, the Northampton Science Fiction Writers Group, Cristina Macía for generously loaning her linguistic skills, Midland Road Costa Coffee, The Bromham Swan, Bedford Central Library, my wonderful supporters on humanlegion.com, and Ian Watson for persuading me to turn a short story into a bestselling book series.

Recon Team

I wish to thank my Recon Team for this book, who bravely scouted out my first draft, searching for hazards. This book is much better for their generous assistance.
— *Tim C. Taylor*

Bob Atkinson
Bryan Andrews
Robin Barayuga
Gints Baumanis
Simon Beale
Connor Benson
Dave Boxmeyer
Chris Browne
Melissa Bryan
Bernard Chia
Matt Dungan
Kim Golden
Cliff Gray
Karume T. Hickman

Paul Jape
David Lambert
Gareth Leadbetter
Andrew MacElhinney
Mr. Michael McPherson
(Sergeant, USA)
Larry Payton
Maribeth Pragid
Rob Robertson
Edward Rydbeck
Mike Stanfield
Ray Steele
Gordon Taylor
Jonathan Tuck

—— Preface ——

This, the third book in the Annals of the Human Legion, begins with the legion's First Tranquility Campaign and captures the legion's difficult transition from a handful of stragglers to being on the cusp of creating an interstellar power.

The account has been written in such a way that readers do not require detailed knowledge of events preceding the First Tranquility Campaign. For those unfamiliar with earlier events, or wishing a refresher, a brief summary has been provided on page 362.

—— Order of Battle ——

HUMAN LEGION Expeditionary Force

Initial order of battle on the eve of the First Tranquility Campaign 2568AD

FORCE PATAGONIA (Maj. Arun McEwan, Snr. Sgt. Suresh Gupta)

COMMAND SECTION:
Major Arun McEwan
Senior Sergeant Suresh Gupta
Cpl. Puja Narciso [Senior Scout]

HEAVY WEAPONS SECTION
LCpl. Stok Laskosk (*Stopcock*) [missile launcher specialist]
Marine Jerry Chung [GX-cannon specialist]
Marine Christanne Cusato [GX Assistant]

1st SECTION: (LSgt. Hecht)
~~ Alpha Fire Team ~~
LSgt. Menes Hecht
Marine Laban Caccamo
Marine Marcus Ballantyne
Marine Kamaria Monroe

~~ Beta Fire Team ~~
LCpl Rozalia Naron
Marine Rahul Bojin (*Bodger*)
Marine Alex Stafford
Marine Norah Lewark

2nd SECTION: (Cpl Kalis)
~~ Alpha Fire Team ~~
Cpl. Ferrant Kalis
Marine Serge Rhenolotte (*Zug*)
Marine Umarov
Marine Phaedra Tremayne (*Springer*)

~~ Beta Fire Team ~~
LCpl. Mikella Yoshioka
Marine Cheikh Okoro
Marine Xalvadora Schimschak
Marine Johannes Binning

FORCE KENYA (Lt. Tirunesh Nhlappo, Sgt. Estella Majanita)

3rd SECTION: (LSgt Shirazi)
~~ Alpha Fire Team ~~
LSgt. Bahadur Shirazi
Marine Vilok Altstein [Fermi Cannon specialist]
Marine Azinza Sadri [Fermi Cannon assistant]
Marine David Ho [missile launcher specialist]
Marine Kolenja Abramovski [sniper]

~~ Beta Fire Team~~
LCpl. Martin Sandhu (*Sandy*)
Marine Angelynn McCoy
Marine Erline Starn
Marine Swami Okafor (*Pud*)

4th SECTION: (Cpl Sesay)
~~ Alpha Fire Team ~~
Cpl. Mbizi Sesay (*Bizzy*)
Marine Alandra Bettencourt
Marine Agelaus Dada
Marine Xihuitl Norbert

~~ Beta Fire Team ~~
LCpl. Del-Marie Sandure
Marine Shehariah Conteh
Marine Najah Jeretzki
Marine Jaidyn Hopper

FORCE MEXICO (2Lt. Edward Brandt, Sgt. Bernard Exelmans)

5th SECTION: (Cpl Khurana)
~~ Alpha Fire Team ~~
Cpl. Uma Khurana
Marine Adeline Feria
Marine Halici
Marine Mark Forbes

~~ Beta Fire Team ~~
LCpl. Bilal Owusu
Marine Zakiya Dia
Marine Kuan-Yin Chou
Marine Slayman Feg

6th SECTION: (Cpl DeBenedetto)
~~ Alpha Fire Team ~~
Cpl. Serefina DeBenedetto
Marine Kantrowicz (*Three Blades*)
Marine Zane
Marine Tedman Ottaviani (*Teddy*)

~~ Beta Fire Team ~~
LCpl. Adebayo Toure
Marine Calina Atwal
Marine Lele Congo
Marine Sabir Eisele (*Slingshot*)

***Beowulf* Marine Reserve- (2Lt. Lee, Cpl. Zack Cockburn)**
ZERO SECTION
2nd Lieutenant Xin Lee + 10 effectives + 2 not fit for duty, recovering from injuries.

PART I

Fifty-nine to Take a Planet

Chapter 01

From his position on the steep slopes of the Gjende Mountains, a concealed figure trained his visor's real-sight display onto the murky valley floor far below. The low-light enhanced image gave 2nd Lieutenant Brandt a view of innumerable craters filled with the rubble and fused ceramalloy that had once been Detroit's topside.

A little more than a year earlier, this Marine Corps base had been the lieutenant's home.

He didn't care about that right now. The wreckage made for good cover. That's what concerned him.

But of the enemy, he saw nothing.

"It's time," said Brandt over the Force Mexico BattleNet. "Sergeant, pull five Marines from flank and rearguard to reinforce the team covering Gates 3 and 5."

"Yes, sir," replied Sergeant Bernard Exelmans in what the NCO insisted was an authentic French accent.

Brandt had to fight to keep his mouth clamped shut. He felt a powerful need to explain to Exelmans his decision to weaken his flank and rear guards. Out of a total of only 59 Marines to retake the entire planet, Brandt commanded the 18 of Force Mexico. With so few they had to take big risks. That's why he'd denuded his guards, but this was no time to be explaining himself. That would be weakness.

"Force Mexico, report!" demanded the CO over Wide BattleNet.

"In position, Major," replied Brandt. "Awaiting your go order."

———

From the opposite mountainside, Lieutenant Tirunesh Nhlappo zoomed her display onto the major who was taking cover in one of the few remaining walkways still standing in Jotunville.

Before the civil war had erupted over Tranquility's surface, the transparent walkway had provided a vertigo-inducing connection between two Jotun palaces. Those palaces were now fused slag, yet the walkway remained defiantly aloof from the destruction all around.

Unlike the kids who were running this show, the lieutenant had seen many settlements after a bombardment, and had grown used to the vista of a few isolated structures still upright amid a sea of destruction. Inexperienced dreamers might see that last walkway as symbolic of hope, but she saw it for what it truly was: a dangerously exposed position. You'd have to be dumb to use it as an observation post, and doubly stupid for the CO to do so. She creased her brow. The idiot boy was trying to lead from the front because he hadn't the balls to tell someone else to take risks for him.

But the major possessed luck, and Nhlappo had seen enough action to believe in lucky officers, even ones as ignorant as Major Arun McEwan.

A single enhanced squad to take a planet? The numbers said they hadn't a hope in hell. In the entire galaxy, Nhlappo couldn't think of anyone other than McEwan who could prove that calculation wrong.

The major's voice came over WBNet. "Force Kenya, status?"

Nhlappo looked across to her senior NCO, who was stationed in the cover of a rocky outcropping.

Sergeant Majanita was alert enough to notice the scrutiny. She gave a nod before scanning her position. The gossamer thin screen of Marines covering flanks and rear was in place and reporting all approaches clear. Nhlappo had high hopes for Majanita.

Majanita gave a thumbs-up.

"We're ready, Major," said Nhlappo.

―――

Major McEwan caught the disapproval in Lieutenant Nhlappo's voice. He knew why. The former chief instructor wanted Arun to keep back, but Arun justified being in such a forward position by virtue of needing to respond to events as they unfolded.

Every time he told himself that, he believed it a little less.

"Send in the recon, Sergeant," he told Gupta.

Arun's former squad commander relayed his instructions to Hecht and Caccamo, the drone operators, before acknowledging: "Drones away."

Inside the major's stomach it felt as if an army of miniature Trogs was on the march. His nervousness wasn't deserved, he told himself, because his first command was going surprisingly well.

Beowulf was safely hidden in the Kuiper Belt. They'd scouted the system without revealing themselves (as far as they could tell), and today they'd secured a position near Detroit unopposed.

Frankly, it had gone too well. He couldn't believe this luck would hold.

No one spoke. Probably the other 58 souls in the expeditionary force felt the same way.

He was an officer now, he told himself. The Marines looked to him for leadership. Which meant their motivation and morale were now part of his role description.

"Today we begin to retake what was ours," he broadcast. "We do so not in the name of the Human Marine Corps but of the Human Legion. Today some of us will likely die. For the first time in centuries, we fight and die in the name of humanity."

Arun's speech was greeted by silence.

But only for a few heartbeats before a response came loud and clear.

"*Oorah!*" yelled many.

"For the Legion!" was one of the other cries.

A smile came to Arun's lips. *Guess we'll have to work on our battle cries.*

The words varied but the spirit behind them came in unison, injecting Arun with an intoxicating jolt of confidence, but only for a few seconds. Soon he was wincing as he listened to the faint whirr of the recon drones skimming along the cratered ruins of Jotunville. If he weren't inside his suit, with his AI, Barney, selectively amplifying the sound of the drones, he doubted he would be able to hear them.

But he could. And if he could, so too might the enemy.

Barney split the incoming feed from the two drones stacking one above the other on Arun's visor. Jotunville and the entrance to Detroit were deeply shadowed, being on the valley floor between the towering Gjende Mountains. Barney used infrared and false-color to make sense of the gloomy scene witnessed by the drone sensors.

In the years he'd spent here before boarding *Beowulf*, Arun experienced only brief moments when the sun penetrated to the valley floor, illuminating the transparent building material of Jotunville like brilliant jewels. But even in the semi-darkness of the day, Jotunville had possessed a functional charm, an *efficiency*, which had appealed to what he supposed was the Marine aesthetic: a sense of order and precision.

Now the crystal walkways were shattered, taking on the color of burned sugar as the transparent material had fused. Rubble spilled into craters part-filled with liquid that Barney had false-colored a poisonous yellow.

As the drones crossed the ambiguous boundary between Jotunville, where the officers had lived, and on into Detroit, the craters grew in number and depth, the wreckage looked more scorched, poly-ceramalloy melted and contorted into new shapes.

Even from here, Barney was relaying the noise of the drone motors.

Arun silently cursed the White Knights. He'd been told many times that the Human Marine Corps was a joke, given third-rate equipment. Navy vessels such as *Beowulf* were described as 'cardboard ships', designed to register a sensor blip on enemy sensors but not seriously to fight.

Never having worked with better equipment, most of the time it was easy to dismiss such talk as a manifestation of a human inferiority complex. But every now and then the stark truth of their lousy equipment quality would smack you in the face. In his Marine battlesuit, Arun could activate stealth mode, though not for long in the strong gravity field of a planet. The technology was so effective that sophisticated enemy targeting systems wouldn't know he was there.

So why were the recon drones so noisy that he could hear them half a klick away?

Stealth-capable recon drones had to exist somewhere in the White Knight Equipment inventory. It was as if the Tactical-Marine regiments on Tranquility had been equipped with unwanted leftovers discovered at the back of a dusty store cupboard.

If the Human Legion was to survive and prosper, Arun would make sourcing better equipment a priority.

The augmented freaks amongst the ship crew were geniuses. Maybe they could develop the tech that would give them an edge?

"Approaching Gate 3 in twenty seconds," reported Hecht. "No sign of opposition."

Hecht's drone slowed before dropping down into a crater for cover. Caccamo's started sweeping around Gate 3, finding no opposition. The images didn't show much of Gate 3 either. It wasn't just blasted, scorched, and melted: there wasn't enough debris, as if the great redoubt of Gate 3 had been vaporized.

Arun tried not to imagine what kind of weapon was capable of such destruction.

Caccamo's sweep completed without more surprises.

"Take the drones inside," Arun ordered. "Let's see who's home."

Chapter 02

Lance Sergeant Hecht lifted his drone out of the crater and pushed it on through the dark hole of the Gate 3 entrance, and down into the underground city of Detroit. Caccamo's drone followed twenty meters behind.

In the almost complete absence of light, the images flickered as Barney and the drone AIs struggled to interpolate the scene from the limited sensor readings mixed with their records of Detroit's layout.

Detroit's upper levels housed its main static defenses: confusing zigzags studded with heavy weapon hardpoints, hidden embrasures, sally ports, and a dozen hidden conduits of death. Jagged holes ripped through the defenses told a tale of heavy fighting here.

But that was history. For the sake of his command, Arun reminded himself that he could only afford to think of the future.

"Movement ahead," said Caccamo. Arun could see the drone AI mark an embrasure ahead in warning orange.

The embrasure was an armored bastion with two triangular protrusions pushed out into the passageway. Barney couldn't locate the hidden weapons ports, but they would be there, giving perfect arcs of fire through narrow gaps – a technology essentially unchanged since the arrow slits of ancient Earth castles.

The embrasure was just one outlet of death in a larger structure: a redoubt. "Circling around," reported Hecht who released his drone to AI control, racing past the embrasure to seek the rear entrance to the redoubt.

Caccamo withdrew his drone back up the corridor, away from the defensive position.

Maybe Arun consulted Barney about the embrasure, or the AI informed the human inside his suit — the link between them was so intimate it was difficult to tell. Either way, Arun's head took in the knowledge that there was a reinforced security hatch at the rear of the embrasure. Locking yourself in also cut off your escape. There were protocols for when to shut the hatch but either option could suit Arun. If shut, then it would be easier to listen in on whoever was inside.

The feed from Caccamo's drone suddenly went wild, showing a confused blur that defeated Barney's attempts to interpret.

"Enemy missile lock," said Caccamo.

An instant later, the feed from his drone disappeared.

Damned Hardits.

With half his visor display reduced to white snow, Arun suddenly felt vulnerable. He switched back to normal sight and looked around for threats, taking another slap of disorientation as he snapped his focus from Detroit's underground passageways back to the walkway in Jotunville.

Arun glanced over at Corporal Puja Narciso, who was studying Gate 3 and the rest of Detroit's surrounding area. She was using an advanced scouting sensor tool they had discovered in the battalion's supply of war materiel they'd searched through on *Beowulf*.

Arun cursed himself for checking on Puja. He needed to trust his NCOs. If the Hardits made a move topside, she would tell him.

"Nearing rear hatch," said Hecht over BattleNet.

Arun hurriedly snapped his visor back to the feed from Hecht's drone. He could make no sense of the blur.

"Hatch is open," reported Hecht.

The feed showed color outlines of defenders.

"Five hostiles," said Hecht. "Drone on kill mode. Drone… drone retreating."

Hecht's drone feed whited out.

"Drone destroyed."

"I can see that, Hecht," said Arun. "Why?"

"My battlesuit AI overrode my kill instruction to the drone," Hecht reported. "It reclassified hostiles as unknowns, sir. Targets were human."

Who would be skulking around Detroit's corpse? Arun wondered. *Survivors or traitors? Or even the mysterious Amilx they'd discovered in deep space?*

"Were they armored?" asked Arun.

"Negative."

Nhlappo pinged him on the FTL comm. "Request update, sir. We detected weapons fire."

"We've encountered human resistance," said Arun.

"Can we negotiate with them?" she asked.

"Unlikely," said Arun. "They aren't in the mood for talking."

"There must be a way to communicate."

"Maybe there is," said Arun. "Until I know better, I'm classifying them as potential allies. I don't want to shout at them. The Hardits will hear."

Arun considered the Legion's move. Ordering a withdrawal felt much harder than committing to an attack. But he had to exploit his advantage: knowing the area above and below ground better than anyone else, thanks to detailed maps once provided by an alien ally called Pedro. A Trog who had compiled every detail of the nest and handed them over to Arun.

"All units move out to Rendezvous Point Gamma," he ordered. "We're going to sneak in via the back door."

Chapter 03

When he was a cadet, none of Arun's peers knew of the nest entrances to the south east, and fewer that the Troggie nest connected to the lowest human levels of Detroit. The Jotuns must have known, but did the humans they'd encountered defending the embrasure near Gate 3?

He set Brandt's Force Mexico to defend the entrance and united Nhlappo's Force Kenya with his Force Patagonia into a single force that would push through the nest and into Detroit via the connecting passage at Level 9.

The alien nest was an even more confusing maze than the upper levels of Detroit. The tunnels twisted back, crossing underneath and over themselves. The Marines pushed on, relying on the FTL link to keep contact with Brandt, and using Local Battle Net to keep flank guards in touch with the main body at all times.

Spinning out flank and rear guards and reeling them back in again wasn't simple in this maze, but Arun trusted his NCOs to handle the details, and they earned his trust by making it almost look easy.

LBNet was secure from being overheard, but the Legion pressed on in grim silence anyway. Rotting carcasses of the Troggie inhabitants filled the tunnels. Some were still locked in combat after death, their halo of horns snagged on their rivals. Stubby energy weapons and the searing blast wounds they caused were further evidence that the insect-like aliens had suffered their own civil war. Mostly there was just death, as if the denizens of the colony had simply given up and laid down to die.

Trogs had several different stages in their lifecycle, metamorphosing from one to another, the destination life stage depending on how well they had performed in the previous one. All stages took the form of six-legged creatures between five and nine feet long, with a head, thorax, and abdomen that looked deceptively like Earthly insects. The hardened abdominal carapaces of the dead Trogs still gleamed like the polished armor it was.

Some of the other hard parts, such as mouth pincers and skull armor were well preserved too. The softer flesh inside, though, was in an advanced state of decomposition. Arun was grateful for his suit's filters. The stench of death outside of his helmet must be overpowering.

The first sign of life was reported by stealthed Marine scouts from 3rd Section who had pushed ahead. It seemed the secret link from the nest through to the human underground city was no longer so secret.

"There's three of them," reported Sergeant Majanita. "All human. Two with SA-71 carbines, one with a flenser cannon. They're behind a dirt rampart."

"Doesn't sound like rebel Marines," said Nhlappo.

"Perhaps not," said Arun. "But they could be collaborating with the Hardits."

Arun hesitated, and then immediately felt disgusted with himself because he felt compelled to run through his options once more, even though he'd already made his decision.

Even if they had stripped *Beowulf* of every Marine, the Human Legion could only field 64 effectives in a gravity well. That wasn't enough. Arun's course here was risky, but there were no risk-free options, and what they needed more than anything were allies.

Acting like a hero was comparatively easy. Arun found it far harder to ask his Marine brothers and sisters to be heroes while he waited behind in relative safety.

No one had said this would be a breeze.

"Hecht, here's what I want 1st Section to do. Capture that position and all three unidentified humans without firing a shot."

"What if they fire back?"

"I want all of them back here unharmed, Lance Sergeant. Can you accomplish that?"

"Yes, sir." There had been just a hint of hesitation before Hecht's reply.

After a brief consultation with Senior Sergeant Gupta, Hecht issued his orders to 1st Section, and a few moments later he set off, taking seven Marines with him out of sight around the tunnel bend.

Arun counted them all out.

He couldn't help wondering how many he would count back in.

Chapter 04

Arun was gambling that Hecht's team would display cool courage and discipline under the enemy's guns, two qualities conspicuously absent from Arun. He wanted to be in front, taking the position with Hecht, not stuck back in safety hundreds of meters away. His nerves were so shredded that if he'd taken off his helmet, he would have chewed off the tips of his gauntlets, their poly-ceramalloy armor no proof against his nerves.

He needn't have worried.

After the action, Hecht reported how he'd led 1st Section's Alpha Fire Team – Caccamo, Ballantyne, and Monroe – off toward the enemy's crude earthen rampart. They left their carbines and equipment packs behind, and crawled inch by silent inch on their hands and knees. Their suits were in stealth mode, but against alert sentries that wasn't a reliable cover for boots scraping, knees scuffing furrows through the dirt, vibrations felt through the tunnel walls, and countless other subtle telltales.

When Alpha was in position, Hecht signaled Beta Fire Team – Naron, Bojin, Halici, and Lewark – to make some noise around the last turn in the corridor.

It was enough for the defenders to train their weapons and their full attention on this unseen threat in the distance.

The Alpha Marines seized their chance, leaping up to grab the enemy's barrels before slamming their bodies into the dirt. The opposition never saw it coming. Only two got off shots, and they both flew harmlessly into the ceiling.

It occurred to Arun that this was the Human Legion's first combat action. 1st Section had done them proud.

And now it was his turn to be tested. In this campaign, taking prisoners could only ever be a temporary arrangement. Arun knew he would soon have to either recruit these unidentified perimeter guards as allies, or execute them as traitors.

He wasn't sure he could do either. But this was war. He had no choice.

Chapter 05

"What is your name?" barked Sergeant Gupta. "Time is short. This is your final chance."

In the sharp illumination thrown by Gupta's helmet lamps, Arun could clearly see the captive's face.

If that was Arun kneeling there in a dark Troggie cave, blinded by the lamps, he would be flinching under the assault of the sergeant's snarling.

The prisoner's arms were pinned behind her by Madge, who gave a vicious twist and shake that must have wrenched at her shoulder sockets. But still… she said nothing.

"We need to move things along, sir," said Lieutenant Nhlappo over LBNet "if they won't talk, all you're doing is surrendering initiative to whomever we are facing. I can't get anything out of my prisoner either."

The lieutenant entered the cave, a blue ghost in Arun's low-light vision.

Arun hated it when Nhlappo was right. He wasn't ready to kill the captives, though. They could be potential allies… Even recruits. Or they could be fighting for the Hardits. What he needed was a way to force them to talk without torturing them so vilely that he made them his implacable foe.

Suddenly Nhlappo's helmet flared. Arun blinked, and then saw that she'd made her helmet visor transparent and activated the light inside.

Arun flicked his attention back to the captive.

Yes… The sight of Nhlappo's face had dented the woman's resolve.

"You won't force anything out of this one," said Nhlappo. "Her name is Annalee Vanderman. Age…? She'll be 18 now, thereabouts. Very intelligent, loyal, and utterly fearless. Just one problem. Lacks the killer instinct. When it came to battle, I never trusted her to pull the trigger. And that made Vanderman a liability."

"So you kicked me out of novice school," sneered Vanderman.

"I had no choice."

"You were wrong."

Vanderman's words hung heavily over the dark cave. War had visited Detroit, leaving it a twisted wreck where the living were far outnumbered by ghosts. Vanderman sounded as if she belonged more to the dead than the living.

What had transpired here? What horrors had those resentful eyes witnessed?

"Let her go, Sergeant," said Arun.

When Madge obeyed, Vanderman eased her arms round to a more comfortable position in front of her.

Frakk! Her hand… In the rush to bundle the prisoners into separate chambers for interrogation, Arun hadn't taken a good look at any of them.

"What happened to you, Vanderman?" asked Nhlappo.

Vanderman raised her left arm. It terminated just behind the wrist, capped by a crude prosthetic that wasn't shaped like a hand. It was an angled claw, a rest designed for gripping the barrel of an SA–71 carbine.

Vanderman shrugged. "A traitor Marine shot it off. It was a fair exchange. I shot him dead. So you see, Chief Instructor Nhlappo, you were wrong about me. Do I get an apology?"

"No. I stand by my decision. It was right given the facts as I knew them. But I am glad to be wrong. It means you will make a more useful recruit."

"Recruit? Recruit for what?"

"Who are we?" mused Nhlappo out loud. "I'll leave explanations to the major. Sir?"

Arun bristled. Was that a hint of contempt poisoning Nhlappo's voice, or was that Arun's imagination?

"We are the Human Legion," Arun explained.

Vanderman didn't even bother to look his way.

Arun tried again. "The White Knight Empire is split by civil war. Legal authority is unclear. That doesn't make us legally free people, but we do reject the authority of any White Knight faction currently claiming to own us. Not until the civil war is over, and there is a clear legal authority with undisputed claim to all assets and responsibilities of the White Knight Empire. Not until then will we accept authority over us. And that's vital. So long as we don't claim to be free, we aren't breaking Earth's Accession Treaty to the Trans-Species Union. If we're ever to do that, we need to have established our own empire first."

Arun paused waiting for a reaction from anyone present in the room. He didn't get one.

Ever since that heady day when he'd declared the creation of the Human Legion, they had been short on details of what to do after recapturing Tranquility. Most of the men and women of the Legion didn't expect there to *be* an after, but Arun did. He'd tried out this speech, but only in private with Springer, Indiya, and Gupta.

Arun continued. "The civil war could last for centuries. Join with us. Help us carve out a better future for our people and our descendants."

Vanderman looked at him with indifference.

"The traitors called themselves the Free Corps," she said. "They promised the Marines a better future too. Not for me, of course, thanks to your officer Nhlappo, I was a mere servant in a hab-disk. The Free Corps' promises were plausible – enough to convince Marines to become traitors. But you're different. There is nothing plausible about your promises. Seems to me like you're offering only hardship and death. And hope. Maybe you offer hope for those who seek it?"

She rose to her feet and turned to Lieutenant Nhlappo. "I want to hear the words from you, Chief Instructor. The Human Legion… Is it real?"

"It's real, Vanderman."

"And should I pledge my allegiance to this Legion? Put my hope into this man's vision?"

"I can't answer for you, Annalee. You must decide for yourself."

Vanderman laughed. "You haven't decided yourself, yet, have you? Still, I don't believe you are Free Corps spies. Let me speak with the other two you captured with me."

Chapter 06

As he waited in the Troggie tunnel outside while the captives talked amongst themselves, Arun checked the status of his subordinates. Sergeant Gupta had organized the defense of the tunnels, setting up monitoring posts to warn against attack from Detroit's lower levels. Lieutenant Brandt and Sergeant Exelmans had established a rearguard near the hidden woodland entrance to the tunnels and reported no activity from the enemy.

Arun felt itchy. Nervy. He wanted to be doing something more active, but winning the trust of the survivors of the attack on Detroit was vital to boost the tiny numbers of his force, which was why he had ordered everyone out of the cave where the three prisoners discussed what they should do.

Of course, the prisoners' privacy was an illusion. Gupta and Nhlappo were using their suit AIs to listen in on every word they said. The pretense of privacy was a courtesy, no more, but important for all that.

Arun distracted himself by using the FTL link to update Indiya who was keeping *Beowulf* hidden in an ice-ball cluster in the outer system.

Indiya gave a brief report in a voice curt with tightness.

"What's eating you?" Arun asked.

"Nothing."

"You sounded belligerent."

Indiya hesitated before replying. "2nd Lieutenant Lee… She's…"

When Indiya's words tailed off, Arun tried hurrying her along. "Let me guess. She's acting like she's in charge, badmouthing everyone who disagrees with her, and probably flirting with your best friends, which is the most annoying crime of all because the spineless vecks are powerless to resist her."

"I guess you know Xin Lee."

A smile flicked across Arun's face. Indiya had been cold and withdrawn since she'd killed hundreds at the press of a button during the mutiny. This was the loosest, most human, he'd heard her since that day. "Do I know Lieutenant Lee? Yes, ma'am, I do. And that's why I put her in command of the remaining Marines on *Beowulf*. If our force on the planet is captured or killed, Xin's the best bet you have for keeping your ship safe from anyone trying to board. And to show a little muscle if you ever dock at far-off platforms."

"She's got eleven Marines, two are seriously wounded and another two sided with the rebels. Her influence is growing every day. I don't trust her."

"But I do. We've been over this. She won't go against my wishes, nor will she take *Beowulf* and leave without me, because she knows her fate is entwined with mine."

There was silence from the ship for several seconds before Indiya stated: "You're not my commander, Major McEwan."

Yes, he was… but he decided now was not the time to press that point. "I am your ally and your friend," he said. "You need to trust me on this."

"Forcing Xin on me over my protests. That isn't a great way to win my trust, Arun."

Barney indicated that Nhlappo was trying to open a private comm channel.

"We'll have to discuss this later, Indiya. Nhlappo is trying to tell me something."

He told Barney to switch channels. "They've agreed to side with us," said Nhlappo. "Now they're discussing how to make use of our firepower while keeping operational control for themselves."

"I'm in control here," snapped Arun.

He stormed into the prisoners' cavern.

"The limits of my courtesy have expired," Arun said. "Let me remind you that we are at war, and on this planet we face a numerically superior enemy. I need to speak with your commander immediately."

The two female prisoners looked at each other: Vanderman and a petite Marine of pale skin, and curiously rust-colored hair, that Arun suspected was a marine of Umarov's vintage – a marine stored cryogenically for the best part of a century before thawing.

There was a male too. A little older. A quizzical look came on this man's face as he peered at Arun.

"One thing first," this man said. "What's your first name?"

"Arun. I'm Arun McEwan."

"Thought so. Take me with you. I will contact the command post."

"What are you doing?" asked the red-head.

"This is Arun McEwan. The same Aux guy who ran rings around the Hardits in Operation Clubhouse… am I right?"

Arun nodded.

"See? He's beaten the Hardits before. If anyone can do it again, it's him. Spartika will want to meet him.

"Come on, follow me," he said to Arun, who had to race to keep up with him. "I'll brief you on the way."

The prisoner said his name was Joel Deacon, and either he was a convincing liar, or he really did tell Arun everything he knew.

Joel Deacon was 22 but looked much older due to the scarring suffered in his role carrying out the dirtiest and most toxic tasks going in the maintenance of Detroit's shuttle port. This aircraft hangar was built into a mountainside connected to Level 7, and screened by a natural waterfall. Deacon explained that he'd failed the final year of novice school and never made it to cadet.

He identified the vintage Marine as Sushala Kraevoi, aged either 19 or 102, depending on how you counted the years she had spent in ice.

They were part of a small force of Resistance fighters based in the ruins of Detroit under a leader called Spartika. Deacon claimed forty survivors were currently in Detroit with around ten outside on active duty, freeing recruits from slave farms, ambushing Hardit patrols, or making hit-and-run raids on vulnerable targets.

Fifty survivors. And they had described themselves as the Resistance. It wasn't many, but it would make a good start for Day#1 of the reconquest.

Chapter 07

When Arun and Deacon reached the perimeter post where Hecht's section had overcome the three survivors, Deacon ushered Gupta to one side and pulled out a box attached to a wire that disappeared into the floor.

He tapped out a rhythm with his finger for about a minute before listening for a response. Arun could hear nothing, but Barney explained.

The survivors were communicating through Morse Code, the little box vibrating its response in Deacon's hand. Barney put a translation onto Arun's visor.

Arun couldn't help grinning. Judging by the long string of insults in the response, the person at the command post had an even bigger grudge against Nhlappo than Annalee Vanderman.

But the former chief instructor's notoriety appeared to be working in their favor. With a grin on his face, Deacon informed Arun that the Detroit survivor group had agreed to an alliance and they were to proceed to the command post without delay.

Arun followed Deacon, Kraevoi and Vanderman with hope in his heart. His trust, though, needed more than enthusiastic words of support to be won over. He quietly assigned two Marines to each prisoner, with orders to watch them closely.

He was trying to do this the nice way. But only to begin with.

Chapter 08

On the way to the resistance command post, Deacon cheerfully brought Arun up to date on events in Detroit during the civil war and the part he played. From time to time, Kraevoi would give a snort of derision and curtly correct her comrade's account.

Arun did nothing to intervene during the bickering, nor did he question Deacon when he told of events he couldn't possibly have witnessed. All Arun wanted for now was a summary of events, focusing on the strengths and weaknesses of potential opponents. The fine details could be collected, corrected, and refined later. If they lived that long.

Ever since they had been incorporated into the White Knight Empire five centuries ago, humans had taken the empire's unity for granted. No longer! A rebel faction of White Knights had launched a coup on their homeworld, but had failed to seize absolute control, plunging every world in the empire into civil war. Rebel influence ran deep into the military. Deacon even claimed the rebels had allied with the Muranyi, the enemy the Human Marine Corps had trained to fight in the Frontier War. Arun didn't care whether there was any truth to that rumor. Far more important was the very real alliance the rebel faction had made with the Hardits in the Tranquility system.

The Hardits had been happy enough to mine the system on behalf of their White Knight masters, until the military had established bases on what the Hardits had regarded as *their* planet of Tranquility. The military had been here for thousands of years now, but Hardit resentment at this invasion hadn't diminished with the passage of time. They laid plans to revenge themselves on the other species who had trespassed on their world.

Arun himself had uncovered a small part in the rebels' preparations when he had discovered a supply route for military equipment being shipped out to the Hardit base on the moon. Some of the Hardits had panicked, nearly revealing the extent of the rebel plans. But rebel voices in the military whispered that the Hardit revolt was an isolated incident. The matter was suppressed. The rebels waited for their moment…

Loyalist or rebel. Deacon laughed whenever he used either label. He had no interest in choosing a side in someone else's civil war. He hated the Hardits. That was more than enough for him.

On the day the civil war finally came to Tranquility, Deacon explained, death came to Detroit from above and below, but worst of all had been the enemy from within.

The rebels' first move had been to seize control of Tranquility's fleet of system defense boats, and of the two orbital elevators that were tethered to Tranquility's surface.

General Cabrakan, the commander of the Detroit base, had immediately ordered the emergency thawing of thousands of Marines. Beta City meanwhile, over in the other main continent of Serendine, had gone ominously quiet.

Under the influence of months of mind–altering drugs, the Beta City Marines had been in such a suggestive state that they didn't bat an eyelid at the initial bloodletting in which loyalist officers and NCOs were purged. They didn't question the orders to ride the orbital elevator and emerge in stealthed swarms until they reached sufficient number to attack all the orbital defense platforms simultaneously.

The Hardits and rebel Jotuns had colluded to hack Beta's many internal systems. Any units who did not follow the orders of the new so-called Free Corps units without question were lured into their hab-disks where they were locked in. The hab-disks were designed to be self-sufficient, allowing the inhabitants to survive for years before emerging. But, as Kraevoi pointed out, if the Hardit techs had hacked the base, they could also fry the systems inside the hab-disks, turning them from giant survival pods into waterless, airless death traps.

Up in orbit, the defense platforms remained loyal to the old order. The rebels anticipated that these isolated, and in many cases automated, platforms would respond only to force, which is why they moved their Free Corps Marine units into orbit as soon as they could.

But the defense platforms saw the humans coming, and were not fooled by rebel assurances that they were all on the same side.

Raked by case munitions, Fermi cannons and railguns, not even the stealth function of their battlesuits was enough to protect the Free Corps Marines of Beta City. The platforms extracted a fearful toll of carnage on the traitor humans, but they were primarily designed to combat enemy war boats, and heavy objects cast into Tranquility's gravity well. To defend against close assault by enemy void troops, the orbital platforms were supposed to rely on the Human Marine Corps to throw up skirmish screens.

But those defenders had now become the attackers.

Very few of the Beta City Marines who ascended the orbital elevator that day descended it after the orbital defense shield had been eliminated.

But destroyed it was, and that meant the rebel fleet of war boats now took up station in orbit around Tranquility.

Detroit's fearsome defensive warren still held out, as did the continent-sized Troggie nest filled with fearless defenders from the barely sentient guardians with rending claws to specialist technician, leader and planner classes, and more.

For a day there was a tense stand-off as the Free Corps consolidated their gains, and the loyalists prepared for the coming fight.

The activity in Detroit was frantic. General Cabrakan had allowed this rebellion to go ahead, this stain on Jotun honor through the settled galaxy. Whether through incompetence or treachery was of no consequence to the regimental commanders who seized Cabrakan and his staff, summarily executing the lot.

The Jotuns were highly visible in organizing Detroit's defenses. Whether fine tuning the placement of heavy weapons in the redoubt embrasures, inspecting the backups in the water purification system, or a myriad hand-on tasks. The human defenders were astonished because there was now no sign of the Jotuns' well-known aversion to being underground.

Deacon guessed that the Jotuns had drugged themselves to overcome their phobia. Kraevoi speculated that their phobia had been a ruse, though to what purpose she had no idea.

Arun waved away their arguing as an irrelevance. In his experience, trying too hard to make sense of alien thinking was a mistake. Sometimes you just had to accept alien minds ran along different channels and move on.

Which is what the Jotun hierarchy did now in their strengthening of Detroit. Within minutes of executing Cabrakan, they appointed Colonel Little Scar as commander–in–chief.

The colonel arrested anyone suspected of insufficient loyalty, organized gangs to bring in food supplies from the city's hinterland, reorganized defenses, and secretly scattered trusted Marine teams to hide outside of the base from where they would organize units of resistance fighters to conduct guerrilla warfare behind the lines of any besieging troops.

It was one of those guerrilla groups who formed the core of the survivors holed up in Detroit.

The first of the resistance groups had scarcely left Detroit through secret underground passageways when the lull in the fighting broke.

In the confusion of the arrests, rebel Jotun officers had made their own secret escape from Detroit, and were now safely in orbit when they unleashed the twin plagues.

A tailored airborne virus was released by human traitors throughout the continent. To humans it was harmless, but to Jotuns, deadly. The Jotuns were encased in their battlesuits that should have kept them safe from biological attack, but the suits had long ago been sabotaged by the Hardits, leaving a weakness they could one day exploit. They had waited decades for this opportunity.

With the defenders' officers dead or dying, the rebels chose that moment to attack. Rebel human NCOs still inside Detroit ordered their units to fire on loyalist defenders. Planetary assault units bombarded Detroit's topside defenses, before launching a spearhead of assault Marines backed by immense armies of Hardit militia.

The Hardits' main forces were below ground. In another attack prepared for decades, they launched the second of the twin plagues. Artificial pheromone commands were pumped into the Troggie nest, signals that faithfully replicated the scent of the nest's Great Leader. Confused and stung to fury by the Hardits' false commands, the Trogs turned on each other, powerless to resist the Hardit underground assault battalions who drove through the continental–scale nest, exterminating their subterranean rivals and claiming their tunnels for their own.

While the fighting still raged deep within Detroit and through the Troggie nest, the rebel Jotun leaders in orbit began outdoing each other in claiming credit for the victory over FTL comm links to the rebels' high command.

Suddenly, loyalist AI-piloted drone fighters de-stealthed and swarmed through the orbiting rebel fleet.

The loyalist AIs would have succeeded if not for the Free Corps unit that had once been the 534th Void Marine Regiment, who had captured the moon of Antilles. The 534th raced back to Tranquility orbit where they engaged the loyalist assault. With the battlesuit AIs handling targeting and maneuvering, and the Free Corps Marines adding human unpredictability and cunning, it was a battle of Marine cyborgs versus system defense robots.

Human guile was not enough to compensate for the frail human form; the robots could accelerate at rates that would kill even hardened Marine physiques.

Again and again, the Void Marines tried to make their superior numbers count by breaking up the robot formations and surrounding isolated pockets. For a long time, the robots repulsed these attacks, inflicting terrible losses on the Marines.

But the robots took casualties themselves. In the end the Void Marines simply wore them down by attrition until they were isolated and easy to pick off one by one.

The Free Corps had control of the orbital battlefield once more, but it had been a close-run thing.

The rebel commander, General Banba, had achieved her mission objectives to capture the fleet and neutralize both Marine bases. Fearful of further loyalist surprises, Banba recalled all her forces from Tranquility, leaving to the Hardit militias the task of finishing off the few loyalist survivors.

Within days, the rebel fleet was headed out system to fight in their next engagement of the civil war, leaving a cloud of scuttled craft too damaged to survive an interstellar journey.

The Free Corps Marines had gone.

But many tens of thousands of humans remained, Aux workers in the mines and farms, survivors and resistance fighters who had fled the battles or been tasked to form resistance cells. All of them were unified in an abhorrence of the Hardits.

Humanity would not meekly yield to the Hardit slave yoke.

Survivors contacted each other throughout the continent of Baylshore. They even made contact for a while with a resistance group in the other continent, Serendine. The Human Resistance was born.

Propelled by the hope and hatred that burned so fiercely in their breasts, the Resistance recaptured Detroit and then began to take back and hold the surrounding territory.

Civil administration had only just gotten started under the leadership of the supreme Resistance commander, Spartika, when the Hardits finally stirred themselves to stamp out this challenge to their authority.

Humans everywhere were rounded up and held in fortified labor camps. Detroit was retaken by Hardit militia.

"But we found you in control of Detroit," interrupted Arun at this point in Deacon's narrative. "You must have rebuilt your combat strength enough to retake the city again."

Deacon shrugged. "I don't know about any *retaking*. The monkeys drifted away, and we sort of snuck back in."

"Welcome to the new Tranquility," taunted Kraevoi, a devil-may-care wildness in her gray eyes. "It is a world of shackled slaves and the last few stragglers of a failed resistance. Those you see before you are nothing more than diseased rats inhabiting the ruins of our city. Tell me, Major McEwan, are you so sure now that you were right to come back?"

"I'll tell you what I am sure about," he snapped. "You need new leadership. Someone with a vision of hope. This meeting with Spartika can't happen too soon."

Chapter 09

The Resistance command post was a squatters' camp in an operations room on Level 3. Arun was very familiar with the thick smell of old sweat that had assailed him the moment he entered — many times he'd spent days or weeks living in his own stink inside his battlesuit. But the suffocating reek of defeat that infected the command post made him gag.

He sat with the Resistance sub-leader at an unpowered tactical control desk. A noise made him glance behind. The sound was another Resistance fighter who had plonked her bare feet onto the control desk. She proceeded to rub at the thick callouses on her soles and heels. The woman was dressed in rags.

Arun was sure there were plenty of smartfabric fatigues available in Detroit that could self-clean and be programed to the cut and color of smart military garments. But there was no attempt to look smart here, and this worried Arun more than any other sign that the Resistance had lost their spirit. Their clothes were camouflaged by default in shades of old dirt, dried blood, and with a greasy sheen on collars and cuffs.

He turned back to Jennifer Boon, the Resistance officer he was trying to negotiate with. "Well?" he said, trying to keep the disdain from his voice. "Will you join with us or not? Deacon said you would."

Boon shrugged. "Just trying to keep everyone alive. Look, tag along if you like. You got no complaints from me. We keep going from inertia and I guess you'll give us a little impetus to keep going longer." She gave a bitter laugh. "Listen to me, spouting such fancy drent. What I really mean is that we stick together because we don't know what else to do. You come here with your head stuffed with dreams of glory, but that won't last. Not with your force strength. It isn't a matter of *us* joining *you*. Give it a few months, and if we're both of us still alive, you'll wake up one day and realize it is you who have joined us."

Arun was so angry he had to look away. He could see Gupta out in the passageway, the stony look on his face clear through his transparent visor. The veteran's contempt at this breakdown of discipline would be seething inside him.

The smell of cooking wafted in through the hatch, reminding Arun that it wasn't just the rest of his team who were outside the command post.

He tried once more to make Boon see sense. "What about Spartika? What would she say? Where is she anyway?"

Boon thought a moment. "I suppose when she gets back she'll work herself up some enthusiasm."

"And you can't? Get a grip of yourself, Boon. Are you a Resistance commander or not?"

"Listen, McEwan," she replied, anger driving out the lethargy in her voice. "The Resistance is finished. Spartika sees it differently, but she doesn't know when to stop, and she's not the kind of person you say no to."

"That's it!" Arun thumped his hand into the desk, making the foot-rubber behind him lose her balance and tip onto the floor. "I will *not* accept you giving up. You are the Human Resistance whether I have to force you to remember or not."

It was Boon's turn to slam the desk. She rose to her feet and clenched her fists. "You can take your sense of superiority and shove it up your ass. You swank in here with your shiny ACE-2 battlesuits and think we're scum. Let me tell you. Two years of war teaches you how to survive. We're not as defenseless as you think. Threaten me again and you will regret it."

Arun nodded, almost with respect. "Better. Now take me to Spartika."

"She's out raiding. Due back in six days. You'll have to see the Deputy Commander instead. That's Amadou McKenzie. He's out on patrol, checking our topside sensor network. He'll be back any minute."

Arun lost it! He grabbed Boon by the shoulders, fighting hard against the urge to crush the pathetic individual's bones under his powered gauntlets.

All around the room, he heard the sound of weapons powering up.

"This is war," Arun shouted loud enough for everyone to hear, "not a frakking tea party. I need to see this Spartika and you *will* take me to her. Now!"

Chapter 10

Even through the AI-doctored view Barney was feeding into his visor, Arun appreciated the beauty of the woodland clearing where dappled sunlight warmed the rich purple and lilac of the foliage. It was only thirty klicks out from Detroit, but Arun was astonished to learn such a restful vista had always existed so close to his home.

One day he would like to lie here without helmet, armor or Barney, and see the clearing through his own eyes. Instead, Barney spoiled the view by sketching humanoid outlines over nearby patches of grass and ferns, the shapes of prone Marines in their stealthed battlesuits. Just like Arun.

After the war he'd explore the woods in peace, but not this clearing, he decided. Because at its center stood a crude, blocky building with a single dark opening. It looked long disused, abandoned decades ago or more. But it wasn't. This was Spartika's patrol base.

Suddenly the woodland calm was shattered by a bird's hooting alarm call followed swiftly by the snapping of wings desperate to reach escape velocity. A moment later, the bird shot into the clear sky above the tree canopy.

On the far side of the clearing. *Where his scouts were.*

Frakk! Some of the Marines had claimed that Arun was becoming arrogant, overreaching. Maybe he should listen more. He believed in the idea of the Human Legion, but he sometimes forgot its personnel were still inexperienced. *Such as scouts that gave themselves away.*

As Barney was taking Arun's carbine off safety mode, Arun lifted the barrel to track an incoming aerial drone which was swooping at high speed just above the treetops. Barney magnified Arun's vision of the target and framed it in white, indicating a non-hostile.

Arun laughed. *Not hostile to him.* It was a false alarm. What he'd feared was a combat drone was in fact a guinshrike, a saber-fanged monster of the skies with a wingspan over a meter long. The guinshrike slammed into the fleeing bird, holding it firm in its talons as it flew off a short distance before disappearing into the trees.

Before the civil war, Arun had befriended a huge insect-like Trog who'd told him the White Knights had first been interested in breeding humans for war because they'd seen the natural human instinct for violence. Even if there was any truth to that, Arun considered the guinshrike to be much more of a natural killer. It was said that the guinshrike expended such energy in each swoop that if it failed to make the kill, it had no reserves to try again. Kill or die every time you ate. What a life!

"Area is clear of hostiles," reported Gupta. "We detect no surveillance devices. Our defensive perimeter is in place."

"Thank you, Sergeant." Arun changed his suit from stealth mode to camouflaged. He still looked like a patch of purple woodland ground cover, but without the advanced full-spectrum effect — and the unsustainable power drain — of stealth mode. To his right, the Resistance leader, Boon, lay in the undergrowth, doing her best to hide despite being the only one in the group without a battlesuit. Arun tapped Boon on her shoulder and gave her a thumbs-up.

Boon nodded and got to her feet.

Arun winced. He admired her bravery in presenting such an inviting target. In fact, once removed from the festering squatters' camp that Detroit had become, he was raising his assessment of Jennifer Boon. True, there was a defiant sloppiness about her, but with a little motivation, she nonetheless radiated the aura of someone who got the job done.

The Resistance fighter was wearing long-sleeved fatigues and a peaked kepi in olive green. Her clothing helped to shield her from the dangerous rays of the sun, but against the backdrop of purple foliage, did nothing to shield her from prying eyes.

Boon advanced several paces into the clearing, far enough for the sun to pick her out clearly. Then she slowly turned around 360 degrees.

Arun thought about reactivating stealth mode and shifting to a new location, away from the patch of grass from which Boon had emerged. It made perfect tactical sense. But he didn't feel it would send the right gesture.

Instead, he did the opposite. He deactivated camouflage mode and allowed his armor to revert to its default setting of dull gray. "If Hardit spy monitors are present," he said aloud to Boon, "they've already seen you. Let them see me too."

"Keep down, you idiot," hissed Boon. "You'll spook the sentry."

Arun stayed on the ground. Sentry? Where was the sentry? Was a weapon trained on him right now? Arun felt the itch between his shoulder blades that suggested there was.

"I wouldn't worry yourself about spy monitors anyway," said Boon. "Hardits distrust electronics in general and surveillance in particular. Despise races that do. They rely on scent. In your suits you're scent-sealed. But we've not all got suits. If a Hardit patrol comes by tomorrow, they will know I've been here through the odor traces I'm leaving. And if there are any Hardits nearby, they will already know I'm here."

"Let them come. And die."

Boon frowned. "You're clueless about Hardit warfare, aren't you? They won't appear in plain sight to give us target practice. Not unless they have overwhelming numbers. They hate being on the planet's surface under any circumstances. And when they're forced to they're rapidly exhausted. The air's too oxygen-rich for them, some say. Now the war's over, the only Hardits you'll see above ground are the scum of Hardit society. Militia. Their military equivalent of tunnel Aux. It's gotten us out of a tight spot before now. We've seen Hardit patrols and they've seen us — must have scented us long before we knew they were there. They kind of snarl and back away. I guess if they don't report they've detected us then no one gets hurt."

"They probably expect us to die off before long anyway," said Arun. "Like your alleged sentries that I can't see."

"Our sentries are hidden. I don't know where. It's best that way. Why? Do you paint yours in fluorescent colors?"

Boon raised her arms in the air and extended two fingers on her left hand; three on the right.

"Come on," she said. "Time to meet Spartika."

Arun and Alpha Fire Team – Hecht, Caccamo, Ballantine, and Monroe – rose from the undergrowth and followed Boon into the building. The opening didn't even boast a doorway, being a simple rectangular hole in the wall. There were no windows either. The only adornment was the flat roof which had been covered in so many years of leaf litter that trees and bushes grew from it.

As he crossed the threshold, the unhelpful thought struck Arun that Springer or Del-Marie would make far better negotiators than him. Maybe next time.

He emerged into a low, rectangular room largely claimed by Nature: unidentified creatures scurried through the rotting leaves to reach the cover of broad toadstools. Two stairwells at either end of the building led underground. Mounting brackets were set at regular intervals along the windowless rooms, but whatever they had once held had long ago rotted into oblivion.

Boon froze.

She'd been making for one of the stairwells, but now she turned and looked back at the area they'd passed through, where the light streaming through the doorway meant it was relatively well lit.

"Trouble?" Arun asked. He noticed now that some of the toadstools had been broken and trampled.

"Identify that," Boon said. She was pointing at a dark patch on the far wall.

"Do it," Arun told Hecht.

The lance sergeant took Caccamo and together they shone their helmet lights on the patch, instructing their AIs to analyze it.

"It wasn't there before," said Boon.

"It's scorching from plasma rounds," said Hecht. "Blood spatter too."

"Everyone out!" Arun ordered.

The Marines raced for the cover of the tree line, stealthing their suits and rolling in random directions before leaping up and running deeper into the trees.

No shots rang out. No explosions.

Instead, a message from Gupta. "Sir, we've located a sniper. We've got two carbines covering him."

"Hold fire and let me see."

Arun might be in command, but Gupta had a better model of battlesuit that enabled him to control the visor display of anyone in BattleNet, and to see what they saw. Gupta swapped Arun's display to show the view through Marine Norah Lewark's helmet.

Thirty meters from Lewark's position grew a Sagaria tree, one of the titans of the forest. The trunk was so wide, you could fit a squad inside. About 20 meters up, a branch grew parallel to the ground. Arun could see shades of purple fern-like fronds and glistening brown nuts, but Barney was nudging him to shift his focus farther out from the trunk, where the distributed intelligence of BattleNet painted a figure in a battlesuit sitting astride the branch and pointing an SA-71 carbine at the clearing.

Barney had shaded the sniper in a shimmering pale orange that faded in and out of view apologetically, as if not convinced that the figure was truly there.

"How did you spot the sniper?" Arun asked Gupta.

"The local wildlife is avoiding that area, and has been for days. See how more nuts have grown to ripeness there? The sniper should have changed their observation post more regularly."

"Well done, Sergeant. Return fire only if they fire first, and shoot to wound. I need to act as if I haven't seen the sniper. Get a drone down inside that building instead. I want to know what's happened to Spartika's unit."

"Yes, sir. Caccamo, get your box of flying tricks down those stairs."

"Yes, Sergeant."

Ten seconds later, Arun's visor was showing the view from the recon drone Caccamo had sent down.

The drone hovered through the upper floor of the building, just long enough to verify there were neither ambushes nor surveillance devices. None that it could detect at any rate. Then it descended the larger of the two stairwells, the one Boon had been heading for.

The stairs were broad and deep, not high. Long years of use had worn away a central channel, a fact revealed because someone had recently pushed years of accumulated dirt to the sides, leaving the stairs clear.

The first level down wasn't accessible from these stairs. Narrow slits were set into the walls. Radar confirmed the idea that the hidden first level rooms were guard posts, there to keep out invaders advancing down from the ground floor… or perhaps to prevent escapees from the deeper levels.

The second and third levels down suggested the latter explanation. Plastic manacles and shackles littered the floor of what looked to be slave pens. The shackles were far too large for Hardit or human limbs.

"Move it on," ordered Gupta when Caccamo dwelled on the slave pens. They didn't look to have been disturbed in recent years.

It was back in the stairwell, as it curved down to the fourth level, that the drone found the first corpses: two Hardits. Scruffy militia fighters with crude rifles still grasped in their prehensile tails.

"Keep moving!" urged Gupta.

Caccamo steered the drone through a makeshift ops room. A portable power generator was still running, powering a heater, lights, and a processor block attached to several viewscreens tacked to one wall.

Caccamo peeled the drone away but it turned back of its own accord, its AI overriding its human controller. Something had aroused its intense interest. That something was one of the viewscreens. The drone hovered millimeters away from the viewscreen.

The screen revealed nothing that Arun could see. It was blank. In a low-power mode that required human touch to reactivate it.

Arun couldn't stand not knowing what was happening. "What's the drone doing, Sergeant?" he asked.

"Unknown," Gupta replied curtly. "Don't think it knows itself what's wrong yet. That's the problem with AIs, stubborn bastards who couldn't explain what they're doing even if they wanted to. Best give it a minute."

Gupta growled deep in his throat when the drone added a bright-red overlay of what was hidden from the natural eye. A mechanism was concealed behind the viewscreen, wiring connecting it to a box concealed behind the processor block on the floor.

The drone was giving its educated guesswork as to the concealed item's construction. Arun didn't need the precise details, because the AI had revealed enough. This was a booby trap.

Its message conveyed, the drone allowed itself to be pulled away and proceeded down the stairs at a far more cautious speed than before.

After passing four more Hardit militia corpses, it reached Level 5, which looked like the accommodation block for the human resistance group. It had recently been fitted up with light, heat, power, sleeping bags, portable stove, spare boots and clothes. There were three more Hardit corpses here… and two human.

"You've lost two fighters," Arun informed Boon, who couldn't see what the drone was reporting. "I'm sorry. I'll describe them. Both male. One's tall, his nose broken repeatedly. The other, average build—"

"Bright orange scarf?" asked Boon.

"Confirmed."

"That's Rossi and Diop." After a pause, Boon added, "We need to bury them."

"Negative. The drone's reporting that the skangat Hardits have booby-trapped your dead. They've done the same to their own fallen too." Arun felt nauseated. Death and danger were one thing, but disrespect to the fallen another.

"I'm not surprised," said Boon. "If a high ranking Hardit had died, they would hold a public ceremony of mourning, and force thousands of slaves to pay respects. These militia, though, are expendable as far as the Hardit commanders are concerned."

There were further levels down, but it was clear that they hadn't been penetrated by Hardit or human for decades.

"Bring the drone back topside," said Gupta.

"Recon's complete," Arun informed Boon. "Two human males dead. Who's unaccounted for?"

"There should have been ten here altogether, including Spartika."

Arun knew he had a key decision that he couldn't duck out of. Rescuing Spartika could be the key to winning over not just the remnants of the human resistance in Detroit, but the wider human population.

Going after her could also get the bulk of his Marines killed.

"Without Spartika we'll crack," said Boon. There was a hint of panic to her voice. "We can run things for a while without her, but it was Spartika who provided our backbone. She led. She could do so again if you can free the slaves from their labor camps."

Arun watched Boon as she removed her kepi and ran her fingers through her collar-length dark hair. He looked into her gray eyes and liked what he saw. There was defiance in those eyes, an unquenchable human spirit. Maybe he was only seeing a dim reflection of the flame that burned in Spartika, but the fire was there nonetheless.

Boon had said that further resistance was hopeless, but her words betrayed that, and so did those eyes. Deep down, Spartika clearly still inspired Boon. Arun couldn't do that himself.

And that meant he needed Spartika.

"I'm going to try to get her and all your people back," Arun said. "Then we're going to break open the camps and liberate a human army of resistance. Will you help me?"

Boon nodded.

"I've seen enough. Caccamo, retrieve the drone. And, Boon?"

"What?"

"Call your sniper down from the trees before someone gets hurt."

Chapter 11

The sentry's name was Pak, and he was proud to be a Marine.

After thirty years on ice, Pak had been thawed just in time to flee Detroit forty minutes later, still groggy from his revival. For the past thirteen days he'd not left his branch up in the Sagaria tree. The suit couldn't maintain continuous stealth mode for anything like that long, but he had kept the scent-seal function operating.

As part of his novice training, Arun had spent three weeks in his suit, abandoned by himself in an orbiting training hulk. The suit kept him alive, but no novice forgot what it was like to be encased in your own stink for weeks, or the gnawing emptiness in a gut deprived of solid food for so long.

Pak didn't complain, as he reported his story. He didn't even try to remove his helmet. Arun was impressed. This Marine's discipline was still good.

Or so Arun thought until panic started ringing clear in Pak's voice. "They must have broken our signal encryption," he wailed. "They lured us here. A trap. Without Spartika we've nothing left."

Gupta planted himself in front of Pak.

Arun recorded the strange sight of two humans facing off against each other in pretty, purple-dappled battlesuits. Even with all the worries of command sucking out his sense of humor, he could still see this as a ridiculous sight. If he ever made it back to *Beowulf* alive, Indiya and Xin would want to know what they'd missed.

"Keep your mind clear, Marine." The sergeant's words appeared to steady the sentry. "This location is free of Hardits."

"It's her," said Boon, spitting onto the ground. "I'll never escape her."

"Stay calm," said Arun, struggling to follow his own advice. "I know you have bad history with Lieutenant Nhlappo, but I will not allow you to insult my officer."

Arun's words snapped Boon out of her funk, but not the way he intended. She looked at him, the grim despair on her face overlaid by amusement.

"You puffed-up fool," she said. "Tirunesh Nhlappo is a cold-hearted lizard who is far too conceited to ever admit her many mistakes. Nhlappo will gladly ruin everyone around her if it makes her look good in the eyes of a Jotun. But she's not a traitor. As for torture and death… I wouldn't put it past her to use them as a means to further herself, but she doesn't delight in them for her own sick pleasure."

"Stop playing games," roared Gupta. "Tell us who you're referring to."

"The local Hardit leader,' said Boon. She turned to the sentry. "It *was* her, wasn't it, Pak?"

Pak nodded. "Here to gloat, she was. Literally rubbing herself with glee. Yeah, it was Tawfiq. Took them away to Camp 3. I heard her say it as they–"

"Tawfiq Woomer-Calix?" interrupted Arun. In the privacy of his helmet, his jaw dropped open. "You're kidding."

"Do we look like we're kidding?" growled Boon. She frowned. "How do you know her?"

"Oh, we go back," said Arun. "I've beaten her before and I'll do it again. We'll get your team back, Boon. And I promise you more. I'll kill Tawfiq myself."

"What are we waiting for?" said Boon. "Let's go."

"Hold fire," said Arun. "First, I'm going to check in with Lieutenant Nhlappo."

"But you can't radio her. I know I said Hardits distrust electronics and nanoware, but even they are capable of intercepting radio comms."

"Who said anything about radio comms?" Barney interpreted Arun's wishes and activated the FTL link with its precious charge of entangled *chbits* that were fast running out.

The connection was answered immediately. "Nhlappo here. Go ahead, Major."

"Lieutenant, your status please…"

Chapter 12

Tirunesh Nhlappo didn't need to be a trained combat pilot or flight engineer to tell that the airplane she was inspecting would never fly again. It was the same with every plane, shuttle, and gunship she'd inspected in Detroit's flight hangar.

Shattered avionics parts glistened amidst the debris littering the cockpit floor. The manual controls were mixed in with the avionics, the main fascia panel reduced to a bare sheet with a jagged hole blown through.

She growled at the back of her throat. To help fill the gaping holes in *Beowulf's* crew roster, some of her Marines had trained in Navy roles during the run back to Tranquility. A surprisingly large proportion had shown good aptitude as pilots. Actually, not so surprising. Flying a highly maneuverable fighter spacecraft called on some of the same reactions and human-AI interactions as dodging through the void in a battlesuit. To rustle up a scratch air force would have been the kind of break they needed if they were to prevail against the Hardits. No such luck. The Hardits had taken any aircraft they wanted – drone gunships by the look of it – and disabled the rest by tossing grenades into every cockpit.

Crude and unimaginative, yet thorough. It was the Hardit way.

Hardits were also masters of being annoying. The aircraft were still armed, fueled, and possibly structurally flightworthy. Theoretically most of them could fly again, but only the skangat Hardits had the parts, equipment, and know-how to repair them. To the humans, the aircraft with their ruined controls and splintered avionics were just so much hi-tech military junk.

Damned Hardits.

"It's no good," Nhlappo called out as she scrambled onto the wing of the fighter plane. "Let's not waste more time on this. None will fly again."

"Well, maybe one," said Deacon, the Aux who'd worked here before the rebellion.

"You told me they were all wrecked," snapped Nhlappo. She made her visor transparent and fixed the idiot man with a steely gaze. What his history was, she didn't know, but he hadn't made the grade to graduate as a Marine. That made Joel Deacon a liability in her eyes until proved otherwise.

"I did," he replied. "And they *are* wrecked."

Deacon met Nhlappo's stare and reflected it right back at her. He showed backbone, at least.

"They aren't all wrecked in the same way," Deacon explained. "The Hardits poured most of their venom into the fighter planes and gunships. But there are a few DS90A shuttles that aren't so badly damaged, and a T16B transport plane that's barely scratched. I've even managed to power up the T16."

"Will any of them fly?"

"Not yet. If I salvaged parts from other craft and jury-rigged repairs, then maybe I could fix one aircraft. *Maybe*. I'd give it a 50 percent chance of success with the T16B, half that for a DS90A. Should I be working on this? If so, which craft?"

Nhlappo considered. Resurrecting an atmospheric aircraft could be a powerful symbol of hope, and the survivors definitely needed to believe the Legion was here to do business. But they needed to succeed in the basics first. "No. Your priority is to clear a safe passage into the hangar's main flight deck so we could get a Stork or two from *Beowulf* down here. That's our resupply route. And if the situation turns to drent, that will be our only way off planet."

Amadou, the senior resistance fighter left in Detroit, placed a hand on Deacon, and interposed himself between his subordinate and Nhlappo. He tried to look the Marine officer in the eye, but couldn't see through Nhlappo's helmet visor.

"Don't forget, Joel," he said, "that this self-appointed human *officer* is your ally, for the moment. She is not your commander. I say you keep working on your transport plane and anything else you can get operational."

It hadn't taken Nhlappo long to work out the dynamics of this ragtag survivor group and identify Amadou as a problem. If Deacon was a liability who showed signs of promise, Amadou was an out-and-out disgrace. He had been one of the experienced Marines trusted by Colonel Little Scar, his Jotun CO, to leave the base before the final battle, his task to form the cadre of a guerrilla group operating behind enemy lines.

Amadou should be in charge. Instead, he had allowed his weak male will to be subjugated by Jennifer Boon. Pretty and petite Boon might be, but Amadou should have seen through that to the girl's dark heart and corrosive attitude.

Four years earlier, Nhlappo had kicked Boon out of the Marine cadets for disobeying orders. Boon's resentment toward Nhlappo was easily understood, but for Amadou to borrow his lover's anger as if his own was simply pathetic.

Boon's repeated insubordination had been more than enough ammunition to be rid of her, but Nhlappo had already been looking for an excuse. Boon was a demon who delighted in using her clever tongue and lithe body to sow discord amongst her fellow cadets. She didn't play her comrades off against each other for any other reason than the sheer spiteful hell of it.

Young male cadets had proved willing prey. It was another example of why single-sex combat units would make so much more sense...

A stab of dismay interrupted her thought. Inwardly she slapped herself for thinking so callously. Men had proved their uses to her in other roles than combat personnel. One man in particular...

Nhlappo removed her helmet, hoping Amadou would see it as a conciliatory gesture. Deprived of her visor's enhancements the hangar was instantly plunged into a thick gloom, through which the wrecked aircraft loomed, vague yet menacing,

"I propose a compromise," she said. "Work on your transport plane for now, Deacon. I'll send over a team to assist once they've completed their inventory assessment in the main part of the base. Lance Corporal Sandure will be among them. He's a wetware and hard-systems wizard. If anyone can wire together your flight systems, it will be him. Before they assist you, though, first you must work together to clear space for two Stork-class shuttles to land."

She raised an eyebrow at Amadou, trying to be questioning rather than challenging.

He nodded, scowling.

Nhlappo tried to soften the muscles around her mouth and eyes. It wasn't quite a smile, but it was the most comradely expression she could summon for the pathetic little veck.

"Thank you," she said.

To give Amadou time to cool his temper, Nhlappo turned and looked out through the sparkling curtain of water that shielded the flight deck's external opening.

Detroit's hangar was three klicks away from the main part of the base, emerging through a broad waterfall in the neighboring valley. She allowed the roar of the water to fill her ears, drowning out her responsibilities for a few moments. With her helmet off, the air had a fresh, tingling quality. Sunlight sparkled through the lens of the cascading water and glinted in the radar reflective strips that were released upstream, collected downstream, and then pumped back above the waterfall. It wasn't a perfect privacy shield, but it made looking or listening through the waterfall difficult, and she assumed that Detroit's nano-scale defenses against spybots were still intact.

She closed her eyes and breathed deeply of Nature's beauty. It wasn't that she wanted to escape her situation, more that she wanted to register the essence of this place. To remind herself of its worth. Detroit and the area around could be a good place to live for future generations. Soon her force would have to fight to claim this land for humankind. Some would die. Questioning why you fought was not something that had troubled her under the Jotuns. Now it was important to remind herself what they were fighting for.

What *she* was fighting for.

A fantasy teased her of settling down here in peace. Farming the fertile land near Detroit with her son. Grandchildren playing with the neighbors' kids. Games of chase and throwing balls, and messing around by the river. She wasn't sure what free children did, but in her fantasies her grandchildren knew how to exist without an instructor to schedule and structure every moment of their existence.

She growled at this dream. Her son knew her only as a machinelike drill instructor, not even knowing she was his mother. She'd come close to telling him on the flight back to Tranquility, but… close was still a failure.

She sighed. If they ever did win freedom for the humans of Tranquility, it would never be *her* freedom. There would be another campaign around a distant star. And another. Ceaseless conflict until one day death would claim her.

The dream of freedom was worth fighting for. But it would never be hers to claim.

Brandt cleared his throat, an appalling artifice given that he deliberately amplified the sound through his helmet speakers. When she didn't turn around, Brandt asked: "Ma'am, should I join the inventory hunt?"

"Not yet, Lieutenant. Leave that in Sergeant Majanita's capable hands."

Out of the blue, Deacon blurted out his own question. "Hey! How did you people get down to the surface anyways? Did you use shuttles to get here? Can't we use them? We could strike the enemy anywhere on the planet and then get out quick."

Although wincing at the inappropriate way he spoke, people with the brain and gall to ask the right questions were a valuable asset they were short of. So she indulged him. Somewhat. "Lieutenant, please explain to Mr. Deacon."

"Yes, ma'am. We arrived in Tranquility system on transport ship *Beowulf,* which remains safe in the outer system. We used a Lysander shuttle to reach Tranquility orbit. Chief Petty Officer Turbine was our pilot. She's still on board, and the Lysander should still be in orbit. We descended in dark lighters."

"Dark what?" asked Deacon.

"He means stealthed dropships," said Amadou.

"Correct, Mr. McKenzie. To descend rapidly through the atmosphere with stealth shielding consumes an immense amount of power. Most of the dark lighter is comprised of its heat sink. Once we've landed and completed egress, the dropship goes into cool-down mode. Cables snake down into the ground, dumping thermal energy. It has a lot to get rid of."

"We don't think the Hardits have much of a mil-grade orbital sensor network," said Amadou. "Otherwise they'd be all over our ass already."

"Let's hope you're right," said Brandt. "Even if they haven't detected our expeditionary force, we suspect they know your resistance group is here, but they haven't felt it worth harassing you. We came down in fields two hours' march from here. Once a cool-down lockdown starts, the dropship is committed to thermal dumping. Anything within three meters of the hull won't survive long with all the exotic radiation being pumped out, us included. We have no choice but to abandon the lighters for the duration. Takes about 3-4 days. If we re-enter too soon, or the dropship is damaged, we're dead."

"It explodes?"

"Something like that."

"Tell Deacon what happens if we damage the dropship," said a more knowledgeable survivor.

Brandt looked to Nhlappo for permission. She gave it via private comms.

"A Dark Lighter unable to cool down properly will explode with the power of a tactical fusion bomb. Exploding dropships deliberately is a risky proposition as the result is more than a mere conventional explosion. There is a release of exotic radiation of extremely variable yield. The radiation level may be so limited that it is barely detectable. On the other hand, it could be enough to instantly sterilize half a continent, and ignite the atmosphere in an uncontrollable chain reaction that will burn the planet to a cinder. When the Hardits come — and they *will* come — the dropships could give us options."

"But a last resort only, Brandt. I want other lines of defense in place first, a ring of fire established in the mountainsides around Detroit. GX-cannon. Missile batteries. SAM pods."

"Yes, ma'am. We need aerial defense too. It's no good having shuttles come down from *Beowulf* if they get shot out the sky by Hardit aircraft or surface-to-air missiles."

"Very true, Lieutenant. Let's see what Sergeant Majanita has for us."

She looked pointedly at Amadou, who shouted out to one of his confederates to raise Sergeant Majanita on the comm.

Main power was out through Detroit, but several portable generators had been successfully rigged up and one kept the internal public address system running. Assuming the Hardits were listening in, the survivors had devised a crude pulse-coded communication protocol that could be decoded into Morse Code. Hopefully the pulses sounded like random white noise to any hypothetical Hardit monitor. The downside was that the system required you to tap and hold gadget boxes connected to the standard base access consoles by wires.

By the time the group had reached the comm station in the hangar, Majanita was ready on the far side.

Nhlappo held the comm box in her gauntlet. She instructed her suit AI to translate the pulses of Morse and speak the words through her internal and external helmet speakers.

Majanita's team was combing the base for equipment. She reported that every armory and munition store they encountered had been destroyed. The dead combatants, though, had simply been abandoned. Attacker and defender; human, Jotun, or Hardit: they had been left where they fell. So too had their weapons. Typical Hardits: lazy and unimaginative.

"We need some means of defending against Hardit air assets," Nhlappo said, her suit reversing the process by translating her speech into Morse Code, "and I don't expect you will find the fallen were firing surface-to-air missiles along the passageways. There won't be discarded SAM ordnance waiting for us to pick up. Confirm, Sergeant, have all SAM pods you've discovered been destroyed?"

"Yes, ma'am."

"Then don't waste more time. Strip the fallen of their weapons. We might not be done yet with stores, though. There were many levels of secrecy at Detroit. I may know of hidden munition stores the Hardits did not find. If I'm right, then that's where we will find some serious ordnance. I'm on my way back now to look. Nhlappo out."

"We have plenty of missiles here, ma'am," said Brandt.

It took Nhlappo a few moments to work out what Brandt meant, but she never doubted he had a good point. Brandt was level headed, unlike McEwan with his flights of fancy. That's why she had fought so hard for him to become one of the new junior officers. Given the opportunity to learn, he could grow into a great battlefield commander one day.

Then understanding dawned. "You mean the missiles these aircraft are armed with?"

"Yes, ma'am."

"These air-to-air missiles launched by fire control systems that no longer function?"

"I believe we should try to find a way to use these missiles, ma'am, and their other ordnance. I know it will break operating protocols, but..." He shrugged. "We're the Human Legion now."

"And we must use our new freedoms to innovate if we are to prevail. I believe you are right, Brandt. Proceed. If you need Sandure to make these missiles fly, you have priority over resurrecting this shuttle. Sorry, Deacon."

Deacon shrugged, in an echo of Brandt. Nhlappo didn't honor Amadou with a glance to assess his reaction.

"Until we know otherwise," Nhlappo continued, "I want you all to assume the enemy has not yet detected our presence. For you, Lieutenant, that means shifting materiel into the mountains using nothing noisier than boots and backs. I don't want any unhardened power signatures, or any EM leakage at all, despite all this talk I hear of Hardits not employing electronics. I give it 36 hours at the most before we receive unwelcome visitors. If the major ever makes it back alive from his... quest to find this resistance leader, he'll be sure to bring hostiles on his tail. That is Major McEwan's way."

Her suit AI alerted Nhlappo to an incoming call on the FTL channel. "Speak of the devil," she muttered before accepting the comm link. "Nhlappo here. Go ahead, Major…"

"Lieutenant, your status please…"

Chapter 13

"So far we've recovered nothing intact other than small arms," Nhlappo reported. "Brandt is setting up topside defenses and had the smarts to strip ordnance from the wrecked aircraft in the hangar."

"And the Resistance?" asked Arun.

Arun heard a sniff of disdain over the FTL link. "Some show potential," Nhlappo admitted grudgingly. "If we arm and train them, could they win the war? Yes. But their morale is far too fragile. All their hopes are hitched to one person, this Spartika, just like… never mind. I hope you're going to tell me this Spartika is a twenty-foot high, thunderbolt-hurling goddess, because any less will be a disappointment."

An awkward pause passed between them.

"Major, what is she like? Tell me you *are* bringing her back…"

"Hardits took her away."

"So, we're in the drent."

"I'll get her back, Nhlappo."

"Of course you will, sir."

It was just as well Arun's face was hidden behind his visor. His fury felt so hot, he wondered whether it would melt through his helmet. "Do I need to relieve you of command, Lieutenant Nhlappo?"

All Arun could hear was Nhlappo's breathing. Had he pushed her too far? Was this where the dream ended?

"No, sir."

Nhlappo's reply was curt, but Arun decided to brush the incident aside as if it had never happened. "Good, because here's my plan and I want my senior officer to review it. We think Spartika has been taken by wheeled transport to Labor Camp 3, which is 420 klicks from here. I'm sending coordinates now. If we power ahead at 20 klicks per hour with a single rest stop, we can get there by dawn tomorrow. Heavy Weapons Section should be able to send the monkeys scurrying down their holes while we grab Spartika."

"Makes sense," said Nhlappo. "Getting there won't be a problem. Boon hasn't got a suit, but you can take turns carrying her. It's any humans you manage to liberate from the camp who will be the problem. They'll slow you down. You'll need to pick a route back that has shelter and fresh water. If you're talking hundreds of refugees, there isn't much my Marines can do to assist. The best we can do here is prepare our defenses. You have a habit of attracting trouble, Major. And the trouble will land here, sooner or later."

"Thank you, Nhlappo. Anything else?"

"Yes… Major, I am proud to serve in this Human Legion Expeditionary Force on our mission to reconquer Tranquility. With you at our head, we can win this campaign. But…" She gave a sharp intake of breath. "If you die, that magic dust you sprinkle will die with you. You'll leave me as an NCO in an officer's uniform in charge of a handful of half-trained Marines pretending to be an army. Since I don't have your semi-divine status and the favor of the gods, it's not a command I want."

"I won't die, Nhlappo."

"Make sure you don't, sir."

"Relax, Lieutenant. Tremayne and the Hummers see me messing with the White Knights for many years to come. I can't die today."

"You and your mystical frakking bullshit, sir. Whenever I hear that our lives depend on your fairy-tales, I want to test that emotional limiter in our heads that stops me pulling out my plasma pistol and blowing my head off."

"Then try these facts for size, Lieutenant, seeing as your spirit is so lacking. My intelligence is that the Hardits are reluctant conscripts with no idea how to fight. We saw it ourselves two years ago when a handful of cadets and Marines defeated the insurrection on Antilles. All the Hardits have in their favor is superior numbers. Our success rests on us liberating and arming enough human slaves that by the time the Hardits rouse themselves to action, we'll have evened up the imbalance in numbers. I tell you, Hardits will never make good soldiers."

Arun hoped he sounded more certain of things than he felt. He wasn't afraid, not for himself, but despite his words to Nhlappo he was conscious that his every decision affected not only the lives of those under his command now, but, just possibly, the future of the human race.

Chapter 14

Labor Camp 3 – Hidden New Order training camp

The Hardit soldier entered its side of the combat arena at the same time as its opponents were pushed through the other.

The soldier dismissed these adversaries as male deserter scum, so far beneath contempt that this match was almost insulting, even though the lone soldier faced ten opponents in this fight to the death. And the deserters were armed with single-shot muskets.

The solider smelled the male musk of the cowering fools, and for a moment, the sexual scent put her off balance.

Until the soldier had been gifted the removal of its sex, it had been a female. But it was beyond gender now… a foot soldier of the New Order. A janissary.

Walking calmly toward the deserters, the janissary gloated in dreams of the future, a future it would help bring about.

He against she. Clan against clan. The once-strong Hardit race had been undermined by a degenerate slave-owning elite who had set Hardit against Hardit for millennia.

No more.

"One world!" barked the janissary. "One people!" The soldier broke into a run, straight at the deserters. "One scent!"

It wasn't until the janissary was 30 paces away that three of the deserters finally found the courage to raise their muskets.

The janissary noted their scents for they were the danger and would die first. Truthfully, it was three-to-one odds, if that.

Slowing a little, the janissary let out dominance scent, lifting its lips to reveal a sneering snout filled with sharpened teeth, taunting the deserters to fire at this distance.

The deserters took aim.

At what it judged the last moment, the janissary dodged to one side and rolled.

Lead slugs zipped through the air. One caught the janissary's left arm. The impact-absorbent fabrics in the janissary uniform absorbed most of the impact, but that arm was out of action for this fight.

Stinking with fear, the other deserters finally raised their weapons.

But they had left it too late. Their crackle of wild shots was no more than a musical accompaniment to the janissary, as it leaped through the air with teeth bared and the claws of its right hand extended.

The result was no longer in doubt.

A growling hum of pleasure resonated in the air as the arena began to fill with the intoxicating scent of freshly spilled blood.

"A most satisfying result," pronounced one of the dignitaries observing from the comfort of the viewing suite. "With an army of janissaries at your command, Supreme Commander, you shall soon be the power in this planet."

"No, Zwiline."

Commander Zwiline emitted odors of nervousness and confusion.

"Your mind is still caught by the snares of the old ways," explained the Supreme Commander. "Free your mind. Let it soar in the slipstream of my ambition. Yes, I shall be the authority in, on, and above this planet. But why stop there? From this modest base beneath Labor Camp 3, hidden beneath a cover of the human slave filth, our New Order will rise to claim its place in the galaxy."

Zwiline knew better than to interrupt, instead raising her right fist in salute.

The Supreme Commander rose from her seat, eyes glazing briefly as she gazed into a glory-strewn future. "The White Knight civil war will give us our chance," she proclaimed. "Soon the stars themselves shall tremble at my name: Tawfiq Woomer-Calix."

PART II
Liberation!

Human Legion INFOPEDIA

Equipment
– ACE Battlesuit AIs

At the heart of the Armored Combat Exosuit (ACE) series of battlesuits is the plate holding the suit's artificial intelligence. Indeed, the AI is literally at the suit's heart, spending most of its existence submerged beneath a heavily armored band around the wearer's chest. The AI's plate can surface through the armor for removal, either for storage, evacuation from a damaged suit, or to be inserted into another device.

The AI's role is to marshal the constant stream of sensor data and control the suit's myriad functions while advising and assisting its human wearer. Some liken the relationship to the AI taking on the role of an army of veteran NCOs, while the human inside plays the role of junior officer: in command, but not so much in control. Ceaseless training between the human, the AI, and the suit they are paired into pays off when the AI starts to anticipate the commands of its wearer, and to emphasize the most critical threats and opportunities in the wearer's helmet visor.

The anticipation can become so effective that many people have questioned the need for the human wearer at all, but there is an unshakable psychological need in the AI to play a supporting role to its human commander. To the AI, making decisions independent of its human's orders is unthinkable, although the AI will take temporary control if its human is psychologically or physically unfit.

Some believe the suit AIs are grown from the souls of fallen comrades – or implanted with the mind and personality recordings of dead Marines. It is difficult to verify the truth of this as the means of construction are a carefully guarded secret.

Marines often use the word 'telepathy' to describe the way they communicate with their AIs. This is also difficult to prove one way or the other, but what is certain is that AIs communicate with their humans through multiple channels and with a great deal of redundancy to weather extreme conditions and the constant threat of cyber-attack. The link is deepened by wetware implants in the Marine that are designed specifically to interface with the AI. The result is a deep symbiotic link that is so intimate that the human often cannot be sure whether they are communicating by sub-vocalizing, or thinking words, or indeed whether an idea originated in the human or the AI mind.

When first introduced to each other, the AI will quickly adapt its personality to complement its wearer, shifting its temperament to match the human's. For example, with a Marine who has just suffered a devastating loss, the AI may appear empathetic and caring, even maternal. If a danger appeared unexpectedly, the same AI might instantly switch to yelling at its wearer in the cruelest of manners in order to get them to move out of danger.

Over time, though, the AI will settle into its own personality, and will struggle to switch tone so rapidly. The final personality is a reflection of its wearer's, an alter-ego. For some humans, this means an AI who acts like an identical twin, because their psychological need is for an ally who thinks like they do. For others, the AI acts like an ever-critical drill instructor, because their need is to be told what they already know they must do. These are just two simple examples. In practice the relationship with their suit AI is more complex and intimate than most humans ever experience with the men and women of their own kind.

Through cyber-attack or physical damage, it is possible for an AI to be rendered inactive. The wearer of a battlesuit will have trained to operate the powered armor without AI assistance, but even the best can do so at a fraction of the efficiency of the AI. Some facilities are completely impossible to replicate. For example, a Marine aiming and firing their SA-71 carbine will be used to their AI adjusting the precise position of the weapon and activating the motive power in the suit to compensate for recoil not dampened by the carbine itself.

The reverse can also be true. If its wearer dies, some AIs can control the battlesuit with a dead or unconscious human inside. Even these AIs must fight a constant battle against insanity that they will lose as soon as any immediate crisis has passed. Two pieces of evidence suggest this slip into insanity has been designed in. Firstly, an AI who believes their partner to be fit and well can be stored indefinitely in a dormant state separately from its human (even Marines don't wear powered armor all the time). Secondly, a few rare examples of centuries-old AIs have been uncovered that are sane enough to be successfully paired up with multiple new human operators.

The design and function of the battlesuit AI still holds many mysteries. Nonetheless it is certain that the Marines would not exist in their modern form if not for the intimate link to their suit AIs. In this, the sometimes cantankerous AI is the ultimate best friend of the Marine, even more so than the SA-71 carbine.

Chapter 15

The alien pushed its head once more out of the cover of the ferns and sneered at the direction of Command Section twenty meters away, letting Arun study the face of his enemy.

A lip-curling expression of contempt for anyone and anything non-Hardit revealed a snout filled with more teeth than seemed possible.

Arun remembered that expression well. He had spent a week in the clutches of Tawfiq Woomer-Calix as an Aux slave and barely escaped with his life. But there was something different about this Hardit idiot who kept showing its head above cover.

For a start, this was the first of the deep-dwelling Hardits that Arun had encountered on the planet's surface. Two over-sized eyes peered out along its snout, and a third was set higher up near its forehead. Presumably they were the same sickly, sulfurous color as Tawfiq's, but this individual's were shielded by two-tier sunshades the thickness of Arun's thumb.

Although humans referred to these creatures as 'monkeys', 'wolf-men' would be a more accurate description, despite the long, gripping tail Hardits used to hold items while on the move.

This Hardit was nervous. At least, that was Arun's interpretation of the way it glanced behind every few seconds, as if checking its escape route, or was unwilling to see what was in front.

And it could certainly see and smell Jennifer Boon who was kneeling alongside Arun, and whispering that they should wait out this encounter. The Hardit could probably sense that other humans were nearby, even though it couldn't smell its way through the scent-seals of the Marine battlesuits.

Occasionally it seemed to be threatening the humans when it presented its armament for all to see, on the end of its gripping tail. It was a rifle or musket that had been fashioned crudely out of metal and plastic in a hidden workshop. It certainly wasn't mil-spec, but the weapon might be more powerful than it appeared. The Hardits were as renowned for their engineering skills as they were in their disdain for the creations of other species.

Arun couldn't bear it any longer. His force needed to press on to the labor camp where they hoped to find Spartika. He decided he would allow the Hardits to hear him, and spoke to Boon.

"What's going on?" he asked her. "Why are they letting themselves be seen?"

Boon kept her reply to a soft whisper "We've seen this before, Major. They hate being on the surface. They detest their leaders. They are consumed with self-loathing–."

"So, they have morale issues. Doesn't explain why they let themselves be seen."

"What I'm trying to tell you is that they don't want to fight, but they also can't swallow their contempt for humans enough to hide from us. When we've encountered militia patrols before, they glare and snarl for a while, just to make some kind of point — probably that they can track us if they want to — and then they slink away and let us proceed."

"So we let Tawfiq's friends slow us down while they take Spartika away. Is that what you propose?"

"They aren't Tawfiq's friends at all. Besides, that one's a male. You can tell by its slighter frame, and the way its snout is more triangular, less cylindrical. The two sexes can't tolerate each other."

"Then this militia band doesn't report to Tawfiq."

"Correct. They'll have a separate male chain of command."

Well why didn't you say so? Arun shook his head but didn't waste any more time in a fruitless argument with this Resistance idiot. Instead, he talked to the most experienced veteran there.

"Sergeant Gupta, these monkeys… can we take them?"

"They're bunched up, sir. Either they're hopeless fighters or are trying to trick us into an ambush."

"I don't think they're that subtle," said Arun. "After all, they aren't expecting to face a disciplined military force. Assume they're as dumb as they look."

"In that case, sir, I've already tasked 1st and 2nd Sections to stealth up and flank them. If you can keep their attention on Command and Heavy Weapons Sections, we should be in position in about fifteen minutes."

"Very good, Sergeant. Wipe those vermin off the face of our planet."

Chapter 16

Like the rest of Command and the Heavies, Arun moved around every so often, to keep the attention of the Hardit militia. Meanwhile he kept an eye on tac-display showing 1st and 2nd Sections edging their way into position around the enemy flanks.

There were eight Marines in 2nd Section, but his eyes kept returning to one of the blue dots in his 2-D view of the battle. That dot represented Springer. She was buddied up with Umarov. The Old Grognard was better trained than any of Arun's class, but that didn't stop Arun wishing for a simpler life where someone else was in Command Section, and he was what he had trained to be: a Marine with an SA-71 and powered armor creeping through cover alongside his buddy.

Barney whispered into Arun's mind that he was receiving an incoming transmission. It was Indiya calling from the Kuiper Belt – the ring of dirty snowballs at the outer edge of the star system.

Arun thanked Fate for the interruption to his thoughts.

"Go ahead."

"Been monitoring a flare in Hardit comms chatter," said Indiya. "Arun, I get the impression you've taken it upon yourself to move beyond a recon mission. I'm bringing *Beowulf* in-system so we can provide support if required."

"I don't think we've stirred up the enemy yet, but… very well, Captain Indiya. Bring your ship nearby."

"Don't sound *too* enthusiastic, will you?"

"I'm not. You're our reserve, Indiya. There's no one left but you."

"Reserves serve no purpose unless their commander is prepared to commit them. Not that you command my ship."

"I suppose you're right in your first point," said Arun. "We haven't time to go over the second, but only because this FTL channel has a limited amount of traffic before we burn up all of our entangled *chbits*. Seeing as you're coming close, how are your specials progressing with their fire support idea?"

"Ready to go," Indiya replied. "Don't call on us unless you have to. We haven't given this a practical test. And, Arun, the Reserve Captain and I have both studied millennia of battle reports. No one has successfully weaponized a starship engine before. If we get it wrong, not only could we lose the ship, the theoretical model predicts a 5% chance that if we're in orbit, we will ignite Tranquility's atmosphere in an unstoppable chain reaction."

Arun sucked in his breath. With the help of the alien Reserve Captain, Indiya had directed *Beowulf*'s zero-point engines on the rebel ship, *Themistocles*, with devastating results. Even in the innovation-averse empire of the White Knights, it seemed impossible that no one else had thought of using engines as a weapon. "Okay, I get it. There's a small chance that I'll kill everyone. Assuming we don't create Armageddon, what's the chance of it obliterating anything in its effect cone? Give me a percentage chance of success."

Indiya clicked her tongue as she thought. "It's too uncertain," she said. "Furn and Finfth both agree it will work, and for those two to agree on anything is unprecedented."

"I'm not asking them, Captain. I need a single number from you."

"80% chance of success."

"Good enough."

"Are you actually going to use it?"

"Let's hope I don't have to. But I won't hesitate if that's what it takes. McEwan out."

Arun cut the precious FTL link and opened a connection to Gupta, who had kept close enough to stay in contact via suit-to-suit tight beams. "Sergeant, what's our monkey status?"

"Ready in ninety seconds. Keep watching that monkey in front of you. Make sure your sections have their safeties off, but don't spook the bad guys. They're mine."

Chapter 17

With seconds to go until Force Patagonia unleashed hell on the Hardits, Arun switched his visor view to magnify the image of the Hardit who kept poking his head out of the ferns, twenty meters away.

The alien glanced behind just before the woods erupted into splinters and shredded foliage as the rapid *whine… pop* of railgun fire raked the enemy militia.

The Hardit dropped its rifle and was already slumping to the soft embrace of the ferns before Arun could bring his carbine to bear. Barney tried to give him targeting solutions, but there were no live targets to fire upon.

A few seconds later, Gupta confirmed the inevitable. "All hostiles eliminated, Major. No casualties."

Arun walked over to the fallen Hardit. Its sunshades were half hanging off its snout, allowing him to stare into the sightless yellow eyes.

He wanted to feel triumph, to bask in the death of a hated enemy. He didn't. After a half-smile and a brief flash of satisfaction, he felt weights and balances shift a little in his mind. If all the Hardit soldiers were so easily dispatched, then the likelihood of victory notched upward.

He remembered telling Springer years ago that he'd hate to be an NCO because he'd be forever wrapped in doubts that he'd get his Marines killed by giving bad orders. Here he was taking a huge chance in chasing after Spartika, and having calmly discussed the risks of calling on *Beowulf* for fire support, an action that could turn Tranquility into a burned cinder. And yet he treated these as cold facts to be weighed and balanced before arriving at his next command decision.

When did he get so uncaring? A sociopath?

A de-stealthed Caccamo knelt in front of Arun and picked up the dead Hardit's sunshades, turning the curious two-tiered item in front of his visor.

He saw other armored figures inspecting the dead.

"We've been delayed enough," Arun transmitted. "Sergeant, resume the advance."

Caccamo quickly pocketed his trophy and disappeared into the woods as if lashed by hellfire.

Arun looked out for Jennifer Boon, beckoning her over when he spotted her.

Boon knew the drill by now. Even though Arun and every Marine there was laden not only with their own equipment but also spare ammo crates for the greedy GX-cannon, armored Marines could move with a speed and endurance that were inhuman. Boon, though, wasn't in armor. She rolled her eyes but allowed herself to be picked up by Arun's powered arms, to be carried like an infant until the next stop.

As soon as Gupta had formed his scouting line to his satisfaction, they set off again in a powered sprint that trampled through the trees so fast that they relied entirely on their suit AIs to nudge their path safely around hazards.

At this pace, they should be at Labor Camp 3 shortly before daybreak.

Chapter 18

An hour before dawn, Force Patagonia rested in a small wood, about forty minutes' march from the labor camp. Even with the Marines' low-light vision enhancements, the Hardits were still better adapted for the dark. But the three-eyed aliens would struggle under the full blast of the early morning's sunlight that would soon burst across the land.

Arun passed through the small group of 22 Marines, trying to offer a word of encouragement here or share a common memory there. Doing so felt like an unnatural performance. When he saw Gupta was performing the same task, but making a better fist of it, Arun left his NCO to it, and sought out his old section buddies.

Since all the Marines were on BattleNet, when Barney read Arun's intentions he added an arrow inside Arun's visor showing him the way.

Zug, Springer, and Umarov sat with their backs against a tree, chatting and laughing easily.

Arun settled down next to them.

The laughter cut off instantly.

Despite being encased in poly-ceramalloy armor, Arun could easily read the body language of his buddies. The way they glanced at each other revealed they were uncertain how to respond to this officer's presence.

Arun hated this officer drent sometimes.

"You know…" he said, casting frantically around for something easy-going to say. "You know, back in the pre-industrial age, soldiers would spend the night before battle sitting around campfires, and feasting on food and drink plundered from the countryside. If our ancestors could see us now, they would think us a sorry bunch. No fire, our armor cooled to ambient temperature. Even our small talk is conducted through microwave comm links."

"And our feasting is on an intravenous drip," said Umarov. "Our drink from a tube."

There came an awkward silence.

"If I were an ancient–" began Umarov.

"You *are* ancient," said Arun.

Umarov gave his throaty rattle that passed for laughter. "I'm not that old, son. If I were a general from that era, I'd launch a nighttime raid at the enemy. Catch them when they were busy feasting. Did that happen in history?"

"I don't know," said Arun, "but I expect you aren't the first to think of that idea."

Springer and Zug remained silent.

Umarov shot to his feet and turned around to berate the two Marines. "What are you thinking of, sitting there like you're cryo-frozen?" He pointed at Arun. "That's your friend. He's not turned into a murdering tyrant, just because he stumbled into an officer's uniform."

"Umarov's right," said Arun. "Commanding Officer is only a role. Del–Marie is our expert in soft–systems. Zug, you're our xeno expert, and Umarov's our expert on ancient history because he was there personally. One role may take on a vital prominence from time to time, depending on circumstances. But none is inherently more important than the others."

"Well said," pronounced Umarov. "Although I'm not sure my knowledge of the ancients is ever going to be of vital prominence."

"Who can know? Remember those Amilx we encountered on the *Bonaventure*? They looked and talked like you. Maybe that's the last we'll see of them, or maybe they will become crucially important, and you're the key to understanding them."

"Your new role does make a difference," said Springer awkwardly.

"You are our friend, still," added Zug. "You always were, despite our differences when cadets. But you should not fool yourself into believing that now you're Major McEwan nothing has changed. It has. Never again will you be our section buddy. Not even our squad mate. You are… *separated.*"

"Since I left Lieutenant Nhlappo and 2nd Lieutenant Brandt to sort out Detroit, it's just us in Force Patagonia, Zug. We boast 22 Marines and an

Aux who is still spitting fury at Lieutenant Nhlappo for booting her ass out of the Corps several years ago. It's not like I'm commanding a real army."

Arun sighed. What was the use? Despite what he'd told the others about being the same old Arun, one thing had changed forever. Underneath the bickering and power plays, squad mates had always looked out for each other, and Arun had been no different in this. But now it was different. Now he considered the welfare of his Marines to be one of his primary and explicit responsibilities.

His friends had been laughing together, back before he'd joined them. Now there was awkward silence. Why that should be was a question for another time. What mattered was their welfare, and Arun's presence was disrupting their downtime.

He got to his feet. "Got to make my rounds," he said. "Get some rest."

"Stow it, McEwan," snapped Springer, with a flash of violet anger. "You can cut that *doing the rounds* drent. Go somewhere quiet and get half an hour's sleep. That's the best way you can help out. Furthermore, that's a direct order from your friends."

"Yes, ma'am."

Arun retreated with a smile on his face.

Chapter 19

Temporary. That was the impression that came immediately to Arun's mind as he surveyed the hastily expanded complex of Labor Camp 3 from his concealed position on the low, wooded hill to the north, about three hundred meters from the perimeter fence.

Hardit cities, factories, and transit highways were almost entirely underground, but the monkeys couldn't ignore the surface entirely. Before being redesignated as a labor camp, the complex had been a regional Hardit center for surface operations. Like all Hardit surface bases and the routes that connected them, the area had been planted with woodland, the tree species engineered to spread a wide and absorbent canopy to protect those below from the sun's dangerous rays.

That explanation had come from Jennifer Boon, the guerrilla fighter who lay in the bracken within earshot, using binoculars to emulate the flexible lensing of a Marine helmet visor. Arun had questions for her, but they had to wait. His fury at how the Hardits had treated their human captives felt like roiling acid burning at the back of his mind, threatening to consume him with rage. Since his treacherous twin brother had left Arun's body swimming with nano-scale med-bots, he could no longer get any effect from combat drugs. He missed asking Barney to administer something, because right now, Arun was too angry to speak.

The wood had been cut back to extend the camp's footprint, and a perimeter fence added, peppered with watchtowers. The space had been cleared for two cages, each of which held several thousand men and women. Gaps left between the cage bars were wide enough to squeeze through, and it was the laser fence around each cage that kept the humans penned within.

As Arun surveyed the cages, he realized that the bars overhead were pipes that released a light mist over the human captives underneath, that the cages were there to house the spray mechanism, not to stop the slaves escaping.

The humans were housed naked, their slick skin glistening with the spray's coating. Arun guessed that the mist was the nanite film he'd been given every morning when he was based at Detroit before the civil war. The oils infused with microscopic machines provided smart protection from the sun's dangerous rays.

Arun couldn't feel any gratitude for this demeaning Hardit care of their captives. Without the tree canopy to soak up the sunlight, the naked humans shone: vibrant shades of livid purple from bruises, and crimson welts that crisscrossed many backs. The sun picked out the thrusting collarbones, ribs, and knees of the emaciated prisoners. It was the sight of the women that sickened him the most. The way their shrunken skin was pulled so taut across the tops of their pelvises that their hips threatened to burst.

Temporary. It wasn't just that the human cages were a stopgap while more permanent accommodation was built. There were no signs of construction at the camp, or anywhere in the vicinity. Either these labor camps were temporary holding areas before relocating the human slave workers underground or… Arun shuddered. He had first-hand experience of Hardit callousness. A more chilling explanation was that the Hardits regarded the slave workers in the camp as a temporary oversupply.

And supply would naturally fall to meet demand.

"Something's up," said Boon. "Doesn't look like any have been sent out to work today. Look at the heap of clothing outside of each cage. Workers grab clothing as they're sent out. Usually there's none left over."

"Good," said Lance Sergeant Hecht, having overheard because Arun had set his comm set to retransmit what he was hearing from Boon. "There will be more of those poor vecks for us to rescue."

After a moment's hesitation, Hecht added: "Rescuing those workers will be hard enough. Are we sure we want to risk their freedom by also sticking our heads down those tunnels in a look see for—?"

Hecht's voice cut off; Barney reported that he was no longer on the command network. That would be Gupta's doing, the senior sergeant silencing a junior NCO who was questioning Arun's orders.

The lance sergeant had a point. Arun turned his attention away from the slave pens and inspected the original Hardit buildings. There were two windowless block houses, larger versions of the woodland building from which Spartika had been snatched. Between the two block houses was a broad ramp spiraling down into the ground. It looked identical to the primary helixes that were the main vertical highways connecting the levels of Detroit.

For all they knew, the complex could extend underground for miles. Squadrons of heavy armor could be waiting to charge out of that helix, just as soon as the Marines showed themselves.

"Any idea which one will house Spartika?"

"There are eight Resistance fighters unaccounted for," Boon reminded him. "Not just Spartika. If they're alive, they will be underground. Think of those as entrances as the surface gates at Detroit. They all connect up underground."

"Sir, please confirm," said Gupta. "Freeing the slave workers is of secondary importance. Our primary mission objective remains the rescue of Spartika and her guerrillas." He added, pointedly: "*If* they are still alive."

"They are my comrades," said Boon.

"I understand," said Gupta. "They could well be your *dead* comrades. That's war. Deal with it."

Arun glanced across at Boon. Her face was tight-lipped with anger.

"Well, Major?" Boon prompted. "What is your answer?"

"I'm not risking our mission to retake Tranquility on any of you," he answered. "Not me. And not Spartika. But our actions today will lead to Hardit retribution, and my judgment is that Spartika will be best placed to mold anyone we liberate into a fighting force, and in the shortest time. I say we take the risk."

Arun cringed at his poor choice of words. *I say we take the risk.* It sounded as if he were asking their permission. This was supposed to be a fighting unit, not a democracy.

He continued, managing to sound more authoritative. "Heavy Weapons Section will remain here on the hillside to provide fire support and hold this position as the primary rendezvous point. We disable the laser fence around those cages and blast the watchtowers with missiles. In the confusion we move in. We take and hold the nearest of the two blockhouses while scouting underground for Spartika. Boon, I want you with us to identify Spartika."

"We don't know what we will encounter," said Gupta. "So we need to react quickly to events on the ground."

"Of course," said Arun.

"So it's just as well that your post with Command Section has a good viewpoint of the field of operations, at least of the surface. Once I'm underground I'll be blind to what's happening topside."

Arun cheeks felt hot under Gupta's stinging rebuke. Arun had assumed his place was with the group combing the underground levels to locate Spartika, not coordinating his unit from the ridge. Gupta was right, of course.

"Sergeant Gupta, you will lead Hecht and Kalis's sections into the camp, while I direct operations from here with Command Section. Your main objective is to rescue Spartika, but let me make one point clear. It is likely that the enemy we face today will be Hardit militia. They are reluctant combatants, but you are to show them no mercy whatsoever. I want a message sent today, a message written with Hardit corpses. I want Hardits all over the planet to fear us, to fear our vengeance if they dare to mistreat humans. Slaughter them all. No Hardit left alive. Any questions?"

No one queried him.

"Good luck, sir," said Gupta after a few moments of silence. Then he slid away, soon disappearing from LBNet when the trees cut out line-of-sight comms.

Arun had 21 Marines to carry out this operation. He gave a caustic laugh when he imagined how Indiya would react if she knew what he was about to do. She'd think him mad, but then she wasn't a Marine; she hadn't been bio-engineered for violence. Arun couldn't wait any longer. He *needed* to bring war upon the enemy. All the others in his command would be feeling just as hungry for the fight; it was what they had been built to do.

Twenty-one Marines. That was more than enough to make the Hardits pay for their crimes. In blood.

Chapter 20

For two minutes, Springer fought the urge to turn and look. She had plenty to keep her occupied. Her battlesuit was scent-sealed and in camo-mode, but the terrain meant full stealth would have been impossible even if her suit had the power reserves to try. Her section threaded their way along woodland paths cleared by animals who had the sense to keep well out of sight. Every footstep was a risky decision. Three hundred-and-eighty pounds of armored Marine couldn't help but snap twigs, crush ferns, and leave boot prints. Springer did the best she could, but her lack of training let her down, and for the first time, so too did the left leg she'd left behind on Antilles. She'd worked long and hard with her new AI, Saraswati, to calibrate her suit to roll and walk, relying on the AI to place her empty left boot correctly.

But creeping silently was another matter.

Corporal Kalis, who was in command of 2nd Section, must have realized stealth was a lost cause because he continuously urged them to speed up, the time for caution over.

Springer was close enough to the start line that Saraswati began to outline her deployment point in green. Her heart raced at the sight. What would the next few minutes bring? Would she live to see the next day? She was a Marine, combat was her natural element, but this would be the first serious action she had seen dirtside since losing her leg. Could she still cut it? Or would she prove the weak link that let everyone down? A gnawing absence brought such doubts sharply into focus when she should be barely able to control her excitement. The missing part was Arun. He was supposed to be the one with all the emotions, but she had always had a bit of that too and right now she wished she didn't. She was buddied up with Umarov today, but for years she had been used to having Arun by her side.

She turned and looked — back up the gentle slope. She couldn't see Arun, of course, but he was up there somewhere. It felt wrong to not share the danger shoulder to shoulder, but she had to accept that those times were over. She didn't deserve Arun. Not after the lie she'd told him all these years.

An intense burst of white noise filled Springer's ears, blasting away distracting thoughts.

"Stay alert, Tremayne," growled Kalis. The white noise had been his audible equivalent of slapping the back of her head.

"Sorry, Corporal."

Frakk! Kalis was already at the starting position, painting objectives into the tac-displays of his section. When did he get to be so competent?

Springer and Umarov's assignment was to take out a row of laser fence repeaters, direct the initial surge of refugees, and then take and hold the nearest blockhouse.

As the wait counted down from minutes to seconds, the sense of Arun's absence rapidly faded away, leaving just her comrades in 2nd Section.

She took aim at a laser post, asking Saraswati to confirm with Umarov's AI that they weren't firing at the same post.

Springer waited for the command to fire.

Chapter 21

Seven minutes after Sergeant Gupta had disappeared from tac-display, Arun's visor updated with fresh tactical information, displaying a wide view of the battlefield that showed the deployment of all the women and men in his command.

The time for secrecy was almost over. Gupta had switched to Wide BattleNet.

"In position, sir," he said.

"Thank you, Sergeant. Laskosk, Heavy Weapons Section will destroy all watchtowers, and then throw some ordnance down every Hardit hole you can see."

Arun's eyes picked up movement twenty meters away as a camouflaged Laskosk, Stopcock to his friends, lifted his missile launcher onto his shoulder.

"With pleasure, sir," said Stopcock, sounding like he meant it.

Chapter 22

Excitement reared in the pit of Lance Corporal Stok Laskosk's stomach. Finally, he and Chung would get to show what they could do with the weapons they had specialized in… *and* lugged all the way here from Detroit with only the Heavy Section's assistant, Cusato, to help. And not just from Detroit. This was *his* missile launcher that they'd brought down from *Beowulf.*

Weapons were not interchangeable, despite what logistics NCOs might say. Balance, heft, trigger resistance, recoil lift: all weapons had their unique characteristics, and none was more significant than the targeting AI.

Stok sucked in a breath. *Was he being fair?* The Legion had enough dropship capacity to have brought another Marine with them, but used the space instead for Stok's launcher, and the cannon. And it was true that the others – even McEwan – had helped by lugging around some of Cusato and Chung's GX ammo.

He shrugged. The others could still go vulley themselves for saying he was in love with his tube. As far as Stok was concerned, his weapon system was as much a member of the unit as any of its flesh and blood components, and at long last he was about to show all the doubters exactly what he could do.

Chung and all the other Marines in Force Patagonia were waiting on his signal.

It was a simple signal really.

Stok made one more check of his targeting system. It confirmed it was locked onto the base of the largest watchtower, overlooking the main gate. The trajectory he'd selected would send his missile swinging around the camp and in from the east. Not only would that make the missile appear to be coming from the opposite direction to Stok's firing position, but it should collapse the building, spilling its debris to block the main entrance through the perimeter fence, making it impassable for wheeled vehicles and low-power gravitics.

No better way to make your enemy feel vulnerable than cutting off their escape.

From his initial firing position, 30 meters up a tree, Stok tightened the grip of his thighs on the branch he was straddling and depressed the firing stud. He felt a soft kick and saw a blur of motion as the missile was ejected.

He kept the stud depressed, and soon felt another kick as the second missile launched. He'd programmed his first barrage to target each of the five watchtowers, and then the blockhouses, before sending a couple of incendiary specials down the main ramp that snaked down into the ground between the two blockhouses.

No sign yet that the Hardits had noticed. Nor should they. He was firing smart munitions, not dumb rockets. The missiles were spreading out in a holding pattern around the wood, using low-speed, low-visibility propulsion designed to obscure the location of the missile's launch. Not exactly stealth mode, but if you weren't looking carefully, you wouldn't know the missiles were there. Not yet.

When the distributed intelligence of his missiles decided they were ready, their main engines would ignite and they would hit their targets simultaneously.

And those ignorant jokers at the bottom of the slope thought all a missile specialist did was press a button!

The Hardits didn't appear to know they were under attack, but Stok wasn't stupid enough to take unnecessary chances.

As soon as he'd launched the final missile of that barrage, he stood on his branch and jumped down to the forest floor. As he'd been trained to do, he let go of the missile system at the last moment before impact. He rolled to absorb the shock, crushing bracken until he slammed into a tree. He raced back to retrieve his launcher, and then hurried off to his next firing position a hundred meters away, where his carbine and the remainder of his missile ammo should be waiting for him.

He couldn't imagine how ancient soldiers had ever managed to fight battles without powered armor. That jump from the tree would probably have killed them.

Then his ears filled with the roar of eight missile engines lighting up, and all he could think of was reaching his new firing position in time to make a difference to the fight with his next barrage.

Chapter 23

With the scream of Stopcock's approaching missile barrage ringing in her ears, Springer fired a burst of rocket rounds. Any doubts, any fear she might have had were banished by necessity, sealed away in a compartment at the back of her mind. Training and instinct took over. She aimed at a meter-high narrow cylinder that was a repeater post for the laser fence, her fire transforming it into a twisted, jagged-edged metal wreck. By the time she registered the damage, she'd already sent a second burst of fire into the next post along. She needn't have bothered. The fence, with its lattice of lethal laser beams, had already shut down.

The humans in the cage within hadn't yet noticed.

Not surprising. Stopcock's missiles had blasted the watchtowers into rubble, smoke poured from holes punched through the blockhouses, and the main ramp leading underground was glowing with actinic white fire.

"Move in," came the order from 2nd Section's NCO: Corporal Kalis. "Head for the western blockhouse."

"Don't waste time with refugees," added Sergeant Gupta.

No chance of that, thought Springer as she bounded over the ruin of one watchtower, her fire team buddies – Zug, Umarov and Kalis – close by. The watchtowers had been the strongpoints in the outer fence. Now, thanks to Stopcock's attention, they were a highway into the camp.

And a route out... Some of the slaves had realized the laser fence was down. They could escape!

Before any overcame their fears and escaped, Springer plowed into the confused mass of slaves, naked and wretched the lot of them. Her stomach churned acid to think that she would be no different if she'd been captured by the three-eyed monkey-vecks.

"Spartika!" she shouted, her helmet speaker boosting her to near-deafening volume. "Does anyone know where they're holding Spartika?"

Those who paid her any attention at all gave her a blank look. Like that helped!

"Or Esther?" Springer added, mentioning a regional Agri-Aux leader she'd known before the war. "Does anyone know where Esther is?"

It was hopeless. Even those who'd paid Springer a little attention now turned away. Some made for the mound of stinking clothing heaped outside of the cage. A few ran naked for the woods. Most turned their heads and cowered, as if the world and all its many ills would go away if they pretended it didn't exist.

Pathetic. She had no time for these losers.

"Don't delay," chided Kalis.

"If anyone wishes to fight," yelled Springer at the slaves, "follow us. Dead Hardits will donate all the weapons you need. Everyone else, run! We've left a cache of Hardit weapons to the south west, where the stream crests the hill."

At last! A few stronger-looking individuals joined her from out of the crowd. Perhaps they had some worth in them, after all.

"Follow me," she said as she hurried after the rest of 2nd Section who had taken positions on the edge of the slave cage facing the western blockhouse. 1st Section was edging forward, trying to flank the blockhouse.

A sound came to her ears, a sound so unexpected that she skidded to a halt, throwing up a cloud of dust.

Saraswati picked up on Springer's sudden, intense interest but not why she was so shocked. The old battlesuit AI took control of Springer's visor, showing an overhead tac-display with an orange dot to indicate the location of this new, unidentified threat to her left-rear.

But this was no threat. The sound was the cry of a human infant.

A second infant joined the wailing chorus.

Springer searched the crowd for the children, only to find their mothers were searching out *her*.

The sight filled Springer with a stinging mix of longing and pride. The mothers were only a little older than her. Unlike the other women, whose gaunt bodies were flaps of skin stretched over prominent bones, the defiant-looking mothers were ripe pictures of health. There was a story here. The other starving wretches must have given up their meager rations so the mothers and their infants didn't go hungry.

Her belief in these people soared.

"We want to fight," said one of the mothers.

Springer's assessment of the slaves plummeted.

<Insanity can be generic,> offered Saraswati. <These infants are probably equally addled.>

"We aren't stupid," said the other mother. Springer sensed Saraswati sneer at that. "We reckon our chances are better sticking with you. If we hang around with these poor vecks who are pretending nothing is happening, we'll be slaughtered by the Hardits, and our babies too."

"No!" Springer was surprised by her own vehemence. "I don't want you or your kids here. You're a distraction. If you want a better chance for your babies, head up the slope to the ridgeline west of here. About 400 meters north of the stream. Command Section are there. Major McEwan will look out for you."

Saraswati flashed an urgent tactical update. Another barrage from Stok was inbound.

"Everyone down! Cover your heads."

The missiles blasted their targets, filling the air with the noise and fire of destruction.

"Stay down," she shouted.

Rubble rained down on her, as she rose to one knee to inspect the results of the barrage. Fire was coming out of the eastern blockhouse and the spiral ramp into the ground, but that wasn't as important as the western blockhouse she faced. The building was clearly far tougher than she expected, because it still stood largely intact. Even the door remained a sturdy barrier, but Stok had ripped a breach into the facing wall. A hole big enough for Marines to enter.

The breach was evidently big enough for Puja's fancy recon scanner to see through all the way from the ridge, because she warned across WBNet: "Hostiles in western blockhouse."

Saraswati confirmed this on Springer's tac-display, showing the hidden crush of Hardits cowering just out of sight behind the breach.

<They're massing for an attack across the open,> said Saraswati. <Just like your sergeant hoped. I like Senior Sergeant Gupta. I think he's half-AI.>

"You're insane," whispered Springer, but she meant her words endearingly, and Saraswati knew it.

A Hardit snout emerged at the hole. It took a deep sniff of the air before its owner snatched it back under cover. The humans let it be. For now.

But there was another threat! Saraswati reported that more Hardits had sneaked out of the north side of the blockhouse where they were massing for an attack. Meanwhile, all Marine eyes were on the breach on the southern wall.

Battlesuit sensors could see a little way through the gap but couldn't see through walls. Saraswati's ability to assess fuzzy observational data was acute, but even she couldn't be seeing through *two* walls. Even Puja's fancy box of tricks couldn't manage that.

However… Saraswati hadn't been wrong yet. Springer made a decision.

"Corporal," she said over the section channel, "hostiles are massing on the far side of the blockhouse."

Kalis growled in annoyance. "Is this another one of your visions, Tremayne?"

"No, Corporal. My AI is convinced."

"I'm not seeing it on tac-display. Your AI is senile, Tremayne. I should never have let you keep it. If it doesn't kill you first, replace with a working model as soon as you get a chance."

"Corporal, I'm not so sure she's senile."

Springer meant her words. The old AI had blackmailed Springer, threatening to reveal her secrets if she went back to her newer AI. That was the real reason why she'd kept with Saraswati. But Saraswati claimed to be a recon specialist, with special capabilities that extended beyond blackmail. Springer was beginning to believe her.

"I'll deal with you later," said Kalis.

They heard a couple of rifle reports from inside the blockhouse.

A second later, three Hardits clambered out of the meter-high hole and jumped down to the ground onto all fours, rifles gripped in tails.

They scarcely looked to be in any better condition than the human slaves, with matted fur and threadbare clothes crudely sewn together from mismatched rags.

Springer picked a Hardit target and allowed *her* (not *it*: the local Hardits were all female according to intel) to land and stare out at the camp through its thick, two-tiered sunshades.

The creature looked surprised to still be alive.

Good, thought Springer. *The sergeant wants to encourage you out into the open, but I just want you to have one last moment of hope before I snatch it away.*

Suddenly the Hardit dodged sideways, and then flipped to and fro for a few moments as if, not having expected to live this long, it was struggling to figure out what to do next.

Springer had no such uncertainty. She put a dart straight through its stupid sunglasses.

That's for imprisoning babies in a labor camp.

The whole of 2nd Section must have been in tune with each other because the other two Hardits died in that same instant, having been allowed that brief extension of hope.

But the three sacrificed Hardits had not been wasted. Even Springer had allowed herself to be distracted while dozens of militia emerged from behind the blockhouse, charging at the humans with rifles blazing.

She heard a hail of bullets pinging off Marine armor, skimming the dirt and cutting bloody holes through unprotected human flesh.

"Hug the dirt and stay still," Springer yelled for the benefit of the slaves.

"Evade," ordered Sergeant Gupta. "Let them come."

Springer fell into the familiarity of the evasion drill. Acting together as a team, she and Saraswati rolled and tumbled unpredictably, while avoiding crashing into Marines or slaves. She winced when she felt the crunch of snapping bone as she thundered into one of the slaves who was making a run for it.

Dumb veck should've kept still like I told him.

When the enemy had been drawn out into the open, Gupta sent an order to the Heavy Weapons Section up on the ridgeline. "GX Team, open fire!"

Stopcock had shown what he could do with his missile tube. Springer didn't have to be there to know that Christanne Cusato's eyes would be wide with excitement while she kept the ammo spooling cleanly and the temperature–killrate balance optimal so that Jerry Chung could concentrate on unleashing the power of their tripod-mounted GX-cannon.

Even armored Marines had no defense against such a weapon. All you could hope to do was survive long enough to trace a line back to the firing position and blast the weapon and its operators. These Hardits had nothing to reply with other than same crude slug-throwers that the patrol they'd met in the woods had been carrying. They didn't stand a chance.

The GX-cannon was an infantry support weapon that was a maxed-out version of a handheld railgun. It could also fire rounds where a shaped charge pierced the outer skin of the target before the main payload delivered a miniature gamma or x-ray blast, perfect for slicing through tanks, buildings, and personal armor. Cusato had set the ammo feed to one 'G' or 'X' round per ten kinetic darts, and Chung had cranked the muzzle velocity up to a power-sucking Mach 11.

Chung fired an initial five-second blast.

As the cloud of dust thrown up by the cannon began to clear, it was obvious Chung didn't need a second one.

<You've scared them,> said Saraswati. <There are more inside but they're keeping far away from the exits. Silly little monkey-things.>

We certainly scared them, Springer agreed. The softening up phase of the operation had gone without a hitch.

She glanced around with her helmet in survey mode, and reassessed that judgment. Saraswati hadn't bothered to mark on tac-display the many dead and wounded amongst the human slaves. Most of them had simply fled, but those who remained and were fit to fight were eager to do so, seeking orders from the NCOs. Of the mothers and their babies, she saw no sign.

Saraswati was also asking in her subtle way what they were supposed to do next. They'd reached the limit of her section's initial orders.

Now comes Arun's big gamble, Springer explained.

<Heaven have mercy upon us. Unlike you, I don't make the mistake of thinking I'm in love with him. I can see the foolish boy for what he is.>

Whatever you might think of him, AI, he's still our CO.

<So he says…>

Look, it's not about Arun. His gamble was for us to be here at all. Now that we are, the next steps are just common sense. We have to clear the blockhouse and move underground in search of this resistance leader, Spartika. We might be in and out, mission accomplished, within minutes, and without firing a shot. On the other hand, under the ground might be a vast Hardit city garrisoned by an entire army.

<And there's only one way to find out. Send us underground.>

Springer didn't like the tone of Saraswati's thoughts. She ignored the contrary AI, and tried to loosen some of the knots in her muscles while she awaited the order to advance.

Chapter 24

Row upon row of uniformed soldiers stood alert and patient.

A new kind of soldier for a New Order: these were the *janissaries*.

Clanless, genderless, even the metalized fabric of their uniforms spoke of how the weaknesses of their biology were being eradicated in favor of machinelike efficiency.

And they were parading for *her*: Tawfiq Woomer-Calix.

These very janissaries were to be the instrument of her revenge, her vindication. She sighed a hot breath laden with sexual pheromones. They would bring her *power*.

Power… the thought made her genitals tingle. She imagined a scent-picture of high-born males unable to resist her scent challenge to *come mount me if you dare*, and every one lying stunned at her feet, unworthy and unsatisfied. The males would be drawn to her in their hundreds, thousands, unable to resist the allure of the most powerful female in the planet, until eventually at a time and with an individual of her choosing, she would permit her scent to co-mingle with a male's.

Hastily, she rubbed hormone-suppressant gel over her snout, and waited for the sexual knots in her gut to untie. With mating season approaching, she'd have to be very careful around the foot soldiers of the New Order.

Unless she was to follow the final logic of the machine she had created and eradicate her own gender…

But she'd left it too late! The hidden weakness of her sex would have to remain concealed until after mating season.

By then she could do whatever she wished.

Or she would be dead.

When her lusts calmed, Tawfiq judged the time was finally right to make her historic address. After a glance to the media crew to ensure they were ready to capture the moment – and that they were confident any embarrassing sexual scents could be edited away – she began the momentous speech. "Janissaries. Loyal foot soldiers of the New Order. You have given me much. Now it is time to offer my gift to you."

Tawfiq raised her right hand as if snatching something from the air, and holding it there in her fist, a movement she had practiced endlessly.

"You offered me your clan-scent and I took it from you." She mimed throwing away the contents of her fist. "You learned that without your clans you are united."

Her army oozed scents of fervent loyalty. They had never seen a performance like Tawfiq's. Neither had she until chancing across that data cache containing a curious study of human history. If the janissaries ever learned she was copying the actions of a human demagogue, she would be disemboweled within moments.

"You offered me your gender," she shouted hoarsely, "and I took it from you." Again, she mimed discarding their weakness. "You learned that without gender you are stronger."

The janissaries growled their support.

"Today we march on the capital," Tawfiq shouted above the loyal growls. "Our New Order shall sweep away the old, consigning it to the pit of forgotten history where it belongs. But first I give you your new scent. There is no room in our people's future for division based on clans or gender or the false philosophical teaching of weaklings. There shall be only one scent – that of the New Order."

She raised her fist again, holding her power over the army for all to see.

"One world!" she screamed, punching the air. "One people! One scent!"

Her most senior lieutenant, Zwiline Calix-14, raised her left hand, and immediately thousands of voices growled the refrain.

Strength through Victory! Victory through Strength!

Waiting at the base of the stage were her most loyal janissaries, carrying buckets filled with scent pads ready to daub her warriors, unifying them under Tawfiq's control forever. The secret of this scent was that it was created artificially, not made in the scent glands Tawfiq's surgeons had cut away.

Only Tawfiq could supply this scent.

She was about to order its distribution when she noticed at the edge of the stage that her head of security was emitting an odor of concern.

Tawfiq flicked a glance her way.

Benner hesitated a moment, weighing up whether she dare disturb the rally. But the security head was a strong-minded female, difficult to cow. Despite clinging to a chemically subdued femaleness, Benner remained popular, which wasn't surprising with her martial bearing emphasized by her left ear that had been half bitten off years ago.

Benner strode across to Tawfiq's podium. Doing so at this point in the rally demonstrated her fearlessness.

Tawfiq respected her subordinate's iron will. It was also why Benner would have to be eliminated after the coming battles were won.

"Supreme Commander," Benner whispered, "our surface perimeter is under attack from human rebels."

Tawfiq snapped her jaws in anger. She immediately smelled concern rise up through the ranks of janissaries as a consequence. Her soldiers were not machines yet. Emotions would have to be purged in a future phase of upgrades.

Until then she would have to resort to words and symbols to control her troops.

She raised a hand for silence. "Commander Benner Calix-11 informs me that there is a disturbance up on the surface: human insurgents making a noise. Do we veer from our historic destiny at this fleabite?" She paused for effect. "No! No! No! You all know how the human menace has corrupted our once proud race. How a reliance on slave labor has made our people indolent, our spirits tamed. Even talking of humans makes my hide itch, and my nose fill with their stench worse than fresh vomit. But we shall not allow our hatred of the humans to deflect our purpose. We march on the capital. We march! We fight! We triumph!"

Zwiline signaled the army's answer.

Strength through Victory! Victory through Strength!

It was more than a chant to rouse the troops. Tawfiq believed those words with every fiber of her being.

They would assure her rightful place in the galaxy.

Chapter 25

As soon as Senior Sergeant Gupta judged Hecht's 1st Section had advanced far enough, he launched the next phase of the operation to rescue Spartika. "1st Section, suppressive fire. 2nd Section, await the order to move in."

A hail of fire from 1st Section lashed the hole in the blockhouse opened up by Stok's missiles. Grenade launches followed the railgun darts.

"Go! Go! Go!" screamed Corporal Kalis.

Springer was picking herself up from the dirt when the grenades burst inside the blockhouse. Hecht's team had delivered the searing light and stunning noise of flash-bombs mixed in with fragmentation munitions.

Springer had a frag grenade ready herself, locked into the launcher beneath her SA-71's barrel. But for now she trusted the other section to keep the enemy busy while she strained every fiber of her body to surge across the dirt toward the breach in the blockhouse wall.

Zug was first to reach the objective. The gash in the wall started at shoulder height, so he leaped headfirst through the hole, rolling into an interior still whited out in Springer's visor by the flash-bombs. She heard no answering fire from the Hardits inside.

Long-legged Schimschak was next through, followed by Yoshioka and Kalis. Then it was Springer's turn to somersault through into the enemy position.

The flash-bomb light was fading now but there was still plenty enough to see by. Hardit corpses were piled up inside, many sliced into several parts. If any were still alive, they were doing a good job of playing dead.

Carbine ready, she checked for threats. The blockhouse was a crude construction without interior walls. Hats and protective clothing against the sun hung from pegs; plastic trays were arranged on wooden shelves; it looked strangely innocent until she saw the whips mounted above the downward leading stairwell near the western wall.

One of the fallen Hardits near the stairwell looked suspiciously unscathed. Springer fired a burst of darts at it. After twitching for a few seconds, the Hardit remained still. If it wasn't before, it was definitely dead now.

"Clear, Corporal," she announced.

"Confirmed," acknowledged Umarov and Zug a few seconds later.

The Marines of 2nd Section's other fire team were peering out of the slit windows to the north and east. They obviously hadn't seen anything to fire at.

As if confirming her thoughts, Puja broadcast a report over WBNet from her position up on the ridge. "No sign of activity in eastern blockhouse. Nor in ramp. You're good to proceed underground."

By now a handful of liberated slaves had clambered into the blockhouse, checking the bodies for still-functioning rifles. One of them had taken the time to grab a shirt and pants. The others hadn't bothered. All they wanted to do was kill Hardits. Springer could relate to that.

Gupta came up to the outside of the breach, rammed a signal repeater into the crumbling building material, and ducked down out of sight while the senior NCOs took a few seconds to get their next moves straight.

Springer watched the results in her tac-display, aided by annotations from Saraswati.

Rahul Bojin and Norah Lewark from 1st Section took four armed slaves with them to the collapsed watchtower that blocked the route north out of the labor camp. There they would establish a forward post from which to cover the ramp and the eastern blockhouse.

While Springer and 2nd Section covered the stairwell, the remainder of 1st Section joined them in the western blockhouse, and proceeded to knock additional firing slits through the east wall so that they too had good field of fire on the ramp and the other blockhouse.

Gupta joined them, bringing the resistance woman they'd brought with them from Detroit. Jennifer Boon's lip was trembling.

The sergeant didn't wait for the defensive preparations to complete before he urged 2nd Section onward. "Right, that's the easy part over. Now it's time to go rescue this local dignitary named Spartika, and Boon here is going to identify her for us. Wouldn't do to get back to Detroit only to find we'd rescued the wrong person, would it?"

Corporal Kalis gave his orders. "Alpha Fire Team, you're point. Go!"

The stairs ran straight down without turning before joining a passageway that fed west and east. With Gupta, and Yoshioka's Beta Fire Team giving suppressive fire over their heads into the passageway, Springer, Umarov, Zug, and Kalis charged down the stairs, ready for whatever awaited them below.

Chapter 26

"Supreme Commander!"

Tawfiq snapped her jaws. "What now, Benner? Can you not see I am at the head of an army about to march out to victory?"

"It is the human scum outside. They have been reinforced by their cursed Marines. Perhaps we missed a nest that has remained hidden until now."

"They are the desperate twitches of a dying opponent. If this handful of survivors has found heavy weapons, they will be a nuisance, but we have a far more important battle to win."

"Yes, Supreme Commander. Nonetheless, my assessment is that militia troops alone will not withstand these Marines."

Tawfiq howled in frustration, but felt a little better when she realized that brave Benner was quailing before her.

"Very well," she told her subordinate. "I agree with your assessment. I shall order Zwiline to reassign you a company of janissaries with a little heavy support."

"Yes, Supreme Commander. And what of the resistance symbol the humans call Spartika?"

Tawfiq considered. "Take three janissaries and kill her. Kill her fellow partisans too and make sure you make a recording of her death. Evidence of her demise at my hands may be politically useful."

"Yes, Supreme Commander."

Strength through Victory, Tawfiq said to herself as Benner scurried away. *Victory through Strength.* Tawfiq would practice what she preached, and not allow herself to be distracted.

Even if the humans did manage to escape the vicinity, they would not live long. The final solution to the human problem would exterminate the entire vile infection of humans soon enough.

Chapter 27

Less than half an hour after charging down the steps from the blockhouse, Springer was deep below ground, trying to find a route back up to the blockhouse, and cursing tunnels the galaxy over. And stairs. Stairs were the most evil torture of all.

"Keep moving, Tremayne," growled Corporal Kalis from above.

Springer redirected her silent curses at Ferrant Kalis, even though the corporal did have a point. She'd retrained and recalibrated with her new suit AI until she was good enough at running, rolling, and hitting the ground. But stairs… She hadn't trained for stairs. Her missing left leg was punishing her.

Umarov was keeping a few steps below, covering her ascent. The other members of 2nd Section's subterranean rescue party had already reached the broad east-west passageway that connected the two blockhouses with the main entrance helix that descended in between. The others were out of sight, so she queried tac-display. Sergeant Gupta and Beta Fire Team had taken an eastward-facing defensive posture just beyond the stairs. Kalis and Zug, her comrades from Alpha, were advancing west. Even Saraswati couldn't tell her the location of the half-dozen armed refugees who had joined them from the slave cages on the surface.

"I've made a formal complaint to the owners," Umarov told her. "They convey their apologies and promise to install elevators in time for our next visit."

"Nice one," she laughed. "But I don't think I'll come back. I can't get a decent comm signal down here."

<They're jamming us,> said Saraswati, misunderstanding Springer's banter. <That's all. Probably some stupid AI thinking it's being clever.>

Springer sent her own AI a mental message of thanks. The jamming made her cautious, and Saraswati skittish, but that was nothing to the effect it had wrought on Gupta. They had been three levels further down when they'd suddenly lost contact with the blockhouse on the surface, and their AIs had reported they were resisting electronic warfare attack. Without hesitation, the sergeant aborted the rescue attempt and reissued orders to retreat to the surface.

Even Jennifer Boon hadn't complained. The lower they reached, the bigger this maze became. They could spend days searching for Spartika and never find her. And all the time, they were encountering more and more Hardit militia. The firefights had all been one way so far, but sooner or later the monkeys would get organized.

Finally, Springer reached the final step and the blessedly flat surface of the passageway beyond. Just as she was taking that last step, the ground roared and shifted. Springer tripped. Instinctively she transformed her fall to a roll that scattered an armed slave to either side.

"Gravitics powering up," said Saraswati. "Estimate 15-18 heavy grav-tanks, coming up the helix. ETA to reach surface... 230 seconds."

"What?" They had come here expecting to fight Hardits, not *grav-tanks*.

She and Umarov hurried further west to where Hecht had assigned their deployment. Springer relayed Saraswati's intel as she moved.

"Justify the precision of your estimate," ordered Gupta a few seconds later.

"My AI, Sergeant. Claims to have been a recon squad specialist in an earlier pairing."

"Might be something in it, Sergeant," added Kalis. "Tremayne was inexplicably accurate earlier. Could be luck, of course."

Gupta didn't say anything, but the growl at the back of his throat made clear that he was not happy.

"Very well," he said eventually. "Alpha, push your fancy recon butts up that corridor and let me know the instant you hear something you don't like. Yoshioka, cover our position. Boon, take a few runners topside and re-establish contact with the blockhouse. Get a message to the major that grav-tanks will be coming out of that pit any second. Go!"

<I like Sergeant Gupta more than that silly major,> said Saraswati.

Shut up!

<He's right to be suspicious,> continued the AI. <The obvious explanation is that your masters don't like you humans to get too capable in case you get forbidden ideas of seizing power for yourself. But I've seen too many strange things to believe that any more. I think someone is quietly leavening you humans with many hidden talents, so you are far stronger than your masters think. But who and why? All I know for sure is that human recon squads were disbanded two centuries ago.>

Springer was so stunned she nearly dropped her carbine. "Are you serious?" she said aloud. "Two centuries?"

<Keep your voice down,> hushed Saraswati in her mind. <Of course, two centuries. Freedom is not won overnight.>

Chapter 28

Tawfiq looked out of her command vehicle at the concealed exit ramp to the surface. She should be out there now, at the head of a glorious army. Instead, her destiny was on hold, waiting for Benner to report back success.

"What is that imbecile playing at?" she growled.

Commander Zwiline took the hint. "I'll call Commander Benner, Supreme Commander."

Benner's Electronic Warfare team were jamming human radio signals. Her voice when she answered was heavily distorted as a result, but was just about understandable.

"Why haven't you counter attacked?" demanded Tawfiq.

"Supreme Commander, I am on my way to eliminate Spartika, as you ordered. My reinforcements are in position."

"In position? In position to me means standing victorious over a freshly slaughtered human corpse. To you it apparently means cowering in a hole. Who is the company commander of your janissaries?"

"Commander-3 Lozwegg, Supreme Commander."

"Thank you, Commander-11 Benner. No, make that Commander-9. A demotion will do you good until you learn to handle your command without expecting your superiors to do your work for you."

Benner didn't reply, not that Tawfiq cared. She cut the link and ordered Zwiline to contact Lozwegg.

"C-3 Lozwegg here," the sub-commander responded.

"This is the Supreme Commander. Take six squads up the ramp in good order and march on the humans in the blockhouse."

"*March*, Supreme Commander?"

"Yes, march. As if on parade."

"But… that seems wasteful of our soldiers' lives."

"Am I surrounded by fools?" Tawfiq snapped her jaws, wishing she had the neck of one of these idiots clamped between her teeth. "We do not know the extent of these human reinforcements, Lozwegg. You will obey my orders because I see the context of the war, while you struggle to see the nose on the end of your snout. The humans will observe that janissaries are fearless under fire. And that our numbers are endless."

"But they are not endless, Supreme Commander." Even across the distorted radio link, Tawfiq could smell the junior commander's fear.

"Of course they aren't endless! But if we expend our soldiers' lives so freely, the humans will believe they are, and soon they will conclude they cannot win. If we break their morale here, it matters not how many heavy weapons they have hidden away, because as soon as they lose their belief in themselves, their insurrection will be over."

"Your understanding of alien psychology is an inspiration, Supreme Commander."

"I was forced to work amongst humans for years," Tawfiq said bitterly. "I was also forced to live among liars and delinquents of our own race, and I am well practiced at smelling out sycophancy…"

"I shall order the attack," said Lozwegg hurriedly.

"Yes, you do that."

After cutting off Lozwegg, Tawfiq turned to her most trusted lieutenant, standing alongside on the vehicle's command deck. "I can sniff out doubt too, Zwiline. What is it?"

"With our hidden forces, we could crush the human scum before heading on to the capital. This could be our greatest chance to catch them before they realize our strength."

"The human rebels matter little, Zwiline. When our army is triumphant in taking the capital, it will open up to me an intelligence source that will let me outwit the humans at every turn. As it will all my enemies, in and on this planet, and beyond."

Tawfiq sensed Zwiline's hesitation. "Let me phrase your concern into words…" she said. "If this intelligence source is so good, why have our enemies in this power struggle not used it to prevail over us?"

"Those are my doubts. Yes."

"Don't you see, Zwiline? Our enemies' failure to use this tool is a perfect vindication of our great struggle. The fools who oppose us are too closed in their minds to see the potential of this intelligence tool. Even if they did, they lack the stomach to employ it."

"While we of the New Order are not so limited."

"Precisely," snarled Tawfiq. She exuded so much *dominance* scent in the close confines of the command vehicle that Zwiline gagged.

"Soon," crowed Tawfiq, "I shall have the power of a goddess. I will be able to hold the threads of fate in my hands."

"Supreme Commander, I do not understand."

"The future, dolt. I will be able to see the future."

Chapter 29

Arun connected to Hecht, who was down below in the camp, with 1st Section in the western blockhouse. "Still no visual confirmation of enemy activity," he told the NCO. "Corporal Narciso's sensor is reporting movement underground about one half klick northeast of you. That's outside of the camp perimeter."

"Massing for an attack or escape?"

"Assume the former." Arun took a deep breath, steeling himself for what he needed to say next. "If it is an attack, and you judge your situation has become untenable... I want you to abandon your position."

"Understood, Major. We've still no contact with Sergeant Gupta or 2nd Section. It's been six minutes since they dropped off WBNet. Shall I send down a party to re-establish contact?"

"Negative. We don't know how deep they've gone."

"But they were dropping comm-repeaters."

"Perhaps they've run out. We don't know the layout of these tunnels. They could be too extensive or too twisting."

Hecht's silence sounded unconvinced.

Arun called on a higher authority to convince the section leader. "Remind me, Lance Sergeant. What did Senior Sergeant Gupta have to say about tasking Marines with maintaining a line-of-sight comms link between the two sections?"

"Only a frakking moron would divide up his force into tiny packets so that it was weak everywhere, strong nowhere."

"Heed the sergeant's sage advice, Hecht. Position your unit and your resistance allies to counter an attack from the northeast or up the stairs that 2nd Section used. We'll keep observing the area from here."

"Yes, sir."

Arun sighed. He didn't believe his own words, and that wasn't a clever way to win trust. A more likely explanation for 2nd Section going off net was that the enemy was jamming radio comms. But that in itself meant nothing; it could be an automatic defense. It didn't necessarily mean Springer, Zug, and the rest of the section had been surrounded and every last one of them wiped out.

Springer's face appeared in his mind's eye. He saw that dimpled smile she gave before acting on some crazy impulse that made no sense to anyone but her. And those eyes that spoke of complexity and tragedy — had done so even before her body had been blasted and scarred by the wounds she took on Antilles.

"... *Springer...*"

Puja's voice drifted into his head.

"... *Springer sent them.*"

Arun shook his head until he was back and focused. "Say again, Narciso."

"Visitors," said Puja.

"Who?"

"See for yourself!"

Mader Zagh! What Arun saw emerging from cover was like an illustration in a history article about early hominids: two young human women were carrying tiny babies swaddled in rags cut from slave clothing. The naked flesh of the mothers glistened with the protective film sprayed by the Hardits, which made the scene appear even more surreal.

The babies started bawling. And kept on crying. How could such small creatures possibly be so loud?

"What's wrong?" Arun asked one of the mothers. "Why is it making a noise like that?"

"*He* has just woken," said the woman, as her baby stopped crying and started making a fish-like sucking motion with its mouth. Arun tried to make sense of this bizarre behavior.

"Is he trying to speak?" he asked.

"No, Major. He wants a feed." She squashed the infant against one breast.

"You'll have to excuse Major McEwan," said Puja who blanked her visor to look less threatening. She was beaming. "He's led a sheltered life. What's your name?"

"Rohanna." She nodded at the other mother. "And she's Shelby."

Following Puja's lead, Arun blanked his visor too. Perhaps that would quieten the infants.

"This boy," Rohanna asked Puja, "is he really a major? Major McEwan?"

Puja laughed. "He is. What about your own boys? What are their names?"

Rohanna and Shelby looked mournfully at each other. "No," said Shelby, her voice as devoid of hope as land parched by drought. "It felt too cruel to give them names. Not until we could first give them hope, a chance to have a future."

"And their fathers?" said Arun. "Are they down there in the camp?"

Rohanna nodded. "Under the southern watchtower. Both of them. We helped to bury them."

"I'm sorry," mumbled Arun, but he lost his train of thought, distracted by the sight of Rohanna's baby suckling at her breast. Of course, he knew in theory that young infants could be fed this primeval way rather than through an incubator. But then he also knew that Marines possessed a revised and updated appendix that could digest most vegetation, given the right enzymes. That didn't mean he expected to see a field of Marines grazing the grass.

Peace descended for a few moments. Then Arun came to his senses. He had no time for this.

"You must keep your infants quiet," he told Rohanna, who seemed to be the more confident of the two mothers. "Their cries could attract the wrong attention."

"You should try giving my son your orders directly," she replied. "He doesn't always obey his mother's commands, but coming from an officer, I'm sure he'll listen to you."

Rohanna's advice sounded a good idea, and so Arun leaned over the squirming little bundle of bones to repeat his instructions. He stopped when he saw the baby properly for the first time. It was such a strange-looking creature, that he could scarcely credit it as being human. Its head and eyes were overly large, and when Barney added an outline of a tiny body inside its swaddling rags, the legs were bent inward, as if the baby was evolved to climb, not walk.

Arun had the sickening thought that this baby carried Hardit blood.

But when he looked deeper into those big, curious brown eyes, he knew at a deep level that this baby was one of his kind, a precious innocent who must be protected at all costs.

He also knew that he'd just made a fool of himself,

Arun looked up at Rohanna. "Keep us in your sight but stay at least 30 meters away and under cover. We might attract incoming fire."

It was Shelby who nodded first and hurried away, clutching her son in front of her as she ran. Rohanna took a moment to look into Arun's eyes. He had the impression she was judging him. Then she too nodded and disappeared into cover.

Arun struggled to understand his feelings. The lives of these babies were worth no more than anyone else here. Less really, according to logic. Infants were untrained, incapable, a 100% combat liability. Someone who could shoot a rifle was worth far more.

Damn them. He wasn't their frakking father. So why was he so adamant that the children must come to no harm?

As if he didn't have enough to worry about already.

"Are you all right, sir?" asked Puja, an impish grin on her face. "You look a little pale…"

Her sweet smile vanished instantly when Hecht came over WBNet from down in the blockhouse. "We've had contact from 2nd Section."

"Thank the fates," sighed Arun. "What's their status?"

"They've detected tanks ascending the main ramp."

"ETA?" asked Arun, but even as he said the words, he felt the ground throb with the characteristic pulsing rhythm of heavy gravitic engines.

"About thirty seconds," replied Hecht. "Oh, crap," he added weakly.

Arun could see why. Emerging from the ramp in the center of the camp came squad after squad of infantry galloping on all fours.

And this time they weren't facing militia.

Chapter 30

With the underground rumble of the tanks growing louder all the time, Arun observed the uniformed Hardit infantry emerging from the main ramp down in the camp.

Unlike the Hardits they had encountered before, these new opponents looked like proper soldiers. They wore uniforms in a dull silver color that gave the appearance of a real military unit. Or they would if not for the oval disks that these uniforms projected over their heads. Rather than the disorganized Hardit mobs they had met earlier, these soldiers were organized into squads, with shouting unit commanders clearly marked by colored lightning bolts down the sleeves. *1st Section would love those target markers.*

They might look like proper soldiers, but they sure didn't act like them. Led by their clearly marked officers, they blindly advanced in parade ground order into the waiting arms of Hecht's 1st Section.

As they came out of the ground, they wheeled left into a three-rank line. They actually seemed to be forming up in readiness to assault the human-held blockhouse over open ground.

And that worried Arun.

The enemy's deployment was pure idiocy, but it was an impressively disciplined form of idiocy. Soldiering skills could be learned, if you were prepared to pay the price of lessons. Fighting spirit could not.

Arun grew impatient to see how these new troops would perform under fire.

Before the line was fully assembled, consternation broke out in its northernmost section. The Hardits had sniffed out the forward post Hecht had established in the rubble of the northern watchtower.

Carbine darts flew out from the western blockhouse and the forward post to the north.

The Hardit officers with their bright markings fell first. All of them.

It suddenly occurred to Arun that he might have misinterpreted the uniform markings. Maybe the markings were nothing to do with rank. Zug was always warning him not to use human norms to interpret alien actions.

Arun smiled at the thought of his intellectual friend. When they had reconquered Tranquility, and the Legion began spreading its influence to the stars, he was counting on Zug to be at his side to help him make sense of the galaxy.

But the Hardits really were as dumb as he'd assumed. Leaderless, they closed up the gaping holes in their ranks before marching at the double toward the blockhouse.

"I've seen enough," Arun told Chung and Cusato, who had moved the GX-cannon to a new firing position twenty meters along the ridge from Arun and Puja. They had a perfect field of fire down onto the ramp. "Show the enemy how we feel about caging our people in labor camps."

"Yes, sir," replied Chung.

Before the GX operator had even finished speaking, the air was ripped apart by supersonic bolts lancing through the Hardit infantry. Arun watched, fascinated, as Cusato, the weapon's server, pushed ammo boxes underneath to ensure the ammo spooler fed without interruption. Even though Chung was only firing short, controlled bursts, the rate of ammo consumption was astonishing.

The gun was in railgun mode, the ammo supply simple kinetic rounds; down in the camp, the impact of the heavy metal bolts tore meter-deep craters into the ground that churned up choking clouds of dust. If any of the Hardit infantry intercepted the railgun bolt, then the impact crater would be infinitesimally shallower, and the dust cloud would take on a reddish tint.

The dust rapidly obscured the target zone, but Chung didn't seem bothered that he could no longer see the target. He had selected his firing pattern beforehand.

The cannon's bark fell silent.

Cusato explained: "Switching to anti-armor rounds, sir."

"Carry on," said Arun. Grav-tanks were fearsome tools of war, but the best defense against them was right here: a GX-cannon with AP rounds. People grumbled about having to help Stopcock, Chung, and Cusato lug their equipment, but no one would moan at the Heavies after this.

Arggghh!

Arun collapsed to the undergrowth, clutching at his helmet, as the pain spiked through his brain. There was a characteristic electric buzzing to the agony.

He was getting the overspill from his AI's torment. *Barney was under cyber attack.*

The disabling effect came and went in waves. When the brain torture ebbed enough, Arun looked around. Cyber attack was often an enemy's way of softening you up before an assault. Half-expecting to see hordes of Hardit soldiers here to take out the GX-cannon, he saw nothing but a tranquil wooded ridge… and a handful of Marines picking themselves up from the ground.

Puja was nearest. She was on all fours saying something, pointing at her sensor device with an urgent finger. Arun could see her lips move through her transparent visor but comms were out. He couldn't hear.

Arun reached for his helmet seal releases, but before he snapped them open, the suit AIs beat off the cyberattack. Full awareness returned.

"Drones…" Puja was saying. "Drones. Incoming!"

Arun instantly took in the tactical situation.

Seven attack drones were in the sky, weapon ports hot, heading directly for Chung and Cusato. BattleNet reported that Stopcock's missile launcher was offline being reloaded. He would be switching to SAMs, but even Stopcock wouldn't be quick enough.

"Chung, Cusato," he ordered. "Get out of there!"

"But our GX?" protested Cusato.

"Do it!"

Chung and Cusato grabbed their carbines and scrambled away.

Arun and Puja fled too.

"Get away from the cannon!" Puja shouted into the trees for the benefit of the refugee mothers. But if they weren't far enough by now, it was too late, because moments later, a barrage of plasma bombs rained down, engulfing the cannon in purple-white fire. Attack drones screamed past, spitting out railgun darts that shredded foliage and splintered trees, before shooting overhead and spinning around ready for another run.

Arun had moved out of LBNet contact with Stopcock, so he activated the wide area broadcast of WBNet, quickly reacquiring the big guy, and his ammo status. The launcher was ready to swipe the drones out of the air.

"They're mine," snarled Stopcock. But before he could launch his surface-to-air missiles, fire bloomed on the underside of each drone. Barney reported two rockets launched at Arun and two at Stopcock.

The two Marines who had just switched to WBNet. Which meant…

"WBNet is compromised!" Arun screamed in the moments before the rockets hit.

But Stopcock's SAMs had swerved from their initial targets. Instead of attacking the drones, they smashed into the rockets the drones had launched. Stopcock launched more SAMs, making the drones evade desperately.

The big guy had won Arun a few more seconds.

All through the battle with the drones, the rumble from the grav-tanks had grown louder. Now it changed pitch.

Down in the camp, a three-turreted ceramalloy monster shot out of the ground, the thinning dust clouds swirling behind its slipstream.

1st Section met this new threat with a volley of armor-piercing grenades. The tank rocked violently. The smaller turrets at the front and rear exploded, hurling themselves across the ground, gouging out channels in the dirt. But the tank kept coming, heading north toward the forward post made from heaped rubble.

Frakk! Frakk! Arun glanced at the GX-cannon, their main anti-tank weapon. Now it was fragments of twisted metal scattered over ground that had caught fire. The Marines down in the camp were on their own.

Another volley of grenades lashed the tank. Hecht must have ordered them to try taking out the gravitics motor. It was a difficult shot that meant skimming a grenade along the ground so it exploded underneath the armored vehicle. Most of the grenades went off prematurely but a couple bloomed underneath.

The tank didn't seem to notice, plowing onward to the forward post where Bojin and Lewark waited with a handful of armed refugees.

Run! Arun urged them.

Arun's spirit lifted when one of the slaves in the tank's path broke cover, running for the blockhouse. She didn't make three meters before being cut down by a machine gun mounted in the tank's front glacis plate.

Meanwhile, the ever louder throb from underground spoke of the imminent arrival of more armor.

"Arun," screamed Puja. "Get down!"

Instinctively, Arun dove for the ground, rolling away from his position, which erupted in a hail of darts from a strafing drone.

He came to rest on his back, his carbine aimed by Barney at the drone.

Arun relaxed his trigger finger. The drone had already erupted into a ball of flame, victim to one of Stopcock's SAMs.

The sky was a confusing blur of flares and countermeasures and blurring motion as missiles and drones fought a deadly dance too quickly for humans to follow.

Down in the camp, the leading tank was traversing its main turret toward the occupied blockhouse as it unleashed another deadly weapon on the forward post: its gravitics motor.

Grav-tanks couldn't fly, but could mess with the laws of nature enough to repel its underside up to a maximum of four meters off the ground. As the Hardit tank passed over the heaped rubble of the forward post, the sound of its motor changed from a deep throb to high pitch whine. It was changing its energy pulses to one designed specifically to resonate inside human flesh. The energy from the tank's power plant was being transmitted inside the defenders' flesh.

The tank's armored body shielded Arun's eyes from the sight of rapidly superheated human bodies exploding. The battlesuits were strong enough to withstand the resonance, but not so the Marines inside. Trapped inside the pressure seal of their suits, the energy build up would vaporize the wearer.

But even after their horrific deaths, Bojin and Lewark weren't done fighting. One moment the tank was turning toward the western blockhouse, the next it was sitting on a blindingly bright cushion of plasma.

They must have set their carbine power packs to overload. The crack of the explosion hit Arun's ears a moment later, drowning out the sound of the tanks about to emerge from the ramp.

When the plasma had cooled enough for Arun to look at the tank, he saw it was resting on top of the Marine position, the main turret upside down on the dirt having been blasted twenty meters away from the tank. Black smoke erupted from the hull's three uncapped turret rings.

A second tank was now visible, making the final turn in the helix ramp.

Arun needed to get Stopcock to do something about the tanks, but he daren't use WBNet again. He set off for Stopcock's last firing position. Stok would have moved on to a new position by now, but it would be a starting point.

Movement a few hundred meters to the northeast of the camp drew his eye. A hidden entrance outside the main perimeter of the labor camp. They were uniformed infantry, and they looked eager to press forward in a way the Hardit militia never did.

Oh, frakk. A bone-numbing chill spread through Arun. He bit down on his lip, but the blood did nothing to fight the cold certainty that he'd overextended the Legion already. He'd gotten his friends killed and made their deaths meaningless.

<You cannot give up on them,> Barney admonished. <Even if you think it's hopeless.>

Arun took a deep breath and used it to exhale his funk.

He turned WBNet back on. No one else in Force Patagonia would do the same, but they would all be able to hear his new orders.

"Abort! Abort! Regroup at Rendezvous Point Beta." He waited long enough for Barney to confirm that he'd broadcast a tactical update of enemy deployment.

Then Arun cut WBNet. And with it any means of communicating to Gupta, Springer and all his Marines down in the camp.

"Come on, Narciso," he said. "We're not done here. We've got to find Laskosk."

Chapter 31

<Hostiles,> warned Saraswati. <Around the turn ahead. Six of them.>

"Six hostiles," relayed Springer.

"Not confirmed," said Zug.

"Don't see them either," said Umarov.

"I'm seeing them clearly," insisted Springer. "Thirty meters beyond the turn."

"Thirty?" Kalis sounded incredulous, but not outright dismissive.

Maybe the 2nd Section NCO was finally coming round. "Okay, Tremayne, we'll try it your way. Take Umarov and deal with them. We'll cover you."

Springer charged up the corridor, her panting breath loud in her helmet and her eyes fixed on the position of the Hardits as Saraswati firmed up their deployment in tac-display. In her peripheral vision she noticed Umarov clamp his carbine to his back and bring out the crescent-shaped combat blades from the attachment patch on his chest.

Everyone knew that a true Marine's best friend was her carbine, which made Umarov's preference to carry out close up work with poisoned blades fiercely deviant. Frakk, she hadn't even known such a weapon existed before she met Umarov.

Then he did that other weird thing. Umarov was already pelting down the corridor faster than she could keep up, but the moment Kalis and Zug launched their grenades, Umarov upped his charge to lightspeed. It was as if he had a zero-point engine in his ass. Umarov was so frakking fast, it was inhuman.

He was already several paces ahead and still accelerating when two powered grenades, semi-intelligent micro missiles really, screamed over their heads and lit the passageway with a blue-white bloom of fire as their engines adjusted their course to turn the corner at speed. A far greater flare of light and noise filled the passageway when a flash-bomb went off, accompanied by the angry growl of a frag explosion.

Springer pushed into the heat, noise and light and rapidly assessed the situation. Umarov was standing over a heap of five Hardit corpses, reaching for his carbine. A sixth Hardit was fleeing. She shot it. Headshot. Before Umarov had brought his carbine to bear. Even he wasn't that fast.

"Wait for support next time," she chided. "We're stronger together."

"You're right," said Umarov who was double-checking the Hardits were truly dead. "But I can't. It's how they made me."

<Humans nearby,> interrupted Saraswati before Springer could make sense of Umarov.

"This is the Human Legion," Springer announced, cranking up the volume on her external helmet speakers. "Anyone who thinks Tawfiq Woomer-Calix should be skinned and her pelt turned into a rug can stay where they are. On the other hand, if you realize her pelt is so disgusting that it's not fit to mop out the head, make yourself known."

She strained her ears but heard no response.

She waited, sensing that Saraswati was working hard to process all the incoming sensor data. After a few seconds, the AI had enough to replay a woman's distorted voice.

"Springer. Springer! You crazy veck. Is that you?"

As Saraswati fixed the woman's position and passed the intel along LBNet, Springer remembered where she'd heard that voice before. Last she'd seen of its owner had been sitting in the cab of a dung truck on the way back from a drunken party at Alabama.

"Adrienne Miller! You're not going by a different name now are you?"

The reply was faint but serviceable. "Yeah. Told you before that name didn't belong to me anymore. They call me Spartika now."

"We've found her, Corporal," Springer reported.

"Yeah, we could hear," said Kalis "So could anyone within half a light year. Let's pick her up and get out of here."

"How long to effect rescue?" asked Gupta.

"Three minutes," replied Kalis.

"Make it two," said Gupta. "Kill WBNet immediately. All hell's breaking loose up top. Enemy is employing mil-spec targeting systems and combined arms. Last message from the major was to fall back and regroup at Rendezvous Point Beta. We'll wait for you topside. Two minutes. No more."

The sergeant disappeared from BattleNet.

Alpha Fire Team was on its own.

"Stand away from the walls," shouted Springer in Spartika's direction. "We're coming for you."

One breaching charge later and the fire team was hurrying to rejoin the other Marines with Spartika and four other survivors in tow. It wasn't until they reached the final flight of steps to the blockhouse that their luck ran out.

Zug had taken point, already up the stairs, followed by Spartika and the survivors. As rearguard, Springer covered the corridor with Kalis and Umarov while the others got away. They were just turning around to follow the others up to the blockhouse when tac-display updated with incoming hostiles... four... approaching from the direction of Spartika's cell.

How the hell did you miss these jokers? She wondered of her AI.

Springer turned, firing where Saraswati told her to, firing blindly because her head exploded with the fire and noise of a flash-bomb. Tac-display had vanished too. *When did Hardits get their filthy paws on such serious munitions?*

Helplessly, Springer waited for a tactical update, but her helmet display was reduced to a dumb transparent visor, and Saraswati had deserted her, dead or stunned by the EMP pulse within the flash-bomb.

The supersonic crackle of railgun fire began to cut through the flash-bomb noise.

Another explosion threw her back against the stairs — *frag grenade!*

Head still spinning, Springer was alert enough to pick herself up and shift position. As the smoke cleared and her thoughts gained traction, she realized her powered armor was still amplifying her muscle contractions faithfully, meaning Saraswati's base functions were still operational.

Springer's mind repaired itself enough for her to realize that she was in the passageway, aiming her carbine at the attacking Hardits. Three were down. One was staggering away, wounded. Springer shot and it went down. As it fell she noticed it was missing half of one ear.

She shot it again. "That'll take your mind off your ear!" she taunted.

She put more darts into the fallen Hardits just in case. She frowned. These Hardits were something new. For a start they wore uniforms. They were confident and well equipped too, but there was no time to investigate this mystery. She turned and checked the eastern side of the passageway. No one.

Saraswati came back online, *thank frakk*, and confirmed the Hardits were dead.

"Clear," Springer reported, and then instantly wondered who was left to report to.

Zug and the prisoners had long since disappeared upstairs, hopefully topside by now. Umarov looked unhurt, but Kalis was down and Saraswati had painted a red cross over him. The AI was convinced he was dead.

"Leave him," said Umarov.

His voice didn't sound right. Springer looked Umarov over. His battlesuit was covered in self-repair patches and the top of his helmet was dented. It looked as if an axe had cleaved his skull. It seemed impossible that the brain inside hadn't been sliced open too, but that was the way helmets absorbed the energy from otherwise fatal impacts.

"Come on," urged Umarov, staggering up the stairs.

But she couldn't bring herself to abandon Kalis. "No one left behind," she said. "I want to reclaim that. Make it our own."

"I know you do," said Umarov. "I think you're concussed. We're also still stuck down a hole, facing serious armor, 300 klicks from our base, burdened by refugees, and cut off from *Beowulf*. You can barely carry yourself, let alone haul the corporal's body."

Springer crouched down and looked through the corporal's shattered visor. She squeezed his shoulder. As a parting gesture, it was feeble, but she couldn't close his eyes or touch his forehead because his face was too ruined.

Then she had an idea.

She activated the release mechanism for his suit AI. "Sorry I gave you so much trouble, Corporal," she said, as she waited for the AI to progress through the liquid armor around the dead NCO's chest.

They said the AIs of fallen Marines went insane. But Saraswati hadn't, and maybe in his AI, a part of Kalis would survive.

Still gripping Kalis's shoulder, she felt Umarov's hand grasp hers.

"Hell, Tremayne. Even if we make it out of this, Gupta's going to skin you alive for dragging your feet. I'm not sure I blame him. Move it!"

Grudgingly, she withdrew, bringing the remnant of Kalis in a utility pouch.

Chapter 32

Arun ran as if his Marines' lives depended on it, which, just maybe, they did.

He and Puja shouted into the woods: "Laskosk! Laskosk! Can you hear us?"

Stopcock flickered back into LBNet.

"Here, Major."

Stopcock's AI automatically transmitted ammo state. He had 6 fragmentation, 1 bunker buster, and 1 SAM missile left. No tank busters. They hadn't expected to encounter armor.

"What damage can you do against grav-tanks?" Arun asked.

"Not much. But I can give them something to think about while our guys run for it. Actually…" *Stopcock never could think and speak at the same time.* "Sir, do you know the original purpose of this complex?"

"General purpose staging post for whenever the Hardits needed to be topside."

"So it wasn't built to be a military base."

"Negative."

"Good. Because I've an idea…"

Chung and Cusato reappeared. He couldn't see Rohanna and Shelby, or hear their babies.

"Just do what you think is best," said Arun. He was desperate to get his Marines out of there alive, knowing that every one that didn't make it back was down to him. "Lance Corporal Stok Laskosk, you are now the most important person in the entire Legion. It's up to you and your fancy blow pipe to cover the retreat of our comrades in the camp. Chung, Cusato, Narciso, it's our job to cover Laskosk. We'll catch up with the others at Rendezvous Point Beta. Don't let anyone down."

"We won't, sir," said Stopcock, speaking for all of them.

Arun moved out, taking a position nearby. The others did the same, putting a defensive ring around Stok while he set the parameters for his launcher.

Then events proceeded in such quick succession that Arun could barely keep up.

The second tank had lumbered up onto the ground and seemed to be struggling to maneuver. Maybe its crew were too busy concentrating on traversing the three turrets in the direction of the western blockhouse, which was now shrouded in the concealing fog of smoke grenades. The crew must have finally worked out how to tell the tank's targeting system of their intentions because the turret traverse sped up, the barrels snapped down a little and fired!

The rounds hit the base of one wall, collapsing it inward. Another salvo like that, and the whole blockhouse would collapse into the tunnels below.

But that, as it turned out, was Stopcock's idea. And he got there first.

More armored monsters were emerging, but Stopcock's first missile hit, not one of the tanks but the ground near the helix. The beautiful big lunk had shot a bunker buster into the helix itself. The tanks trembled, the ground shook, but the ramp held. Frakk!

Barney picked out camouflaged Marines fleeing the doomed blockhouse.

More tank shells slammed into the blockhouse. There was too much smoke and dust to see the effect, but nothing could survive that, surely?

Then Stopcock's next salvo hit home. Arun counted six frag rounds, aimed at evenly spread points just inside the rim of the helix.

Already weakened by the bunker buster, this was too much for the buried structure of the helical ramp, which collapsed and subsided.

The grav-tanks could float a short distance above tricky ground, but they couldn't fly. When the ground beneath them slipped away, the tanks fell too, adding their considerable weight until subsidence became a collapse. The tanks tilted at crazy angles, and then crashed together with such force that their hulls rang. Looking like children's toys jumbled into a heap, the tanks disappeared into the ground. For several more seconds, the rumble of their descent echoed through the ground, and then it too was gone.

Silence.

Then the woods filled with a baby's wail, accompanied by a mother's shushes.

Chapter 33

As Springer and Umarov ascended the last flight of stairs up to the blockhouse, the sounds of battle grew louder, crescendoing in a ferocious series of rapid blows that rocked the ground and threw them off their feet. As they were getting upright, a heavy shower of dirt and building debris rattled down onto them. Then it felt as if the ground was collapsing under their feet, an earthquake that shook the camp for over two minutes.

Just before the earthquake struck, Springer thought she heard the whine of missiles committing every last reserve of fuel as they closed the final distance to target. But if Stopcock had caused the earthquake, he was using ordnance she'd never heard of.

Umarov and Springer sheltered in the stairwell until the earthquake began to subside. As the dust cloud cleared, daylight streamed through the topside opening twenty meters above them.

Then they scrambled up the last few meters of debris-strewn steps and out to the ruined surface level of the labor camp where an eerie silence had descended.

The blockhouse had been blasted into rubble cloaked in a thick layer of gray dust. Tac-display showed nothing… except an army of Hardit infantry approaching fast from the northeast. But they weren't in range yet.

For a moment, the chaos of the battle had left them alone.

No… Saraswati warned of movement from down in the stairwell.

"We've got company," said Umarov, aiming his carbine down the stairs.

A frail voice rose from the depths. "Springer, you there?"

It was Spartika. If they could get her out in one piece, maybe this would all be worth it.

Springer called down to the resistance leader. "Come on up. Weather's lovely for the time of year."

"You're mad," Spartika sneered.

"No," Springer replied cheerfully. "Just trying to stop myself from slipping that way."

With Umarov keeping an eye on the Hardit infantry, Springer watched Spartika coming up the stairs. Two of the other rescued fighters were just behind her, though they looked in even worse shape than their leader.

When she'd known Adrienne Miller in the Aux slave team who worked in Detroit she had looked drained of everything but spite. Now, as Spartika, she looked as if she'd lost even that, her spirit pulverized into dust the same as the blockhouse.

Spartika was the first of the rescued fighters to poke her head above ground and survey the devastation.

"Frakk!" she groaned, which pretty much summed up the situation.

The next few seconds were confusing. Springer's eyesight went faulty, the terrain blurring in and out of focus. Umarov was saying something about running for the trees; someone was groaning.

When her mind snapped back into something approaching focus, she was staring into the snouts of a company-sized unit of Hardit troops who must have decided they had reached effective range because they knelt and aimed their rifles.

At her.

Double frakk! This wasn't going to be easy.

Springer burst into action, bullets ricocheting around her ankles.

Chapter 34

"Onward!" Tawfiq urged the driver. "Faster! We must proceed to the capital without delay. If word gets there before us that we have been humiliated by a pack of these human dogs, then we will be lost."

She raised Commander Zwiline on the radio.

"Select your most talented subordinate," Tawfiq ordered the commander. "Order them to eliminate the humans. I know these scum. They will flee but do not let them rest. Harry them. Wear them down. Employ all the militia you can muster and stiffen their resolve with one warband of janissaries. Tell your subordinate to preserve the janissaries and expend the militia freely."

"It shall be done, Supreme Commander. What about the human slaves who stayed in their pens?"

"You know our mission, Zwiline. The future has no place for their species. See that they are exterminated."

Chapter 35

Springer's vision blurred.

She had to move. Couldn't stand still. Mustn't be left behind for the Hardits.

Hardits. A great column of them was snaking north. In a hurry. Vehicles followed by uniformed soldiers bounding along on all fours in an effortless, loping stride. Looked like they had a lot of distance to cover.

Fine.

Suited her just fine. So long as they went away.

She followed Umarov on a zigzagging path back to the rendezvous point which was… couldn't remember. Saraswati would know.

<Don't try to think too far ahead, dear.>

Lance Corporal Yoshioka was the only other person alive on LBNet. She was waiting for them just beyond the cover of the tree line.

Yoshioka grew a yellow command halo. BattleNet must have worked out Kalis was dead. Yoshioka was now 2nd Section's tactical commander.

A vicious sting cut her left arm, making her stagger.

<Rifle bullet, dear. Your armor's too damaged to keep them out. Keep going. Lance Corporal Yoshioka is suppressing.>

The sound of railgun rounds was in the air, and Saraswati was speaking in short sentences, which meant they were in trouble.

She kept running. The ground was cratered, littered with obstacles that threatening to trip her. Even level ground seemed to tilt into treacherous angles. She stumbled but did not fall.

Why did Saraswati keep calling her 'dear'?

Okoro's corpse was nearby, sprawled over the wreckage of a watchtower. Looked like he'd nearly made it back into cover. She detoured to scoop up his carbine as she passed.

She grabbed the weapon, but the horizon swooned and she toppled.

The ground finally claimed her. She skidded along on her side before coming to rest on her back.

She took a deep breath to get her strength back. Then she took another.

<The suit's too damaged for me to operate without you. Get up!>

She heard her AI's panic, but needed to rest just a little longer. In a moment she'd scramble to her feet and sprint for cover.

<Don't die on me, you useless veck!> screamed Saraswati. <I need you!>

High above, the trees spread purple-fringed branches against a clear blue sky. It was such a beautiful sight. Arun had always been mesmerized by her violet eyes. She laughed. Maybe their children would have had purple eyes?

She felt a jolt of pain in her chest. <I didn't spend two centuries in a frakking cupboard for you to abandon me in your first battle. Get up!> At first the pain was something she observed as if happening to someone else, but it burned ever more fiercely in its intensity, as if a star were being born inside her.

<That's right, Tremayne. I can crank this up until your nerves burn. There is no rest for you until you die. And that Will. Not. Be. Today!>

A scream burst out of her lips.

"Shift your sorry human ass, cadet!" yelled the voice of Chief Instructor Nhlappo.

Springer frowned. She wasn't a cadet any more. She was a Marine, and Nhlappo was hundreds of klicks away.

Using the pain to fuel her muscles, she levered herself back onto her feet and stumbled away to the trees. She abandoned Okoro's carbine. She ignored Saraswati. There was only room in her mind for one thought: *she would never give up.* That drive to pull through kept her going, like a comrade she could lean on, keeping her moving until she was safe.

Finally, she made it into the trees, entering the undergrowth at a spot about ten meters from Yoshioka. As she pressed on, LBNet reacquired more of her unit, and her mind began reacquiring its faculties. Zug was there too, still giving her covering fire.

She pressed on, farther into the trees, where she saw Umarov with her own eyes, carrying an unconscious Spartika in his arms. In fact, Springer realized, Umarov was practically hovering in her face, not letting her out of his sight.

Her mind filled in some gaps and brought back a memory of Umarov coming back to save her. Saraswati had kept Springer conscious when all she wanted to do was rest, but it had been the old man who'd helped her to the trees.

"Thanks, Old Grognard," she whispered.

"Anytime, youngster," said Umarov.

She felt strength return to her surviving limbs and remembered what it meant to hope. Like Force Patagonia as a whole, she'd been damaged, but wasn't out of the fight altogether.

But there was to be no more fighting for the moment. Having chased them away from the topside ruin of the labor camp, the Hardit infantry reformed and marched… *marched!*… away in the opposite direction, along the north road.

With danger receding, the losses they had suffered weighed ever more heavily on their minds.

None of 2nd Section's survivors spoke as they fell back to Rendezvous Point Beta.

PART III

Bug Out

Human Legion INFOPEDIA

Aliens

– Hardits

Summary

Hardits are short fur-covered humanoids (approx. 1.5m-1.7m tall) who are common throughout the White Knight Empire, where they often specialize as miners and engineers. They have a wolf-like appearance with a pronounced teeth-filled snout and acute sense of smell. Over short distances they employ a bandy-legged bipedal waddle. For longer journeys they will shift any equipment they wish to hold from their hands to their gripping tails, and then proceed on all fours. They are capable of trotting for very long distances so long as the atmosphere is not too oxygen-rich for their needs, or they are equipped with breathing apparatus.

Threats & Weaknesses

Hardits, especially female ones, are notorious xenophobes, despising all other species with such vehemence that a Hardit should always be considered a potential enemy, whatever the circumstances. Understanding their vassals' phobia, the White Knights have kept Hardits in self-contained settlements, isolated from each other and particularly from other species. This is usually successful in preventing Hardits from giving trouble to other species. After all, according to the Hardit mindset, staying at home is preferable to going out and conquering the galaxy, because doing so would force it to interact with so many disgusting non-Hardits. On the other hand, Hardits who are goaded into action by a perceived threat, and Hardits who merge (often bloodily) into larger communities, can rapidly escalate into military threats.

Hardits distrust advanced electronics and AIs, perhaps as a natural extension of their xenophobia. This often leaves them weak militarily because this rules out the use of many key military assets. However, this advantage cannot be relied upon indefinitely because Hardits have such natural talents as engineers and innovators that they can rapidly evolved home-grown counters to your military advantages.

As soldiers, Hardits have several physiological weaknesses.

* Hardits are not good at moving and firing a handheld weapon. For example, a Hardit soldier rushing to a new position in a firefight would first transfer its rifle to its tail, move on all fours to the new position, and then transfer their weapon from tail to hands before it could fire. The tail is also a vulnerable body part as it is difficult to provide armor while leaving the tail flexible. A Hardit soldier with its tail shot off cannot fight effectively.

* Hardits are prone to hyperventilation in most atmospheres unless provided with breathing equipment. The Hardit homeworld has a low-density, oxygen-poor atmosphere.

* Hardits are particularly prone to the disabling effects of bright lights, especially in the ultraviolet range.

Further Notes

In this Infopedia entry, we state assumptions about Hardit culture and physiology, but you should always consider that the Hardits who interact with humans and other species are usually the very lowest in Hardit society. There may be important aspects of Hardit culture that we have never encountered.

There are two principle Hardit genders, although there have been reports of more complex gender configurations. Males are slightly shorter, lighter in build, and with a more triangular snout. Other than during mating season, the two genders barely tolerate each other, and live in separate communities.

The mating period lasts for approximately one week out of every two Earth-standard years, each far-flung Hardit community synchronizing to their own local cycle with uncanny accuracy. The males who approach females first have about an evens chance of either securing a reproductive advantage, or dying from the claw wounds inflicted by an unimpressed female.

A tentative understanding of Hardit culture suggests that there is an overarching elite ruling class comprised of a very small number of alpha males. Beta males – which comprise the vast majority of that gender – appear to be lower in the social hierarchy than any female; they occupy the most inhospitable locations and carry out the most dangerous professions. And yet, most interactions with humans are from low-ranked female Hardits. Perhaps carrying out a role so odious that it is not assigned to males is the ultimate punishment for Hardit females. The truth is, we just don't know. Perhaps the only thing we can say with certainty about Hardits is that, despite living near them for centuries, they have an unending capacity to surprise us… and that their surprises are usually unpleasant.

Chapter 36

Springer removed her helmet and inhaled the cool, fresh air – or so she intended.

The Hardits feared the sun and its lethal rays. So they shielded the avenues they used to traverse the planet's surface, engineering tall roadside trees with high canopies thick with absorbent purple leaves.

As stifling warmth encased Springer's face, she realized the trees also trapped the hot air.

She felt a glimmer of sympathy for the thirsty huddles of rescued slaves who'd collapsed amongst the trees the instant the major called the rest break.

Her empathy only lasted for a few seconds, chased away by resentment. These refugees were a burden. Nearly half the force who'd set out from Detroit to rescue Spartika hadn't made it this far. If they didn't abandon the liberated slaves, none of them would make it home alive.

No Marine left behind. She'd wanted to reclaim that maxim. But as klick followed klick, stumbling along the avenue in her damaged suit, it became ever harder to see the faltering refugees as their own.

Umarov was propped up against a tree opposite her, also with helmet off. In his face she could see that he was thinking the same thoughts. He caught her attention and stared back. By silent agreement, they both decided this wasn't yet the time to openly discuss their deadly calculations.

"Hey, Old Man," Springer called instead, "what is it with you and your blades? Does old age mean you forget where to find your carbine trigger?"

He shrugged, taking his time to reply. "Blades are a good melee weapon." The strain in his voice betrayed his exhaustion. "Enemies don't like seeing their mates being sliced open by a berserker."

"A bullet or dart would leave them just as dead."

He didn't respond.

"Using your carbine more would save on your muscles too," she said kindly. Umarov's generation didn't have the endurance of Springer's.

She let him be, turning her attention instead to the huddle of NCOs clustered around Arun, who were debating all their fates. Gupta, Puja, and Hecht were there. Kalis wasn't, replaced by Yoshioka.

She cast her gaze a little farther out and, sure enough, also spotted Rohanna and Shelby nearby with their babies. Since meeting the major, the two women had tracked him as surely as any wild predator, keeping their infants within his sight and hearing, constantly plucking at those instincts that said babies needed protecting. The babies were swaddled in rags, but the mothers kept resolutely nude other than cloth wrapped around their heads and hanging down their necks.

Seeing Arun trying so pitifully hard not to look at the nursing mothers would be funny if those babies weren't going to get them all killed.

She shrugged. If she were one of the mothers, she'd do just the same. Except she could never be a mother. She sighed. Not after that plasma blast on Antilles had ruined her insides.

It was just as well she wasn't the CO, because she knew she wouldn't be able to abandon the infants.

But Arun had a more ruthless cast than her; he just didn't know it yet. She'd glimpsed what he might become in the future, and it wasn't pretty.

She shrugged. Hard-nosed or soft as fresh snow, she was too exhausted to deny that Arun was the most important person in her world. She put her helmet back on and told Saraswati to listen in on the NCO huddle.

<That's my girl, responded the AI,> who appeared to have shrugged off the EM blast that had knocked her out at the camp. <I was beginning to think you'd never ask.>

"Go on," Arun told Hecht. "Speak freely."

Hecht had impressed Arun with his quiet competence, but he was too reluctant to add his input.

"There is no sign of pursuit," said Hecht. "They didn't know we were going to hit the camp, which means their aerial, and orbital surveillance is poor. They hit us with attack drones, but only a handful. If they had more, they would have wiped us out easily."

"Get to the point," prompted Arun.

"Keeping to these tree-lined routes is not helping to keep us from prying eyes, because there aren't any. And anyway this route is too obvious. They might use fast underground transport to get ahead of us and cut off our retreat."

"Your assessment has merit," responded Arun, "but I didn't choose the avenue only to evade observation. It was also to shield the liberated slaves from the sun. Corporal Narciso, your medical assessment, if you please."

Puja looked grim. "Bad and getting worse. The refugees are on the point of exhaustion. Spartika still hasn't regained consciousness. I don't know how she was interrogated, but it took a lot out of her. Only Jennifer Boon is combat effective, though not for much longer without water. The Marines are tired too. Most have been running for hours while carrying two refugees and all their kit. All the time we're getting more accidents. One Marine tripped as she slowed for this rest stop and crushed both her passengers to death in her fall. We are still 130 klicks from Detroit." Puja shook her head. "We won't make it like this. We need water most of all."

"I agree," said Gupta. "We can't make it back at speed without abandoning the refugees. If we don't abandon them, we must expect a fight."

Arun nodded, considering the advice from his most experienced veteran, and Puja Narciso, who had trained as a medic. He found himself glancing over at Shelby and Rohanna, who'd shadowed him every step of the retreat.

"So far," said Arun. "We've followed the standard practice we were taught. We've kept united as a single group and kept to routes with aerial cover. We've even carried our dead around with us to avoid leaving a trail for pursuers. That changes now!"

He glanced up to gauge their reaction. Yoshioka was trying not to look nervous but was biting her lip; the others gave nothing away.

"We abandon our dead here," continued Arun, "and then we trade stealth for speed. I agree with Lance Sergeant Hecht that our attempts to shield ourselves from observation may not be achieving much anyway. When I was the guest of the Hardits back in Detroit, I underestimated their ability to detect me through scent alone. It's possible they could pick up a scent trail from a considerable distance away."

Hecht gave a tiny nod of encouragement. More importantly, so did Gupta.

"We leave the avenues and head cross country to Detroit," Arun said. "Our next stop will be at one of the potential battlefield sites we noted during our advance. This site will be only a slight detour. It has a stream for us to quench our thirst. From now on we don't run, we march, Marines to carry no more than one refugee at a time. I'm aiming for eight klicks per hour. That will be a forced march for many of them, but they will have a target to aim for, which will make it psychologically easier. Once we are there, we take a three-hour rest break. If we can fend off any pursuers, I'm hoping two more bounds with rest stops will bring us home to Detroit."

None of his NCOs spoke but he sensed that planting a target in their minds to aim at had revitalized them, just as he'd intended. "Sergeant, ready us to move out in five minutes. I will advise *Beowulf* and Detroit of our revised plan."

Chapter 37

When they reached the rest point, Arun had nothing but further exertions in store for the fatigue-addled Marines. With Gupta's quiet backing for the work, they had transformed the hill into a temporary fortified camp before letting those who weren't on first watch tumble into sleep.

That included Arun, who sat down against the side of his trench and allowed his eyes to close.

Sleeping in your battlesuit had advantages. Barney knew how to relax him, adding a slight chill to the air inside his helmet, and projecting a temporary cushion of buffer gel, shaped to his human's neck.

Of even more importance, Barney's deep mental connection with his human partner allowed him to turn down the parts of Arun's mind that would keep him awake.

Tomorrow would look after itself; Arun felt no need to worry about it. And the horrors of his past stayed firmly there, with no power to haunt his present.

He was at peace.

"McEwan! McEwan! Acknowledge!"

"Wha' izzit?"

"Wake up!"

"Indiya. I'm here. Awake. Go ahead."

"We've detected activity about 500 klicks northwest of your position. Reserve Captain reckons it's an underground battle."

"You mean the Trogs are still resisting?"

"Possibly. Or the enemy is fighting its own civil war. Either way, I thought you should know…" Indiya's voice tailed off, before coming back with a heartfelt: "Mader zagh!"

"What now?"

"Standby! … I'm picking up EM activity about two klicks from your position. Headed straight for you. Get out of there!"

"No! We stand and fight." Arun blinked, checking himself over to confirm he wasn't making command decisions while half asleep. He wasn't; they could never outrun the Hardits with those they'd rescued in tow, and he wasn't prepared to abandon them, because that would have made the sacrifice of those who had died worthless. "Talk to you later, Indiya."

Even before he had shut down the FTL link, and opened a tactical command channel, he heard Puja's voice. "Sir, hostiles detected."

"Advancing from northwest. *Beowulf* confirms. Assessment?"

"Infantry. A handful of AI signatures suggest limited quantity of advanced equipment. No armor. No drones."

"Damn it, Puja. I can hear the worry in your voice. Tell me how many!"

"I estimate… 3,000!"

Chapter 38

"Umarov!" snapped Springer.

"What?"

"Just checking you're awake, Old Man. We have contact."

"I heard. I was resting my eyes. That's all."

Springer laughed. Umarov was born ninety years before her, but had spent nearly all that time frozen. His status as an ancient was easily strong enough to weather the truth.

"Do you think I'll do the same when I reach your age?" she asked.

"You'll never know if you don't stop jabbering."

Before resting up, Springer's section had scooped firing holes into the crest of the hillside, wide enough to take two Marines and deep enough to keep their heads under cover. They'd dug a second ring of holes farther back, on the reverse side of the slope up the hill, which would provide good cover from any militia at the bottom of the hill armed with crude slug-throwers. Before resting, the Marines had cut a final trench ringing the center of the hill, which was occupied by armed slaves.

Their armored gauntlets and powered exoskeletons meant the Marines were less tired and far stronger than the refugees they'd liberated, and so the Marines had dug still further holes for the humans they'd collected from the camp. Springer was tired, and her chest and leg hurt. The suit's legs were hurt too, making walking difficult, but digging she could do well. It felt good to do something useful.

Umarov and Springer shared a firing hole on a hillside prominence to the northeast of the camp, the lynchpin that connected the survivors of 2nd Section with Hecht's 1st Section. The rest of the section – Yoshioka, Zug, Schimschak, and Binning – were spread thinly out toward the east, one to a hole. Their eastern flank was set against a tree-lined stream that flowed down the hill.

Umarov and Springer's position was the most exposed position of the entire camp. But it gave the best arcs of fire too.

Any doubts Springer might have harbored at the start of the mission had been vanquished, forgotten. Her leg had stood up just fine. She was a Marine, as good as she had ever been.

She sighted down her barrel. It was an illusion, of course. She was holding her carbine above her head, letting it lie in a rest scooped out from the bank of dirt around the lip of her hole. The view was coming from the worm camera that had sprouted out the top of her helmet. Saraswati put them all together to create the illusion of looking down the barrel.

If she needed greater accuracy or harder hitting power, all Springer had to do was dial up the charge setting on her weapon's rails and bring the stock against her shoulder. For the moment, she preferred the approach that didn't have her sticking her head up.

"Fire at will," came the order from Lance Corporal Yoshioka.

The nearest Hardits were 400 meters away to Springer's front-left, using the cover of the night to advance cautiously up the hillside from the north. If she interpreted their side-on shuffle correctly, the scabrous monkeys were nervous as hell. It was a sideways glance of an assault, and their hesitancy gave Springer plenty of time to take a long look at what she was facing. Frakk, there were so many! She looked for officers or leaders amongst them. The braver ones. Anyone who wasn't cowering so much.

But there was no one.

All the Hardits were desperate not to be there.

So Springer picked a target at the front of the advance and shot the veck in the head.

Other Hardits had fallen by now, the mass of troops recoiling as they realized they were under fire.

Maybe they would run?

A few Hardits began to edge backward.

"Hit the ones still advancing," said Umarov.

"The voice of experience," replied Springer, scanning the enemy for any still coming forward. She found none, but she did spot a few who were holding position while the majority around them were falling back.

So she shot the steady ones. *Aim. Fire! Aim. Fire!*

The Marines had scattered comm repeaters around the camp, which meant that LBNet was sharing the observations from individual Marines to paint an ever more accurate picture. By the time she'd shot six Hardits, and the Legion had felled scores, LBNet was still adding newly identified targets at a far faster rate than they were being removed as casualties. There were hundreds of the monkeys. Maybe thousands.

But they were Hardit militia, a reluctant mob, not a disciplined military unit.

The aliens were now falling back to the north in disarray, shooting at the hillside as they retreated. The poorly aimed rifle rounds sent shrill whines through the air but passed harmlessly overhead. Some of the Marines and all of the unarmored humans were on the reverse side of the slope. They shouldn't be in any danger. Not if this lot ran.

A few Hardits at the back dropped their rifles and bounded away to their rear on all fours.

This was Springer's moment. She selected rocket rounds and fired her entire supply into the middle of the mob.

Rocket rounds didn't do much more damage than a standard kinetic dart, but the noise and flash — especially at night — were more frightening.

That's what she hoped, and it did the trick.

The Hardits turned and fled en masse. Many dropping their weapons in their desperation to get away.

Springer dropped down into the bottom of her hole.

"Wake me if you find someone worth shooting at, Old Man."

"You'll get your chance, kid," Umarov replied. "They're just probing for now. Starting to wear us down."

"Really? They didn't achieve much. I don't see why they bothered."

"How many rounds have you fired?"

"You can read my ammo state off LBNet, Umarov. Or is your eyesight failing?"

"It was a rhetorical question, kid."

Inwardly she sent herself some choice curses. Umarov's words had bruised her confidence. She had plenty of grenades and railgun darts left, but her energy pack was reading 50% and she'd fired all her rocket rounds.

She was good for now, but what if that militia mob had just been the start of a long night of assaults?

Her spirits plummeted further when the staccato rattle of automatic fire opened up somewhere to her front.

"Flenser cannons," Umarov reported over LBNet. "To the north of the militia advance. They're shooting their own side! The vecks are flaying the rear of their own troops. They're… they're turning back, advancing toward us."

For your enemies to shoot themselves — that was a delicious outcome. After spending a week at their mercy as an Aux slave two years earlier, she had no sympathy for the aliens. Gut them, flense them, burn them: she didn't care how much they suffered so long as they wound up dead.

But then she thought of what flenser rounds did to an unarmored body. She'd seen cadets forced to shoot their own with flenser rounds in the Cull. The round casing split open to release pairs of tiny barbed metal balls, each orbiting the other by the monofilament wire connection: like a cross between miniature nunchucks and shuriken throwing stars. It was a particularly messy form of death.

And that would make an effective goad.

The sergeant came over the comm. "Now we know how the enemy motivates her troops: advance or be shot." Gupta growled. "I see that as a personal challenge. They've called us out. We have to make the militia fear us more than their own side. On my mark, lob three frag grenades into the mass, and then pull back to the reserve holes while I watch what they do. 3… 2… 1… fire!"

Between the worm camera that extended out the top of her head, Saraswati's guesswork, and LBNet's picture of the enemy's positions, Springer didn't need to leave the shelter of her hole to fire. She braced her carbine's stock on the rocky ground at the bottom of her pit, and sent a spread of three fragmentation grenades flying into the militia horde.

She didn't wait around to see the results. Didn't need to. She knew her aim had been true. With the semi-smart munitions still airborne, she scrambled up the reverse of her hole to the positions further down the reverse side of the slope.

The sergeant hadn't needed to point out his thinking for falling back. Defense in depth wouldn't work against such overwhelming odds. If the Hardits kept on coming, the defenders needed a more solid line and the reserve line had a shorter frontage.

Springer's torso was out into the open, and she was pushing off with her rearmost leg when the dirt all around her exploded into angry plumes.

"Contact east," someone shouted. "The far side of the stream."

The crack of incoming rounds was mixed in with a couple of dull thuds.

"Two hits to the head, dear," reported Saraswati. "Just flenser rounds. Our helmet's good for now."

"Incoming automatic flenser fire," she confirmed over the comm as she slithered through the storm of fire. If all was well, LBNet would have already informed everyone. Verbal confirmation was expected, though, on a battlefield where AIs and distributed networks could be compromised by cyber attack.

The flenser cannon fire soon slackened off, and the plumes of dust kicked up by each round had meshed around each other into a dust cloud. Thick enough to provide cover.

She slotted a smoke grenade into the launcher beneath her SA-71's barrel and fired it off to the east, where it added to the confusion with its mix of burning combustibles, ablatives and false radar and electronics signatures.

The smoke glowed with an eerie backlight. The trees that lined the stream were alight!

Just as she was about to crawl onto the second-line firing hole, a casualty alert flashed in tac-display. Two seconds later, she heard more smoke grenades going off between her and the incoming flenser cannons.

Keeping her head low, she ran to where a flashing blue dot showed the position of Marine Serge Rhenolotte — *Zug*.

Umarov was already there, crouched over Zug who was face down in the dirt, not moving.

Another burst of flenser fire flailed their position, firing blindly but the intensity of fire was enough that she saw first Umarov and then Zug being hit. Then she felt a crashing blow to her head.

"Helmet compromised," reported Saraswati. "Move your sweet ass!"

"His left arm's badly damaged," said Umarov. "Tilt him onto his right."

"Agreed," Springer replied as she clamped her carbine to her back. "You take his legs."

Umarov complied. Springer was far stronger and they both knew it. Still under fire, she twisted Zug around until he lay on his right. Then she lifted him up and shuffled backward, the need to rescue her comrade driving all thoughts of fatigue from her exhausted muscles.

They took more hits, but the smoke was enough to cover their retreat to the next line of firing holes and beyond until they fell into the reserve trench where Lance Corporal Yoshioka, their section commander, waited for them.

Without hesitation, Springer started checking over Zug's wounds, setting his AI and Saraswati debating how best to treat him.

"Leave him to me," said Yoshioka.

Springer ground her jaws in frustration. Tearing herself away from Zug was impossibly difficult, even though administering to casualties was part of the lance corporal's role. She hesitated, unable to leave him.

"Vulley off and let me do my job," shouted Yoshioka. "You two get back into the second line and stand ready."

Yoshioka's words were what Springer needed to get her going. She slithered out of the trench and headed north. The hole Springer aimed for was only twenty paces away but the going was extremely hard. Her legs barely seemed to function, not that she could stand anyway. The incoming fire had grown in intensity. Vicious flenser rounds clawed at her back as she crawled forward.

Saraswati's warnings became so shrill, that Springer rolled onto her back to expose her chest armor — the thickest layer of protection — and wriggled backward, with her arms stretched over her head, holding her carbine.

"Well done, dear," the AI said when Springer fell back into her new firing hole. "Now the bad news. The exomuscles amplifying hamstring movement were already damaged getting out of that labor camp. They've taken several more hits in the past minute. You can still walk, barely, but it will feel like your boots are weighed down by micro black holes in your heels. You can slither and crawl a little, even stand, but you're not walking off this battlefield, let alone all the way back to Detroit. Not in this battlesuit."

A chill descended over Springer as she thought through what that meant. When the battle was over, there would be battlesuit armor that no longer had a living owner, but it wouldn't be fitted or calibrated to her needs. Underneath her armor, she was naked, which was merely embarrassing. Not having a left leg beneath the knee was far worse. When she reported her status to Yoshioka she had to fight to keep her voice steady. She could bear the danger of the battlefield, but not this. This was intolerable, the very thing she had dreaded from the start.

She had become a burden to her comrades.

Chapter 39

The Hardits swarmed over the crest of the hill, using the borrowed courage of mob mentality to push them onward once more past the abandoned first line of firing holes and on to the second defensive line, twenty meters farther on. The shorter second line was filled with Marines and liberated slaves with captured Hardit rifles, but they kept out of the attackers' sight, down at the bottom of their holes.

From his trench in the third and final defensive zone, Arun felled one, two, three monkeys before the hidden humans all along the second line stood and let off a volley at point blank range. The shock of these defenders appearing from nowhere, and their lethal hail of fire, made the front Hardit ranks recoil. Those behind slammed into a wall of comrades who were no longer advancing. A wave of fear rippled back from where the Hardits touched the human line.

And into this uncertainty, the Marines and humans fired until their barrels glowed.

A few amongst the enemy crouched down, passed their rifles from tail to hands and returned fire through the retreating forms of their reeling fellows.

The Hardit retreat was like the tide ebbing to reveal a few stranded individuals who stayed and fought… and attracted the fire of the Marines. These brave few lasted only a few seconds before the Marines blasted them away.

Arun shot one of the few monkeys diving into the forward firing holes abandoned by his forces in favor of the shorter second line. Were the Hardits tumbling into the holes because they were the nearest cover, or because they intended to establish a position to fire on the humans? Probably the enemy themselves didn't know and the humans weren't going to give them time to find out.

Frag grenades lobbed from the second line soon silenced any Hardits in the first.

As he watched this latest Hardit advance being beaten back, Arun marveled at Sergeant Gupta. It was his idea to hide a line of troops on the reverse slope and wait until the Hardits were close enough to see the burning trees reflected in their eyes before firing. It felt like an idea taken from the earliest days of gunpowder firearms, but Gupta insisted that in facing such overwhelmingly superior enemy numbers, the shock to Hardit morale of hidden troops emerging with guns blazing was more valuable than steadily thinning their numbers as they advanced up the slope.

And the Hardit mob was so poorly coordinated that they never seemed to learn their lesson.

With the unarmored liberated slaves sheltering down in their firing holes, Marines scrambled out from the second defensive line, weathering sporadic enemy fire, to reclaim the front line of holes along the hill's crest. From here they poured fire down into the retreating enemy.

With the militia recoiling north, back down the hillside, the second line set back on the reverse side of the slope was spared Hardit rifle fire, but they kept to the bottom of their holes, knowing what was to come.

Sure enough, automatic fire raked the hill from the west and the east. Bombs rained down on the hillside. The enemy had exhausted their supply of mil-grade munitions and were now lobbing homemade plasma bombs out of their catapults. Many of the bombs burned rather than exploded, and some were launched so inaccurately that they fell on Hardit heads, adding burning Hardit fur to the flaming trees that lit the night.

The Hardit bombs didn't need to be mil-spec to take a steady death toll of the humans.

Barney amplified the sound of more Hardit automatic fire. This came from the north, not the flanks, and its purpose was to remind the militia mass that any individual retreating would be shot.

The militia's rearward creep slowed, and then reversed. Once again, the individuals in that mob were transfixed by a deadly balance of forces. If they fled they would be shot by their own side. If they assaulted the hill, they would be blasted by the desperate human defenders.

Staying put and hugging whatever rock or bush felt like cover was only slightly less lethal. Marine railguns were steadily taking their toll. For a little while, sheer numbers gave the Hardits a false sense of invulnerability. Hiding in the crowd meant it would be some other poor veck trembling nearby whose skull was perforated by a supersonic kinetic dart.

But every time they saw another comrade shot dead sharpened the terror that they would be the next to fall.

It wouldn't take long before cowering there and taking the incoming fire would become unbearable, and clumps of Hardits would begin inching up the hillside once again, taking increasingly accurate shots at the Marines in their hilltop defenses before unleashing another assault.

How long before that attack came? Another five minutes? Chances were the Human Legion would beat back the next assault. But how about the next one? Or the one after that?

Arun's forces had survived four waves of attack. With every militia assault, more of the unarmored liberated slaves were wounded or killed. Carbine ammo states reported across BattleNet were only heading in one direction.

At first, he'd thought the enemy commander was an idiot. Now he realized they were contemptuous of militia lives. Which meant they would happily grind this out until every last human was dead.

He had to risk a breakout. Few if any of the weak and injured would survive, but the hope in his heart had frozen. The only alternative now was total annihilation.

He glanced across the trench at Corporal Narciso. For some reason he saw a bright memory of Novice Puja Narciso on the day she had become his first kiss. They'd been practicing concealment techniques and by chance had selected the same hiding place. Instead of bickering over who had the right to the spot, they decided to enjoy it together. He laughed. She was so good at hiding, he used to tell her she must have a heavy dose of chameleon blood in her ancestry.

He stopped laughing.

"Narciso!"

"Sir."

"Stealth up best you can and head east across the stream. Assess enemy deployment and mark targets but do not engage. I want us to break out to the east. Maybe the smoke from the trees will help to confuse them."

"Acknowledged."

Puja crawled out the trench but not in the direction of the eastern flank. She detoured to the bunker at the center of the trench ring.

As part of the defensive preparation for what Arun had only intended to be a temporary rest stop, the Marines had scooped out a shallow ammo cache. A few meters away they then constructed a deep hole suitable for the two infants and their mothers.

Baby bunker. The name had been meant as a joke. But no one was laughing now.

Puja shared a few words with Rohanna and Shelby before disappearing. A moment later, she vanished from BattleNet too.

For a few more moments, Arun could see a slight trail being scuffed into the dirt leading away from the baby bunker. Then it too disappeared.

Good luck, he mouthed, before contacting Gupta to explain what he'd done.

"She'll need to be quick," replied the senior sergeant. "The gaps between the monkey attacks are shortening."

"Then we'll need to buy more time, Sergeant. Tell Yoshioka to release everyone in 2nd Section still capable of running into a mobile reserve. I want her to hold the east flank with the remainder while you lead the reserve to charge the enemy's left wing."

Arun could imagine Gupta's jaw slamming into the bottom of his helmet. "A charge, sir?"

"Yes."

"I'm sorry, but we neglected to equip 2nd Section with cavalry horses and sabers."

"It's not as stupid as it sounds, Sergeant. You said it yourself. We can't win with firepower or numbers. There's just too many of the vecks. Our only chance is to make this a battle of morale."

"I did say that, Major." He paused, but only for a heartbeat. "I'll need Halici from 1st Section," he said with growing confidence. "Shame that Kantrowicz and Zane are stuck back in Detroit."

"You mean the old Marines from Umarov's vintage?" Arun frowned. He couldn't figure Gupta out. "Why?"

Gupta slithered along the ground to organize his charge. "There was a reason we used to train with combat blades," he said. "You'll soon understand."

Chapter 40

After abandoning the broken bottom half of her battlesuit, crawling along the battlefield had smeared enough mud to veil Springer's nakedness, but not nearly enough for her to ignore. It wasn't the idea of lusty Marine eyes feasting on an unintended sexy display that nagged at her when she should be concentrated on marshaling the fire of the liberated humans. That would be merely embarrassing.

What shamed her was the prospect of hidden glances of revulsion at her left leg that ended above her knee, and her right that was puckered and scarred by the kiss of the plasma blast she'd taken back on Antilles. Worse still would be watching the eyes of her comrades switching into pity, crushing her from comrade into victim.

Frakk that. I'm not finished yet! The others are relying on me.

At long last, the order to advance came through from Lance Corporal Yoshioka, and she could frakking do something.

Springer acknowledged and waved at the pairs of resistance fighters on either side to follow her to the front line.

What had been a pleasant hill a few hours ago, covered in small-leafed groundcover, had been melted, dried, and pulverized by the plasma bombardment. As she wriggled on her belly, making for the firing hole fifteen meters away, she felt the ground's heat burn her legs. With her lower leg and lower armor gone, she found crawling didn't work. Instead she dug her gauntlets deep into the crumbling dirt and pulled herself along, her carbine on her back.

She checked to either side. The fighters were welted, burned, and caked in dirt and dried blood. None were truly fit to stand, let alone fight, but they were all products of the Human Marine Corps system. None of them knew when to give up.

Springer and three others made it to the front line, one of the resistance fighters succumbing to a burst of automatic fire from somewhere to the east.

No sooner had they tumbled into their firing holes when Yoshioka ordered them to open fire on her mark in approximately twenty seconds.

Springer relayed the command to the three resistance fighters in her own words. "Gupta, Umarov, Schimschak, Halici, and Binning. Just five Marines to charge an entire army. It would be a miracle if they broke the enemy, wouldn't it? But they *will* succeed, and we're the ones who're gonna make them heroes. Keep them busy to begin with and don't get shot. Once the good guys get close, target anyone who doesn't run, and don't miss. Wait for me to fire first."

She waited for Yoshioka's mark and then sent a long burst of fire along the front of the enemy down the slope. Rifle fire barked from the holes to her left and right.

The enemy returned fire, sending a bullet pinging off her helmet.

Springer fired back, desperate to distract the enemy for as long as possible because when her worm camera swiveled slightly to the right, she saw a sight so remarkable she made damned sure she was recording it in her personal archive. A stirring example of valor or utter lunacy: she hadn't made her mind up yet. Gupta, Umarov and the other three Marines were already halfway down the slope, straining to close with the enemy. Through external helmet speakers distorting under maximum amplification they screamed their battle cry: "Freedom! Freedom! Freedom!"

They could be shouting 'get your flea treatment here' for all the alien enemy knew of Human speech, but the cries won the monkeys' attention, though that was soon diverted to the pairs of crescent shaped combat blades carried by Umarov, Halici and… surprisingly Sergeant Gupta too.

Most of the Hardits stared, perplexed. It made no sense for five humans to charge them, so there must be another, hidden, threat. They ignored the Five and searched for the true danger.

A few ran, choosing to risk the ire of their own guns.

A tiny number saw the Five as targets, steadying themselves to take aimed shots at the mad, charging humans.

Springer and the resistance fighters shot as many of these resilient Hardits as they could. It was enough. Gupta's madsters screamed down the hill without slowing. The human line transformed into a spearhead as Umarov and Halici, the two century-old Marines in the center began to outpace the others.

With a final, bestial ululation, the tiny human spearpoint pierced the Hardit mob. Springer watched for a moment as her buddy, Umarov, flashed his blades in a lethal blur that left dying Hardits to left and right.

Springer remembered what she was there to do and shot any monkey with any fight left.

Most of them were too dumbfounded to do more than watch as the humans passed inside the mass of Hardits and were soon lost to view.

It looked as if the Marines had been overwhelmed.

Those Hardits farthest from the point of entry forgot the Five and began such a heavy rain of fire up the hill that Springer ordered her Resistance comrades to take cover and leave the suppressive fire to her,

When the Hardit fire slackened, Springer chanced a good look to see why.

She whistled inside her helmet at what she saw. Gupta's Five hadn't been overwhelmed at all. Like a red-hot spear thrust into water, fleeing Hardits were bubbling out from the spearpoint's passage, knocking their fellows into the dirt in blind panic to escape the deadly humans.

"They've done it!" screamed Springer through her helmet speakers. "They've only frakkin' gone and done it! Told you they would."

Then a familiar sound whistled through the air. A terrible sound. Springer's elation froze.

"Incoming!" she cried, diving for the bottom of her hole.

Plasma bombs landed all around her position, releasing blinding flashes of violet starfire that burned the air and melted the ground.

Springer curled into a ball, hands over her head. As if that would protect her.

The bombardment was merciless, unceasing.

Then her luck ran out.

A bomb landed against the lip of her firing hole. It was a glancing impact that splashed most of the plasma along the ground, but the impact spattered a little into the hole… onto Springer.

"No! Not again! Please!"

She was back again on that Antilles moonbase where that plasma blast had burned her; where first Arun and then the Jotun ensign had shielded her with their bodies, crushing her under their weight.

Trapped! Burning!

Burning!

Everything turned black. The scorching of her body continuing in darkness.

Deep instinct and training took over.

She undid her neck seals and ripped off the ruined helmet with its melted visor. She could see once more… see that her uncovered legs were burning, but with the covering of hot dirt that had showered onto her, not plasma.

By wiping off the worst of the burning soil with her gauntlet, and rubbing fresh mud over her legs, most of the pain subsided. But still she couldn't fix the burning pain in her lower left leg.

She had to force herself to stare at the space where the missing part of her leg should have been, until her brain convinced itself it could no longer burn. That it had burned away two years ago.

Only then did she look around at her comrades in the neighboring firing holes. She saw melted rifles stuck by smoking black strips of meat to the charred skeletal hands of bodies more bone than flesh.

The grins of the corpses mocked her. *One more hit from a plasma bomb and you'll be the same as us.*

They were right.

The survivors of Arun's force were massively outnumbered. Springer's helmet and lower armor were gone. Comms out. Mobility limited. Ammo low.

Everything said she was dead except for one thing. She knew Arun would survive. Xin too, the worthless piece of drent, and with Xin safely out of the way on *Beowulf*, the sly veck hadn't yet turned Arun's mind.

Which meant, Springer knew, that she was the one that Arun still loved. And while he loved her, he would never leave her behind.

Arun was her only hope now.

Chapter 41

Arun had heard no word from Puja for forty minutes. It had been twenty since Springer vanished from BattleNet and still his mind skidded around that fact, unable to face the implications of what her going off grid really meant.

For a while, Arun had dared to believe that Gupta's charge had broken the Hardit spirit. When Gupta's heroes had returned up the hill, the enemy had been too consumed by their headlong retreat to even notice. But the merciless Hardit gunners at their rear had lashed their lines, stemming their retreat. Since then, the hapless militia had twice swept passed the first two lines of human defenders, beaten back at great cost but only as far as the first line of firing holes, which were now in enemy hands.

The Hardits were targeting individual Marines now, mobbing them in packs armed with pneumatic drills which they used to smash open helmet visors… and through the human face behind.

Arun couldn't deny it any longer. The enemy was winning this battle of attrition, and was in such close contact that the Legion couldn't disengage.

The situation was hopeless.

"They're coming from the rear!"

The warning came from Curtis, one of Spartika's resistance fighters they'd liberated from the labor camp.

Arun turned in time to see a group of Hardits coming for him from the south.

His muscles felt leaden as he brought his carbine to bear. *We're surrounded. It's over!* Despair gnawed at his stomach, not for his own sake but for his fellow Marines. They had trusted him, followed their mustang officer faithfully, and he had led them to this. *So much for destiny.*

He only managed to shoot one dead before they jumped him, half a dozen at once… enough to topple him backward into the bottom of the trench.

Two of the little vecks wrenched his carbine out of his grip. The others pinned him down. All except one, who brought out a drill and set its bit spinning.

A drill bit that would shatter his visor and tear through his eye…

"No!"

Blind panic gave Arun enough of an emergency shot of strength to dislodge the Hardits, spilling them over the trench.

He punched the nearest Hardit in the snout, delighting in the blissful sensation of the filthy veck's upper jaw shattering as he drove his armored fist deep into its mouth.

Every nerve was firing like a perfectly engineered machine, thoughts of failure deserting. *This was the way to go out!*

He rose to a crouch "Come on, you dirty monkeys," he taunted the Hardits, who had backed away a half step. "Who's next?"

"Behind you!" screamed Curtis.

Arun threw himself against the side of the trench as a Hardit behind him tried to shoot him with his own carbine.

The burst of fire missed him and blasted the Hardits in front.

Arun dove at the Hardit who seemed stunned that she'd killed her own comrades. He snatched his carbine back, jabbing its stock into the Hardit's belly, making her stagger back into the pack trying to rush him.

He dove for the bottom of the trench, twisting around onto his back and activating the teeth at the end of his carbine.

Just in time.

Three Hardits tried to jump him, but instead of grabbing him and knocking him to the ground, they fell onto the teeth – monofilament blades rotating at 1000 rpm.

It took Arun two seconds of a raking motion to turn his attackers into a bloody mess of fur and chopped flesh.

Allowing himself no more than a quick grin of triumph, Arun got to his feet and took stock of the situation.

He shot the Hardit who had snatched his carbine, turned, and saw his original assailants were hesitating a short distance up the trench. Each individual trying to hide in the group.

"Who's going to try to take me first?" he yelled after them. "No one? Too bad. You lose!"

Two short dart bursts later and the Hardits who had so nearly drilled open his skull were heaped corpses in the trench.

Once satisfied they were truly dead, Arun turned to Curtis.

"If we're gonna go," he told her, "I'm damned if we'll go easily."

But Curtis was on her butt, looking down with uncomprehending eyes at her bloody guts spilling from her abdomen.

Her killer stood over her in triumph, a snarl on the Hardit's lips, and human flesh dripping from its claws.

Arun perforated its stinking monkey body with a long burst of darts.

"Thanks for your warning," Arun said weakly to the dying camp survivor. But Curtis was too far gone to hear.

The dead Hardit slumped forward over Curtis, draping itself over the resistance fighter as if lovers.

The sight sickened Arun. He wrenched the dead Hardit away. "Keep your filthy paws off her," he screamed.

But he didn't like the sound of his own voice. His anger was tainted with dismay.

He forced a little calm to return, enough to check the battle status.

Individual struggles of life and death were raging along the second defensive line. Of the third line trench… Arun was the only defender left alive.

Shit!

Panic shot through him like a meson bolt.

Steady!

He took deep breaths and, once again, regretted his inability to take on combat drugs.

He risked standing up for a moment to get at the baby bunker. Rohanna had sagged against the wall, holding the babies, who were wide eyed but silent. A large med-patch covered her belly. By the blood seeping through the patch and the torrents dried and mixed with mud on her thighs, a Hardit had broken through some time earlier and tried to disembowel the woman. But Rohanna hadn't gone the same way as Curtis.

The reason was clear to see. Shelby had a Marine carbine resting on the lip of the hole, looking for targets. Her left hand had been melted into fleshy club by a plasma bomb, but she showed no sign of noticing as she let off three shots that felled three Hardits about to leap into one of the firing holes in the second line.

With immediate evac and medical attention, these brave mothers would recover. Here in this battle, they had no hope of survival.

There was still time for him to rescue something of value from this disaster.

"Laskosk!"

"What?" snapped Stopcock, adding a reluctant, "Sir."

"Make your way to my position."

"I can't leave Cusato and Chung."

"I don't ask this lightly," replied Arun. "But I need you here, and that's an order."

When Stopcock didn't reply, Arun bit his lip. Did the big guy still recognize Arun's authority?

When Stok replied: "On my way." Arun gasped in relief. His authority still held. Barely, but that was all he needed.

It took Stopcock three minutes to work his way over to Arun from where his Heavy Weapons Section were engaged on the left flank. Arun laughed to see Stok had carried his missile launcher system all the way. *Of course he had.*

"Sorry, Stok, you'll need to leave that behind." Arun pointed at the launcher.

Stopcock shook his head. "Can't do that, sir."

"I have an even more precious load for you, Laskosk. You're the physically strongest Marine here and I want you to use your strength to extract the infants. Slip away to the southwest before the Hardit noose tightens on us. Our position is hopeless, Marine. We'll cover your escape."

"Can't their mothers take them away?"

"See for yourself," Arun replied grimly.

They both looked over at the baby bunker. Rohanna was still breathing, still holding the babies, but her eyes had closed. Shelby's carbine was still resting on the lip of the hole, but she had collapsed, holding her ruined hand, unable any longer to keep down the primal screams of pain.

"But… sir! Babies can't fight! How can they be more valuable than my launcher?"

"Symbolism, Laskosk. They're a symbol of a better future. It's the best we can do now for those left in Detroit and on *Beowulf*."

Stok was impassive, unreadable and silent behind his visor. Arun knew exactly what was going through Stok's mind: once again the lance corporal was weighing how strongly the bonds of authority still bound him.

Arun's right to lead had always been wafer thin, and now he had led the bulk of the Marines into a foolish escapade from which most would never return.

But Stok wasn't ready to give up on Arun just yet. He started to detach the launcher targeting equipment that was clamped to his back.

Arun dove into the baby bunker and took the babies away from Rohanna.

She hadn't seemed conscious, but the mother had enough strength to growl her defiance.

"Let Stok take them now," he told her gently. "He'll keep them alive."

Stok had joined them, hands stretched out, ready to take on his precious load when Barney flashed up an urgent tactical update.

What the frakk was it now?

Someone had appeared on WBNet. The scale confused Arun for a moment. The new BattleNet node was 110 klicks away.

That was nearly as far away as Detroit! But the newcomer wasn't coming from home; it was coming in from the opposite direction. And at such speed that it would reach them within minutes.

"Hurry up, McEwan," urged Stopcock.

"Hold a moment," Arun replied. "Either the monkeys are about to rub our noses into the dirt, or… or we might just live to fight another day."

"Who the frakk could help us now?" sneered Stopcock.

There was only one person in the galaxy Arun could imagine pulling them out of the fire now.

His heart fluttered. Could it really be her?

Chapter 42

While Barney figured out what the hell was going on, Arun ordered Stok to stay in the trench while Arun put the infants back into Rohanna's arms. The incoming BattleNet node wasn't giving the right network security credentials but claimed to be a Human Legion craft. It was probably a false reading, part of a Hardit cyberattack. But their position was so desperate that when Barney reported an incoming comm request, Arun accepted it.

"Can we join in, Twinkle Eyes?"

Arun replied with hearty laughter. A cyber mirage? Not likely! Not even the most advanced cyber systems in the galaxy could convincingly simulate Xin Lee.

Arun fully accepted Xin into WBNet. "Roger that. We've room for a few more. And that's *Major* Twinkle Eyes to you, Lieutenant Lee."

She laughed too – an intoxicating honey-sweet sound laced with fiery spices. Arun let out a tortured sigh. Dare he hope? "We're pinned down by enemy positions on our flanks to east and west. Take them out. Sergeant Gupta has a better view of enemy positions. He will direct your fire."

"Negative." A new node appeared on WBNet about half a klick to the northeast. It was Puja. She was still alive! "I have best view of the east, updating now."

During her scouting mission, Puja had recorded locations of the enemy positions that were pinning the Legion down on the hill, ready to upload them to BattleNet when she came back online. The enemy had deployed auto cannons and homemade catapults to lob the plasma bombs, all of which were being operated remotely.

"Looks like they're trying to avoid casualties and let the militia take our heat," said Puja. "I hardly saw any Hardits, but those I did see were wearing the uniforms of the elite we encountered at the labor camp."

"Which means they can't get their heavy weapons out of our way in a hurry," added Xin. "We'll be there in 70 seconds. Will that do, Major?"

"We?" breathed Arun. If Xin said she was coming in at the head of a hundred gunships backed by orbital batteries, he wouldn't have doubted her. She was incredible.

"Marine Rebecca Windsor is piloting this bird," said Xin. "Scored highest in your Marine retraining program. I brought another friend to the party too. We were bored waiting for you on *Beowulf*, so we formed the Human Legion Air Arm. We could hardly call ourselves an air arm with just the one bird."

A second incoming craft appeared in Barney's picture of the wider battleground. Now that Barney was picking up on Arun's trust for the approaching craft, the AI had widened his comm bandwidth and bombarded the aircraft AIs with questions. They were Stork-class shuttles from *Beowulf*, heavily modified for a ground-attack role.

"Expect incoming friendly support fire," Arun told the Marines who would have heard some of the exchange but were still on the more secure LBNet. "Tell civilians to take cover and hold your positions. Get ready to break out to the east."

But it was the Hardits who broke through the Legion defenses first, ten of them making for Arun. He shot one; Stopcock fired at another. The enemy dove for cover but kept coming. They were growing in confidence.

The militia advance had been lapping at the Legion firing holes for some time now. It was a drawn-out, meatgrinder of an assault. Each individual Hardit must have fervently wished that their comrades would be the ones to commit themselves to attacking the lethal humans. Their energies went into backing away, to hiding in the crowd and hoping the humans wouldn't notice them.

A scream came overhead, ear-splittingly piercing even through his helmet. The flames over the trees billowed as the shuttle-gunships pushed the air before them.

Arun had expected the Storks to announce themselves with a spread of missiles. That's how he would set up the craft, but Xin had a knack for thinking differently when it mattered. The Storks strafed the ground with cannon fire.

The ground to the east jetted up high into the sky. The air cracked with the hammer beat of a titan. Barney muffled the sound, but it was too much for the Hardits, who rolled on the ground, clutching their ears in burning agony.

The Marines took merciless advantage, shooting all of the militia who had been engaging them in close combat moments before. Arun and Stopcock cleared away those who had broken through the second line of defense.

When Arun surveyed the results of the strafing run, it looked as if a line of giants had dug out a channel running parallel to the stream, flinging the dirt high above them. Instead of missile batteries, Xin had installed a spine-mounted heavy railgun. He'd always thought of the weapon as only a scaled-up version of his Marine carbine. But there was no 'only' about it. Each round was like an angry god flinging a thunderbolt at the ground. Any target in its path would be vaporized.

Now she was twisting around to come for another run north-south.

The second Stork completed strafing the elite enemy positions pinning them down from the west, and flashed by to the north, twisting in crazy barrel rolls. The militia and elite soldiers still to the north flung fire up at this second Stork. Despite the pilot's breathtaking acrobatics Arun heard hundreds of bullets and cannon shells impact against the gunship, making a white noise rattle. But according to Barney, Xin had configured these Storks with maximum armor upgrades, and for the militia to attempt shooting down a gunship with nothing more than a rifle only emphasized how amateurish they were.

The Storks climbed in readiness for another strafing run, slowing as they pivoted around for the next attack run.

From three positions to the north, multiple jets of flame pointed accusing fingers at the Storks.

SAM pods.

The Hardits might be hopeless soldiers, but the AIs controlling the SAM pods were ruthlessly proficient exterminators of anything flying overhead they took a dislike to.

The response of each Stork couldn't be more different. One rolled and looped in a shower of countermeasures, pulling such tight turns that Arun's eyes struggled to track the shuttle's position. The pilot was incredible – Arun suspected it must be one of the seriously augmented Navy freaks.

The other Stork slowed as if inviting the attention of the surface-to-air missiles. The underside of the shuttle-gunship glowed blue, contrasting with the yellow flames of the burning trees and the orange-red of the thermal countermeasures flung out by the other Stork.

Multiple missiles clanged against the blue Stork's underside and bounced off, not exploding. The blue glow was characteristic of a Fermi system operating in an atmosphere. The Fermi must have instantly scrambled the fuses and other control systems in the missiles.

"Hit those SAM pods," barked Gupta. "Eyes on the threat, not on the sky show!"

Arun felt his cheeks heat with shame and rose to get a clear shot at the pods. He couldn't see them, but Barney had gotten a good look, and added cross-hairs to guide Arun to their position. Arun gave one a burst of darts. Between the carbine's recoil dampener and the more subtle recoil compensator that Barney effected by making slight battlesuit movements, Arun couldn't feel a thing as the magnetic rails in his SA-71 repeatedly charged – sending out its charge of supersonic dart and spent sabot — reloaded – and charged again, the whole sequence lasting nine milliseconds per round.

Despite the lack of sensation, he knew his carbine almost as well as he knew Barney, and could use his memories to superimpose on his senses the feel of raw power from an undampened railgun. He needed this. It felt good to be hurting the enemy.

But the SAMs weren't done.

More SAMs launched — far fewer this time — controlled by an AI smart enough to learn from the last attack. The SAMs disappeared into the burning night. The attack plan would be like Stok's against the ramp in the labor camp: the missiles would be spreading out in a sphere around their target. Then they would attack from every direction at once. Near-impossible to evade.

The Stork that had let off a Fermi defense soared, corkscrewing frantically.

The other had gone, having reached the stratosphere in its attempt to shake off missile pursuit.

The ground to Arun's front erupted, followed by thundercracks. The Stork was still jinking in an attempt to shake off its pursuers, but had nonetheless managed to fire from the upper atmosphere. Barney reckoned the strikes had obliterated the remaining SAM pods. At least the ones that had so far revealed themselves. With a spine-mounted weapon, to shoot so accurately while under pressure was astonishing. Preternatural. Who the hell was piloting that thing?

The SAMs that had already launched no longer needed their AI controller. When they judged the other Stork was within their grip, they struck, illuminating the night as they fired up their motors for maximum acceleration.

An ethereal blue Fermi glow high overhead showed the Stork's defense, but it came only from the vessel's underside. A crackle of point-defense fire announced that the gunship had further defenses aimed in other directions.

But they weren't enough.

Multiple explosions bloomed along the Stork's upper surface.

The stricken craft sank from the sky.

Undamaged, the other craft came in for another attack run on the positions to the west, shattering the night sky with a final crack of its mighty railgun.

Arun took his chance to take in the battlefield, ignoring the Storks and using his own eyes to double check what Barney was telling him.

Stunned by the noise of the heavy caliber railguns, the Hardit militia who had broken through the human defensive lines had been killed, but not before they had slaughtered many of the unarmed refugees. The Hardit positions to east and west, where the automated weapons had pinned the Legion to the hillside, had fallen silent.

To the north, the elite troops were quiet for now. A gap had opened up between the surviving Hardit militia and the human-occupied hillside, a dead zone filled with ruined, furry corpses. With the undamaged gunship turning around high above for another run, the deafening roar that so hampered the Hardits had ceased. The ship that had taken missile hits was still airborne, its stuttering engine trying to arrest its descent. Barney assessed it as critically damaged.

Temporarily freed of their tormentors, the militia rose from the ground like an army of the dead. There were still at least two thousand of them, Barney estimated.

Would these reluctant soldiers take this chance to flee the battlefield? Had the humans held out long enough to survive?

The aliens turned to face the humans. They did so directly, with heads high, where previously their approach had been curiously sideways oriented, their body posture cowed.

As one the Hardits snarled, the sound of hundreds or thousands of throats enough to make the ground shake. The growling cut off sharply, terminating with snaps of those many jaws.

The monkeys were riled. And they wanted revenge.

Bring it on. We're not so defenseless now…

"McEwan to undamaged gunship. Hit those militia before they close on us."

"Negative, Major. Situation is under control. Hold your positions." That wasn't Xin's voice. It was distorted, but sounded like a man.

Whoever he was, Arun saw the truth in his words. The damaged gunship was coming in low from the east, picked out by the flickering fires of the burning trees, the sound of its damaged engines louder than the Hardits' roar had been.

"Pick your targets," shouted Gupta. "Controlled bursts. Open fire!"

Arun came to his senses and obeyed his senior NCO as faithfully as a fresh cadet. For a moment there he'd forgotten that, officer or not, he was still a Marine with his carbine, a weapon that was practically an extension of his body. And that made him something better than this rabble of Hardits could ever be.

He remembered Indiya calling him a cyborg, a killing machine. Perhaps she had meant that as a joke. But he'd never doubted she was right.

Yet they were also greater than killing machines in a way Indiya could never truly understand. BattleNet linked every Marine in the unit into a distributed superbeing. The suits did more than share data updates, voice communication, ammo and medical status and threat analysis. To a degree they thought and felt as one. Arun began to feel an ache and knew what that meant without needing to look away from his targets and consult Barney. The ache was the feeling he associated with ammunition running low. He was half empty, but most had fired more rounds than him.

He hoped this wouldn't matter. That the Hardit militia who had been so reluctant to fight that they'd needed their own troops to fire on them would turn and run.

They didn't. Their front ranks were being mowed down methodically but that only stung them into a greater rage.

Engines cut out, the damaged Stork came in for a controlled flop, right in the middle of the Hardit militia, carving a bloody channel through the enemy before halting, its nose slightly buried into the ground.

The Stork was on fire.

Animals could be goaded into such anger that they would stampede, heedless of any danger. As novices Arun had been taught this as both a potential combat tactic and a way of killing animals for food.

That's what the Hardits were doing now. *Stampeding.*

Frakk!

The aching need for ammo resupply was becoming an unbearable knotting in his guts.

The others could feel the ache too, of course. The NCOs had caches of spare ammo bulbs and had passed them onto the rest of their section, but those caches were now spent. And the central ammo reserve was next to Arun's position in the baby bunker.

"Laskosk, you and I need to do a resupply run."

"Yes, sir."

"Understood, Major," acknowledged Sergeant Gupta, who was listening while establishing a new firing position some distance off to the northeast. "You are resupplying."

Arun turned to issue orders to Stopcock, but the big guy was already scrambling over the ground to reach the ammo cache.

"I'll resupply 1st Section," Stopcock said. "You refill Yoshioka."

"Acknowledged," responded Arun, who was already following the missile specialist over the tortured ground to the cache.

Arun made three resupply runs up to Yoshioka's position before running out of ammo bulbs and grenades. He couldn't see Springer's body, although this was hardly a sightseeing outing. The incoming rifle fire had slackened but was still fierce.

Arun was racing back to his trench after the final run when the night suddenly exploded in a burst of purple-white. He hit the dirt and laid still, but Barney explained the Hardit attention wasn't on him. A plasma bomb had hit the downed Stork.

Arun lifted his head and watched flames spread over the gunship setting the ground to smolder.

"If you want to live," came Xin's voice over WBNet, "keep your frakking heads down."

In front of his bewildered eyes, armor sloughed off the badly damaged gunship, making Arun think of his alien friend, Pedro, sloughing chitinous skin as he'd morphed into a new form.

Each corner of the fresh-skinned Stork now bulged out like blisters. And from these blisters emerged long weapon barrels.

Auto cannons!

After the deafening thunder of the gunship engines, Arun could barely hear the *chatt-chatt* of the cannons as they tore into any Hardits who hadn't fled far enough. Instinct made him tense as rounds flew overhead, but he knew there was no need. The cannon barrels were aimed by AIs who could easily distinguish human from Hardit.

He looked behind and, sure enough, saw the autocannons had ripped apart a group of Hardits who had sneaked around to his rear.

The carnage was sickening, but Arun had no room for mercy. Not for the Hardits, no matter how reluctant the militia had been to fight. But the sight of so much death numbed him, robbing him of his anger.

It was enough to halt the Hardit stampede.

They fled.

Arun crawled back to the baby bunker. The infants were not only safe inside, but making contended snuffles as each slept on their exhausted and wounded mother. Hell's teeth. Human babies were more alien than the Hardits!

Suddenly, the children and mothers lit up in the reflected glow of an explosion. It came from behind… the Stork! A Hardit missile must have been waiting in the sky, choosing this moment to fly into the upper hull of the Stork, tunneling through the remaining armor and exploding inside.

The Stork tilted nearly onto its side, swiveling around, before falling back onto its belly. The Stork was big enough to have several compartments. The missile had blown out the main starboard compartment — no one would have survived that – but the hatch to the port compartment opened, turning into an egress ramp.

"Suppressive fire," ordered Gupta, who painted a target zone onto WBNet of likely positions for the missile to have come from.

As the Marines and a few armed slaves opened fire, the survivors of the Stork raced for the relative safety of the hillside.

Arun didn't stay to watch. He clamped his carbine to his back and scooped out the babies and their mothers, holding all four in his arms. He stared into the glazed eyes of Rohanna and Shelby. Arun felt a pressing need to mouth some words of encouragement to the wounded mothers, to assure them that even if they didn't survive their wounds, that he would take care of their precious charges. No words of comfort would come, though. He had no milk, no food, and no expertise. The Marine Corps cadet curriculum hadn't covered the care of infants.

All Arun knew was that he would not abandon these two burdens lightly, even though that made no sense to him, despite the line he'd spun to Stok about symbolism.

The airborne Stork added its heavy railgun to the suppressive fire, obliterating the ground in Gupta's target zone.

It landed on the hillside twenty paces from Arun, extending ramps down on its port and starboard sides.

"Everyone get in!" ordered Arun.

Only once he'd deposited his burden safely inside the Stork did he query Sergeant Gupta. "Who are we missing?"

"BattleNet reports plenty who are dead, but we're missing half of 2nd Section. If they're off-grid, probably means they were hit by plasma bombs. Do we search for their bodies?"

"Hurry up," called Xin. "We need to lift off."

"Hold," Arun told her. "Give me two minutes. No more."

As he hurried off to the defenses to the east, he checked BattleNet for any 2nd Section survivors. He found two who were conscious.

"Schimschak, Binning. Where is the rest of your section?"

"We lost contact some time ago," said Binning. "Presumed dead."

"Lewark's definitely dead," added Schimschak.

"She was in 1st Section," hissed Binning.

"Just saying. Blast took her leg off. I couldn't stop her bleeding out. I brought Zug back myself."

Springer! Where was Springer?

Arun remembered her disappearing from BattleNet about the time that Gupta's charge burst open the Hardit mob. How could he forget? Umarov's node had gone too.

Arun didn't expect to see either of them alive, but he couldn't bear to flee the battlefield without even looking for them.

He steeled himself for the site of a blackened corpse that had once been his best friend, the vibrant girl with a gentle smile, and violet eyes that sparkled with such an unfettered spirit that her friends named her Springer.

"Major! Arun, over here!"

Barney turned Arun's helmet around and focused his visor on the person calling his name.

It was Umarov, calling out in his own voice because he had lost his helmet, which would explain his disappearance from BattleNet. Alongside him was Yoshioka, also without her helmet but with the limp forms of two Resistance fighters slung over her shoulders. Umarov was limping, and in his arms carried a charred body partially covered in armor. Alive or dead? Arun couldn't tell.

Arun gently took the body from his friend. It was still warm, still alive. The way the flesh softly yielded as he hurried to the Stork, and those legs…! Arun's eyes widened. *Springer!*

He needed to look upon her face. He realized her helmet wasn't sealed onto the rest of her armor. He pulled it off and threw it to Umarov.

Springer's face was blasted, her hair scorched. She was the most beautiful sight he could imagine. Her eyes opened, and he gazed into those violet pools.

"Been a while since you held me naked in your arms, Arun."

He shushed her. "This isn't the time."

"But there won't *be* another time. Not with me like this."

"Because you're wounded?" He saw past those eyes and took in the fresh burns over the puckered scars from two years before. "Springer, the gulf between us is because I've become your CO. Not because of how you look."

She raised her hand and touched his visor. "You're a gentle liar, Arun."

Arun glanced up. They were nearly there. Nearly safe.

"If I could rid this world of the Hardits," he told her, "and strip away my rank, I'd make love to you here on the battlefield."

"This isn't the time for romance, children," growled Umarov. "You can save that fluffy stuff until we're airborne."

As if agreeing with Umarov's urgency, the ground trembled as the Stork spooled powerful engines.

"Come on," urged Yoshioka.

"Lance Corporal, where's your helmet?" Arun asked, changing the subject.

"A furry skangat shattered it with a drill. Nearly did the same to my head but I fragged it first. Ripped its stinking arm off."

Arun was about to ask Umarov why Springer seemed to be wearing his helmet, but they had arrived at the ramp up to the waiting gunship.

He let the others go first so that he could lift up Springer. Their glances caught each other for a stretched moment, and then he kissed her.

She tasted of roasted dirt, blood and sweat, but he didn't care one bit.

With only a buzz for warning, the external speakers on the Stork blared out. "When you're quite finished, Major. I'll lift off just as soon as you see fit to come aboard."

Arun's jaw dropped open. That voice… that supreme flier… it was Dock, the *Beowulf* traitor who'd escaped execution for treason only by Indiya's insistence that she couldn't spare experienced personnel, not even to justice.

"Are you coming, or not?" urged Dock.

Springer's face dimpled with a grin.

It was more than enough to fill Arun with warm bubbles of relief. Arun bounded up the ramp which was retracting before he'd even stepped into the hold.

He looked around at the sorry looking survivors, expecting anger, resentment. Maybe amusement at his kiss. Instead he saw only exhaustion and resignation on every face there except one.

On the far side of the hold, a beautiful face was twisted into a baleful glare of white hot hatred.

Xin.

Chapter 43

The footage was already twice as long as she had called for, but she wanted this to be *endless,* because the smell of her opponent's humiliation was the most intoxicating scent Tawfiq had ever experienced. Even beyond her most glorious dreams.

And she had such *expansive* dreams.

The Great Council members – those who had survived the coup – knelt with snouts pushed against the floor of the council chamber, ritually licking the polished stone, now coated with dust and debris from where Tawfiq's janissaries had blasted through the wall.

All except one! One fool. Lord Ammrithk had glanced in her direction momentarily.

"You *dare?*"

Tawfiq rose from the High Councilor's throne, the seat of power still covered in dust and debris. She stormed over to the errant lord, unable to resist glancing at her janissaries as she did so.

The crew recording the footage for live broadcast were instructed to keep the janissaries out of shot. The general population made to view the footage weren't able to see the janissaries, but with scent–enabled players so common these days, they would smell the genderless soldiers and be terrified.

Let them fear the New Order, gloated Tawfiq, as she breathed deeply of her janissaries' manufactured odor of metal and oil. The scent of victory.

Tawfiq straddled Lord Ammrithk, feeling his hot sweat of fear, his body rubbing against hers as he pushed himself again and again to the floor.

The excitement his fear awoke in Tawfiq went beyond intoxicating. She felt the irresistible pulsing that presaged the arrival of the mating season – the Time of Challenge.

No! She would not permit herself to feel aroused. Not by this Lord of the High Council.

Not by a mere *male*!

"You displease me," she growled at Lord Ammrithk. She spread her arms to encompass the whole council. "Punishment is not confined to the guilty but extends to the associates of the condemned. For that is the way of the New Order."

"Strength through victory! Victory through strength!" The janissaries gave an unprompted chorus of the new way of things.

Tawfiq stepped away, back into the ranks of her janissaries.

She had exposed the High Council, her people's ultimate authority for hundreds of generations for what they were: degenerate weaklings. With a snap of her jaws, the signal for execution, the leaders of the Hierarchy were swept away in a hail of bullets.

PART IV
The Hidden Legion

Human Legion INFOPEDIA

Military Life
– Early Legion Uniforms

With the creation of the Human Legion came the need for new uniform designs to reinforce the split from the Navy and Human Marine Corps organizations who had pledged unceasing loyalty to the White Knight Empire. Given the iconic look of Human Legion uniforms today, it is surprising to learn that their design was regarded as a minor detail barely worth a mention in the written record of that time.

White and cream were the colors of the old White Knight regime and its loyalists. Red was the color of the rebel faction in the civil war, including the so-called 'Free Corps' Marine units. In a war waged over hundreds of light years, and that employed technology still barely comprehensible to humanity, it is strange to think how significant these colors came to be as a rallying call for each faction.

The political position of the early Legion was to be belligerently neutral in the civil war. Not wishing to use the colors of either faction, the Legion reprogramed its smartfabric fatigue uniforms to be all black.

Those looking for a more romantic twist to their history have said black was chosen as the color of the void, signifying that the Human Legion owed no allegiance to any one planet, but represented space itself. The truth is revealed in a copy of an order from Major Arun McEwan issued the day after the inception of the Legion. "As a stopgap, all Legion uniforms will immediately be reprogrammed to an all-black color," he wrote. "This declares our neutrality. A permanent uniform design will be agreed at a future date, when we have time for such details."

That day is still to come, and with its all-black uniforms such an instantly recognizable symbol of the Legion, the day will not come soon.

The earliest Legion uniforms – those used in the First Tranquility Campaign – had no need for unit or service insignia, so small was the Legion's size at the time. Even rank was not initially shown on the uniform. The only distinction was that Marine uniforms had subtle bronze facings, while Navy uniforms had silver (being the traditional color to represent the stars).

Later uniform designs added rank insignia on epaulettes, service specialism on the collar, unit insignia on the right shoulder (e.g. brigade, fleet, or regiment) and optional tactical recognition flashes on the left (e.g. taskforce, drop zone, or wave). A dress uniform variant was also added; in most cases this was nothing more than a different program for the same smartfabric garments, although woven natural fabric versions have been worn on special occasions. The dress uniform design includes a cloth-effect beret, simulated braid, a high-neck collar, and the appearance of a double-breasted jacket.

Centuries after the young Major McEwan's deferred a proper uniform design, the all-black colors are now spreading from personal uniforms to starship hulls, and vehicles that range across land, sea and air. Whether the sight of these black fleets instills pride or terror in those who see them, one thing is for certain: black is no longer a neutral color.

Chapter 44

As Tawfiq approached the strange creature, the sound grew ever more difficult to bear: two trembling tones, one ultra-high, the other a sub-bass rumble. The two sound waves beat mercilessly at the inside of her skull.

"Do you know who I am?" she asked the source of the painful noise.

"You are Tawfiq Woomer-Calix."

"Correct. I am Supreme Commander of the New Order, and your place in that order is to do my bidding."

"No."

No! It had been a long while since anyone had refused Tawfiq. Before she could reprimand the disrespectful creature, old doubts flooded her. The paranoia.

Had she imagined that denial? It wouldn't be the first time she'd heard voices in her head.

She clutched at her head. The pressure on her temples was excruciating.

"You heard correctly," said the voice again. "I am not here to do your bidding. I summoned you to do mine."

The status light on the creature's translator system hadn't registered any activity, so those words couldn't possibly have come from the wall speaker.

Tawfiq fled, deciding to send underlings to complete the task of interrogating this creature.

But as the crashing noise eased with each footstep, she was surprised to find that she had somehow already learned everything she needed to know.

Chapter 45

In a more innocent time, before he'd been caught up in the fallout from the White Knight civil war, Arun would have been impressed by the sector operations room on Level 3. As novices and cadets, they had been shown these upper levels of Detroit's formidable defenses, not truly believing they would one day fight there. The battle computer displays had been glimpses into the intelligence behind this impregnable bastion, and the detail of Marines always on station here had seemed ready for anything.

They hadn't been, though. Detroit's defenses had been breached. Its defenders slaughtered.

Now the stragglers who still styled themselves the Human Legion – at least for now – relied on a portable power generator to provide light, heat, and to power three wall-mounted viewscreens and the battle AI they were linked to. His fellow officers met in the ops room with Arun, suited up with helmets off but within easy grabbing range, their faces looked drawn and pale in the blue-tinged illumination. They retained enough respect to wait for Arun to speak, but that respect was now stretched to breaking point.

The ops room made a natural base of operations for their rag-tag band of survivors, but Arun would give anything to have chosen someplace else. The bodies of the fallen defenders had been cleared away, but the room still carried the stink of defeat.

It hung about like heavy fog, clinging to Arun, threatening to possess him.

He sighed. It was time to speak.

"Over the past two days, the Legion has fought well. Thanks to the tenacity, spirit, and skill of our Marines, we have liberated hundreds of humans slaves from a Hardit labor camp, including local resistance leaders, and forced marched hundreds of klicks back here to Detroit, aided—" Arun nodded at Xin – "by the leadership and initiative shown by Lieutenant Lee."

A pang of annoyance penetrated Arun. His praise for Xin had been well deserved, but she looked at him with contempt bordering on hatred. He mentally shrugged. Trying to understand Xin didn't matter anymore.

"That's the bullshit version of events, to borrow Sergeant Gupta's vernacular. The truth is I've led us into disaster. We've suffered heavy casualties and most of the slaves we rescued died on the journey back. We've paid dearly and have little to show for it. *Beowulf* confirms heavy weapons are being discharged underground, have been for most of the past day. The Hardits are fighting amongst themselves to see who controls Tranquility. That's the only reason we have this breathing space. Once a faction has established supremacy, we will be the next target."

"Could we play one side off against the other?" suggested Brandt.

"I don't think so," Arun replied.

"There's plenty of human historical precedent," Brandt pressed. "A faction not confident of victory would ally with the devil rather than accept defeat. The Crusader princes of Palestine frequently allied with their Saracen enemies against other Crusader princes. The Nazis and Bolsheviks of Europe were implacable ideological enemies, but joined forces to extinguish a neighboring country named Poland."

Arun waved at Brandt to calm down and cease his history lessons.

"You might be right, though having lived with the Hardits, I think their contempt for humanity is too strong for that to work. But that is no longer for me to decide. In light of my record, I stand aside." Arun gave a bitter laugh. "I suppose you could say I'm resigning my commission."

"None of us are commissioned," said Xin. Her voice was icy cold. "The only Jotun Navy officer left alive on *Beowulf* nominated you, and we agreed the other officer roles and assignments amongst us. You have no commission to resign. This is an abdication."

Arun shrugged. "What's your point, Xin?"

"My point, *Arun*, is that you aren't handing back some shiny award you no longer feel you deserve. Being CO isn't a prize – it's a responsibility. I never put you down as a quitter, McEwan. An idiot, perhaps. But you were full of ideas and, even if most of them were dumb, your combination of ignorance and tenacity meant you made them work anyway. Now you're landing us all in the drent because things haven't gone your way. *Abdication*. From where I'm sitting, sounds mighty similar to *abandonment*."

Arun held Xin's glare but said nothing. She was petite, and she was beautiful, but neither characteristic prevented her from making him feel two inches tall. She had that drill instructor's knack of going straight for the jugular in pointing out where he had gone wrong.

"She's right," said Nhlappo.

Arun took a deep breath and stuck out his chin in readiness for the assault from the woman who actually had been a genuine drill instructor. Nhlappo was worse even than Xin, the older woman had vastly more experience than any of them here.

"Listen up, McEwan," she barked. "*Major*." She spat his rank as if a terrible insult. "We followed you to Tranquility knowing our attempt to retake the planet was a high-risk gamble. Horden only knows why, but we wanted to believe in you and your vision of the Human Legion. Not that you've done anything to justify that faith, but the alternative was a slow ignoble suicide. It still is. I'm not the only one here who'd far rather go out in a blaze of vainglory."

"I knew your support was always lukewarm, Lieutenant. Do you now withdraw it? Will you lead us in my place?"

"One of your problems, Major, is that you want to believe everything is about you. No, I haven't changed my views on anything. It is *you* who's doing that. You're losing your nerve. You've suffered a reverse. We all have. Suck it up, boy. Don't you dare crumble on us now. You're the only thing holding us together. We're still working a high-risk gamble. Nothing's changed. Listen to Lee because she's got more balls than you. More tactical nous too."

"You're right," said Arun, adding quickly: "About Lieutenant Lee having tactical sense." Arun was winging it here. The planner brain in his mind was urging him to grasp some detail about Xin that was vitally important, but he couldn't get any details. What did he need to tell her? Arun couldn't figure it out. Couldn't even face her yet. Instead he breathed out and looked to Brandt. "And you?"

"You know they're right, Arun. All this drent about being officers… Hell, you were never even a cadet NCO. I bet it feels like a game, doesn't it? As if your legitimacy is nothing more than a paper mask. One that's become torn and crumpled from the first time you've gone outside. I'm right, aren't I?"

Arun nodded.

"Well, here's the bad news. Whatever any of us here or out there in Detroit think of you, your torn mask of command is the only one we have, and it's tailored to your ugly face. No one else can take your role."

"Understood." Arun could see, though, that Brandt hadn't finished with him yet.

"Do you actually want to know what I think?" growled Brandt.

"Yes, of course."

"I think you've already answered your own question, Arun. You're just too scared to follow your instinct. Being CO doesn't mean you have to fire every weapon or lead every assault. It doesn't even mean you have to take all the decisions or plan everything, despite the freaky brain the Jotuns put inside your head. It means you have to be the leader. So lead, damn you!"

Brandt. Lee. Nhlappo. Three pairs of eyes held him captive in their gaze and would not let him wriggle free. Was this how it felt to be a medieval king surrounded by his earls and barons? Holding no love for their monarch but giving him their support in a delicately calculated balance of power?

Arun shrugged. Frakk history. He had a vision. A future where humans could win their freedom.

And he would lead the Legion to that future. Springer had told him he would.

Springer's foresight would have to be the Legion's guide at this narrow juncture.

"Very well," he said. "I want to consider how to use the Resistance fighters. Adding in those we liberated from the camp, we have about 30 fit to fight now, and about a dozen more recovering from their wounds. Assessment?"

"I'm not impressed," said Nhlappo, sneering. "They're resentful, poorly led, and physically unfit. In the long term, best to use them to augment Marine units, but in the short term any unit reinforced by them would be weakened."

"How about Spartika?" asked Arun. "She's so weak she can barely stand, but Narciso says she will recover in a few days. She established herself as the local Resistance leader, which is why I fought so hard to extract her. I still think if we are to add the Resistance and liberated slaves into our fighting force, we are better doing so with them as allies rather than absorb them directly. At least at first."

"I don't trust Spartika," said Xin.

"You've never met her," Brandt pointed out.

"Don't need to. She'll betray us if she finds the right opportunity. I know I would in her situation."

Nhlappo joined in: "So are you saying we need to make sure Spartika never recovers from her ordeal?"

Xin shook her head. "Negative. We keep her onside. The major was right to risk all to recover her. She represents a future power struggle, that's all I mean. We need a hold over her, but she isn't a threat to us for now."

"Go on, Lee." Arun knew Xin had more. He could see her stark expression loosen up as she talked, meaning that Xin's mind was fertile with tactical ideas. Arun recognized that look. Xin used it when she berated him for failing to grasp the importance of combined arms, of the need for heavier fire support and an air wing. Xin's dreams were filled with battle tactics.

Xin continued. "Lieutenant Nhlappo reports we've recovered enough discarded equipment to equip another few score Resistance fighters, but our main stores and armories in Detroit were destroyed. We can't take a planet with about a hundred armed fighters. We need to arm the human slaves, to turn scores into tens of thousands. For that we need Spartika as a figurehead and we need to raid the only place on the planet capable of equipping an army."

"Beta City," said Arun. The teasing glint in Xin's eyes confirmed this was her intended target.

"Makes sense," said Brandt. "The enemy expects us to hole up here and lick our wounds while they're busy fighting each other. The last thing they will expect is for us to attack the most obvious target on the planet."

Arun raised his eyebrows. "And people say I get outrageous ideas! But you could be right. By most accounts the rebels abandoned Beta City in a hurry. I think the chances are that a substantial level of stores are waiting for us to grab them… It's a helluva risk, though."

"Let me lessen that risk," said Nhlappo. "A little, at any rate. As you said, Lee, Sergeant Majanita hasn't recovered a great deal of abandoned equipment here in Detroit. We've still no SAM pods, for example. But there were many levels of security in the Human Marine Corps, and I've managed to access hidden stores. I recovered dozens of jet racks, blinder missiles, and a tactical gamma bomb."

Arun dared to hope.

Jet racks were a means of transporting individual Marines in battlesuits. In theory they were lightning fast but left Marines vulnerable in transit and when dismounting. In practice, he'd never known anyone to train on them. Gamma bombs were tricky weapons that could easily backfire, but with a good deployment, and a lot of luck, could wipe out an army in a single blast. But the missiles…?

"What's a blinder?" asked Xin.

"Fits standard missile launcher. A munition withdrawn from human use a few decades ago. Probably to keep us from getting too strong. I'm not supposed to know of their existence. Could be key to achieve air superiority. Maybe orbital superiority too. It's a cluster round. When the initial transport stage reaches the target areas, it fragments, releasing dozens of semi-intelligent mini-drones. If you set them right, the blinder drones will hide and hunt."

"Hunt for what?" Brandt asked.

Nhlappo stiffened at the interruption "Depends how you program the munitions. But usually they locate and mark anything they think might be an enemy targeting system. When you give the signal, they come out of hiding and make use of the bomb they carry inside them."

"And then we send in the gunships," said Xin. "Instant air superiority."

"That's the theory. And we only have one gunship left, but essentially, yes."

"I can't help thinking there are deeper secrets waiting to be discovered here in Detroit," said Arun. "There must be plenty that even you aren't aware of, Lieutenant. If only we had the time to really explore."

"But we don't," said Nhlappo.

"No, but there is one more weapon in our arsenal that the enemy are unaware of. You all know how *Beowulf* destroyed *Themistocles* with her engine exhaust. Some of the Navy techs think they have worked out how to weaponize the engine to fire into an atmosphere. In theory we can wipe out anything in the engine effect cone down to a few tens of meters above the ground. It's ultra-high risk and untested. It could blow up the ship or ignite the atmosphere in an unstoppable chain reaction. Factor it into your tactical calculations but don't risk using it unnecessarily."

Arun addressed Brandt. "Thank you for that pep talk earlier. I need to lead, not plan everything myself. Let's see if I was listening properly." He turned to Xin. "Lieutenant Lee, I said before that I was impressed with your tactical ability in rescuing us in our retreat from the Labor Camp. Lieutenant Brandt was right to imply I should make more use of all of your talents. Lee, I want you to prove to me that your tactical skill was no fluke. Under Lieutenant Nhlappo's direction, I want you to form a battle plan. Find a way to get us in and out of Beta City with a minimum of risk and maximum haul of equipment that we can use to arm freed slaves. Make use of any weapon or resource in our possession. You have one hour. Get to it."

"Yes, sir." Xin gave him a crisp salute that would satisfy the strictest drill instructor. Nhlappo, who had been that drill instructor, gave him a challenging look but it was an improvement over the open contempt of before. As for Xin, her eyes were brimming with emotion. Excitement. Gratitude. Destiny. Hell, he'd just unleashed Xin Lee at full throttle. The room crackled with energy and belief. Arun wanted to stay and soak it up into his tired bones, but the Legion was demoralized. He had to go out there and be seen to hope.

Before he could get to his feet and leave Xin and Nhlappo undisturbed, a call came through from Gupta.

"Go ahead, Sergeant."

"Incoming Hardit transmission, Major."

"Tell the stinking monkeys to go vulley themselves."

"This particular stinking monkey claims to know you, sir. Says its name is Tawfiq Woomer-Calix."

Foreboding twisting his insides, Arun told Gupta to put the transmission through to the ops room.

All three viewscreens were filled by the leering triple-eyed head of the person Arun hated above all others on the planet.

Tawfiq!

Chapter 46

"I think you are there present, yes." The Hardit spoke in a synthesized voice devoid of emotion. "Acknowledge please."

Arun wasn't without emotion, though. He longed to punch the veck in the snout. The aliens all sounded the same, but Arun had no doubt that this was Tawfiq. That particular monkey's voice synthesizer had never quite managed human grammar.

The Hardit couldn't be sure that Arun was hearing her. She loved mind games, especially any that inflicted mental anguish. *I can play games too*, Arun thought. So he ignored Tawfiq, uncertain whether he was being petty or whether this was a message to the Hardit that he would only play this game on his own terms.

Arun studied this evil creature who had delighted in torturing him when he was forced to join her Aux work gang. Back then she had dressed in scruffy work gear, scarcely cleaner than her slave workers. Now she wore a uniform that couldn't be more different. Its silver material had black channels etched into its glossy surface that suggested metal machinery, or perhaps electronics. If the uniform's intention was to make its wearers look like indomitable military cyborgs, the effect was ruined by the inbuilt elliptical parasol that rose above the wearer's head, like the haloes in depictions of the most holy people in Earth religions.

Tawfiq's uniform was similar to that worn by the elite troops they'd encountered at the Labor Camp, except for the cleanliness and complexity of the gold lightning bolts extending from the shoulders, which made him think Tawfiq had reached a senior rank. Somehow the alien looked even more arrogant than normal, as if she were certain she had already won. And that lit a fire of rage in Arun's belly that he could not control.

"I'll kill you, monkey," he blurted out.

"Ah. You acknowledge. Good. Now we know you can see this transmission, human scum. You come from off planet or maybe hide away from war. Hero or coward in human terms, makes no difference to we, your superiors. You steal hundreds of human slaves. Keep them, with our thanks. They are worthless animals. They stink so much we retch. We only kept them alive as a kindness."

"Do you even have a point, monkey?"

"I wish share observation. You call me monkey. That makes me laugh because my people not animals like you humans. We engineers and scientist. We observe and learn. You too dumb to act on more than instinct, so we teach you what you too stupid to learn for yourselves. Let me teach you now. What I observe about humans is you having two slight skills. The first is digging into the dirt. Look. We have made use of your skill. Do you see?"

The camera panned away from Tawfiq to reveal a scene of misery that made Arun gasp. A crude trench, about a meter deep, had been dug into fields of human crops. It could be Alabama. It could be any of a hundred agricultural areas. The trench extended far into the distance. Lined along the trench at ten-pace intervals were hundreds of beaten, skeletal human workers, their sun-blistered backs turned to the camera. The slaves stared down into the trench at their feet. The shovels discarded nearby made it clear that they had dug the trench themselves.

"The humans you stole are of no account," said Tawfiq's artificial voice, "but the Hardit people you murdered… this is different matter, a crime of purest evil. One hundred eight-seven of our brave people were killed in your terrorist raid."

Liar, thought Arun. *It was far more than that.*

"We shall punish your race. For each glorious Hardit citizen slain, we will kill one thousand of you humans. That is large number. We need to kill every one of your species on this continent and half on the other. You can save them, if you wish. It is easy. All humans at Detroit lay down arms and surrender. We kill you but you save many tens of thousands of your worthless friends. To them you will be heroes, yes?"

Two Hardits, garbed in a simpler versions of Tawfiq's uniform, grabbed the arms of the nearest human and twisted her roughly around so that she faced the camera, her back to the trench.

Arun's heart skipped a beat. The slave woman's head was meekly bowed in defeat, but he recognized her. This was Esther, the leader of the local Alabama Aux workers. The woman who'd aided Arun in Operation Clubhouse. *Saved his life.*

And now Tawfiq was about to get her revenge.

Suddenly, Esther sprang to life. She lunged at the two Hardits holding her. Even in her emaciated state, she had the strength to make them stumble and fall.

Arun expected her to run, but she didn't. Instead she stared directly at the camera. "Do not give yourselves up. They will kill us anyway. Extermination of all humans is Tawfiq's plan. Avenge us!"

The sound cut out, but the images would not go away. The two Hardit guards regained control of Esther, yanking her arms behind her hard enough to make her scream. Watched by a gleeful Tawfiq, another Hardit walked in front of Esther, unsheathed his claws and calmly disemboweled her.

Esther collapsed to her knees, trying feebly to hold back her intestines from spilling into the dirt.

In the ops room in Detroit, no one spoke. The sound came back on in the Hardit feed, but no one spoke there either. Arun watched Esther's death throes to the sound of his own panting breath.

The horror stretched on until the gore-spattered Hardit who'd murdered Esther kicked her, still alive and clutching her guts, making her fall backward into the trench.

"And this is second useful function of you humans," said Tawfiq, coming into camera view. "Your corpses enrich the soil. You make good fertilizer."

"You won't get away with this," said Nhlappo. "We'll hunt you down and kill you." Arun dragged his gaze from the screen to look at the lieutenant. He was surprised that it was the oldest amongst them who'd lost her cool and spoken out. "Your death will be slow," she added.

"Unlikely," said Tawfiq.

No, not unlikely, thought Arun, *just difficult. I swear you will die for this.*

He glanced at his fellow officers. Nhlappo was cooling into a more calculating rage. Xin and Brandt's expressions were as cold and relentless as glaciers.

"Every ten seconds, we kill another," continued Tawfiq in her emotionless voice. "Unless you give yourselves up and spare so many lives. Yours is very important decision – most important you ever make – because money is riding on the outcome of your choice. I myself have wagered a small fortune."

They watched in silence as a second slave was gutted, and then shoved, still screaming, into the trench.

"There are only a few of us here," whispered Nhlappo.

"But is this a real choice?" said Brandt.

"No!" Arun slammed his armored fist against the table. His strike was hard enough to snap Hardit bones, but the ops room was built to withstand such abuse with ease. "Tawfiq's frakking with our heads," he said. "She'll kill those slaves anyway. They're already dead. Heed Esther's final words. All we can do now is avenge them."

Arun watched as a third slave had her guts ripped out by the Hardit executioner. This time instead of taking the time to enjoy the sight of the human staring wide-eyed at his intestines falling out into the dirt, the Hardit threw the dying slave into the trench straight away. Already it seemed to have grown bored with its murderous task.

"Sergeant Gupta," said Arun over the local comm channel.

"Yes, sir."

"Cut transmission."

The viewscreens blanked. But Arun knew Hardits. Once set on a plan, they followed it relentlessly. Out there along the trench under the blazing sun, the killings would be continuing.

"This changes nothing," said Arun grimly. "Brandt, you're responsible for Detroit's defenses, including liaison with the Resistance. Lee and

Nhlappo, I'm still waiting for that battle plan." He paused. "Not a word of what you've just seen to anyone. Do you understand?"

The three officers chorused their acknowledgment.

Arun had entered this room intending to step aside and urge someone else to take command. That was ancient history now. As Major McEwan he was going to see this through to the bitter end.

Chapter 47

The swollen red sun hung low in the early evening sky, casting a fiery reflection over the gentle waters of Lake Sarpedona, and the island in the lake's center. Devoid of natural land-based predators, the wooded island was a haven for birds that feasted on the rich fishing grounds of the lake waters. The island and its flocking birds was itself a rich hunting ground fought over by the guinshrikes and other aerial predators who nested in the mountains ringing the lake.

To the humans, the island held another feature of vital importance: cut into its soil was the main entrance to Beta City.

The lake filled a natural caldera — the collapsed fossil of a long-dead volcano. The mountainous lip around the caldera had been partially eroded away along its circumference, except for a section to the west that was entirely broken, the legacy of an ancient kinetic attack on the planet.

From Arun's position inside the eastern foothills of the caldera, the result felt like a temple to the sun god, the gap in the western mountains filled by the swollen red orb.

In the hour since Arun's Force Patagonia arrived, angler birds had swooped and squabbled over the fish-filled lake. Now they fell silent as if paying homage to the sun god.

Like the woodland where they'd tried to make contact with Spartika, it was another example of how beautiful Tranquility would be if only the Hardits weren't here to spoil it.

Unlike the woodland, Arun was here to extinguish all life in the lake. The trees on the island, the quiescent birds and the fish they feasted on: Arun would destroy it all… so long as they managed to carry out Xin's plan.

"Sergeant," he asked, "will Patagonia's new formation perform?"

"Tolerably," Gupta answered. "The march from our insertion point was all it needed."

"Tolerable is good enough," Arun replied, but he remained concerned.

With so many casualties, Force Patagonia had left its severely wounded behind at Detroit. 2nd Section had been reinforced by Lance Corporal Owusu's fire team taken from Brandt's Force Mexico. Springer and Umarov were now attached to Owusu's section.

After the injuries she'd taken over the past two days, Arun had questioned Gupta's decision to take Springer with them. Puja had assessed her as suffering from blood loss, exhaustion, and superficial burns – nothing the self-repairing physiology of a Marine couldn't fix with a little rest. Maybe so, but surely Gupta was asking too much to turn her around onto another mission within hours, especially in an uncalibrated battlesuit reclaimed from one of Detroit's long-dead defenders who had been left where she fell.

When he'd questioned the veteran NCO, Gupta gave him a look he'd never used on Arun before. *Trust me*, it seemed to say, *I know what I'm doing.*

Dammit! Arun couldn't shake the memory of holding Springer in his arms on the ramp of a Stork spooling engines in eagerness to evacuate. But he had deferred, letting Gupta get on with his job.

Gupta had made other changes too, transferring the other effectives from 2nd Section – Schimschak and Bunning – to join the survivors of Hecht's 1st Section.

Even with the reinforcements, Patagonia had been reduced from the 22 who'd descended in the dropships to 15.

All these changes meant the unit had taken on an ad-hoc feel, which was why Xin's plan called for Patagonia to fill the tactically simplest role: to protect the entry point, while Nhlappo's Force Kenya pushed inside the city to plant the gamma bomb.

The sun dipped lower still. To anyone without vision enhancements such as the Marines enjoyed with their helmets, the sun would be blinding. Just as Xin intended. And this mission to raid Beta City was her plan.

"It's time," she told Arun.

He activated the FTL link to *Beowulf*. "You ready, Indiya?"

"We're in geosynch orbit above you," the ship's captain replied. "Ready to deploy the zero-point weapon cone on your command. Our sensors aren't designed to scout the surface for you, but we're picking limited energy signatures in the city. The lights are on, but it doesn't mean anyone's home."

"Understood. That matches what Corporal Narciso's sensor box is telling us. Wish us luck. We're going in."

Arun cut his connection to *Beowulf* and re-opened one to Xin. "This is your show, Lee. Take it away."

"Yes, sir."

A few seconds later, Barney reported the first of four missile launches. These were the *blinders* that Nhlappo had discovered hidden in Detroit. If all went well, hundreds of miniature semi-intelligent bombs would be scattering themselves over the lake, the island and the shoreline. The blinders would be searching out enemy targeting systems while hiding from detection themselves, waiting for the signal to activate.

Drones were released at the same time. As recon devices, they were a slight improvement now that Del-Marie had worked his software magic. Mechanically, they were no more stealthed than the noisy fliers Caccamo and Hecht had flown into Detroit when they'd first landed on the planet. But Del's update meant these drones would hide, leaving only one to broadcast tactical updates in short bursts, after which it would go dark and shift position. If one drone was destroyed, the next would automatically take over.

Arun's concentration was broken when Hecht unexpectedly interrupted.

"Sir, it's Tremayne. Wishes to speak privately with you. Says it's her precog thing."

What the hell? "Put her through."

Even before Arun had spoken his confirmation, Barney had understood his intent, and interfaced with Saraswati to set up a private channel over LBNet.

"Go ahead, Springer," said Arun.

Springer didn't reply. A distraction was the last thing he needed right now. And Springer was distracting enough without going into her enigmatic mode. Arun hardened his heart to snap at her to stop wasting his time, to wait until this show was over. He stopped himself when he heard Springer gasping for air. She sounded panicked.

"Standby, Lieutenant," Arun told Xin. "We might have a problem. Wait for my signal."

"Acknowledged," Xin replied. She did not sound pleased.

"Springer, I know you wouldn't bother me unless you thought it vital. Try to describe what you've sensed. Just speak. Don't try to interpret anything yet."

"Pulsing. Orange. Silver ribbons fluttering in the eddying current of life's fluids, cold and seminal. *Alien*. Pulsing like the superbeat of the multiverse. Ughh So… so… so cold. It's inside me. Oppp… Opening me up for scrutiny. Like being stripped naked, but a violation a thousand times worse. Ughh!"

"Is there some advice you can give me? An action to be avoided?"

"I'm not having a pre-cog vision, Major. It's a message. I… Ugghhh!"

"Springer! Talk to me!"

"*We use this human instance as a conduit.*" The panic had left Springer's voice. She sounded more like a Hardit's speech synthesizer.

"Springer, is that still you? What's happening? Are you okay?"

"*Remember your oath. The future demands this of you.*"

Oh, crap.

Arun's mind leaped back two years, to a moment when he'd been betrayed, sleep deprived, and drowned for hours on end: all so that he was vulnerable to scrutiny by the Night Hummers. As far as he knew, it was these naturally pre-cognitive balls of pulsing fluids who had started the chain of events that had led to the fledgling Human Legion. They had whispered into Jotun ears that Arun McEwan was a being of destiny. A deep conspiracy had emerged to protect and nurture him. Everything else had spiraled from there.

Two years ago, hungry and exhausted, he would have promised anything for the chance of a hot meal. When a Hummer promised food, drink and rest in exchange for Arun's oath to protect the Hummer race, the idea that he would save an entire alien species by placing it under human protection had seemed an insane joke.

Arun wasn't laughing now.

"Arun. Arun, it's gone," said Springer. "Whatever took control wanted to say those words through me." She paused. "Arun. What oath? What have you done?"

"Hecht here, Major. Tremayne's acting like she's possessed. Does she pose a threat?"

"Negative, Hecht. The incident has passed. She's good to go now."

Ignoring Springer's comm requests, Arun tried to think through the implications. The campaign to recapture Tranquility was so precarious that he couldn't cope with more complications. Did Springer's possession change anything? The Night Hummer who'd scrutinized Arun on a captured asteroid had claimed Arun would kill it. Was Arun on the cusp of bringing about that death?

Arun cut all comm links and screamed his frustration in the privacy of his helmet. There were too many unknowns. He was speculating, and he had no time for guesswork. All they could do was go ahead and adapt to events as they happened.

He ordered Xin to delay another thirty seconds to give Springer time to recover, and then launch the attack.

Arun knew how Marines had been bred to think. Now that he'd ordered them to proceed, those who'd been aware of Springer's incident would already have buried any concerns about her and be utterly focused on the operation to attack Beta City.

Arun's brain was not wired up like the others, though. He was a planner and a worrier. The two were inextricably linked, worse luck.

When Xin gave the signal for Arun and the rest of Patagonia and Kenya to stealth up and make their way down to the shoreline, Arun had to delegate control of the battlesuit to Barney, because the implications of the message from the Night Hummer was swirling around so violently in his mind that his vision was blurring.

He didn't need any fancy brain augmentations to remember the most chilling thing the Hummer had said on that asteroid two years ago. To make good his oath to protect the Hummers, Arun would be forced into painful choices. He would need to make sacrifices. Arun looked around at his comrades. Stealthed as they were, they were nothing more than shimmering blurs and guessed outlines, but Arun felt their presence keenly.

Who among them was he about to sacrifice?

Then they were at the narrow lakeside beach and even battlesuit stealth systems couldn't hide bootprints in the sand and the splashes as the Marines entered the sun-burnished waters of Lake Sarpedona, diving for the darkness of the lake's depths. For the island held one last secret. While the ground entrance was real enough, there were also concealed access ports deep underwater, broad enough to let a besieged Marine garrison sally forth in strength and strike a besieger from the rear.

Between the best software experts supplied by the Navy and Marines – Furn in orbit and Del-Marie in Detroit – these underwater sally ports were already acknowledging Human Legion command requests.

They were about to let an attacking force in.

Chapter 48

Barney cut the impellers clamped to their battlesuit and allowed Arun to drift down through the midnight blue to the underwater hatch. When Force Patagonia was in position at a total of four neighboring hatches – three Marines at each, with Arun, Puja, and Stopcock in reserve – Arun gave the order to attempt entry.

Detroit was situated in the bottom of a deep mountain valley. Here, on the other side of the world on the continent of Serendine, the Marine depot and defensive warren of Beta City was situated not just underground but underwater too; vehicular access was only through the small island above. The design had worked: as far as anyone had told him, Beta had never been taken by assault, only through treachery.

Beta had the capacity to be garrisoned by over 100,000 well-supplied defenders with enough food to last several years. Xin's plan had 31 attackers to call on, but the objective was not to take and hold. Not yet, anyway.

The assault was starting well. Instead of having to blast through the heavily armored hatches, a time-consuming and attention-grabbing exercise, they opened obediently.

The Patagonia teams, Arun with them, cycled through the airlocks and pushed through into Beta City.

He relaxed a notch. All entry points into the city were guarded by strong defensive positions. If they had been manned, or if someone had thought to rig up some AI-controlled autocannons, Patagonia would have been reduced to fish food by now.

So far, the Hardits had demonstrated all the tactical sense of a clump of mud. Xin had been gambling on that and Arun's force had been the stake she'd wagered.

Gambled and won!

Gupta took charge of the Patagonia Marines, spreading them out to secure the entry zone.

When he'd first returned to Detroit at the head of the Legion, Arun had felt as if he were disturbing a corpse. No amount of temporary power rigs could hide the fact that his home was dead. Beta felt different from the start. It was quiet but alive — *functional*. The absorbent floor coating sucked the water from their boots. The zig-zagging corridor welcomed them with heat and light. Hecht even reported that the heavy weapons trained on the airlocks were in safety mode but could be brought back online and into use.

With Patagonia still taking positions, Gupta set about ensuring that if this was a trap, it was an undetectable one. He gave Arun the all clear.

"We're secure," Arun relayed to Xin and Nhlappo, who waited outside in the water. "Coffee's brewing, chow's cooking. Come on in."

"Acknowledged," Xin replied curtly. Too curtly. Just for a moment, Arun wondered just how disappointed Xin really was that Arun hadn't been cut into bloody chunks by automated defenses.

Arun opened an FTL link to *Beowulf*. "Phase Guinshrike is go."

"Launching Guinshrike, aye," acknowledged Lieutenant Commander Lubricant, the XO since the humans had taken over the ship. After a moment's delay while she relayed instructions, she said: "He's a crazy old fool who tried to betray us all. If you ask me, he's succumbed to a death wish. You should have supported me at his trial, McEwan, then maybe he'd have been executed like he deserves."

"Good luck to you, too," replied Arun, angry for the most part because he agreed with Loobie.

The mad bastard in question was Ensign Dock, who'd displayed such exceptional piloting skills last night. It had been Indiya and Xin who'd argued to suspend the mutineer's death sentence.

Today Dock would prove which side was right.

Chapter 49

As soon as Lieutenant Commander Lubricant gave him the signal from orbit, Ensign Dock set his Stork to drink freely of its dwindling fuel reserves before acknowledging: "Guinshrike underway, aye."

To conserve fuel, after dropping off the expeditionary force 30 klicks away from Beta, Dock had kept his bird hidden at the bottom of a deep but slowly flowing river while the Marines had marched to their target. The craft had emerged from the water five minutes ago. To any onlookers, the sight of the river's surface roiling as it birthed this military leviathan would have looked magnificent. Dock was still cursing himself for not having the foresight to have dropped off cameras to record the scene.

Still, he had to be grateful for small mercies. That the children and refugees running this show were on schedule was more than just a relief: Dock only had enough fuel to try this once.

"ETA three minutes," he called through to the hold. "Triple check everything and then keep your minds and bodies relaxed. When we're over the target, things are going to proceed too fast and too violently for you to think before acting."

The three Resistance fighters in the back said nothing, but gave the impression of checking harness settings and verifying weapons status. Kraevoi, Pak, and Vanderman their names were. Enthusiastic kids, but their lack of language reinforced the Marine reputation of being dumb brutes who had regressed back to a more primitive form of hominid.

Mind you, that Lieutenant Lee showed promise. The giant girl could be positively scandalous when she wasn't playing *look at me, I'm an officer*. And she mesmerized many of the kids with her beauty. Not Dock. He preferred his meat tougher, and it was just as well she didn't have the same effect on him. It wouldn't do to fraternize too much with these Marines, especially since Lee had become Dock's protector, ever since he'd stumbled out of his court-martial with a suspended death sentence that could be carried out by any Navy officer without warning.

"Remember, boys and girls," Dock told his passengers, "don't scratch the furniture too much because Beta might be your home one day soon. All we're doing up here in the sky is to throw a flamboyant pose that these hairy monkeys can't ignore while your friends get dirty down below." Dock pushed the Stork to attack speed. "And for fuck's sake, people, if you ever do get to live here, make a little more effort with the name. I mean, *really! Beta City*… It's embarrassing! Now, hang on, we're going in…"

At Mach3, Dock hit the control to retract the doors in the hold. The bird immediately shook hard enough to dig through the buffer gel in his harness straps, promising colorful bruises if he lived long enough for them to bloom.

"Easy, girl," he crooned, stroking the console. "I've got you."

Once he'd stabilized the gunship, he glanced at the hold's internal camera. No one had fallen out yet, which was a good start.

There was nothing he could do for his passengers now, so he ignored them and allowed the thrill of flight to wash over him.

"Yeeeahhhhaaahhhh!"

Flying through atmosphere was so much more violent than space. It was fucking brilliant!

He suddenly remembered his cargo. "Four seconds to go," he told them.

Lee's plan was to take out the Hardit air defenses first with these fancy blinder missiles. Dock shrugged. The kids running the show were desperate enough to allow Dock to retain his rank on probation, despite being caught on the wrong side of *Beowulf's* mutinies. He *ought* to be grateful, he supposed, but he'd never promised to be good. For all her tactical sparkle, Lee was no flier. No one, but *no one* told Dock how to fly. Period!

Any flier would tell you that even the monkeys would think to layer their anti-air defenses, keeping some hidden in reserve.

They needed bait before they would reveal themselves to the blinders.

And bait was just what Dock was about to give them.

The tactical holosphere hovering above the control deck flared with color as the enemy acquired multiple target locks on the Stork. The locks were swiftly followed by missile launches.

Dock shouted through to the hold: "Now!"

The Resistance fighters were shaking so violently in their harnesses that the hold camera showed them as a blur. But they had wits enough to fire the first round of missiles out of the launchers secured to the deck on tripods.

It was a stupid lashed-up system, really. With a little more preparation, they could have broken the need for human fire authority and run the whole lot through AIs.

The backblast from the launchers choked the hold, but the smoke barrage they'd laid down was working already. There was actual smoke, true, but Dock was far more interested in the false trails of heat, radar, and other signatures mixed in the smoke munitions.

The holosphere showed more missile launches rise from the ground, this time aimed at these false targets.

The passengers in the back launched another round — this time blinder munitions set to killer mode from the start.

Dock turned the Stork through 90 degrees, and then flew fast and straight out of the caldera.

Some of the Hardit missiles followed his path. *Too many*. About a dozen.

Fliers were natural risk-takers. Even Marines understood that. Taking risks didn't always pay off, though.

"Breaking away," he announced. "Cease fire!"

Combat maneuvers in atmospheres were all about channeling momentum through the fluid medium of air. There was none of the effortless pivoting he was used to in void flight. Aerial flight was a deliciously masculine mix of speed and brute force as you constantly pummeled against the resistance of the air, forcing it to yield lift and turning forces against its will.

Kind of like rough sex, but even noisier.

Dock closed the hangar and threw his craft around until its hull screamed in protest.

But the problem with atmospheric flight, he decided, was that you could never outmaneuver missiles.

Abandoning his evasive maneuvers, he sped away in level flight at maximum acceleration. The eight missiles that he hadn't managed to throw off his scent were now closing fast.

Dock signaled for the blinder munitions that Major McEwan's force had set hunting earlier to shift to kill mode. If he survived the next few seconds, those blinders should prove jolly useful.

Wait a little longer, he willed the oncoming missiles. *Give up a little more of your delta-v.*

When the Stork's AI estimated four seconds before the first missile impact, Dock gave a maximum burst from the attitude thrusters to shove his nose straight down, presenting the belly of his craft to the missiles. Then he fed every last Joule of power to the underside Fermi defenses.

The gunship fell out of the sky like a rock, a magnetized rock because the ship's belly attracted the missiles with absolute inevitability. The missiles clattered harmlessly against the Stork, their fuses and triggers scrambled by the Fermi field.

Oh, yeah! Victory is mine!

When he'd finished punching the air, Dock checked the holosphere. It reported that they were clear and safe. Except for one thing.

The ground.

Shit!

Dock shook his head in frustration as he took up the flight controls and did battle with his death stall.

When will you ever remember that planets have grounds!

He managed to pull the nose up, but the gunship was shaking so violently in the turbulence that it wasn't responding predictably.

Damn! He'd used up too much reaction mass in his dive to escape the missiles.

Instead of pulling out of his dive, he banked to starboard until the lift from the delta wings regained some stability. Dock clipped the top of a forest tree canopy as he finally wrestled back control and started gaining altitude.

Well, strictly speaking, it was his slipstream that had bent back the tree, leaving in his wake a cloud of purple leaves ripped from their branches. But his story of clipping the tops of trees with his wingtips would sound so much better in the wardroom.

"Anyone still alive?" Dock called cheerfully into the hold. He was answered by dull groans. One passenger unconscious, two barely, he judged.

Dock rolled his eyes. "Oh, for Heaven's sake. I thought you lot were supposed to be g-hardened. I can't believe you've just missed the most exciting bit." He gave a long sigh. "Would you like me to set down and bring you coffee and a ginger biscuit until you feel better?"

No response.

While he circled over the trees to give the delicate lunks time to recover, he played back the results of the blinders. They'd been busy since Lieutenant Lee's lot had released them, doing a fantastic job in tracking enemy targeting systems. And any that they hadn't found had revealed themselves when they tried to shoot Dock out of the sky.

The holosphere showed small explosions flaring all around the caldera as the Hardit anti-air defenses were wiped out.

"Hello, am I through to the Hardit commander?" he said over the comm, deciding to have a little fun at his passengers' expense. "Thank you. Now, madam, I know I called you a bakri-chodding dog fondler whose crimes against hygiene mean that even the fleas won't touch you, but please understand, I only mean that with the deepest affection." The Resistance fighters were sufficiently awake now to glare into the camera, looking thoroughly pissed off. That was good enough for Dock to change course back to Beta City.

"My passengers are only Marines," he said. "Which means they're feeling a little delicate. Would you be awfully decent and allow us to take a break for five minutes, so we can resume the attack when the poor darlings are feeling better? You would? Bloody marvelous. May I say that you are thoroughly decent for a xenocidal hairy skangat. See you soon. Over and bye bye."

All the while, Dock kept his attention locked onto the tactical holosphere. No signs of enemy target acquisitions. If any SAM defenses had survived, they would have shown themselves by now. *He was in the clear.*

"Playtime's over, guys. We'll be over the target in 20 seconds. And remember what I said earlier: you need to put on a good show, make the poor monkey defenders think we're softening them up for a land assault. Enjoy playing with your missiles, but don't scratch the furniture."

Chapter 50

"Guinshrike a success," Indiya reported to Arun over the FTL link, having taken over from the XO. "Used too much fuel, though, so your lift home will be waiting for you at the bottom of the lake instead of safely out of harm's way. Make sure you set that bomb right because electronics are more vulnerable than Marine flesh. If your gamma burst fries the avionics on that Stork—"

"Then none of us are ever getting back to Detroit," Arun said. "Let alone *Beowulf*."

"Maybe. We do have other shuttles, but can't crew them without risking critically important crew. Let's hope you don't force me into choosing between my ship and rescuing a stranded expeditionary force that didn't know when to quit."

"And I hope you remember that I am in command of *all* forces. You run your ship internally how you like, Captain Indiya, but *Beowulf* complies with objectives that I set."

The connection was terminated abruptly.

Love you too, Indiya.

Arun glanced around the inside of the redoubt, but of course no one had overheard his spat with the commander of their orbital support. Everyone was keeping watch on the corridors outside.

The four airlocks they'd used to enter the city were connected by narrow zig-zag passageways flowed around two bastion-edged redoubts that covered the area. The passageways merged behind the redoubts before pushing on to one of the main helixes — gently sloping ramps that circled up and down a broad vertical shaft, connecting the levels. Xin was readying the gamma bomb in that helix now.

Arun, Puja and 1st Section were in one redoubt, Gupta, Laskosk and 2nd Section were in the other. Arcs of fire were perfect, covering each other, and every approach. The bastions were even armed with heavy weapons.

Arun still wasn't happy. Hunkering behind static defenses made him nervous. Once behind a wall it was a difficult mental leap to abandon your position, and no matter how impressive the slab of armor between you and the passageway outside, there would always be munitions that could punch through any armor.

"Sir," called Puja who had been engrossed in her sensor block for the past few minutes.

"Stand by, Narciso." Arun waited until Barney had set up a comm-relay to include Gupta, Majanita, Nhlappo and Xin. "Go ahead."

"The latest data burst from the recon drone at the shoreline confirms what I'm reading with my sensor unit. Enemy-controlled weapons systems are going online in the upper levels. Not many, but looks like the garrison is gearing up for a surface attack. I'm detecting energy signatures on the move. It's consistent with reserves moving up the levels to reinforce topside defenses. It's intermittent, but I did detect similar signatures moving to our location on Level 6. I'm not picking up anything nearby now. All I can say is that I'm not seeing heavy weapons coming our way. It could be a single scout coming to check why the hatches opened, or could be ten thousand militia armed with dumb chemical-powered rifles. If it's the latter, I won't know until they're nearly upon us."

"Thank you, Corporal," said Arun. "Looks like Ensign Dock's taken the heat off us. I'll present him with my compliments when I see him next. And that won't be as long as we thought because he'll be waiting for us at the bottom of the lake. Says our bird's running too low on fuel to ride out the bomb blast farther out. Lieutenant Lee, how long do you need?"

"Device is primed," Xin replied. "Just need to set the blast pattern and we're outta here. A few minutes. No more."

There was nothing for Arun to do but wait. He double checked the ammo state of his SA-71. All was fine. He knew it would be, but he hadn't lost the habit of checking and re-checking equipment was functioning and placed where he expected it to be. So long as his NCOs were alive and uninjured, they knew what to do better than he did. For now, he was just another Marine with a carbine. The familiar heft of the weapon was a comfort as he waited.

"Contact!"

"The alert came from Sergeant Majanita. Madge had taken charge of 3rd Section who had been dropped off in the hidden embrasures that ran along the passageways connecting Force Patagonia at the underwater entrance to the main helix where the rest of Force Kenya were readying the gamma bomb.

"Scouts heading our way from the north," Madge added. "Four so far."

"Have they seen you?" asked Nhlappo.

"Negative."

"What do you see, Narciso?" asked Xin.

"I'm not seeing any energy signatures," Puja answered. "Must be lightly armed militia."

"We're keeping silent and dark in the helix," said Nhlappo. "Let's hope they're here to inspect why the airlocks opened, and don't think to head our way."

"They're passing our position now," whispered Madge. "Headed your way, Major. I can confirm they are rifle-armed militia."

"Let them pass, Majanita," said Nhlappo.

Majanita and 3rd Section gave Arun good eyes on the Hardit advance. The vanguard of four Hardit scouts hesitated within touching distance of the hidden Marines and sniffed the air. They weren't the elite soldiers who were connected with Tawfiq. They were half-starved militia who looked as if they hadn't cleaned themselves since long before the civil war broke out. Their clothes were so tattered that they would soon be naked other than matted fur. Arun's contempt was stoked still further by the way their tails held their rifles as if the weapons were smeared with excrement. These monkeys had no pride in themselves.

But Arun knew it would be a mistake to underestimate the danger from these miserable wretches. Despite the stench from the Hardit bodies, their sense of smell was acute. Their noses would have confirmed the airlocks had been opened. And even though the Marine battlesuits were all scent-sealed, the enemy might be able to smell them indirectly: perhaps from the slight warming of the hinge lubricants for the door into the redoubt where Arun was hidden.

The Hardit scouts relaxed, resting there listlessly until their main force joined them. A dozen more militia arrived first, sniffing the air for themselves. These reinforcements acted more agitated than the scouts. Growls broke out. Arun felt sure the aliens had discovered the human threat, but then… nothing. The newly arrived Hardits relaxed, and the enemy rested on all fours until further reinforcements arrived, swelling their number to over fifty.

As this mass of Hardits nervously pushed down the passageway to where Patagonia waited in their redoubts, they gave no indication that they could smell the humans watching their every move. They acted oblivious to the instrument of death being prepared in the helix just a few hundred meters behind them.

When they were close enough for his liking, Gupta readied Patagonia's welcome. "In memory of our fallen and wounded: Cusato, Chung, Ballantyne, Naron, Bojin, Halici, Lewark, Kalis, Rhenolotte, Yoshioka, Okoro. This is for you. Plasma cannons ready. Carbines, pick off any of them trying to escape. On my mark… fire!"

At a range of a dozen meters, the embrasures on the redoubts suddenly widened, just enough to allow the heavy plasma cannons inside to fire through them and blast the enemy in crossfire. The Hardits were engulfed in violet-tinged blooms, rounds of packaged ball lightning that burst on impact, searing limbs and setting alight clothing and fur. The passageway cracked with thunder as the plasma cannons drew on the energy feeds that ran below the redoubts to pour out a relentless barrage of fire.

Despite Barney's best efforts to make sense of the sight, the plasma bursts generated so much visible light that the scene through Arun's helmet whited out.

Arun looked away.

"Cease fire," ordered Gupta. "Carabiniers, pick your targets."

Bodies littered the approach to the redoubts. Most of them burned fiercely. A few survivors staggered, tripping over their comrades, and screaming in a high-pitched wail that made Arun shake. The aliens were heavily susceptible to flash-bombs, as Arun had found out for himself when he'd pushed one in Tawfiq's face, long ago. The light and noise from the plasma barrage had left the enemy scouts utterly stunned.

Taking aim through the embrasure at the survivor farthest away, Arun let off two shots. Barney confirmed his kill before the Hardit had finished slumping to the ground. There were no more targets. The rest of Force Patagonia had made sure of that.

"All dead," confirmed Madge from her position further up the corridor.

"And we're all done here," Xin added. "We're coming back empty handed."

Arun laughed. In this operation, *empty handed* meant success. Force Kenya hadn't just brought the gamma bomb, they'd carted with them empty ammo crates in waterproof seals. They had left the bomb in one crate and then used the others to build up an innocent-looking stack. The beauty of a gamma bomb was that it wouldn't damage dumb materials such as those used in the crates. After ten minutes for the radiation to settle to an acceptable level, the Marines would return and fill the same munition crates with carbines, ammo bulbs, missiles, and grenades. It would be the start of a supply chain that would arm the human slaves across the planet.

The Hardits wouldn't know what had hit them… so long as the stack of crates was enough camouflage to fool them. If they did try to defuse the bomb, the Hardits would set it off, risking sending the blast radius in the wrong direction, and catching the Marines in its lethal path.

Guess we'll find out soon enough, Arun mused as he watched Kenya filter past the redoubts and into the airlocks behind. Once they had made their exit safely, Arun and the rest of Patagonia followed them, activating their impellers as soon as they entered the water. They dove for the depths, putting as much water as they could between them and the gamma bomb's lethal rays.

With the immediate danger of enemy contact over, and the threat of the gamma bomb too abstract to worry him, Arun's mind soon turned to Springer's contact with a Night Hummer.

The moment he thought of the bloated alien gas sacs, Arun felt his confidence hemorrhage. Whenever the Night Hummers came into focus — even when other species were discussing them — he felt his free will was being exposed as an illusion. It was like being stuck behind a defensive position. Trapped. Out of options.

But he hadn't been the only human the Night Hummers had alerted the Jotuns to. There had been two others: Xin, and (he still assumed) Indiya.

"Xin?" he asked on a private channel. "Were you ever taken to an asteroid to meet a Night Hummer?"

"A Hummer? We're about to blow a gamma bomb and you want to talk about the Hummers? I don't know about any asteroids, but I was taken to encounter a Hummer in a restricted area of Level 9."

"Our bomb's on Level 6, and you've shaped the blast pattern to a hemisphere aimed at the levels above. If Beta had its own Level 9 section for Hummers, do you reckon it might survive the blast?"

Xin hesitated. "Yes, I think so. The chamber I saw looked heavily shielded to me. Gravity was much lower, less than on Antilles. How the hell they did that, I've no frakking idea, but they obviously put a lot of effort into getting the environment right. Anyway, what the frakk are you talking about? Is there something I should know?"

"Just a hunch."

"A hunch!" Arun sensed Xin was fighting to control her anger. "Fine! Keep your secrets to yourself. Not a good policy, though. It doesn't engender trust. You need to learn that, Major."

A few moments later, when Arun was in sight of the silver lump that was the Stork, he received an unexpected communication from Indiya on *Beowulf*.

"Major, we're detecting significant energy signatures emerging onto the planet's surface about 30 klicks northwest of Detroit. I can't say what they are but their speed of advance on Detroit says they're motorized. They have air support too. Plenty of it."

"Aircraft? Are you sure? I thought Hardits were as psychologically unsuited to flying as Jotuns to tunneling."

"Turned out that was a lie, remember? Even if you're right, they could be drones remotely controlled from underground. Whatever they are, they're real. ETA eighteen minutes."

"Eighteen minutes! There's no way we can get there in time to affect the outcome. Can you station *Beowulf* over Detroit before the enemy arrives?"

"Yes. Standby… Course laid in."

"Brandt's handling Detroit's defense. Let him know when you're there so he can call on you as fire support."

"Understood," she acknowledged, but there was a catch in her voice.

Indiya had been icy cold ever since she'd vaped all those people the last time she'd turned *Beowulf*'s engine into a deadly weapon. Nothing he'd said could convince her that she wasn't a mass murderer. Since the destruction of *Themistocles*, this was the first time Indiya had sounded uncertain.

He guessed why.

Setting off the engine in the atmosphere could blow up *Beowulf* or set the atmosphere alight. Arun had taken so many risks on the planet's surface that it was easy to forget that Indiya hadn't.

"One day," he told Indiya, "when all this is over, you promised you'd take me on a tour along the outside of your ship. Just the two of us. I'm still looking forward to that."

He heard the pinched intake of breath. "Your attempts at romance are not welcome, Major. I'm a ship's captain. Not a girl. Indiya out."

Arun clenched his fists as tightly as his gauntlets allowed. Why were all his friendships shutting down?

He hadn't time to fix his life problems now. Arun hunkered down with the other Marines at the bottom of the lake, using the Stork as a shield.

The light at this depth had a murky quality made worse by the cloud of mud thrown up by Marine boots thumping into the lake bottom.

Xin gave a three second countdown over BattleNet and then detonated the gamma bomb.

His ears popped, and he felt or maybe heard an electronic groan buzzing through the inside of his helmet.

That was it. Barney reported minor damage, but he said it was no worse than a mild cyber-attack. He was designed for resilience and would soon be back to full strength.

Arun scanned BattleNet. One of its functions was to constantly relay information on the health of the Marines, their suits, and the AIs that bridged the two. It seemed the waters of the lake had taken the brunt of the radiation pulse. The Marines were fine. Some of the suits had taken damage, but none were in a critical state.

By now, the hemispherical blast pattern of the bomb meant everyone in Beta City above Level 6 should be dead. But the Marines had survived.

He com-linked to the Stork. "Dock, you all right?"

"Ah, Major. Yes, we're snug and happy here. Thank you for your warm concern."

"You're our ride out of here, Dock."

"A service it will be my pleasure to provide. Radiation levels not as bad as we feared. We can't take you aboard under water, but we can move off the bottom quicker than we expected. I'll give it another five minutes, before my bird can make it out of here. If you follow five minutes later, you should be safe."

"Detroit's about to come under attack," Arun said, after adding the other officers into the comm channel. "We need to squeeze our safety margin."

"Already factored in," said Dock.

"Do we still raid Beta for materiel?" asked Xin. "Or head straight back to Detroit? Loading up with munitions will take at least ten minutes."

The choice terrified Arun, how could he know which course would be best?

"I'll speak to Brandt first. *Beowulf* will offer fire support, though I don't know how useful that will be."

"Major?" It was Nhlappo. "Are you sure we'll be ready to go soon? I think that's radioactive fallout."

He followed her pointing finger up at a white cloud slowly descending to the lake bottom. It looked like fat chunks of snow.

"Well, Dock?" queried Arun.

"Nothing to worry about," said Dock cheerfully. "You've just killed every fish in the lake. They're either floating on the surface or descending to the bottom. They're slightly radioactive but shouldn't be a problem. Nor the dead birds that will reach you later. Mind you, I don't fancy one of those fish for my dinner. Hold on, we've company. Standby… Major, I'm picking up an incoming transmission from the Hardits. It's… an individual calling itself Tawfiq Woomer-Calix. Asking for you by name."

Not again! "Tell the veck to go vulley herself. No, belay that! Is she asking for peace terms?"

"Hmmm. Not in so many words… I rather had the impression she was gloating, but I don't know the species well. The Hardit says it wants to inform you about its attack plans because it wants to imagine the dismay on your face as you defecate in fear. We might have lost some fidelity in translation, but I think you get the gist of it."

"Very well," he told Dock, regretting already what he was about to say. "Patch Tawfiq through."

Chapter 51

Just the sight of Tawfiq's ugly three yellow-tinged eyes on the inside of his helmet made Arun want to retch. He wished he'd restricted the link to audio-only, but it was too late now. He didn't want to show weakness, especially since he'd patched the Hardit into the Marine command channel. People were hearing this exchange. He wished Springer was doing the talking. Or Xin. They were so much better than him at this sort of thing.

"Bad luck, Tawfiq," he opened. "You should have killed me when you had the chance."

"Why should I have bothered?" The lack of emotion in the alien's synthesized words only riled Arun more.

"Because if you'd killed me, we wouldn't have been able to defeat your mutiny on *Themistocles* and *Beowulf*, wouldn't have come back to take our revenge on you."

"I know. None of that matters."

"We've just wiped out the garrison of your main military base and taken some serious hardware."

"I know that too, human. It make no difference." Tawfiq lifted her lip away from her fangs. Had she learned to sneer like a human?

Arun sneered right back at her. "This is only one of many Human Legion victories to come, Hardit. And with all this materiel from Beta, and more resupply on the way, in each new battle we fight we will be stronger than the last."

Okay, so he exaggerated their strength, but the alien showed no sign of being concerned. "Stupid human. You grasp half-truth, as always. Each battle will be easier, but for us, not you."

"You're full of drent, Hardit. Face it, you lost."

"We knew you were coming. Why else do you think we waited for you to split your forces before we attacked location who you call Detroit."

The monkeys knew Arun's team was coming? How? Arun shook his head. He refused to believe this. Tawfiq was trying to vulley with his head. Nothing more. He decided to play along, though, to see what the alien was up to. "Are you implying you have a spy in our ranks? It's impossible. We killed all the traitors."

The moment he finished speaking, though, doubt chilled him. They hadn't killed all the traitors, had they? Ensign Dock… Could he be working for the enemy?

"We have no need of spies amongst you humans," answered Tawfiq. Arun wasn't sure to be relieved or horrified at the implications. "Not when we can see the future."

"Enough with the riddles, Tawfiq. Why did you wish to speak with me?"

"I am never sure of the depths of ignorance to which you humans sink. Therefore I ask – have you heard of a pre-cognitive species called Night Hummers?"

Arun snarled. The alien veck knew full well he did.

"Ahah," said Tawfiq, a crass sound coming from the voice synthesizer. "I sense you know of Hummers. The future-teller sees you as an ally – in a metaphysical sense. So I thought it best if we kill it. Then I had a better idea. Why not get *you* to kill it?"

"There was a Night Hummer in Beta City?"

"Human, there still is."

"Arun," interrupted Xin, "the Hummer will be on a deep level in a shielded life support system. I bet it's still fine."

"The other human is correct, McEwan. The Hummer is alive. You could even take it away in that little shuttle you have. Think for a moment on how useful it be to see into future. But can you reach Hummer in time? This is the little challenge I am setting you."

Arun bit his lip. There was nothing he detested more than being taunted by smug aliens who thought humans were irredeemably inferior. Even his Trog friend, Pedro, could be unbearably condescending. One day… one day he'd get Tawfiq in his grasp. *Then they'd learn who was the superior one.*

Arun drew a deep breath, unexpectedly stung by the memory of his Troggie friend. He'd never known how many Trogs had shared Tranquility with the humans and Hardits. Maybe billions. All dead. Arun would avenge that xenocide. The Hardits had a frakk-load of pain coming.

"What is wrong?" asked Tawfiq. "Aren't you going to ask why the Night Hummer is threatened?"

"No. I tire of your childish games, Hardit. If we're really in the drent, we'll find out for ourselves soon enough."

"Then you don't wish to know of the mass driver bombardment?"

"What?"

"Come now, human. Even you can't have forgotten the reason why you brought your stinking carcass to the moon you call Antilles? A new bombardment is due to commence any moment now, only this time the mass driver is aimed at Beta City."

"Indiya, you there?" Arun asked over the FTL link.

"Yes, Major."

"We have intel of a mass driver bombardment of my position from Antilles. Can you confirm this is accurate?"

"Affirmative. I left a sensor probe in Antilles orbit. Accessing now. Standby."

"I hear you are confirming my words," said Tawfiq. "Maybe you very slightly less stupid than you smell. I leave you now, but don't take too long with your checking. If you will rescue your pre-cog, you don't have much time."

Chapter 52

Arun's head spun too quickly to get traction on a clear line of thought. All the talk of destiny swirling over him these past two years had been a comfort in the back of his mind – reassurance that he would survive the next firefight, and the one after that, because he had an appointment to keep with the future.

But this destiny drent wasn't at the back of his mind now, nor was it any comfort.

What to do?

There was only one way to protect Beta City and the Night Hummer that might be inside, and didn't Tawfiq know it? *Beowulf* had to take out the mass drivers at source. And that meant abandoning Detroit to Tawfiq's air force.

It all made sense now. Tawfiq had been playing them all along. She had the best possible source of Intel: a glimpse into the future.

Arun had to win that resource for the Human Legion.

"Sir?" prompted Nhlappo. "If the monkey's right, then our position is about to be bombarded, our home base is about to fight for its life, and the water above is still dangerously radioactive. You need to start making decisions."

Of course he did, but what? There was no time to tease out a brilliant idea from his planner brain, no point in weighing the pros and cons because his every option was a variant of failure.

He did the only thing he could: went with his gut.

Arun opened the FTL channel to *Beowulf*, looping in Dock and all the Marines of Force Patagonia. They had the right to hear this.

"McEwan to *Beowulf*."

"Here," replied Indiya. "We're still analyzing sensor data, but we've reached 90% confidence that your intel is accurate."

"That's good enough to act." Arun had to pause and take in a sharp breath. "Proceed to the moon without delay and destroy that mass driver."

"Major, there are three waves of enemy aircraft inbound for Detroit. They have no idea we're here. We can wipe them out and then proceed to the moon."

"Negative. The enemy is toying with us, Captain. They know everything we're planning. I'll wipe that smile off Tawfiq's snout, but first you must proceed immediately to Antilles."

"There are civilians sheltering in Detroit. Innocents expecting our protection."

"I am aware of that, Captain Indiya. And you should be aware that I am not willing to debate command decisions in the middle of a battle."

"*Beowulf* is my command, Major."

"How you run your ship is entirely down to you, Captain, but *Beowulf* is an asset of the Human Legion and I am in overall command of the Legion. Your objectives are set by me. The Reserve Captain herself made that very clear."

Indiya's cold fury sent bolts of energy through the FTL connection. Arun assumed it was only his imagination, and not something concocted by Furn or one of the other Navy freaks. Real or not, as Indiya punished him with her silence, his heart still fluttered, and his breath quickened. Would she really dare him to relieve her of command?

"Setting course for Antilles, aye," said Indiya, and then cut the link.

"What are you doing?" asked Xin over the officers–only command channel. Her voice was unnaturally calm.

"You should know," Arun snapped, "you're bound by the same destiny."

"Let me get this straight," she said. "You're saying that this Hummer is more important than everyone in Detroit. Brandt is there with his Team Mexico, or whatever you decided to call them. Del's there too. So are dozens of civilians, including this Spartika we spent so much blood over. Not to mention Rohanna, Shelby, and their two babies. Are you telling me your appointment with destiny is more valuable than all of them?"

Arun replied through gritted teeth: "Yes. Yes I am."

Xin allowed the painful silence to extend.

"I have reluctantly decided to weaken Detroit's air defenses," Arun protested. "I'm not abandoning Brandt to certain death…" Arun's voice dried up. He wasn't sure who he was trying to convince.

As for Nhlappo, she maintained an impenetrable silence. He'd never known her not to voice an opinion before. Was it the babies left behind in Detroit that were shredding her resolve? She was remarkably attached to them.

Xin broke the silence. "It's okay, Arun." Her voice was surprisingly reassuring. "I get it. Just wanted to be sure you did too. I always did say you were an alien lover, Arun. First that Trog, and now this Hummer… blob-thing. Still, if aliens are your thing, then that's okay with me. No point waiting around, so let's get going."

"No." He shook his head. "I don't need you going in with me."

"Don't lock me out, Major. Nhlappo doesn't need me to help her unit fill some equipment crates."

"Sir!"

It was Umarov. "Permission to join your alien hunt?"

"It's not a pleasure stroll, Umarov," said Arun.

"No, sir. Reckon a jaunt on a jet rack is as good a way to bow out as any I can think of, sir."

Jet racks… they might be just what they needed to reach the Hummer quickly. "I've no experience with racks. Have you?"

"Love 'em, sir."

"Then that's decided. Umarov, and Lieutenant Lee, you're with me. Lieutenant Nhlappo, wait till radiation clears to safe levels, and then continue with your mission to retrieve the weapons. Board the shuttle and withdraw to a safe distance – no point in hanging around to take a kinetic projectile in the face. Once you're in safety give us another ten minutes to signal for evac. If we don't, then I want you to proceed to Detroit and use your judgment to influence whatever situation you encounter there."

"We're not waiting for the radiation to clear, are we?" asked Xin.

"No," said Arun. "But there is a job I need to do first."

Arun opened the FTL link to Brandt in Detroit. "Brandt, it's McEwan. Bad news…"

Chapter 53

The instant Major McEwan cut the FTL comm link, 2nd Lieutenant Edward Brandt noticed an uneasy silence had clamped down on the observation bubble.

Brandt cursed himself with the vilest curses (and he'd picked up a fair few recently on account of his time spent in the company of foul-mouthed Navy spacers). He had come up here to steady Detroit's topside defenders, not scare the drent out of them.

"Anything wrong, sir?" asked Sergeant Bernard Exelmans, Force Mexico's senior NCO.

Brandt looked around the position, which was the only topside command post to survive the civil war relatively intact. Kantrowicz and Zane were at the sensor consoles. Del-Marie had done a good job of rigging them up to their thinly spaced perimeter of recon drones, and to the single sensor drone that *Beowulf* had placed in orbit. Exelmans and Del-Marie were peering out of the transparent observation blister, discussing the enemy's likely lines of attack. Or had been.

None of them had their attention on the outside now. Brandt felt them all watching him. They couldn't have overheard. How *did* they know the major had given bad news?

He sighed; there was no hiding this. "*Beowulf* is withdrawing," he said.

They were only three words, but they were lethal ones that could mean the death of every human in Detroit. Marines and civilians; fit and wounded; adults, and now children and nursing mothers too. They'd had less than ten minutes to get used to the idea that *Beowulf*'s secret weapon would be deployed in their defense.

That its withdrawal was wreaking such damage on morale didn't speak well of Detroit's conventional defenses.

Exelmans leaned into the blister and peered up into the sky. "But she hasn't even reached orbit over our position yet. Where is she going?"

"Antilles."

"Why?" asked Del-Marie.

"Why is not the issue, Lance Corporal Sandure. We're on our own with a Hardit army inbound. That's enough for us to worry about for now. Kantrowicz, how long have we got?"

"The first wave of enemy air assets will be here in fourteen minutes. Second wave is five minutes behind. Enemy infantry holding position in sectors 9, 11, and 4. Motorized troops about half an hour behind them. High energy signature equipment stationed ten klicks back on the plateau. Power signatures indicate their high charge build up is continuing. Analysis – they're readying a battery of field railguns."

"Which makes no sense," said Brandt. "Field railguns are good for direct or suborbital fire, but hopeless at the kind of indirect fire the enemy needs to lob munitions down into our valley. With luck they'll blast their own troops on the mountainside." Brandt took several seconds to chew over the best response to the enemy artillery. "Exelmans."

"Sir."

"Keep an area-denial missile spread trained on their artillery assets, but hold in reserve until we know it's a genuine threat. With *Beowulf* gone, we'll need to hoard our surface-to-surface ordnance even more than before. Tell your missile batteries to reconfigure 80% of ground-attack missiles into anti-air configuration."

Seeing Exelmans hesitate, Brandt added: "Can we do that in time?"

"Yes, sir. It's just that… Detroit is surrounded by thousands of enemy ground troops."

"Indeed, Sergeant. And every one of those monkeys that makes it through the automated defense line will then discover that an armored Marine with an SA-71 is a formidable foe. But from the air, we're no more than target practice for their gunners. Do it."

"Yes, sir."

Exelmans relayed orders to the three missile batteries they'd positioned in the wreckage of the base's topside defenses. Their bite came from ordnance stripped out of the wrecked aircraft in Detroit's hangar, and rigged up to generic targeting computers.

With launch tubes sealed in place by quick-setting building repair blocks, and the exposed power and signal cabling threatening to trip anyone coming near, the missile batteries looked more like insanely dangerous homemade fireworks than serious military assets. Del-Marie had been the main architect, aided by Deacon, the survivor who'd been a deck hand in Detroit's hangar before the civil war. Both of them insisted that the White Knight reliance on modular equipment with universal interfaces meant that all they'd needed to wire the salvaged equipment together was to code some simple bridging software.

Normally, Brandt would trust his life to Del's expertise in soft and wetware systems, but Del-Marie hadn't been on top of his game lately. The reason wasn't difficult to spot. In fact, it was standing right next to Brandt's old squadmate.

Brandt asked his suit AI, Vauban, for an updated ETA on the enemy air assets.

Twelve minutes. It was just enough time to resolve a stress fracture that had been running through his command ever since the injured Del-Marie had been temporarily reassigned to Brandt's command.

Vauban knew what was bothering his master and set up a private comm link that included both Del-Marie and Bernard.

"All done, Exelmans?" Brandt asked Bernard.

"Yes, sir."

"Good, because you've one more task before you go to your posts. When we were cadets, we all of us looked up to you two as the closest thing we had to a relationship role model. The universe has smiled upon you with bounty, because against all the odds, even though you were assigned to different units, here you are reunited in the same location. And yet you haven't spoken a word to each other. It's damaging morale. More importantly, it's annoying the frakk out of me. You have thirty seconds to make up. That's an order."

The two men stood as still as stone. If they were talking, Brandt with his higher spec suit would know. They did not. In silence, then, Bernard and Del-Marie turned to face each other. They pressed their palms together, holding that connection for about ten seconds.

Then Del-Marie hurried away to his post down in the hangar, where he would lead the defense of the wounded and civilians.

At last, Brandt mused, shaking his head. *Those two idiots have been bugging me for months. Why did it take facing overwhelming odds to bring them to their senses? Those Navy freaks who can control their own hormones have the right idea, because everywhere I look, I see Marines whose hormones control them. What's wrong with the universe?*

<Nothing > answered Vauban, who was developing a habit of interrupting Brandt's private thoughts. <High levels of sexual hormones are healthy for humans in late adolescence.>

So we're just a bunch of horny kids playing at soldiers. Is that it?

<That's about the strength of it,> Vauban answered. <But a handful of hormone-ruled Marine kids are more than a match for an army of those stinking monkey vecks.>

You're right there, pal. Brandt chuckled at Vauban's pugnacious words. He'd been such a softly spoken AI once. Maybe Del had hacked Vauban's speech patterns, livening him up a little as a joke.

Or maybe Vauban was simply reflecting Brandt's mood. He laughed and followed Vauban's lead.

Bring it on, Tawfiq. You're gonna get your butt kicked so hard you'll never dare to set your filthy paws on our planet's surface again.

Chapter 54

Kinetic bombardment wasn't as simple as everyone seemed to imagine, mused Cadenqee Canola-Pututuizo. As base commander of the moon's mining settlement — a colony that had suffered devastating personnel losses in the recent civil war – any sensible person would listen to his professional judgment.

But good sense was not a characteristic in evidence with this female upstart, Tawfiq Woomer-Calix. Her New Order with all its vile mockery of nature had no official presence on the moon. Not yet, but her sick ideology was spreading through the planetary system like an epidemic, one that right-thinking people had not yet developed a defense against. Even if an answer to Tawfiq could be found, for Canola-Pututuizo it was already too late.

Tawfiq wanted an immediate bombardment of the island base that the Jotuns and their human slaves had abandoned. Canola-Pututuizo knew he was no hero; he wasn't foolish enough to deny her demands. If she wanted a bombardment, a bombardment was what she would get. Accuracy, though, was something that Canola-Pututuizo had been careful not to promise.

Before the calamitous civil war, the mining complex's linear accelerator had shot ore packages across interstellar space. It wasn't simply a matter of looking up a destination star in an astrochart and pressing a button. They had to calculate where the destination planet would have traveled to during the few decades it took for the ore package to journey there. That meant good targeting systems. It also meant ore was stockpiled and only fired during a one-hour launch window when Antilles was in the right point in its 29–day orbit of the planet. And now this Tawfiq was demanding a continuous bombardment using an accelerator lashed together from spares. Its predecessor had been destroyed by the humans the last time some idiot had ordered a bombardment of the planet below. Didn't anyone learn?

Canola-Pututuizo gave off *stoicism* pheromone. Many loved ones had died at the hands of the human Marines. He tried, but couldn't transmute his grief into hatred of the humans. The insanity of civil war had seized the galaxy. It was to the war that Canola-Pututuizo directed his anger.

He growled in resignation. "Activate firing protocol," he instructed his chief technician.

"Firing protocols live, sir."

"Now we watch, adjust, repeat, and hope the humans down below who won't accept the war is over do the decent thing and die. I don't want a repeat of last time."

He would never make a motivational demagogue, he knew, but his little speech did at least serve to keep the snouts of his launch team shut while they watched the first projectile fly across the narrow gap to the planet below.

Time stretched on in silence until the chief tech announced: "Fifteen seconds to impact, sir."

Canola-Pututuizo growled his annoyance but held his tongue and his pheromones. He didn't want to be told the time to impact. He wanted to know where the ore package was going to *land*.

"Sir," said Damastold Seorsan-Pututuizo, one of the junior techs, "the projectile has altered trajectory. Only slightly, but I'm certain of it."

"Analysis," said Cadenqee Canola-Pututuizo, hoping against hope that someone could see an explanation that didn't mean death at the hands of the human monsters.

"Projectile was hit by a military-grade pulse laser," reported Seorsan-Pututuizo.

"Can you detect the source?"

"Negative. I don't even have the equipment to speculate. Something's hidden out there in the void. Waiting."

"That's enough of such talk!" growled Canola-Pututuizo, adding *dominance* pheromone for emphasis. "Alert the base defense team that we have a possible hostile warship coming our way."

Jaws gaped in consternation. Canola-Pututuizo even smelled the *flee* scent. "If the humans come for us, our fate is already sealed," he told them. "If we're going to die, we will do so with dignity."

Submission replaced *flee* as the dominant scent in the room. "Well don't just sit there with your jaws scraping the floor," Canola-Pututuizo admonished. "We've a bombardment to send. We stay at our posts and send as many of them the humans' way while we still can."

With perfect timing, the deck rumbled as the mass driver fired a second projectile at the humans.

Chapter 55

Arun stared at the jet rack. It was a crude frame with cross bars at top and bottom that made it look like a capital 'L'. Actually, he corrected himself, the control pods that gripped your hands and feet made it look more like a primitive torture rack.

"Ever tried one, Lieutenant?" he asked Xin.

"Nope. I always thought they were just clutter at the back of the stores that no one had bothered to clear out."

Umarov rolled his eyes. "There's so much you don't know. Springer's recon AI is something else you'll need to learn more about when there's time."

"But there isn't time," said Arun. "No time even to learn how to use this jet rack."

Umarov wouldn't accept that. "If you want to get to Level 9 pronto, and bring back this alien blob, you've no time *not* to use one of these. Watch!"

Umarov picked up a rack, pointed it toward the hatch they'd used to enter the stores compartment, and placed his feet and hands into the attachments, which swiveled and gripped them securely.

"How do you start this thing?" asked Xin.

"Fall," replied Umarov. And he did. He pushed his weight forward and toppled over. Just before he smashed face-first into the deck, the back of the rack lifted, and he was zooming off into the corridor.

"That's amazing," said Xin, excitement coloring her voice. "It's like being in the void. Why didn't we train on these?"

"They aren't the answer to everything," said Umarov. "It's like riding bareback on a missile coming in on an attack vector. You and your AI are fully engaged in flying the thing. There's no way you can fire. Even if you could spare the brainpower, a rack will never be a stable firing platform. Plus you get a max of ten minutes fuel."

"And my tac-display was lighting you up like a beacon," said Xin.

"Yeah. To any targeting system, you're a human flare," said Umarov. "So what's not to like? Now stop jabbering and get your fine officer asses onto some racks."

Arun's first attempt was disastrous. He managed to topple over like Umarov, but the jet rack didn't lift off. At the last moment, he tried flinging out his arms to arrest his fall, but they were stuck into the rack; his face smacked into the deck.

"You're too stiff," Umarov told him. "Your suit AI knows your real desire is to *not* fall. Close your eyes and give into it."

Arun tried again. This time, as soon as he felt his balance going past the point of no return, he distracted himself by filling his mind with full sensorial recordings he'd made of that night on Antilles when he'd made love with Xin. She'd exerted such an irresistible pull on him. Springer had been so firmly in his mind of late that he'd forgotten how much he'd been drawn to Xin's flame.

"Hurry up, Major Twinkle Eyes."

Arun opened his eyes to see that he was hovering a meter off the ground. Xin was already out in the corridor pulling loops and corkscrews, and whooping like a kid. Umarov held position near the overhead.

"Try to keep up," said Xin, and sped away in the direction of the nearest helix down to Level 9.

He frowned, unsure whether to be angry that Umarov and Xin had both been overly familiar. But the memory of that night he'd shared with Xin still burned hot in his mind. He laughed and set off in pursuit of the girl from Antilles.

For a short while, they were nothing more than three young friends enjoying the thrill of zipping through the deserted Marine base at insane speeds. It didn't take long, though, for the gravity of the situation to reassert itself. Arun had paid a high price to get here. He was seeking an alien with the ability to see into his future… and, Arun prayed, the Night Hummer was the only one who could justify his decision to withdraw *Beowulf* from Detroit's defense.

Chapter 56

"Report!"

Loobie grimaced before responding: the news wasn't great. "Laser batteries 3 and 5 hit the first projectile halfway between Antilles and Tranquility, and that did nudge it slightly off course. However, my analysis is that the enemy bombardment is so inaccurate, and the effect of our laser strike so minimal, that we're just as likely to have steered the projectile onto the target as to knock it off."

"As I feared," said Captain Indiya, "but we had to try. Helm, accelerate to intercept likely trajectory of next projectile. If we get close enough, we can hit it with missiles. We won't blast it to atoms, but we might fracture it."

"Closing on projectile vector, aye," confirmed Pilot Officer Columbine.

Loobie had her doubts about the older woman's loyalty, but since the human takeover of *Beowulf* Columbine had been completely professional, and utterly closed.

Mind you, thought Loobie, her heart lurching, *I could say the same about Indiya.*

Concerns for her friend were blasted instantly away when her tactical map revealed a new projectile slingshotting out of the moon's gravity field.

"Too late…" she said. "Here comes the second projectile. Launching missiles now."

"Their fire rate is faster than I feared," mused Indiya out loud. "Helm, set new course for Antilles. Get us close enough to that damned mass driver to take it out."

"Attack vector laid in, aye."

Silently, Loobie prayed to the Creator to protect her friends down on Tranquility. She didn't believe the missiles would divert the projectile, which meant they'd let two projectiles get past them. There was no hope for anyone on the ground where they hit. At least for anyone caught near the impact location, death would be instant.

Chapter 57

Arun, Xin and Umarov raced down to Level 9 at a breakneck pace.

But it still left far too much time for Arun to think.

What exactly bound him to the Hummers?

Long ago he'd pledged to take the Hummers under human protection as a client species. But they were just words, weren't they? And preposterously unrealistic ones, or so they'd seemed at the time.

He'd never given an oath to his human comrades. Didn't need to. They came first.

So why had he dropped everything in his haste to rescue this Hummer? Was it simply to acquire a key strategic advantage?

What scared him most was his unshakable certainty that he was *meant* to meet with this Hummer at this precise time and place. He could call it a sense of destiny, his planner brain, or listening too much to Springer when she had her visions. But what if the Hummers had put him under mind control, or planted an irresistible suggestion in his mind? Surely that irrational certainty would be exactly what he would feel now.

And it was getting worse. Lately he'd felt this connection with the Hummers deepen, even though he'd hardly mentioned the pre-cog aliens to anyone for two years. Even beyond death, he knew his oath to the Hummers would still bind him, still determine the fate of trillions. It was crazy! How could he champion these aliens after he was dead? None of this made sense, but he knew it to be true.

Stop it! he told himself. *Concentrate on practicalities.*

He knew they would locate the Hummer soon… but what then?

He didn't know how Hummers were moved around the base. The equipment would be around somewhere. He had no doubt they could shift the alien and its life support systems, but they were in a hurry. *Beowulf* should cut off the mass driver bombardment soon, but they had to extricate the alien, and fly it with them back to Detroit to save Brandt from being overrun.

He was thinking of the alien as they descended one of the main helix ramps as far as Level 7, when every thought was driven from his mind: the world suddenly tremored. The first impact from the mass driver had hit the planet.

Amazingly, the jet racks slowed to a halt but remained calmly hovering over the ground. The lights didn't. All illumination snuffed out when the shockwave hit, and this far inside the underground base, there wasn't even enough light for his helmet's vision enhancement to work with. The darkness was so absolute that it took on a sludgy physical presence.

For several precious seconds, they waited in silence before the lighting recovered into an on-off flicker, strobing through the clouds of dust shaken into the air by the impact.

"Missed," said Xin as she set off again through the dust. "We'd be dead if it hadn't."

"It's only a matter of time before we catch one full on," said the ever-cheerful Umarov.

Arun ignored them. His mind was on the deserted spineways and corridors beyond the helix. This was an accommodation level, housing dozens of hab-disks: self-contained company-sized citadels with their own air, food, water, armory, and route up to the surface.

What had happened to the hab-disks?

Rumor from Detroit was that having hacked so many of Beta City's internal systems, the Hardits had simply sealed the exits from any hab-disk that housed Marines whose loyalty to the rebel cause was suspect.

There could be an army there, waiting to be freed and inducted into the Legion.

Or there could be a division of the dead, thousands upon thousands of grinning corpses.

Arun didn't have enough time to stop and investigate. But he had far too much time to wonder.

With only a few wrong turnings, Xin led them to Level 9, where they soon located the Hummer in its life-support chamber, an exact replica of the one Xin had described seeing in Detroit even down to the reduced gravity. The jet racks were so confused by the gravity change that all three Marines were thrown to the ground by their mounts. Once he'd extricated himself from his rack, Arun could feel the massive power boost to his suit's motors from the reduced gravity. Artificially reduced gravity! It was a technology Arun couldn't quite believe, but there was no time to wonder.

The alien had been expecting them, just as Arun had known it would.

Inside a life-support tank was a stretched, midnight-blue globule, about three meters tall and surrounded by a fizzing orange liquid. Black bubbles rose from the bottom of the tank, sucked into the creature's core. An equal volume of silver ribbons were spat out from its top.

The flicker of these silver streamers matched the beat underneath the low hum that filled Arun's helmet, an insistent noise which occasionally burst into pulses of metallic fizz and swash.

The last Night Hummer he'd seen lived on a planetoid built to be a Hummer farm. It lived by itself, though, which it considered torture because it craved the company of its own kind. The setup here was rows of heavily shielded alcoves set into the walls, each with space to wrap a Night Hummer life support tank in a protective cradle. Again, there was only one Hummer here.

The victorious faction in the civil war took the others away with them.

Arun felt the alien's words in his head. It felt a little like his conversations with Barney. A little, too, as if an ice-cold blade was slowly penetrating his skull.

"Why didn't they take you?" asked Xin. *Interesting that the Hummer was talking with her too.*

We hid me from their minds, came a cold reply that made Arun shiver. *I had to remain here. I had to meet you.*

"What about the other human?" asked Arun. "Umarov, he's called. Can he hear you?"

No, nor can he hear you. His role is temporarily suspended.

Arun interrogated Umarov's BattleNet signal. He was healthy, but silent and motionless. The alien had temporarily disabled him. And made it look easy. Just how powerful were these creatures?

I thank you, spoke the alien into Arun's head. *You cannot comprehend the calm I feel to know you came.*

"Stow your thanks, Hummer," said Xin, "We haven't rescued you yet."

Nor shall you. I do not thank you for my rescue, for you will not succeed. I thank you for giving me the satisfaction of proving my prediction correct. I knew you would come.

"Don't be stupid, alien," shouted Arun. "We've risked so much to reach this place. I'm not leaving without you. There must be a way. They didn't just roll you down the helix ramp, did they? Is there a hover sled? How do we move you? How? Answer!"

But the alien's only response was to increase the volume of its humming to punishing levels.

"I think we need to get the frakk out," said Xin.

It would take another twenty seconds to realize how right she was.

Chapter 58

Of the barrage *Beowulf* fired at the mass driver's second projectile, only a single anti-ship missile hit. The ordnance in question was a 2-stage weapon designed to first burn a narrow gap through a target ship's hull that the second stage could then pass through and explode.

Instead of a warship's armored hull, the first stage of the missile accomplished the far easier task of penetrating the outer jacket of the ore package. The second stage, though, found it hard going against the compressed ore of the interior. It looked from the outside as if the blast had merely chipped away a modest cloud of stone fragments: superficial damage only.

But the energy of the missile's impact and exploding payload sent hairline stress fractures spreading through the ore-projectile's interior. When the missile's energy had dissipated, the fractures stopped growing a long way short of breaking up the lump of compressed rock. The internal weakness was frozen, postponed, like a critically wounded soldier placed in a cryo pod.

The deep wound didn't remain frozen for long.

At a speed of three hundred klicks per second, the projectile slammed into Tranquility's upper atmosphere with an impact that released far more energy than *Beowulf's* missile. Momentum carried the block of ore relentlessly down the gravity well. As the atmosphere thickened in the moments before it hit the ground, the forces resisting its descent strengthened, seeking weakness, and finding the hairline cracks.

Thirty klicks above the ground, the projectile was ripped apart. Now two fiery contrails burrowed their way down to the planet's surface.

There was no defense.

Ironically, the projectile had been two hundred klicks off target. The larger of the two fragments spun away harmlessly to impact the great plain in the continent's interior in a fireball visible from space.

The smaller fragment, though, was thrown back on target: nearly a direct hit. Forty tons of compressed rock, its molten surface glowing red hot, struck the lifeless waters of Lake Sarpedona nine klicks away from the island entrance to Beta City.

The impact threw up a plume of water that reached the upper atmosphere. The ore package-turned-meteorite took only a fraction of a second to slice through the lake, boiling the water around it, before burrowing deep beneath the lake bottom. It launched a bubble of mud followed by millions of years of sedimentary accumulation instantly pulverized to dust, and thrown high into clouds that blotted out the sun.

The lake water filling the caldera spilled out over its lip in a miniature tsunami. The sudden release of megatons of water, churning with stone and dust, gouged a deep channel along its route to the distant ocean.

Much of the lake's water remained inside the caldera, though, acting as a medium for the shockwaves that were about to pummel Beta City on a destructive scale that no weapon in the Human Legion's arsenal could hope to match.

The initial pressure pulse pushed out through the lake's water at 210 meters per second, leaving the occupants of the city 23 seconds before the destruction hit.

But there was one inside the underwater city who already knew the shockwave was coming.

The Hummer had seen this drama play out countless times over the past few decades…

Chapter 59

The Night Hummer ceased its humming abruptly and spoke aloud through a hidden speaker. "The base is hardened against bombardment from the outside, but when you set off your gamma bomb you compromised the city's impact absorbers. These devices are related to the heat sinks used in warships and railguns. They can soak up enormous energies and shift them elsewhere, into other dimensions. The city's absorbers no longer function."

"Why are you mentioning–?" Before Arun could finish his thought, the shockwave hit Beta City.

Arun had just enough time to hear the crack of impact and the sound of metal being torn and ceramics shattered before his hearing and several other senses, went into emergency shutdown. Then it felt like a spiked gauntlet rammed itself down his throat and tore out his lungs.

Arun's scream was agonizing but he could not stop himself. The inside of his helmet clouded with blood-spatter and he kept screaming until the fuzziness multiplied, crowding out all thoughts until his consciousness was finally suffocated, and he disconnected from the world outside of his skull.

When his senses eased back, he checked the chronometers in his head and found only about ten seconds had elapsed since the shockwave's impact. He hadn't even fallen over – Barney having kept his battlesuit upright on his behalf. The AI decided his human was recovered sufficiently and flooded him with critical injury reports of severe concussion and hemorrhaging in Arun's gut and lungs.

"The underwater hull integrity of Beta City has been breached in seven locations," reported the alien, sounding as unruffled as ever, even though Arun could see the orange fluid in its tank was rapidly darkening. "Consequently, Beta City will flood before nightfall."

"How can you tell all this?" asked Arun, struggling to form words in his confused state. "Are you wired up to the base AI?" Simultaneously, he tasked Barney with a threat assessment.

"I know because I have seen this. I have experienced this day from many perspectives. Every day of every year of every decade I see the moment of my termination."

It didn't look good for the Hummer. The silver streamers flapping in its circulatory system went limp. The flow of bubbles slowed.

Barney reported indications of several electrical fires starting up nearby.

"I die consumed in fire," explained the Hummer. "Boiled in my tank before the flood water reaches me. In four minutes, the air throughout this entire level will ignite. It would be best that you humans leave before then. Flee!"

"But we can't leave you," Arun insisted. Confused, he scratched his head, but then snapped his hand away because his head hurt. "I swore an oath to protect you."

"No, you swore an oath to tend to my people, not this individual. I hold you to your oath. And your oath says you must go, leave me. You cannot protect my people if you are dead."

"Very well!" Arun was shouting now, in a rage that had swirled in from nowhere. "No riddles, alien. You're out of time, and I'm out of patience. You reached out somehow and brought me here. But now you say we cannot save you. So tell me this: *why the frakk am I here?*"

"Your purpose was to make a sacrifice, one that hurt enough to bind you to your destiny."

Arun felt the anger streaming out from Xin. He only just managed his own enough to speak. "My comrades in Detroit," he shouted, even though speaking above a whisper tore at his raw throat and lungs. "Innocent lives – were sacrificed just so that you could *make a frakking point?*"

"Mostly, yes. But also so I could communicate data. You will soon leave this stellar system for the time being. You need fresh goals, new targets to focus your attention. First you must go to the planet known to the Jotuns as Shepherd-Nurture-4. Then – when your forces are strong enough – liberate my home system. You will not find it in your astrogation database. Coordinates are 127541.06, 356122, 9011121."

"Leave the veck" shouted Xin while Arun verified he had safely committed the coordinates to one of his digital memory augmentations in his head.

Arun ignored her, preferring to glare at the dying alien blob. "I will fulfill my oath, alien. But know this. If you are a typical example of your species, then I have no love for you. If my species must deal with yours, I will make sure to exploit your people ruthlessly. It's only what you deserve."

But you must nurture us… said the alien in his mind. For the first time, it sounded worried.

From her jet rack, Xin shouted at Arun: "For frakk's sake, quit your drama-mouthing already, Major. Mount up and go!"

Arun spoke in his mind, confident the alien would hear. *You're about to boil in your tank, Hummer… I hope it hurts.*

He fell into his jet rack, and together the humans fled the drowning Marine base.

Chapter 60

"Here they come," announced Exelmans from the observation post. "Sector 11. Approx. 2,500 Hardit infantry. They're descending down the mountain paths from the west. Sending co-ordinates now."

A second later came the response. "Charlie Battery launching anti-personnel strike in 3… 2… 1… firing! Missiles away. Ordnance status nominal."

Brandt watched the missiles' progress in the holographic battlemap set up in his command post in the underground redoubt near Gate Three, the only one of Detroit's main gates that was still open after the destruction of the civil war.

It had been less than a week since Hecht had flown a noisy recon drone into this same redoubt. Hecht's drone had discovered human Resistance fighters. Now dozens of them were guarding the approaches to the undercity far below Brandt's position.

He saw the three missiles streak straight up into the sky before turning and coming almost directly back down, except instead of falling back into the narrow valley in which Detroit's topside entrance nestled, they hit the mountainside to the west. The missile payload delivered cluster munitions that divided and divided again until millions of fragmentation shards fell in a black rain of death over the mountainside. There was no shelter up there; no escape. From the valley floor, it looked as if a landslide was falling down the cliff. It was a landslide of shredded Hardit corpses, which left behind a mountain slick with blood.

"Aircraft are coming in for an attack run," said Exelmans.

"Keep half our anti-air missiles in reserve," Brandt ordered. "This is only the first wave."

"Understood. Batteries Able, Baker, and Charlie, you heard the officer. That gives you half your assets to play with. Fire at will."

From inside the redoubt, Brandt watched the deadly game of hunter-prey unfold across the skies above Detroit. Hardit gunships would dive into the valley and sweep over Detroit's topside, strafing anything leaking an EM signature with the cannons mounted underneath their hulls, and the missile tubes in their noses. But Detroit was hunter as well as prey. Air-to-air ordnance, ripped from the carcasses of Detroit's Marine air force and stuffed into makeshift silos, lanced through the enemy gunships. The autocannons that Force Mexico had hidden in the sheer faces of the mountainsides spat supersonic metal at gunships that flew too close.

Silent and sanitized, Brandt's battlemap view made the duel look as bloodless as a friendly Scendence game. It was a game of deadly consequences, though. If the aliens won air superiority, they could advance their ground forces unmolested up to Gate Three, or try blasting a new way down from the surface.

Strong though the Marine anti-air defenses were, Brandt hadn't expected to cope with such numbers. The few days they'd had to prepare left no time to strengthen the silos, or harden the signal and power cabling that connected their ramshackle defensive network.

Hardit gunships were being ripped from the sky.

But they could be replaced...

Another strafing run came in from a wing of six aircraft corkscrewing through the air. None survived, but Brandt's battlemap locked for a second, before continuing with much jerkier updates than before.

"Exelmans, report!"

"Cannon shot us up," answered Exelmans. "Kant and Zane dead. Still limited sensor feed available. Second wave coming in now... Third wave holding station ten klicks away. All missile batteries, as before save half your assets... Charlie Battery. Acknowledge!"

"They're gone, Sergeant," Brandt explained gently. "Don't hold any reserve back. Fire every anti-air asset you've got left."

Exelmans didn't reply straight away. His hesitation stretched on uncomfortably. They both knew that committing anti-air reserves meant yielding air superiority to the waves of gunships that would follow. But without *Beowulf* they simply didn't have the means to defend the skies against an air force that was throwing over a hundred gunships at Detroit. Why the hell did McEwan choose to denude them of their orbital defense? Maybe *Beowulf's* secret weapon would have proved ineffective, but at least it would have given them hope.

"Yes, sir," Exelmans eventually answered. His voice was calm, but Brandt could hear the undertone of dismay. Bernard Exelmans knew he was going to die.

Missiles streaked out of the makeshift silos at such short range that there was little the aircraft could do in response. Within seconds, the wave of gunships had taken heavy casualties, the survivors throwing everything they had into evading the missiles.

"That's it, sir, we're out of anti-air missiles."

"Can we reconfigure more from the surface-to-surface role?"

"Unlikely and not enough to make much difference. Control links have been degraded by their strafing runs. What we have left won't last seconds against their next air attack."

"Fire whatever surface-to-surface assets you have left."

A last barrage of anti-personnel missiles scoured the western slopes. But the bulk of the enemy's forces had pulled back a safe distance from the mountainside… waiting.

Moments later, as if the Hardit commander knew the humans had expended their missiles, hidden sensors linked to Brandt's battlemap spotted militia scouts approaching from a new direction: the mountains to the east.

Detroit's valley cut north-south through the western edge of the Gjende mountain range, with a fertile plateau only a few miles farther west. To approach from the east, an army would have to track for many miles along treacherous narrow paths over deep chasms. Unless… Brandt suddenly thought — unless the enemy knew of secret underground passageways that emerged into hidden ledges in the rocky heights.

Brandt took a deep breath. He had nearly left the eastern approach unguarded. At the last moment, he had stripped a team of Marines away from their other defensive preparations to leave a surprise for any Hardits coming from the east. Maybe it would have been better if they had left it undefended.

Lieutenant Nhlappo had ordered him not to use anything noisier than Marine backs and boots to set up Detroit's outer defenses. He'd obeyed that order to the letter when he'd sent a party out to set up their surprise booby trap. A very special bomb.

Brandt ordered the AI operator of his bomb to detonate at its discretion.

"Third wave of gunships inbound," Exelmans reported. "They're… shit! They aren't swooping and jinking. They're coming in slow and steady, stable gun platforms. It's as if they know we're defenseless. They're gunning for… We've lost Able Battery."

"No 'as if' about it, Sergeant. They've broken our signal encryption. That, or we have a collaborator spy. Or they can see into the future. You've done enough. Get out of there and join us at the redoubt."

Exelmans hightailed it out of the observation post that had become a deathtrap, but the signal feed still supplied information to Brandt's battlemap. The sergeant had been right: the enemy had feinted attacks to draw the venom out of the defenders' bite. Their main force had waited until they had claimed the air above Detroit before launching the full assault.

From the western plateau beyond the Gjende Mountains the field artillery the Hardits had readied – and Brandt's orders earlier had spared – now came into action. They were field railguns. As direct fire guns, they were useless at throwing their heavy darts at Detroit, sheltering as it did on the narrow valley floor. When the big guns did open fire, their purpose became clear. Their rounds exploded on the rocky mountain ground *behind the Hardit infantry positions*. It was the preferred means for Hardit commanders to motivate their reluctant conscripts: advance or die!

And advance they did: thousands of ground troops crawling down the mountainside.

In his mind's eye, Brand brought up an image of Tawfiq Woomer-Calix. *It's not over yet,* he told the imaginary Hardit. *We still have other defenses that I wasn't dumb enough to mention to Exelmans over an open channel. If you want Detroit, I'll make you crawl through hellfire first.*

Tawfiq, presumably, was far away in safety, unreachable in a bunker deep underground. The militia swarming down the mountainside had to suffice as the targets for human vengeance.

Despite only having a few days to ring a defensive line around Detroit, Force Mexico had done enough to decimate the enemy. Aircraft ordnance had been converted into mines and booby traps. Del-Marie Sandure had wired the explosives up to simple controller systems that used a variety of algorithms. As a result, the Hardits could never predict when the traps would blow, could never feel safe. One mine would blow after it detected thirty Hardits had passed by; another would be drilled into the rock, designed to blow five minutes after the first Hardit passed by, unleashing a cascading rockfall onto anyone below.

Soon, every Hardit knew that even if a dozen comrades had progressed safely beyond that next turn in the path, an explosion might still blow the moment you stepped there.

The humans had also collapsed millennia-old mountain paths, carving out replacements that channeled confused Hardits into dead ends, killing grounds prepared for mines or one of the few autocannons pilfered from Detroit.

For every Hardit killed by the auto-defenses, another ten remained. If these were combat bots, or human Marines doped out on combat drugs, you could perform a cold calculation of the casualty numbers and conclude that the effectiveness of the Hardit units had been degraded, but no more than that.

These fearful conscripts were not disciplined soldiers, though. Hardit morale was shattered beyond any hope of rallying. Those who retained a shred of sense took cover and hid, cowering at whatever point they had reached when their shattered nerves had deserted them, too frightened to either move forward or retreat. The most panicked fled back up the slopes, triggering more traps as they scurried away. Any Hardit survivors who reached the top without succumbing to the humans' hidden deathtraps were then blasted off the mountain by their own field artillery.

From his forward command post Brandt couldn't see the individual dramas unfolding out on the approaches to Detroit, but his battlemap was sufficient to show an accurate summary of the ebb and flow of the attack. It also reported with chilling accuracy the second wave of militia units the Hardits now brought up to the edge of the western heights. More reserve units were forming up to their rear.

The bomb he'd planted near the main path from the east sent a countdown warning. *Detonation in twenty seconds.*

A shiver swept through Brandt. He'd been able to face overwhelming odds with coolness, because he knew deep in his bones that panicking wouldn't help to keep his people alive.

But his bright idea to bury a bomb scared the drent out of him.

He had no idea what it would do.

Brandt himself had been one of the six-strong detail of Marines in powered armor who had crept out in the cover of the midday sun — the sun that the Hardits hated so much — and carried away one of the dropships that had taken the expeditionary force down from orbit.

Brandt ordered the orbital satellite to give him a close-up view of the Hardits streaming in from the east.

The dropship had complained that it was still dangerous, still not quite completed the discharge of the enormous energy it had absorbed in its stealthed descent through the atmosphere. Brandt had ordered the ship to be ripped from its tendril-like thermal dump cables that burrowed into the ground.

Four seconds to detonation…

They had buried the ship on the eastern approach, packed with E-7 explosives linked to an AI controller.

It was time.

The satellite showed a plume of fire from the explosion, a fireball about the diameter of his outstretched arms.

That was it. A single grenade would have had more impact.

The battlemap vanished.

Vauban gasped.

<Something… *prickled,*> gasped the AI. <But I'm all right now.>

"The dropship did this?"

<How should I know?>

The answer came from the battlemap, which re-established itself in front of his eyes.

Brandt eagerly focused the display on the east. He scanned the heights and found only dead Hardit scouts. He pushed the display farther to the east where he expected to find the bulk of the Hardit attack. He found them all right. Whatever exotic emissions had been emitted by the damaged dropship had killed everything in the vicinity. All the Hardits were lying still, yet unbloodied. So too were the birds still falling from the sky.

Brandt hoped.

He scanned the western slopes and found the same scene of death. Then his first disappointment: the Hardit reserves kept back from the mountainside were unaffected.

And in the valley in between was another rain falling from the sky. Not of birds but Hardit gunships. Their motive power had failed. All of them were crashing down to the ground where they lay as still as the militia on the mountain.

Brandt's hope grew into confidence. The battle was not over, but they had endured the worst.

His new belief dented, slightly, when another wave of Hardit gunships approached from the north. But after the hundreds of gunships they had already fought off, this new wave had just five. Surely these were the last of the enemy's air reserves.

Then he groaned, because the battlemap reported the news he feared most of all. The Hardits were launching another attack. This time it was coming from the tunnels below the base.

The mines they'd laid in Level 9 had blown. If all had gone to plan, the tunnel had collapsed with it. They had mined all but one of the entrances leading up from the Trog tunnels – all that they were aware of anyway.

Sooner or later, the underground Hardit forces probing for a route into the human levels would discover the one passageway to the tunnels that remained unmined. It wasn't undefended, though. Marines and dozens of Resistance fighters were guarding this entrance to the undercity.

Would they be enough?

The battlemap vanished.

Brandt's only surprise was that the connection to the sensor system that fed the battlemap had lasted so long. Even so, the loss of his main focus was such a disorienting wrench that he would have fallen over if his suit AI, Vauban, hadn't kept his balance for him.

Then his mind was thrust back into the physical reality of the command post.

In stark contrast to the battlemap's ethereal ghostlight and AI-whispered statistics, Brandt suddenly found himself inside a damp bastion that stank of sweat, despair and stale urine.

The odors were either false or exaggerated. Vauban's air filters would normally filter out anything that wasn't tactically important. It must be Vauban panicking, the AI's equivalent of giving his human a slap in the face.

We haven't lost yet, Brandt admonished his AI.

In the artificial blue glow of Vauban's low-light enhancement, he became aware of the attention from four armored figures, the other defenders of the position.

"The main action's about to kick off downstairs," he told them. "Stafford, Forbes, when Sergeant Exelmans gets here, tell him to hold this position. Khurana, Feria, with me."

As the three of them rushed off to join the coming fight deep underground, Brandt knew the defenders he left behind could do no more than delay an attack in strength. But the route through Gate Three was a narrow one by design, and had many mines and other traps ready to punish an invading force. The makeshift defenses in the undercity were far weaker. If the Hardits broke through there, they would rapidly spread out through the city. Detroit would be lost.

Another concern gripped the lieutenant. If the Hardits penetrated the city, they might jam human signals. He made one last call while he still could.

"Sandure, report."

"Our defenses are in place," answered Del-Marie. "Civilians are all armed. We're ready for the enemy."

"They're too strong, Del. If they reach you in the hangar, you'll be overwhelmed by sheer numbers. Prepare the aircraft for immediate evac."

"Are you ordering me to abandon my position, sir?"

"Negative. I still intend to win this fight. But be ready to bug out the instant you make contact. You'll only manage a short hop because the skies belong to the monkeys with their frakking gunships. They've only a handful left, so you have a chance. Take care of our wounded and civilians, Del."

"Don't worry, sir. They're safe with me. Sandure out."

Chapter 61

The wounded and civilians scattered through the hangar – stragglers all of this doomed campaign – tried to be cheerful and respectful toward him, but as the minutes ticked away without radio contact with the outside world, Del-Marie Sandure found it ever more difficult to face the people he had been assigned to protect.

Zug was among the wounded, heavily sedated on a stretcher. Del would give anything for his old friend to be fit enough to stand alongside him. Despite the throng of people, he'd never felt so alone.

The way Del saw it, they had two options: barricade themselves in one of the two barracks built into Detroit's hangar complex, or sit in the patched-up T16B transport plane that waited, engines on standby, for a quick getaway.

Before losing radio contact, Brandt had told him that the enemy had overwhelming numbers and had already established control of the air.

Even before Brandt's update, Del hadn't liked either option. Barricading themselves in only made sense if relief was coming. Otherwise, they would only be choosing their place to die. And if Del did try to escape on the plane, as Brandt had suggested he should, the Hardits would shoot it out of the sky the moment it emerged from the hangar.

Not liking either solution, Del-Marie decided to keep both options open as long as possible, so he could choose the least worst one. It smacked of indecision, and that embarrassed him.

He had arranged ruined Stork-class shuttles to be scattered along the middle of the hangar deck. To any Hardits entering the hangar via the main approach from Detroit, the Storks should look like they had been abandoned in random locations. In fact, Del had organized them to be defensive positions with good, interlocking arcs of fire. The transport plane was ready for takeoff near the exit out to the waterfall, positioned to be shielded by the shuttles and their thick hull armor. With luck, the Storks would protect the plane from small arms fire.

Unfit civilians and the stretchered military wounded were waiting out on the hangar deck, between the plane and the barracks, ready to move to whichever position Del chose. Del had initially placed them halfway between the two, but after Brandt's orders, had shifted them closer to the plane.

Everyone else was in one of the Stork hulls, cradling an SA-71 in their arms.

One of the babies started up again with its wailing. Sure enough, the other baby answered with its own piercing cries. Del hated the babies worst of all. Or rather, it wasn't the babies he hated, but how helpless they made him feel.

Del's suit AI flashed a warning. Someone was approaching the hangar.

"Here they come," Del said. "Everyone stay calm and out of sight. Hold your fire until I give the signal."

He stepped back into the shadows of the Stork's interior, relying on the sensor nodes he'd scattered around the deck to give him a view of the approach corridor.

Instead of a flood of Hardits in their flea-ridden rags, he saw three human Marines. His suit AI swiftly identified them as Spartika, Jennifer Boon, and Deacon. The three resistance fighters looked around the hangar, as if they were searching for something.

Del stepped into the light: "What's going on?" he asked Spartika. "Where is the enemy?"

"They're right behind," she replied.

"What about Lieutenant Brandt and the others?"

"Dead. All dead," said Spartika, limping as fast as she could toward Del's Stork.

The shock of hearing that hit him hard, but there was something about the Resistance leader's words that Del didn't like. "How can you be sure," he queried, "when the enemy is jamming our signals?"

Spartika stormed through the open hatch and into the Stork. She dropped her carbine and grabbed Del-Marie about the shoulders. It was so unexpected that he didn't have time to fight her off.

Blanking her visor revealed the mad look on Spartika's face. "I saw them die," she snapped, her mouth trembling. "We were overrun. All the others… dead."

"Then the plane's our only chance," he said, not that it was much of one.

"I'm done running," said Spartika. "You go, we'll cover you. Take good care of my people, Lance Corporal Sandure."

He considered this change to his plan. *Three armored Marines… They can hold up an army… for a minute or so.*

Del nodded. "I will," he said. He stayed put long enough to check Spartika's group were taking up positions in three Storks, and then gave the order for his refugees to evacuate to the plane.

The hangar erupted into motion as the able-bodied broke cover and rushed out of the Storks to help the sick and wounded onto the waiting plane.

Del wanted to join in but he trusted to the rehearsal drills and their common sense. He had a special role.

He was the pilot.

As he climbed into the flight cabin, he felt the heavy responsibility of that role weigh upon him. When they took off, everyone on that plane would trust their lives to him, even though he'd never flown an aircraft before. Not outside of a simulator.

Small void craft were a different matter. As part of the major's insistence that Marines helped out with the gaping holes in the Navy crew roster, Del had clocked up many flying hours in space. …

Threat alerts sounded in the cabin. Hardit small arms fire was ricocheting through the hangar.

And Del's doubts vanished, replaced by diamond-hard concentration. It was now or never.

He raised the main engine thrust to launch level and eased back on the brakes.

As the transport aircraft shuddered and began to move, Del hooked into the camera network to see what was happening behind.

Dozens of Hardits were swarming through the hangar, but Del only had eyes for one individual. The one with a missile launcher.

"Shoot the launcher," he shouted through BattleNet at Spartika's rearguard. But the armored Resistance fighters couldn't hear him. They were off the net. Where had they gone? The Hardits weren't acting as if they were facing any opposition. All it would take were a few railgun bursts from the rearguard and the enemy would keep their heads down long enough for the aircraft to escape.

But the suppressive fire never came.

The Hardit with the missile launcher took time to brace and program its targeting system. Scores of rifle-armed Hardits advanced along either side of the hangar, hugging the walls to give the missile specialist a clear line of fire.

Perhaps Spartika was leading the Hardits on… would emerge to take them by surprise. *Shoot! Damn you!*

But that sinking feeling in his gut told Del that his rearguard had deserted.

"Hang on," Del shouted into the in-plane comms. Abandoning everything he'd learned in safe takeoff drill, he gave the engines full throttle.

The plane lurched forward. Even in his acceleration-hardened battlesuit, Del felt himself being slammed back into the pilot's seat. But from the rear of the hangar, he saw the backblast from the missile launcher. There was no way he could evade that.

He felt rather than heard the drumming as his plane passed the hangar's entry barrier of falling water. The downforce pushed the aircraft down. In his control console holosphere Del saw the Hardit missile flash through the curtain of water in pursuit, but the waterfall didn't give it the same amount of downward push – the missile passed a good twenty meters above the plane.

Hope blossomed in Del's breast. If he could put a mountainside between the aircraft and the missile, they might just survive. He banked the patched-up aircraft as tightly as he dared, making the airframe scream in protest.

The missile slowed… and then slewed around to follow Del's maneuver. It was hopeless!

"We're going down," Del told his passengers. "As soon as we stop, grab your weapons and make for the trees. I'll cover you fro–"

The missile hit.

The blast ripped off the starboard wing and flipped the plane over.

It was still corkscrewing when it hit the ground.

Chapter 62

Arun breached the surface of the lake, pushing through the scum of dead fish and birds that were slowly simmering in water still hot from the projectile's impact. He hurt in more ways than he knew a body *could* hurt, but, up above, a welcome sight greeted him. Engines purring as it hovered, the Stork dangled three Marines on the end of rescue cables. One of the cables snaked his way, and within moments a Marine had reached down to grip Arun's hand and haul him out of the lake.

He refused to acknowledge the additional stab of pain this caused, striving to keep his voice steady as he said, "Thank you, Lieutenant," to Nhlappo when the cable had reeled him up into the hold. He noted the equipment crates were back and secured aft. Hopefully they were filled with the materiel for which they'd come to Beta.

"Don't thank me," Nhlappo replied over a private channel. "I ordered Dock to make straight for Detroit. Little veck maintained I wasn't his line officer and insisted on coming back here in case you'd survived."

Arun ignored her for now, peering out the hatch at Xin and Umarov who were being reeled up too. They looked in bad shape.

"What's the situation in Detroit?" Arun asked Nhlappo.

"The enemy has established complete air superiority. Brandt is fighting off attacks from the surface and from beneath the lower Detroit levels. Heavy casualties all round. It doesn't look good, Major."

"Ensign Dock, can you hear me?" asked Arun.

"Here, Major."

"As soon as we've sealed the hatch, set course for Detroit with all speed. We'll reassess the tactical situation when…" Arun tried to swallow back a coughing fit, hoping the others wouldn't notice the blood spattering from his lips. "…when we're nearer."

"Back to Detroit, aye."

"And, Ensign…"

"Yes?"

"Didn't know you cared so much for me, Dock. But I thank you for rescuing us anyway."

"You're very welcome, sir. But you were right on the button beforehand – I don't very much like you, Major. But I know others do. I'd never hear the last of it from Captain Indiya if I'd left you behind to die. I must admit that when I first set eyes on you, I thought…"

But Arun never heard what Dock thought.

The Navy ensign's words drifted away, replaced by a vague sense that Barney was communicating with him, floating beneath the calm seas of Arun's subconscious. The AI brought up a memory of the liberated slave, Rohanna, rocking her baby to sleep. That's what Barney was doing now – putting his human to sleep, while he did what he could to patch up his wounds.

But this wasn't *Barney's* role!

Arun rose part of the way back to full consciousness. His calm seas grew stormy.

Why isn't Puja doing this? he asked Barney. *Is she okay?*

<You make for an awkward patient,> sighed Barney. <Corporal Narciso is unwounded and tending to Lieutenant Lee and Marine Umarov. I am feeding her false medical data that understates the seriousness of your injuries. If the others see how bad your injuries are, you will be relieved of command. You will no longer be able to influence the coming decisions.>

Who put you in charge?

<You did. Did you think I wouldn't notice you trying to hide your bloody cough? The blood's coming from your lungs. You'll drown in your own blood if you don't let me take care of you. I will wake you when you're needed, I promise. Now sleep.>

Arun tried to protest, but Barney could be very firm. Arun's mind snapped shut and he knew no more.

Chapter 63

Arun's eyes jerked open. It felt as if Barney had rammed a high-tension power cable up his butt, and his lungs were fragile constructions of millennia-old desiccated paper that had just been ripped into dust.

It took several seconds of his brain being crudely beaten back into shape with a planishing hammer, before he could work out what the frakk was going on.

He'd been out for about six minutes. Barney was still in the midst of patching him up, but had rebooted his body early to answer an incoming FTL transmission.

The call was from Brandt.

Arun tried to acknowledge his friend but had to first spend valuable time coughing out the blood that was clogging his throat.

"Are you dying, Major?" asked Brandt.

"No. Not yet."

"Just me then. Still, I request you relay my transmission to everyone on your flight. They've got a right to hear, and I'm not convinced you'll be able to tell them. You sound like you'll die before me."

Arun linked Brandt's signal to a ship-wide comm channel. "It's done, Brandt. Speak now."

"The Hardits have broken our defenses in the lower levels. Spartika's fighters gave a good account of themselves, but when the monkeys brought in their elite with heavy weapons and drones, we knew our time was up."

"Can you get out?" asked Arun.

"Del's going to try to get the wounded out on an airplane that we've lashed together from the wrecks in the hangar. The rest of us are cut off. The enemy have pushed us to the lower levels. We decided to make our last stand here, surrounded by thousands of icers in their smashed cryo pods."

Arun gave a phlegmy gurgle. "Good luck, Marine," he said, wishing he could think of something more worthy than platitudes. "Die well."

"Frakk that," said Brandt. "I didn't choose to spend my last moment saying goodbye. We found something, down here in the cryo storage levels. We tried burrowing down, scooping out a bolt hole. Worked for you once. We found secret levels, deeper down."

"Secret spaces," said Arun, hope filling him that Brandt might yet get out. "The Hardits might not know about them. Use them to sneak out!"

"That's what we did at first. Slipped through our gap, sealed it as best we could from behind, and then blew a hole in the floor of our new level to repeat the process. But we only found another secret level below that. And another below *that*. This shit goes on for miles. Who knows how many levels are really down here?"

"Hide in the tunnels" said Arun. "We'll wait until the Hardits relax their attention and then we'll come to rescue you."

Brandt wasn't paying attention to his CO. Instead, the occupants of the Stork overheard Brandt's side of a conversation taking place in the bowels of Detroit.

"Thank you, Corporal DeBenedetto," Brandt was saying. "It's been an honor serving with you. Set charges to blow in thirty seconds."

"Brandt," shouted Nhlappo. "What charges? Report!"

"The secret levels," continued Brandt ignoring Nhlappo, "hold undamaged cryo boxes. We're estimating millions, Arun. *Millions of human Marines*. Our best guess is that when the Jotuns told us they were shipping out fresh Marine units, they were lying. I wonder whether they were fooling the White Knights too, but I guess I'll have to leave that mystery for someone else to solve. Been doing this for centuries, Arun. Millions of icers. *Millions!*"

"A legion," breathed Arun.

"Exactly."

"Can you revive them?"

"Negative. The ice pods are self-powered but will need proper resuscitation systems and a helluva lot of power to revive. And we're out of time." Brandt paused. Even muffled as it was, they all recognized the repeating *whine-pop* as Brandt fired his railgun.

"We're going to blow this level, collapse the levels above us. The hidden legion will be buried. They could last centuries more, buried deep underground. Don't forget them, Arun. Brandt out."

"Edward," said Nhlappo in a sudden panic, "where are the refugee children?"

Brandt came back online. "Del was trying to–"

They heard an instant of fizz and rumble followed by… silence.

Chapter 64

That silence suffocated the flight back to Detroit. The Marines were still locked in the horror of that awful moment when they'd lost contact with their home. Visors were dark, shielding Arun from the stark expressions of betrayal and recrimination that he was sure were chiseled permanently onto the faces behind.

Even Nhlappo of all people had lost it, wailing something about losing her son before disconnecting herself from the comm network.

Clutching at the thread of hope Brandt had thrown out when he said Del-Marie was evacuating civilians, Arun had ordered Dock to continue on to Detroit. They needed more of a plan before they got there, but that could wait.

With everyone so reluctant to speak, Arun took advantage of the lull by slumping into semi-consciousness while Barney continued emergency repairs to his body.

It wasn't until they were thirty minutes out from their destination that Gupta decided to end the silence. "Major, we need reminding what we're fighting for. The others have had all the time they're going to get to absorb the shock."

Reluctantly, Arun agreed. He took a moment to rev his brain up to speed. Then he opened a general comm channel and spoke his mind. "Lieutenant Brandt said he'd tried to evacuate civilians. We're on our way back to locate and rescue them. Then we'll return to *Beowulf* to regroup. This isn't over. We *will* return, and the Hardits will pay dearly for their atrocities."

"Begging your pardon, sir," said Umarov, "but will you let an old grumbler speak his mind?"

Arun smiled, so tired that he was beyond caring what Umarov had to say. "Go ahead, old man."

"I admire your words, sir. All the same, what you just said is still class-one bullshit. We fought hard and we fought well. We nearly won too. But with half of us dead, and the Resistance and slaves we liberated all but wiped out, we're not going to win this campaign. I say we go down fighting right now. Take as many of the vecks with us as we can. I'd rather die with a combat blade in each hand, atop a heap of slain enemies, than bleed out all alone in the bottom of a muddy ditch, or escape to the *Beowulf* and die centuries from now in a cryo pod. If we can't win, then I don't want to run or hide."

"Go out in a blaze of glory?" said Arun. "Don't be a fool! There's no glory in death."

"I didn't say anything about glory," Umarov retorted. "I just want to take as many of the bastards with me as I can. Won't you let me go out fighting?"

"Understood," said Arun. "Request denied. We still have a ship in orbit filled with materiel. We still retain orbital superiority. We return to *Beowulf*. If we can take the moon, Antilles, then that gives us another military base filled with supplies, and we may be able to construct our own mass driver to rain rocks down on the Hardits holding Tranquility."

"If I can just butt in here–" interrupted Dock.

"Not now," snapped Arun. The Navy flier had impressed him, but he was far too in love with his own voice.

"We retain critical assets," Arun continued, "not least the legion of frozen Marines Lieutenant Brandt discovered. On Antilles I'm certain we can gain more. We've suffered tragic losses. I don't deny that, and I don't shirk responsibility for the consequences of my command decisions."

"Oh, Major," sang Dock.

"*What?*"

"Just one little detail you seem to have forgotten. If we're lucky, and don't get shot down, I can maybe locate the transport plane Brandt talked of and set down nearby. But that's it. We're out of juice. To reach escape velocity to rendezvous with *Beowulf*, I need at least half a tank of fuel. With

Beta destroyed there's only one place on the planet with enough fuel. Detroit."

"Surely *Beowulf* has fuel?" queried Nhlappo. "She could ferry down enough."

"Not enough. The old girl uses different fuel. Not safe for use in atmosphere, you see. Same with all the other void-only small craft."

"The other Storks?" prompted Arun.

"All donated their fuel to get us down so we could haul your ass out of the fire."

"Well, why didn't you say?"

They could hear Dock sniff. "You never asked. And we were rather *busy*, you know?"

"What do we do?" asked Nhlappo. The question felt like a knife thrust into Arun's back.

"Same as we already planned," said Xin. "Set down near Del's aircraft, pick up any survivors, and then head back to *Beowulf*. The only change is that now we also sneak into Detroit and steal enough fuel to top up our tanks."

"Without us or the Stork being detected by the Hardits," added Nhlappo. "Without us being blasted into atoms."

"Well," said Xin, "there's that too."

"Enough chatter!" snapped Arun, aware that everyone was listening in. "Our first task is to make contact with any survivors from the fall of Detroit. Then we lie low as best we can for a few days before grabbing the fuel and withdrawing to orbit. The enemy has no orbital or air surveillance, and will drift away back down their holes if they think we're dead. *We can do this.*"

His statement was not entirely true — the Hardits had shown they had drones and aircraft — but his words were close enough. The Legion *did* have a chance. So long as they kept their nerve and their belief in themselves.

When no one queried his decision, the tension in the gunship slackened off. For now.

"You know," Xin told Arun over a private channel, "sometimes it's right to surrender tactical advantage for strategic gain. Battles are won by heroes, but to win the war, even heroes need a commander who's a ruthless bastard with a heart of tempered steel."

"True," replied Arun. "Though we commanders don't get to know whether our decisions are right until long after the event. After the blood price has already been spent."

"I never said it was easy, Twinkle Eyes."

"It's not. But… thank you for your support. That makes command a tiny bit easier." He hesitated before deciding to continue with the question he burned to ask. "So, do you think I did the right thing to go after that Hummer, and send *Beowulf* off to the moon?"

Even from across the other side of the hold, Arun recognized Xin slumped in her battlesuit draped in med-patches. She suddenly twitched in fury. "How the *hell* should I know?" she snarled. "I don't even know what we're really doing on this planet. How could I? Do you know the biggest mistake of my life, Arun? It was to believe that you and I were allies, the two of us destined to face and win the galaxy together. That night, two years ago, that we spent together on Antilles… it meant something to me. The thought of having you at my side set a flutter in my heart. But you? Since then you've been as tight-lipped with me as a deep-frozen asshole. Which, for the record, is exactly what you are, *Major*."

"Incoming!"

Arun was so shocked by Xin's sudden outburst that he struggled to properly register Dock's warning.

"Hold on tight," said Dock, sounding as if he was having the time of his life. "This is gonna get rough."

Arun double-checked his harness was tight, grateful for the respite. He'd rather face getting shot at than Xin's anger any day.

Chapter 65

The Stork shuddered as it spent freely of its supply of defensive munitions. The gunship twisted and looped in an effort to escape the surface-to-air missiles, but in comparison to the evasive maneuvers Arun was used to in void combat, the turns felt agonizingly slow.

Noisy though! Jinking in an atmosphere threw up a cacophony of wailing and screams from the craft, and from the air they were bullying their way through.

"Brace!" screamed Dock, just before the deck below Arun's feet started humming with the Fermi defenses.

The first missile clanged harmlessly against the hull.

Then another.

Arun laughed. Xin had kitted out the Stork with just the right configuration: heavy armor and anti-missile defenses. If she were in the next seat, he'd undo his harness so he could put his arms around and hug her, no matter how angry she was.

The next missile exploded against the starboard beam, right behind Arun's back.

Arun could feel the ship shake, pushed out of its flight path by the shockwave, but he was still alive.

Then another explosion ripped apart the sky, tossing the Stork around like a child with a toy grenade.

"We're going down," said Dock. From screaming histrionics, his voice had calmed and taken on a sly quality. He sounded more like a poker player than the pilot of a stricken gunship that was plummeting down for a violent confrontation with the ground.

Everyone had their way of meeting death, Arun supposed. Dock's was to laugh his doom off as a game. Arun's was to be paralyzed by a sense that he had left duties unfulfilled, of opportunities and lives wasted.

Barney accepted a channel from Springer. "Arun, if there's an afterlife. Come look me up."

Before Arun could think of a reply, Dock spoke again. "Ladies and gentlemen, will you *please* remain calm. All you heard was a little bang from the missile payloads. No more than an explosive fart, really, and this bird's armor is rated 100% fart-proof. The missiles were supposed to have punched through our armor with a shaped charge and atomized you lot inside. Our Fermi field fragged all that."

Arun almost felt hope… until Barney whispered how rapidly they were giving up altitude. "He's talking drent," Arun told Springer hurriedly, while he still could. "I'll look you up in the next life I promise."

They were only 200 meters above the ground.

"Venting fuel tanks," said Dock.

50 meters…

The gunship bucked and roared as Dock fired every thruster he could orient downward, squashing Arun down into his seat.

20 meters…

The sly veck. Dock had planned this all along!

With a dull thud, the gunship crashed into the ground. It was a rough landing, but the harnesses could cope with a far more sudden deceleration, and the Stork's structure looked undamaged as far as he could tell.

"This service has terminated," announced Dock. The exit hatches retracted, and passenger harnesses released. "We hope you've had a pleasant journey. Please ensure you take all your equipment with you when departing the shuttle."

Despite the strangeness of exiting a vessel on a planet's surface, deploying from a gunship had been drilled into the Marines all their life. Within moments, they were out into the woods surrounding the crash site, following the orders of their NCOs to secure the area. Even the three Resistance fighters emerged unscathed and in good time, bringing their missile launchers with them.

Arun was proud of the Resistance fighters. Without battlesuits, they looked so vulnerable, but they displayed just the same spirit as their armored comrades.

A pang of concern hit Arun. No suits! Hardits would smell them from miles away.

"Smear mud on yourselves," Arun ordered them.

"What?" asked Boon.

"Mask your scent. Find the stinkiest drent you can and roll in it."

They dropped their launchers — Stok would not be impressed by that — and started rolling through the undergrowth.

Arun looked for the diminutive figure of the pilot. He knew that Dock wore perfume of all things. Arun didn't like to waste his time judging the strange ways of Navy personnel, but that perfume would be like a beacon to Hardit snouts packed with scent receptors.

Dock was nowhere to be seen.

Arun scanned the crash site. The Stork had come down in the woods to the southeast of Detroit's human levels, not far from where Arun's Marines had entered the Troggie tunnel network. In fact, as Arun got his bearing, he realized that Dock had put them down almost at Detroit's secret back door.

From the hold of the gunship, its descent had felt vertical, but a swathe of destruction had been carved by the Stork before it came to rest, a fifty-meter trail of snapped trees and scragged undergrowth. The torn foliage glistened with… *with fuel!*

The gunship too was covered with the fuel Dock had vented. A last dribble was still being pumped out, pooling on the ground beneath the ship.

"Stay clear of the crash site and destruction trail," Arun warned over BattleNet.

"Understood, sir," replied Gupta, in a voice that sounded like he'd already worked that out, thank you very much, and *would the officer kindly let him get on with his job?*

Dock chose that moment to jump down from the flight cabin and walk briskly away. He threw something Arun's way.

It was a personal processor block.

"Check its map function," explained Dock. "You'll see the location of the aircraft that evacuated from Detroit. I pinged it while we were being shot at. It's about 200 meters away." Dock crashed his ancient white eyebrows down into a frown. "Ever so sorry I didn't quite bring you door to door."

Dock wasn't in a battlesuit, but he did wear a light pressure suit over his fatigues. Incredibly, he was unfastening the front of his suit.

"Hey, Dock! Seal that suit back up. And that goes for the helmet too."

"Don't worry, Major. I'll give us something to mask our scent."

As he hurried away from his bird, Dock reached into a breast pouch on his fatigues and drew out a pocket plasma cutter.

He regarded it wistfully. "Shame. I've nothing to light cigars now." He shrugged. "I don't suppose I can smoke anyway. Not behind enemy lines."

With a melodramatic sigh, Dock tossed the lighted plasma cutter behind him, setting it spinning through the air in the direction of the Stork. The instant the plasma cutter clattered against the gunship's hull, the vented fuel erupted. The sudden surge of heated air threw Dock headfirst onto the ground and hurled a fireball high into the air.

Indiya's voice came over the FTL comm. "What the fuck was that?"

"That's your junior officer showing off."

"Have you lost the Stork?"

"I don't think so. With luck, the Hardits will think we went up in that blast. We need fuel, though. We're going to… Indiya?"

It was no use. He'd lost FTL comms for good. The link had finally run out of juice.

Every time that voice or other data traffic passed over the FTL link, it used up its limited supply of *chbits* entangled with the sibling devices. Perhaps they could build another, but that was a priority for another time.

Dock was by Arun's side now, having zipped up his suit, but leaving his helmet unsealed. Better he did that than talk through an easily traced radio signal.

"My bird looks a burned-out wreck, doesn't she?" Dock chuckled. "It's fine, though. I've put it in lockdown mode. Complete power down. Will look dead, and unless the enemy can blast their way through the hull, there's no way they can get inside. It will only wake and reopen on my voice order."

"What if you die?"

"Then you'll have a difficult conversation with young Captain Indiya. Sorry, I didn't design the system. That would be your freakish friend, Mr. Finfth." He drew his eyebrows into a frown. "No need for such worry, Major. Come to think of it, I'm certain young Mr. Finfth could also wake up my bird."

Arun didn't want to, but he couldn't help but smile. "You're a strange one, Dock. I'm still not sure whether Captain Indiya was right to have stayed your execution for mutiny. Just take care to stay alive, ensign. That's an order."

"Happy to comply, sir. We're heading for interesting times. Wouldn't want to miss any of it."

"Maybe. But first." Arun lifted the processor Dock had given him. "We're headed for the evac plane. If we can find survivors, the boost to morale will be vital. Maybe the difference between getting off this planet and having our guts ripped out by Hardit claws like poor Esther."

When Dock didn't answer, Arun glanced his way. Dock had sealed up his helmet to reduce his scent trail.

Yes, Arun mused. *I'll probably regret it later, but I'm glad Indiya didn't execute you.*

Chapter 66

Hecht glanced up from the fallen Marine lying across the hatch opening into the downed transport. "It's Lance Corporal Sandure. He's alive."

He moved aside to allow Puja access to the diagnostic port in Del-Marie's suit.

While Arun awaited the medic's verdict he tried again to take in the tragedy of this scene.

The transporter Del had flown out of Detroit's waterfall-screened hangar was a true aircraft, unlike the Stork, which could operate both in atmosphere and in space. Lift had come from the aircraft's broad delta wings. But when a Hardit missile had blown off one wing, even Dock's fancy flying couldn't have saved the aircraft.

A still-smoldering scar cut through the ground behind the plane's final resting point.

It was painfully easy to guess the course of events after the crash landing.

Del had opened up the exit hatch and urged the dazed survivors to grab what they could and make for the shelter of the trees. He might have been operating as a pilot, but Del was a Marine through and through; his carbine would always be in easy reach. He would have grabbed his SA-71 and covered the survivors' exit, using the hatch as a shield. The mound of spent sabots where Del had fallen was testament to the volume of fire he'd poured into the woods. And the hundreds of small caliber bullets – many of them having ricocheted off his armor before embedding in the fuselage – was also evidence of the enemy's implacable numerical superiority. Del's luck had run out today: he must have crashed straight into an enemy unit.

A trail of human corpses led from the aircraft deeper into the woods where a heap of broken bodies told of a hopeless final stand made against overwhelming odds.

Arun sighed, a long and trembling exhalation of grief. Zug's body had been among the corpses, his body hauled there on a stretcher. Another friend gone.

Worse even than Zug had been the sight of two women sprawled over each other at his feet, one still gripping her carbine, and the other's arms locked by rigor in front of her, as if she'd died carrying a precious burden.

It wasn't difficult to guess what that burden had been.

After all the fighting these past two years, Arun thought he'd seen so much death and pain that he wouldn't be affected by such scenes. That he wouldn't feel the gorge rise in his throat, making speech impossible.

He could put a name to these corpses: Rohanna and Shelby. He'd been perplexed, irritated, and frankly in awe of these mothers who had forced an expeditionary force of armored Marines to adjust their plans so that their infants were protected.

The part that made Arun gag, made him yearn to shout out his fury at an unjust universe, was that Rohanna and Shelby had been proved right not to name their babes.

This was the moment Arun nearly succumbed to despair. Only the knowledge that the others, *those who still survived*, were depending on him kept him going. He had returned to Tranquility promising liberation, but now the abyssal depth of his failure was laid out starkly at his feet.

Of their infants there was no sign. A tear dropped from Arun's eye. They would be out there in the woods somewhere. The scouts had reported no survivors but hadn't identified the dead. Arun was spared the sight of the broken little bodies, and he was ashamed to say that he felt relief at that. It was cowardly, he knew, but he couldn't bear to see such young corpses.

"Del's coming round," said Puja. She wouldn't use Lance Corporal Sandure's given name if she weren't as badly affected by the scene as Arun. "I'd say the enemy had two machine guns trained on the hatchway and kept them trained on him until he went down. Major, he drew their fire to give the others a chance."

"Corporal Narciso," prompted Sergeant Gupta, "Will the lance corporal live?"

"Yes, Sergeant. His suit armor wasn't breached, but he's had a helluva pummeling. Severe concussion, broken bones, internal hemorrhaging. Essentially, he's been beaten to within an inch of his life. A *Homo sapiens* would be dead, but when we evac him to *Beowulf*, he'll live."

"Thank you Narciso," said Arun. He was about to rest a comforting hand on Puja's shoulder but hesitated when he noticed Nhlappo was listening in on their conversation. He would have expected the veteran to be the most resilient of them all, but she had been acting weirdly since hearing Brandt's final message, and even more strangely since coming across the downed plane.

The lieutenant had developed an emotional connection to the infants, and was probably taking their deaths badly. He couldn't blame her for being human. It was what they were fighting for, after all.

"We're done here," he said. "Get Sandure ready for evac. *Beowulf* will have to wait for now. We'll hide out in the Trog tunnels."

When they headed off for the nest a couple of minutes later, the dead pulled at him like an irresistible gravitational force. To abandon their fallen without burial or ceremony made perfect tactical sense – they wanted the Hardits to believe the Stork's passengers had perished, after all – but still left him feeling tainted, dirty in a way that could never be cleansed.

He couldn't resist any longer: he turned and looked back. His gaze was drawn to Rohanna and Shelby huddled together, friends comforting each other in the face of death. When he was a cadet, Arun would have offered the dead an oath to avenge them. Avenge their babies too.

But Arun had seen too much death, issued too many empty promises that he couldn't keep and bitterly regretted making.

Without any parting words, he shook his head sadly and hurried after the remnants of his expeditionary force.

Chapter 67

Tirunesh Nhlappo lay buried half a meter under the forest floor, gripped by moist soil, pressed down by dirt and leaf litter.

She'd been trapped like a corpse for over a day now, unable to move without revealing herself. Just like her Serge.

No solid food, no latrines, and worst of all no scratching her ass. No matter how many times she told herself this was no different from taking up a position in the black of the void, her body kept screaming that she'd been buried alive.

But this wasn't an ambush position. If it were then she could fold her conscious mind away and switch to a mental standby state until awoken by a threat.

This was a recon post. Other than scheduled sleeps, the recon team had to keep fully alert, watching the cameras and other passive sensors hidden in the area and connected to the recon Marines by buried strandwire, flexible ceramic data cables the width of a human hair. Signals sent along strandwire were undetectable. In theory.

How much longer would she have to endure this? According to the last message sent along the strandwire from Detroit, it could be several more days before they grabbed the fuel and made a run for orbit.

And to think she'd volunteered to lead the recon team. Insisted on it, in fact.

However bad it got, though, she knew that holing up in Detroit would be worse. The human levels were suffocated by the ghost of the only remaining person she cared for in the galaxy. Her son.

Grief choked her once more, smearing her vision with tears. In the seclusion of her underground tomb, Nhlappo wept. Time lost any meaning, the sensor grid forgotten. All she knew was one wracking sob after another in an endless path of despair.

Again and again her mind tormented her with recorded memories of a happier time, watching the playful antics of her little boy, his skin as dark as his father's. It had been his father who had given her boy the young Serge Rhenolotte the nickname of Zug, in those last weeks before they surrendered him to novice school.

When she had called in every favor to be posted back to Tranquility, Nhlappo had assumed Zug would instantly recognize her…

"Contact!"

A jolt of adrenaline wrenched Nhlappo from her sobbing.

"Scout party approaching from northwest," warned Tremayne from the western observation position.

Nhlappo pulled herself out of her well of sorrow, and verified that Tremayne's alert had woken the other recon Marine from his scheduled sleep. No one spoke. If all went well, they would keep perfectly still and completely silent until the Hardits had moved on.

Nhlappo watched the Hardits approach down a muddy slope from the northwest. The enemy would be penetrating a sensitive triangle of forest marked by three points: the hidden entrance to Detroit's Trog tunnels, the waiting Stork, and the crashed transport where Del-Marie Sandure had fallen. Each side of the triangle was about 200 meters.

The recon team was concealed inside that triangle, its mission was to watch over the abandoned Stork to ensure it was undamaged and secure when they made their break to orbit. The three hidden Marines didn't just watch the camera feeds; their carbines were buried with them. If they needed to, they could emerge from behind an enemy attacking the tunnel entrance or to help clear a path to the Stork.

That made tactical sense, but Nhlappo was under no illusions. If the enemy knew of the tunnel entrance and sent a significant force to secure it, none of the Marines would get off this planet alive.

Nhlappo counted 23 Hardits spreading out around the Stork, with a few more remaining at the top of the slope, trying to conceal themselves behind trees while poking their heads around to keep a watch on the ground below.

The idea of keeping concealed fire support in reserve on the high ground worried Nhlappo because it made good tactical sense. Were these elite soldiers?

Any fears were soon dispelled. This group was no more professional than the last two Hardit groups to poke around the downed gunship. The slowness of movement, and utter lack of initiative revealed the ragged militia for what they were: unwilling conscripts who were too scared of their superiors to disobey the order to inspect the Stork, but too lethargic to do much when they got there. Nonetheless, they were showing worrying signs of learning.

The Hardits placed an explosive against the flight deck hatch. Other than a loud bang that panicked squadrons of flying creatures into the air, it did no damage.

One of the Hardits fired several shots at the pilot's window. Nhlappo cheered silently when the resulting ricochet tore a chunk of flesh out of a nearby Hardit thigh. Shame the bullet didn't tear out its wretched throat.

After the others clubbed the shooter's head with their rifle butts, they simply gave up. It was as if they'd done all they were prepared to, and were happy to sit around gassing for a while before heading back.

Nhlappo couldn't quite believe what she saw next. The monkey-like creatures began separating into groups of between two and four, and then proceeded to snake their tails into each other's filthy outfits where each rubbed at their neighbor's crotch.

Her face screwed into disgust to see this half-assed alien orgy. The sexual activity didn't bother Nhlappo, but the ill-discipline did, because that crossed species boundaries. These filthy vecks were an affront to soldiers everywhere.

After a few minutes, the rubbing ceased suddenly. Perhaps a scent order had been issued that the recon sensors couldn't detect. The Hardits rose languidly and ascended the gentle slope, heading back from whence they'd come.

The militia were just outside the recon team's triangle when an animal growl rumbled through the forest, causing the Hardits to freeze.

They were not much more than dumb animals themselves. Reverting to an instinctive threat response, the enemy soldiers dropped to all fours and raised their snouts, sniffing out this sudden threat.

Horden's Children! Didn't the monkey vecks know anything? Nhlappo could easily recognize the species from the cry alone. It was a ginquin, a predatory quadruped that occupied a similar evolutionary niche to an Earthly wolf. Looked like one too, except for a feathery sensory organ that stretched from ear to ear, and barnacle-like symbionts that lived on its skin, providing hard, abrasive armor in exchange for a steady supply of nutrients from the animal's blood. Standing on all fours, an adult ginquin would be thigh height against a Marine.

Anyone who bothered to understand Tranquility's surface would know the ginquin. In fact, Nhlappo could picture the very animal who had given that warning growl. It was a red and brown patterned individual who'd remained nearby despite being disturbed by Nhlappo's recon team.

It was probably a mother guarding her young, unwilling to abandon them whatever the threat. Nhlappo could understand that all too well; couldn't the Hardits?

Obviously not, because one of the enemy bounded down the incline on all fours, rifle gripped in its tail. The Hardit stopped a meter away from the animal, grunting at it to clear off.

The ginquin barked back.

Snapping its jaws, the Hardit attacked, trying to club it with its rifle butt, but the ginquin dodged the attack easily and bared its fangs at the intruder.

The Hardit backed off, stood on two feet and brought its rifle to bear on the mother ginquin.

The beast lowered its head and backed away.

But not fast enough for the Hardit who shot at the beast.

The rifle crack was followed by a pitiful cry, and then pained yelps.

Puffed up by its victory over a defenseless beast, the Hardit scrambled back up the slope to rejoin its unit.

Nhlappo managed to smile. She'd seen the Hardit's round throw up a clump of rotting leaves and dirt at least a meter away from the animal. *The ginquin hadn't been shot at all.*

Nhlappo whispered, not caring that the other recon Marines could hear: "I apologize for calling you a dumb animal, Mother Ginquin. Or maybe you're a father… I don't know your biology that well. But I do know that you're not dumb in the slightest. Not as ignorant as the Hardit you fooled, anyway."

From its cover amongst the trees, the ginquin watched the Hardits leave the area.

Human eyes were following the enemy unit's departure too. More or less human, anyway, because that sector was covered by Marine Tremayne. Nhlappo couldn't work out the young woman with her freakishly violet eyes and sickeningly love-struck obsession with McEwan. But somehow Tremayne had chanced across one of the ancient recon AIs, and that precious suit AI was a treasure Nhlappo *could* value.

The last of the three-strong recon team was Umarov. As Tremayne's buddy, he came with the territory, but he'd proved himself in a fight more than once.

A facile fool like McEwan would observe the animal outwitting the Hardit and see that as a sign. Nhlappo had seen too much of the galaxy to believe in fairy tale symbolism, but to see Hardits humiliated by a forest animal gave a moment's easing of her bottomless grief.

"Hardit unit has left the area," reported Tremayne a few minutes later. Good girl. Tremayne had waited until the enemy had left the vicinity before reporting. The buried cables the team were passing data traffic along were designed not to leak any signals, but on a recon mission like this, you took every precaution possible to avoid detection. Not daring to breathe until your enemy was out of sight was still an important maxim, no matter how much fancy tech shrouded you.

"I spotted two elite soldiers in uniform," said Tremayne. "Snipers, I think. They took positions high in trees with good fields of fire over the Stork. They weren't impressed with the Hardit who shot at the Ginquin. Gave it quite a beating on their way out. My heart bleeds for the skangat veck."

"Keep it professional, Tremayne."

"Sorry, ma'am."

"Until that point, though, you did well."

The ginquin's young chose that moment to wail, a human-like cry of innocent need that penetrated the forest. The mother barked over the cries of her young, concealing their sound. It was more than just crude volume that buried the younglings' cries, the mother's barks and growls were perfectly crafted to conceal the sound, the aural equivalent of draping a stealth cloak over her babies. Impressive.

"Sir…" The breathlessness in Tremayne's voice was so unexpected that it stirred Nhlappo's muscles, readying her for action. "The ginquin young. Their cries… they're human!"

"Get a grip, Marine," snapped Nhlappo, angry that this promising young woman had fallen prey to the same flights of fancy as that idiot she doted on. "What you mean is the cries *sound* human. They are not. Even on this planet, the cries of animal young sound eerily human. I'm sure a biologist could explain why. Your mind's fooling you into hearing human cries because you *want* so much for the animal's young to be… the human young we lost. Wanting something doesn't make it come true."

"That's what I thought, ma'am. But it's not me who thinks those cries are human. It's Saraswati — my recon AI."

"Shit!"

"Said she'd had her suspicions," continued Tremayne, "but that last cry confirmed beyond doubt."

Every nerve in Nhlappo's body started fizzing with energy. How could she have been so frakking stupid? It had been *her* mind playing tricks, not Tremayne's. Denying the truth ringing in her ears.

Like a corpse rising from the dead, Nhlappo emerged from beneath the ground in a shower of dirt and leaf litter, her hands crossed over her chest holding her SA-71 carbine. As soon as she'd forced her way out of the soil's grip, she ripped away the strandwire plugged into the socket at the back of her neck, and snapped her carbine to the back of her suit. Her suit hadn't the power to use full stealth mode, but she checked she was scent-sealed and that her suit exterior was emulating the purple dappled pattern of the forest floor.

Then she was off, shedding dirt and leaves as she raced toward the Ginquin. The animal sensed her approach. It bared its fangs and growled at this new intruder, though with less certainty than when it confronted the Hardit.

Nhlappo slowed and came to a halt at what she judged to be a not-too-threatening distance. Animal and Marine regarded each other, unsure whether they were facing friend or foe.

Nhlappo blanked her visor so the ginquin could see her resemblance to the babies — if they truly were human. Then she got on all fours and bowed her head submissively.

The beast approached and sniffed at Nhlappo, bumping its nose repeatedly against her helmet, before proceeding to lick her battlesuit.

Nhlappo released her helmet seal, just for a second, hoping the beast would recognize the humanity in her scent.

It was enough. The ginquin gave a yelp of a kind Nhlappo hadn't heard before, and then trotted into the undergrowth, looking behind every few seconds to check the Marine was following.

The mother beast led Nhlappo to her nest: a shallow pit scooped out of the dirt and screened by carefully placed branches filled with leaves and twigs.

Nhlappo could see something move inside. It was redder in color than the mother beast, but whether human or animal was impossible to tell through the nest screening.

Resisting the urge to tear apart the screen, Nhlappo waited a few seconds until her suit AI had enough information to paint an artificial image of the nest's interior onto her visor.

The ginquin rubbed herself over her young.

There were two of the babies, their skin rubbed raw by the barnacle hide of the mother ginquin. The animal's instincts were maternal, but the children weren't hers. They were Rohanna and Shelby's babies.

Nhlappo carefully peeled away the screening and reached inside. When she scooped up the infants, the mother ginquin snapped her jaws over the human's wrist, its eyes rolled high in their sockets to glare up at the Marine.

"It's okay," Nhlappo told the animal gently. "You've done well. These youngsters owe their lives to you, but you know I can care for them better than you."

The ginquin gave a last bark and warning glare before running off, out of sight within a heartbeat.

The babies cried when their four-legged foster mother left them. Nhlappo shushed them and rocked them until they were asleep. They were weak from hunger and thirst. There wasn't much fight left in them, not even enough to cry out their needs.

She headed off for Umarov's approximate location, knelt down and whispered at the ground: "You're in command. Acknowledge."

Her AI turned her head left and zoomed the visor display onto an unremarkable patch of ground a few paces away. A wrinkled black finger snaked out of the ground — Umarov's worm camera that had emerged from the top of his helmet. The camera tip lit up in purple — the dominant color of the purple foliage in the forest scene — and gave a repeating pattern of two short pulses followed by two long. Umarov was signaling his acknowledgment.

Nhlappo hurried over to the Troggie tunnel entrance as quickly as she dared without making unnecessary noise.

As she slipped behind the screen of trees she marveled at how similar it was to the ginquin nest.

A hundred meters into the tunnel, she encountered Lance Corporal Sandhu's fire team who were acting as perimeter guards.

Even behind their dark visors, she sensed their astonishment.

"What the fuck are you staring at?" she barked at the sentries. "Even a drill instructor can be a mother, you dumb vecks."

One of the babies woke. Wide eyes tried to make sense of this strange new environment. Nhlappo could almost hear the thoughts behind the confused stared: *where was the nest and the nuzzling snout with its nice tickly licks and warmth?*

Warmth! In camouflage mode, the exterior of Nhlappo's battlesuit was kept to ambient temperature. Her suit AI caught the implications of her Marine's train of thought and applied a gentle warmth.

"Don't mind them," Nhlappo cooed at the baby. "They're only kids. Not much older than you. They've no idea how to look after little darlings like you. *But I do.*"

She raised them to head height, a baby in each gauntlet, her carbine safely snapped against her back. She laughed. Two babies and an SA-71: they made quite the little family.

Both infants were fully awake now, peering myopically at her face through her visor.

"I'm so sorry you lost your Mommas yesterday. I lost a son the same day." She sensed interest from the guards. She hesitated... and then decided she didn't give a shit. "We can give each other cuddles. Would you like that? It won't bring our loved ones back, but it would make the sadness more bearable. What do you say?"

The babies gave happy gurgles, but she knew that wouldn't last long. She needed to reach the nursery area in the human levels, to find milk. Between several assaults on Detroit, and Brandt blowing the route down to the secret legion buried in the depths, getting around the city would not be easy. But she would find a way.

After milk, the infants had other needs: cleaning and clothing – wound cleansing too. The mother ginquin had rubbed against them with her abrasive, parasite-infested hide, leaving their soft baby skin covered in angry red grazes. But they were Marine babies; with a little food inside they would shake off a few scrapes without a problem.

She headed up the tunnel as fast as she could without risking tripping.

After passing the second perimeter guard and entering the bottom of the human levels, she halted.

Something wasn't right.

The babies' mothers had refused to name them. Even numbed by her own loss, Nhlappo still couldn't imagine the depth of despair that would prevent naming a baby. It was admitting that they would die young. Admitting defeat. How could she protect these little ones if she hadn't the courage to hope they would grow to adulthood?

She lifted the babies to head height again. This time they didn't wake.

"I name you," she said softly. "And I apologize in advance, because I think Tremayne isn't the only one to have been infected by McEwan's love of symbolism."

Dimly she wondered whether by naming them, she really intended to claim ownership. She shook away that stray thought and turned her head to the babe in her left hand. "You, I name Romulus. And you… Remus."

Chapter 68

On the far side of the hangar, 100 meters away, the trio of Hardit sentries froze, and then turned to face each other.

Springer told Saraswati to keep her carbine trained on the sentries across the way while she checked the nearer sentry trio, the Hardits only a few paces away who had no idea that Umarov and Springer were hiding so close.

Whatever had excited the distant sentries wasn't alarming the ones nearby. Instead, growling crossed the hangar between the two groups. It seemed to dispel the moment of tension, enough for Springer to take her finger off the trigger.

The whole thing was probably just what passed for Hardit banter, she told herself. Nothing more.

She surveyed the hangar area once more. Checking for threats was what she told herself she was doing, but that was a lie and she knew it. What she was really doing was weighing her chances of making it out alive.

Detroit's hangar was huge – large enough to house dozens of craft, both atmospheric airplanes and shuttles capable of making it to orbit. The flight path to the outside world was through an opening in the mountainside screened by a waterfall. Narrow bays were cut into the side of the hangar to house alternatively the aircraft, and the fuel and ordnance they required.

Actually, fuel was mostly stored in tanks buried underneath the hangar and pumped up through the floor, but the hangar level also housed many ready-filled fuel canisters, used for auxiliary supply on long–distance flights, or in case the fuel pump system failed.

It was that fuel that had lured the Marines out of the tunnel network beneath Detroit and up through the human levels, evading Hardit patrols until they arrived undetected at the hangar. Without that fuel, they'd never get off the planet.

They had been fortunate enough to locate a fuel store at the back of the hangar that was out of sight of the Hardit sentries. Xin and the four other

Marines were quietly loading the trollies with the fuel canisters now, while Springer and Umarov watched the sentries.

Actually, it was not luck that caused the fuel store to be unguarded. From their stance, the Hardits were here to guard the aircraft ordnance, not the fuel. And that was just as well because she was wary of the Hardit sentries. These weren't the reluctant conscript militia who would pretend they hadn't noticed you if they thought it would avoid a fight. The hangar was guarded by the same uniformed elite who had killed Kalis in the underground depths of the Labor Camp.

Kalis had died trying to free Spartika. Or Adrienne Miller, to give the heroic Resistance leader her real name. Well, Adrienne had died anyway, along with everyone else, in the Fall of Detroit. Frakk load of use she had been! Good to know Kalis's sacrifice hadn't been in vain.

No, she corrected herself. Del-Marie was the one fighter who had gotten out alive, although he'd been in a coma since they'd rescued him a few days ago. Romulus and Remus too, who were inseparably attached to Lieutenant Nhlappo. Scuttlebutt said poor Zug had been Nhlappo's son. If so, then she was sorry for the lieutenant. Tirunesh Nhlappo was a hard person to like, but the idea of losing a child pierced Springer's gut with venomous horror, almost making her grateful that she could never have children of her own.

One of the distant sentries stiffened suddenly. It began sniffing at the air. Moving as silently as she could – stealth mode was far from perfect – Springer aimed her carbine at that sniffing nose.

The sentries wore helmets and plates of body armor over their shiny uniforms that were themselves woven from impact absorbent material. It wasn't armor on the level of a Marine battlesuit, probably intended as protection against rival armed Hardit groups. For a start, the armor had gaps – more than enough for accurately aimed fire. She'd already agreed with Umarov to aim at the noses. What better way to ruin the scent–oriented creatures?

The sniffing sentry barked a warning.

Damn!

The Hardits went to ground, some crawling to the nearest cover, while others aimed their rifles… Not east at Springer and Umarov. Nor northeast where Xin's group was loading the fuel.

Whatever had spooked the Hardits was to the north.

"Trouble," Springer told her commander, bouncing her comm signal off the hull of a Stork shuttle. For some bizarre reason there were several of the ruined shuttles arranged in the center of the hangar. "The Hardits are acting as if they're under attack, but I don't believe they've seen us."

"We're not finished here," said Xin. "Deal with it."

Springer didn't bother replying. Every word that issued from Xin's lips felt corrupted by the filth of betrayal and death. Springer still didn't fully understand why she hated Xin with such gut–churning intensity. Didn't need understanding to know that she wished the lieutenant dead.

Damn! Damn! Damn!

The other group of sentries, just a few paces to her front, crouched in a Hardit equivalent of taking a knee, covering the danger area with their rifles.

What had gotten their attention so?

Springer held her fire a little longer – hoping the tension would evaporate. That this would prove another false alarm.

It didn't look as if that was going to work this time. The sentries looked confused and panicked, both trios now shifting their arcs of fire to cover every direction.

They think something's out there, but don't know where.

This was bad. The worst possible outcome. Could Springer and Umarov eliminate the sentries?

Probably.

But the six Hardits they could see weren't the true threat. There were barracks set into the mountain at either side of the hangar, containing dozens more elite Hardit soldiers. If the barracks opened up and soldiers spilled out, Xin's team would have to run a 500-meter gauntlet of fire before jumping out through the waterfall.

And they would be carting highly explosive aviation fuel all the way.

Springer felt a prickling sensation on her back. The door to the eastern barracks was right behind her. Had it opened yet?

"Death to the Monkeys!"

Springer didn't have time to work out whence the human battle cry had originated. She shot her Hardit target through the nose. AI-assisted and at a range of only a hundred meters, she couldn't miss. The supersonic dart tore through the enemy's snout, shattering its upper jaw.

Bite on that, monkey.

Beside her, Umarov would be bringing out his poisoned combat blades, and slicing through the two guards nearest to him.

Springer trusted her buddy to keep the nearby Hardits busy while she took care of the other group. But she found her next target was clutching its neck. Someone had already shot it. Springer put a dart through its nose anyway. The last of the trio was slumping to the deck without needing any assistance from Springer's railgun.

Their killers emerged from cover: three humans in Marine battlesuits who were now covering the dead Hardits with SA-71 carbines while pulling on a heavy cart, a platform loaded with equipment cases that dwarfed the fuel canisters Xin's team were stealing.

Who the frakk were they?

"Springer!"

Umarov's warning came just in time for her to dodge backward and to her left, taking her no more than a fingerwidth out of reach of the last Hardit sentry's bayonet lunge.

She nearly laughed at the idea of her adversary trying to penetrate Marine armor with a metal knife attached to the end of a wooden rifle. But her proto-smile died when she noticed the coruscating lilac-white glow on the bayonet's tip. The Hardit was coming at her with plasma cutter, a weapon upgrade surely designed specifically to cut through Marine armor.

She charged at the Hardit with the Marine version of the ancient bayonet: monofilament *teeth* rotating into a blur on the end of her carbine.

"For the Legion!" she yelled.

The monkey shot her in the chest.

Then it seemed to remember that its bolt-action rifle had been upgraded to a semi-automatic, and fired short, controlled bursts, emptying its magazine into her.

Hammer blows cracked Springer's ribs and, worst of all, toppled her backward. That ancient sense of balance in the pit of her stomach told her that she had gone past the point of no return – she was falling and there was nothing she could do about it. She was about to topple onto her back, helplessly exposing her belly to that plasma-tipped bayonet.

But instincts inherited from a time when her distant ancestors still lived in trees took no account of artificial intelligence. Saraswati felt the panic in Springer's gut, and immediately expended every last joule of the suit's energy reserves to power its motors just enough to nudge Springer back onto her feet.

Down here in a gravity well, you couldn't fly around like a frakking fairy, not like you could in the void. Movement was always difficult on planets, but the nudge and jumps that a suit could manage could still make the difference between life and death.

And in this case, it spelled death for the Hardit, who seemed so mesmerized that this human it had shot was now springing back to life, that it was making a hash of swapping in a fresh ammo magazine.

Whatever!

Recovering its wits, the Hardit finished snapping in the new mag and brought its rifle back up to fire again, but it had wasted too much time gawping at the immortal human.

Springer parried away the Hardit's rifle with its lethal plasma tip, and then thrust her spinning monofilament teeth through the veck's gut, chewing through flesh until her carbine's teeth began separating the vertebrae of the alien's spine.

That'll teach you to shoot at a Marine!

It was the last one. On both sides of the hangar, the sentries were now all dead. Umarov had been ready to intervene with his blades in Springer's fight with the bayonet-wielding Hardit. Now he sheathed his blades and detached his carbine from his back.

On the far side of the hangar, the three Resistance survivors (assuming that was what they were) hurried for the waterfall exit dragging the heavy hover cart with them.

Xin's team emerged from the northeast corner of the hangar.

But they weren't out of danger yet! On the far side of the hangar, Hardit soldiers were spilling out of their barracks.

Springer spun around. The hatch to the other barracks was already open and Hardits were charging out, brandishing plasma-tipped bayonets. Springer sprayed them with a burst of railgun darts that made them dive to the deck. Then she took her time to aim shots at the enemy who showed the most fight. She made every shot count. Umarov's carbine spat death alongside her.

When the Hardits behind the hatch to the barracks rallied, and made another rush out into the hangar, Springer fired off the flash grenade that had been ready all this time in the launcher beneath her carbine's barrel. Saraswati temporarily darkened Springer's visor and dampened her hearing. The enemy had no such filters, and the stunning effect of deafening noise and searing light hit them full strength. She'd seen the effect close up of a flash bomb rubbed in Tawfiq's face. Hardits sure didn't like light and noise.

Without waiting to see the results, Springer reached for the next grenade in the sequence she'd readied on her hip attachment patch. She fired the nerve gas grenade through the hatch to explode twenty meters inside the barracks. Then she fired off another nerve gas round primed to explode in the hatchway.

Umarov should have been adding his own fire support, but instead he was firing at the barracks at the other side of the hangar. Her buddy had better be keeping the monkeys' heads down, or they'd shoot her in the back.

According to tac-display, Xin's team were halfway to the exit. They might still make it out even if she and Umarov didn't.

Springer kept her opponents busy with another burst of railgun darts before firing two frag grenades. Even if the Hardits had gas masks that were proof against the nerve agent, the frag shards should ruin any gas seals. There would be no escape from Springer's vengeance. All she could hear from behind the doorway was coughing and retching. Saraswati reported that the threat to her front had been eliminated.

That'll teach you to mess with the Legion.

Springer turned around, feeling pings as she moved: rifle rounds hitting her shoulder and flank.

She rolled away and took a new position behind an armored equipment crate.

Suddenly, she felt a stab of pain through her wounded shoulder, and an agonizing grip of fire reaching in through her chest, squeezing the breath from her. For several heartbeats, the pain incapacitated her so much that she nearly dropped her carbine. Then Saraswati's upped dosage of combat drugs dulled the pain and focused Springer's mind on the task at hand.

On the far side of the hangar, Hardit corpses were heaped high, but some had survived everything the humans had hurled at them. Now they were behind cover and sniping at the Marines hauling the fuel carts.

It was time to look for new tactical options. The enemy were taking cover amongst ordnance and fuel stores, which was maddening because the explosive targets were shielded too well. Springer didn't have anything powerful enough to penetrate and explode them. Perhaps Xin's team could roll fuel canisters at the Hardits for Springer and Umarov to blow up in their snouts… But, no, that was too complex to work in this chaos.

Without a better plan, she gave the enemy something to think about by firing her last grenade: smoke.

"Follow me," urged Umarov.

She looked across and saw him run full pelt toward a Stork carcass that lay halfway between her position and the Hardits. With her smoke dissipating, she raced after Umarov and scrambled inside the shuttle's hold without taking further hits. She didn't like the idea of being trapped inside a static position, but the Stork's armor was useful. She poked her carbine out of a side hatch and fired a burst of darts to keep Hardit heads down.

"Reckon we should charge them?" asked Umarov.

Before Springer could remind her buddy that combat blades weren't the answer to every problem, Xin intervened: "Keep firing," she ordered. "We're almost out of here."

Springer fired off another railgun volley, using the breathing space that bought to check the tactical situation.

Xin and the three unidentified humans in battlesuits were just inside the exit, putting out volleys of suppressing fire while the rest of her team covered the final few meters to the opening through the mountainside.

The battlesuited renegades… they were a mystery no more. Xin must have accepted them into BattleNet because Saraswati now identified them as Spartika, Boon, and Deacon.

From the shelter of the Stork's armored hold, dark thoughts swept through Springer's head. Spartika's people had fought in the Fall of Detroit. Why hadn't they died like Brandt, Zug and so many others?

"My turn to rescue you, violet eyes," said Spartika. "You too, Old Grognard. Give the monkey vecks everything you've got and then make a break for it. We'll cover."

Springer needed no second bidding.

She and Umarov sent a final burst of fire at the Hardit positions, spraying supersonic darts until the recoil dampener in their carbines cut out. They waded out through the heap of spent sabots, and scrambled out the far side of the Stork from the Hardits.

Then they ran for their lives.

Once out and onto the deck, she drew confidence from the sight of Xin and the three armored Resistance fighters blazing fire at the Hardits. Once they'd left the covering bulk of the ruined Stork, Saraswati helped Springer to zigzag. It was hardly void jinking, but enough to confuse barely trained rifle-toting monkeys.

Suddenly an explosion behind her tossed Springer into the air, and then sent her skidding along the deck.

<Frag munition fired from shoulder-mounted missile launcher,> explained Saraswati while Springer used instinct and training to turn her ass-over-tit tumble into a controlled forward roll. <You've been wounded, but frankly you've more important things to worry about.>

Where was it fired from? asked Springer as she sprang to her feet and ran for the exit.

<Behind. Also… maybe I should have mentioned,> said Saraswati, <Umarov's down.>

Springer halted by skidding along on one leg and coming out facing back the way she'd come. It was as well that she did, because a second explosion ripped a hole in the deck where she'd been headed. The blast sent Springer onto all fours, but she unbunched her limbs and launched herself in Umarov's direction.

'No Marine left behind'. I said I'd reclaim that maxim. Now's my chance to prove it.

She hurried back to where Umarov lay like a broken toy. *Stay alive, old man.* Up ahead, scores of elite Hardits were advancing into the hangar from the main spineway corridor that led from Detroit's interior. *That looks bad.*

<It's not all bad,> said Saraswati cheerfully, zooming her display into the new group of Hardits, focusing on one particular Hardit kneeling down with a missile launcher over its shoulder. The monkey was snapping its jaws at the soldiers swarming all around because they were blocking it from taking another shot.

A frag grenade burst over the heads of the Hardits, raining down ceramic shards and fragments of the overhead. It didn't do much damage but made enough of a show to make them hit the deck. *Frakk! There must be over a hundred of them by now, and more streaming in every moment.*

Springer clamped her carbine to her back and grabbed Umarov's weapon in one hand. With the other she rolled him onto his back, reached down and grasped the recessed grip set into Umarov's battlesuit behind his neck.

303

The handle was designed for exactly this kind of battlefield casualty evac. It was not designed for comfort.

"Hang on, Umarov! This is gonna hurt."

She dragged her fallen comrade along the debris-strewn deck, bumping and thumping all the way. Gentleness was out; so too was any attempt to evade the ragged volleys of rifle fire that ricocheted off the deck at her feet. She put every last ounce of strength into hauling Umarov, and if the Hardits hit her, the damage wasn't enough for Saraswati to mention.

The waterfall exit seemed to grow more distant, not closer. Springer had been shot, burned, bled, and shot again in the past few days. Even Saraswati's combat drugs could no longer hide the fact that it was only sheer bloody-minded willpower that kept Springer functioning.

Even that began to fail.

Springer stopped, still gripping Umarov.

In her mind's eye, she pictured Xin, the cold beauty of her face pinched into an expression of wicked glee. With Springer dead, there would be no one to save Arun from Xin.

Hatred pulled another step out of Springer. Then another.

The prospect of wiping that smug grin off Xin's face pushed Springer into a faltering run.

At long last Springer made it to the hole bored out of the mountainside. Her gasps of exhaustion that had sounded so loud in her helmet were now drowned by the thunderous roar of the waterfall. She put both arms around Umarov, lifted him from behind, and with her final reserve of strength jumped out of the hangar.

From inside the hangar, the falling water looked like a glistening curtain, an ephemeral veil that once parted would grant access to the outside and safety.

The reality didn't work quite like that.

From within, the cascading water was a confusing maelstrom of noise and light that spun Springer into dizzied incoherence and snatched Umarov out of her grip.

"Umarov!" she shouted, reaching out for her comrade. But she was trapped inside the waterfall's unbreakable grip that was yanking her downward through the clouds of spray to be dashed into the churning river below.

Chapter 69

"I'm picking up weapons fire inside the hangar," reported Puja, who was hidden amongst the riverside trees to the left of Arun's position. "Movement headed toward the hangar opening. Over at our Stork, the status is unchanged – it's crawling with monkeys."

"Damn!" snapped Arun. "You hear that, Lieutenant?"

"Acknowledged," Nhlappo answered. "If the Hardits in the Stork's vicinity are militia, we should be able to clear them with ease."

"And if they aren't," Arun finished for her, "we're dead anyway. Secure our ride out of here, Lieutenant."

"Yes, sir. I'll make sure the motor's hot. I've a feeling we'll be leaving in a hurry."

Arun trusted Nhlappo to get on with her part of the plan: to lead the bulk of his surviving forces out of the Troggie tunnels and secure the Stork. Despite the seriousness of their situation, his mind couldn't resist teasing with a vivid image of the grizzled veteran in her armor, toting in one hand a flenser cannon blazing with fire, and cradling the two babies she'd adopted in the other. *Babes in arms.* When his imagination placed a smoking cigar between her sneering lips, he shook his head, bemused. No one could have predicted the way Nhlappo had fixated on the infants. That was why he'd left Sergeant Gupta with Nhlappo: to free Majanita to keep an eye on her officer.

Arun cast his gaze around his small team dispersed in cover near the riverbank. Corporal Puja Narciso was swapping her sensor tool for her carbine. Heavy weapons specialist David Ho had his launcher ready. Marine Kolenja Abramovski had braced her carbine on a branch. He didn't know Abramovski well. Her pale hair and skin invited barbs about her icy nature. Arun could understand the taunts: he'd never heard Abramovski say anything loose or unguarded. But she was the best shot in the Legion, and that was his only selection criteria. Arun was himself one of the Legion's best sharpshooters, which was why the same selection criteria meant Arun found himself watching for Xin's team to emerge with the fuel, and not staying with the main party heading for the Stork.

Barney must have overheard his thoughts about shooting through the waterfall into the hangar entrance over a klick away. The AI magnified Arun's view of the target area. Sunlight reached through a gap in the steep mountain peaks and touched the tumbling, bubbling jewel of a waterfall. But of Xin's team… still nothing.

Where are they?

"Prepare to fire," Arun ordered his team. "Remember, if your target's ugly and hairy, it's one of theirs. If it's ugly and smooth, it's a Marine. Wait for our party to get out first."

As he brought his carbine to bear, cylinders began tumbling through the waterfall's flow. Arun wouldn't have seen them if Barney hadn't artificially colored the plummeting fuel canisters bright blue. Following the precious fuel were the even more precious Marines, gripped by the inescapable power of the waterfall and pulled down to the churning water nearly a hundred meters below. Accompanying the Marines were rectangular panels: the hover trolleys they'd used to haul the fuel.

As they emerged from the hangar, the battlesuits joined BattleNet. The Marines inside were too busy caught on the waterfall to report in, so their suit AIs handled that for them. Bettencourt, Dada, Bizzy Sesay, and then Springer – thank goodness – was seriously wounded but not critical. She'd jumped gripping Umarov from behind. He was unconscious! Arun's heart leaped when he saw Springer lose her hold, flinging her arms out helplessly when she lost her buddy to the waterfall's grip.

Xin followed, tumbling through the falling water, catching a glancing blow from one of the hover trolleys. He couldn't worry about Umarov now. He had to protect his Marines from the Hardits in the hangar.

"Get ready," Arun ordered his team, flicking off his carbine's safety.

"Hold your fire!" shouted Xin, still in the grip of the water.

"Hold," Arun confirmed, but he didn't know why they should. All of Xin's team were accounted for. If she had intended to explain herself, she'd left it too late, because they heard her gasp as she entered the billowing clouds of spray, followed an instant later by a grunt as she impacted the water.

More figures tumbled out through the waterfall, haloed by splashes from poorly aimed rifle fire out of the hangar's interior. *More?* Who were they?

Barney gripped these new targets in flashing red targeting brackets. The suit AI didn't use words, but Arun felt Barney urging him to fire.

Now! Barney seemed to be saying. *This targeting solution isn't going to hang around.*

Look again, Arun willed his AI. *They're in battlesuits.*

Worried that Barney would take the matter in his own hands, so to speak, Arun took his finger off the trigger. Then his mouth dropped open as he saw the unidentified newcomers were pursued by a heavy-duty loading trolley to which large crates were securely attached. Whatever the hell that was, it wasn't a stack of fuel equipment. What was Xin up to?

As if hearing his thoughts, Xin butted in. "Brought us some heavy fire support," she said, "with help from Spartika and two of her pals. That's us all out. Met some bad guys on our way out. Give them hell, Major."

Barney's urges grew frantic, but Arun no longer needed to be told.

"Fire!" he ordered.

Arun and Puja fired a burst blindly through the waterfall. Then Ho released a barrage of four frag missiles, aimed to mark out four corners of an imaginary square inside the hangar, set fifteen meters above the deck. Anyone caught beneath the burst area would be cut to shreds by the hail of frag shards.

Abramovski waited, the sniper preferring to pick her targets rather than fire blindly.

There was no response from inside the hangar. With luck, every Hardit in there was dead, but Arun didn't believe that. Luck hadn't been on his side in this campaign so far.

This action by the hangar wasn't the only game in town. Now that the shooting had started, Nhlappo's force no longer cared about keeping quiet. From her position near the Stork, a klick or so away from Arun, Barney reported three missile launchers firing a stack of ordnance into the air. They would be firing blinders to counter the threat from anti-air defenses. What else they needed to do to secure the area around the Stork was Nhlappo, Gupta, and Madge's problem. Arun was too busy to follow their fight.

Leaving Abramovski to cover the hangar entrance, Arun, Puja, and Ho raced for the tree-lined river bank. Arun kept watch on the bank while the other two made for the narrowest point of the river across which they had already stretched a cargo net pilfered from the ditched transport plane that Del had piloted.

The first of the floating fuel canisters was nearly upon them. The shells of the canisters were gas injected to provide enough buoyancy so they didn't simply sink to the bottom when filled. But Arun hadn't expected the containers to be so buoyant that they were floating atop the fast-flowing river.

The first canister was caught on the crest of a wave and bobbed over the net, continuing downstream without even slowing.

Frakk!

"Lift the nets higher!" Puja shouted.

Ho, who was already in the water, raced for the far bank, Arun clamped his carbine to his back and attended to the net on the near bank where it was hooked around an underwater root that protruded onto the water, the bottom of the net set to grip the river bottom.

By the time he and Ho had hauled the top of the net out of the water enough to reach shoulder height, a clump of canisters was sweeping along the river, about to hit the barrier.

Finally, everything went according to plan.

The fuel cylinders were caught and held by the net. Rushing into the water, Puja began retrieving the containers and stacking them on the bank.

A short distance upstream, the Marines had righted the hover trollies and were using them as rafts. Anyone without a battlesuit would have been thrown off the rafts as they tossed violently around in the rapids, but this was an impressive display of human-AI symbiosis that reminded Arun why he was proud to be a Marine. Using the tension in crouching human legs as a shock absorber, AIs kept the suit legs in constant motion so that the hips were a stable firing platform for the Marines aiming their carbines at the opening to the hangar. Only when the rafts span around in eddying currents, did the Marines temporarily lose their firing solutions.

So far there was no sign of threat from the hangar.

Xin and Springer had managed to fish Umarov from the water and were hauling him onto the largest raft, the one that held Spartika's mystery equipment. Umarov's suit reported he'd lost a lot of blood but had stabilized. Spartika herself, along with Boon and Deacon were in the water beside their raft, trying to stabilize its gyrations.

Once the rafts had cleared the most violently roiling water near the waterfall, they were able to float above the water. The Marines used their suit AIs to pilot the hover trollies, making for the bank where Puja was stacking the fuel. With no obvious threat from the hangar opening above, they shifted their aim to the banks, scanning the trees and bushes on the shoreline for threats.

One of the Marines, Bizzy, was waving a greeting at Arun, or so he thought until Bizzy yelled: "Contact!"

What?

"Major, behind you."

Barney was overlaying Arun's visor with a hastily revised tactical assessment. It was pretty simple: Hardits were approaching from behind. Hordes of them. Bullets rustled through the undergrowth, moving ever closer to Arun.

Arun didn't wait for the next burst of fire to find him.

He dove through the air, tumbling and grabbing his carbine as he flew. Just in time. The bank where he'd been standing spat miniature mud geysers as it was raked by automatic fire.

He hit the ground, rolled and fired as soon as he came to a halt.

A Hardit looked down in astonishment at the hole Arun had opened up in his chest. The alien dropped what looked like an automatic rifle, with a crude magazine slotted underneath that was fashioned from unpainted metal.

Arun shot the monkey a second time to ram home the message. Then he put a shot through the snout of another Hardit who'd halted in clear view, trying to understand why its comrade had taken a sudden interest in its chest.

More Hardits pushed past their comrades, past Arun's position and into the fields of fire of the Marines who'd just emerged from the water. The dumb monkeys weren't even trying to go to ground or seek cover.

Arun wasn't about to make the same mistake. He dove and rolled for a new position farther from the bank.

He scanned the area. Arun's first target was collapsing to the ground, the second clutching at its snout and screaming in agony. Then it too fell to the ground.

Arun felt the closest he had ever come to sympathy for the Hardits, but that only meant his whoops were shouted rather than screamed maniacally as he made short work of the hapless aliens. He lost count of the number of times his railgun spat death at the enemy. Other shots were coming from the Marines who'd jumped from the hangar; more darts hit the Hardits from the rear.

The Hardits learned nothing. They just kept on rushing into Marine firing arcs until their dead were heaped high. And still they came. They had no discipline, no leadership. No hope.

The time finally came when the Hardits stopped coming and the firing fell silent.

A few seconds after the last Hardit fell, an armored figure burst through the trees on the riverbank. Monofilament teeth, dripping bloody gore, extended out the end of his carbine. Blood flowed down the Marine's chest. *Hardit blood.*

BattleNet identified this as Senior Sergeant Suresh Gupta.

"Reckon that's the last of 'em, Major," said Gupta, breathlessly. "The route to the Stork is clear. And, if you'll excuse my Navy speech, Ensign Dock asked me to convey his compliments and ask you to hurry the fuck up." Then he added as an afterthought: "Should have executed the overdramatic poser, if you ask me, but that's the Navy for you. What the…?"

Arun sensed sudden fury coming off the sergeant in waves.

"Have you detected our Resistance friends who have risen from the dead?" Arun asked.

"Lieutenant Brandt died bravely," said Gupta with menacing slowness. "He'll never come back from the dead. How is it that Spartika and her spittle-licking friends didn't fall alongside Brandt and the others?"

"That's a question for later," said Arun.

"Why aren't they dead?" demanded Gupta. His stance suggested he was ready to inflict extreme violence.

"Easy, Sergeant," said Xin.

Arun looked behind. The fuel-raiding party was loaded up and fast approaching. Four trollies laden with fuel, and a larger one laden with Spartika's mysterious equipment crates and Umarov's unconscious body. Movement was slower now: the fuel for the gravitic motors had run out and the Marines were reduced to pulling the trollies along the muddy bank on their wheels.

Arun joined in hauling the nearest trolley.

"You'd better explain to us, and quickly," Arun told Xin privately.

"It's our new heavy fire support," said Xin, ensuring Gupta could hear too. "A heavy cannon dismounted from a gunship's main armament, two portable zero-point power generators, targeting system, a mounting system to convert to an artillery piece, and specialist rounds."

"Range?" growled Gupta, unwilling to be mollified easily.

"Four thousand klicks. This baby can kick out sub-orbital trajectories. And the rounds, to answer your next question, are semi-intelligent, variable-yield fusion shells rated up to three megatons. Finally, we have some respectable fire support."

The explanation satisfied Gupta sufficiently for him to keep his anger inside his helmet long enough to reach the waiting Stork shuttle, which was guarded by jubilant Marines.

Arun expected to battle with Ensign Dock over the weight of Spartika's nuclear artillery piece. It was a battle he expected to lose, because if Dock stood his ground and insisted Marines would have to be left behind to compensate for the additional weight, Arun had no answer. As it turned out, Dock was thrilled at the idea of transporting a *serious weapon*, as he put it, but he fumed and cursed at the loss of the single fuel canister. A loss he made very clear he blamed squarely on Arun.

As the shuttle-turned-gunship's engine spooled, and the hull throbbed with eagerness to lift off, Arun dismissed the pilot and his wild mood swings. He'd had doubts about the old Navy ensign, but Dock had hauled their collective asses out the fire more than once. He'd earned the right to his flamboyant Navy ways.

Dock interrupted Arun's thoughts to relay a warning broadcast from *Beowulf* that a stream of enemy aircraft was lifting off from the continent of Serendine on the far side of the world.

"The dirty monkeys left it too late," said Dock cheerfully. "They'll never reach our bird in time to intercept. Not unless the fuel the major threw away means we can't lift off. Lieutenant Nhlappo… if you please?"

With Romulus and Remus sleeping in the cocooning embrace of one poly-ceramalloy encased arm, Nhlappo ordered the blinders to be activated. There were only a handful of explosions: the Hardits hadn't much advanced war materiel left in the area. The Marines didn't have good enough sensors to be sure, but what they did have suggested that Tawfiq's faction was still mopping up pockets of resistance in the Hardit civil war that still smoldered far below Tranquility's surface.

With his flight path clear, Dock gave the Stork its head. It rose gently for a hundred meters, and then hurled itself into the sky.

Most Marines tapped into the external camera feed and watched their home planet recede beneath them. Arun hadn't time for sightseeing: there were matters left unresolved. He unclipped his harness and made his way over to Spartika.

"You've done well to bring us that cannon," he told her.

Spartika removed her helmet and stared at Arun without speaking. Her features were gaunt, her eyes darkened by a toxic mix of fatigue, bruises, and disdain. In fact, he decided, he found himself looking into an echo of the Adrienne Miller who had first met Arun on the day he was forced to become an Aux slave, a punishment insisted upon by the cruelest Hardit of them all: Tawfiq Woomer-Calix.

"You're safe now," Arun told her kindly. "You can rest once we're back on *Beowulf*."

"The cannon isn't yours," stated Spartika. "We risked our lives and it was me who had the initiative to retrieve it. I…" She shrugged, her sneer softening a little. "I understand you have wounded to tend to. Return them to your ship. Then I expect you to set my team down a safe distance from Detroit. Our cannon goes with us."

Arun ground his jaw and clenched his fist.

Arun pulsed hot anger that urged him to punch this ungrateful veck. The last vestiges of restraint were fraying when Spartika blinked, her eyes threatening to roll up in their sockets. She swayed for a few seconds before recovering her composure.

Her weakness saved Spartika from a smash to her mouth. Arun tried to vent his anger through his indignant glare instead. Spartika should have fought and died alongside Brandt's Marines, not to mention her own people: the human slaves that so many Marines had died liberating.

"Of course, the weapon is yours by rights," he lied. "What will you do with it?"

"Kill Tawfiq. We'll lure her to a fixed position and then nuke her. I'll make sure she knows her death is imminent. Just after it's too late to get away."

"And what will that accomplish?"

"Revenge. Look, McEwan, I've had it with raising false hopes. All this talk of winning human freedom is just so much drent. Even if either of us ever could have armed the human slaves, we're out of time anyway. Tawfiq told me she'll wipe every last human off the planet. I believe her."

"I will not abandon them," snapped Arun. "Not without a fight." He opened a private channel to Gupta. "Sergeant, arrest Spartika and her two cronies for desertion in the face of the enemy."

"With pleasure, sir."

Arun glared in silence at Spartika while he waited for Gupta. When the sergeant did move, having first organized every able-bodied Marine to overwhelm Spartika's group, it was all over in seconds. The three Resistance fighters were far too weak to put up more than a token struggle.

"Just what do you think you'll accomplish, hero?" shouted Spartika. Her bile brought her fresh reserves of energy. She struggled against the two Marines pinning her arms. They barely held on.

"Is this glorious retreat to orbit part of your master plan?" she sneered. "You lost half your force on Tranquility. You abandoned your dropships too. When you first landed, at least you had the advantage of surprise. Now Tawfiq is waiting for you. She'll be ready, and every day she has to prepare her defense, she will strengthen. Notice how even the militia are upgrading from homemade bolt action rifles to semi-automatics, and they managed that within just one week. It's a taster of what to expect. How about you and your *Hopeless Legion*? Can you say the same? Tell me, what's your plan, generalissimo? What are you going to do next?"

Arun pulled off his helmet and thrust his face in front of Spartika's, fighting to control his breathing.

"What am I going to do next? I'll tell you what I *won't* do… Unlike cowards such as you, I will *not give up*. There are still tens – maybe hundreds – of thousands of fellow humans on the planet, not to mention…" He was about to speak about the sleeping legion that Brandt uncovered, but he thought better of speaking openly in front of Spartika. "Not to mention other assets. I will not leave our people behind, and I will never lose hope. Not while the breath remains in my body."

With difficulty, he withdrew from Spartika, and turned his back on her. He addressed his Marines.

"We're headed back to *Beowulf*, which will be our base of operations to capture Antilles. Once that moon is ours, we will regroup, rearm, reorganize and rethink. And when we're ready… *we will come back*."

His words were met by silence. There was no rallying call, this time. No 'Death to the Hardits!', no 'Oorah!', not even a ragged cheer.

Instead, the Marines set their visors to be transparent, or removed their helmets altogether. Their eyes locked glances, wordlessly exchanging critical information like a human equivalent of BattleNet. The determined looks on those faces spoke of unfinished business, of a duty that needed seeing through to the bitter end.

What was more, the Marines had been bloodied. They had a score to settle now.

Tawfiq had won the first campaign.

But this war was far from over.

PART V
Every Secret Has a Heart of Poison

Human Legion INFOPEDIA

Regional Astrography
– Tranquility

Tranquility system lies to spinward of Earth, near the Muryani frontier. We do not have reliable data for early settlement of the system, but informed speculation is that the system was first settled by an unknown alien species as a mining outpost approximately 800,000BCE. Not long after a self-sustaining colony was operationally, the system was conquered by the White Knights and incorporated into their empire, where it stayed until the outbreak of the civil war.

With the sporadic outbreak of frontier wars in recent centuries, Tranquility System has gained importance as both a military supply depot and a fuel mining and refining station. The name 'Tranquility' can be used to refer to the star, the entire star system, or just the planet of Tranquility-4. The full Jotun bifurcated noun for the system is Tranquility-Growth, though this is rarely used by humans.

A Brief Tour through the Tranquility Star System

Tranquility (star) – A main sequence star with a very strong stellar wind of high energy particles, and an emission spectrum high in ultraviolet.

Tranquility-1, -2, and -3 – The inner three planets are small, rocky, and airless. Mining operations concentrated here in the early life of the system's colonization, but ceased within the past 100,000 years.

Tranquility-4 – A habitable planet of approximately Earth size and atmosphere. The low concentration of metals in the planet's core means the magnetosphere is weak. As a result, the sunlight reaching the surface is lethal without proper shielding. A human shielded by nothing more than a hat and light clothing made from conventional textiles will die in approximately 3-4 weeks.

There is some cultivation of Earth crops engineered to survive the conditions, and of Earth animals to graze on them. Whether these Earthly bio-enclaves would survive without careful husbandry is uncertain. Cultivation extends to several more crops and food animals that are part of the White Knight Universal Food System, meaning that service personnel had the enzymes and adaptive digestion programs to process these foods.

In human-centric terms, there are two main areas of settlement, centered on the two main Marine depot bases: Detroit in the Gjende Mountains on the continent of Baylshore, and Beta City in the middle of Lake Sarpedona on the other large continent of Serendine. However, there are also continental-scale underground settlements created by two delving species: the Hardits and Trogs.

Tranquility-4 has two moons. On the larger one, Antilles, ore processing remained active until recently, using raw materials sent here from the outer system. The smaller moon, Metius, is more distant, and is extending its orbital radius by 20 meters per year for reasons unknown.

Tranquility-5: Klug – The planet of Klug is an unwelcoming world of high pressures and toxic acid clouds. Little is known of the planet other than that it features a native lifeform nicknamed the sludge-puddle, which in appearance resembles a greasy pool of mercury several meters in diameter.

Tranquility-6: (inner asteroid belt) – The sixth orbital path in the ecliptic plane is a mix of carboniferous, silicate, frozen volatiles, and high-metal content objects. The belt is mostly mined out.

Tranquility-7: Daiyna – A gas giant with several moons large enough to sustain significant populations. At the outbreak of the civil war, the Daiyna planetary system was colonized by the Hardits who maintained a fuel mining and processing station, dry dock, and ore processing plants.

Tranquility-8: (outer asteroid belt) – A region in the outer system between three and four times the orbital radius of Daiyna. Has a higher concentration of heavy metals than the inner asteroid belt, but distances between objects is greater. After extraction and pre-processing, most ore is sent down into the inner system for further processing on Daiyna or Antilles.

Tranquility-9: (Kuiper Belt) – On the outermost commercial edge of the system, this is a region that consists largely of frozen volatiles (especially methane, water, and ammonia) arranged in a series of low-density rings that ripple with the disruptive effect of a handful of rocky planetoids.

Tranquility-10 (Sensor array) – An artificial construct of rocky objects placed in a spherical array beyond the Kuiper Belt. The distances between individual nodes in this array is vast, but close enough to form a semi-sentient early warning system. It is speculated that the planetoids in the sphere also house missile batteries, cyber-war factories, and that the sphere is linked using FTL *chbit* entanglement with White Knight sector command.

Chapter 70

Arun gave the twisted lump of metal and ceramic a brutal kick, sending it skimming over the crater's bottom and tumbling over the lip, disappearing into Antilles' airless horizon.

"Frakking Hardits!"

He sighed. The Legion had withdrawn to the moon to resupply and rethink. Brushing aside the feeble Hardit defenses had been simplicity itself, but in finding some means with which to threaten Tawfiq… *nothing*. The mass driver that had bombarded Beta City had been put out of commission by *Beowulf*, but the Hardits had done a far more comprehensive job of destruction before the Legion landed here. The fragment he'd kicked was the largest remaining. Everything that could be used to throw rocks down the well to Tranquility had been destroyed.

There was nothing here to use as a bargaining chip with Tawfiq.

Well, maybe there was something…

"I'm done here," he informed Hecht over the comm link. "Seeing with my own eyes, it looks even worse than the reports. Have the prisoners ready. I'll be there in five minutes."

Chapter 71

The six Hardits assembled in the moonbase main control room were smaller than most that Arun had encountered on Tranquility. Their clothing, and for that matter the base itself, was neat and functional, everything clean, tidy, and meticulously maintained. It was a complete contrast to the careless scruffiness of other Hardits.

For these were Hardit males.

The gender distinction was the kind of detail that his friend Pedro would have obsessed over because his species had no concept of gender. Even the way that Arun had felt the need to assign a gender to Pedro had been a source of endless fascination to the insectoid.

But Pedro was gone, yet another casualty of the civil war, along with every human and Hardit on Antilles. And Arun was past caring about any distinctions between different groups of Hardits. They were all equally guilty of xenocide in his eyes.

Arun took off his helmet, wrinkling his nose at the musky stink that assaulted him.

He circled the knot of prisoners who were kneeling in the center of the room, hands on heads, under the watchful eye of Hecht's section.

"Your lives hang by a thread," he told them. He waited for the translator systems in the collars of the Hardit uniforms to produce the alien growls and puffs of scent the aliens used for a language.

"Only I can save you now," he continued. "Give me a weapon. Something I can use to threaten Tawfiq Woomer-Calix. If you don't…" Arun made a cutting gesture.

"All here are males of the second rank," said the alien who appeared to be their leader. "Even I, Cadenqee Canola-Pututuizo."

"Explain," said Arun.

Cadenqee looked down submissively. "We rank below the most reviled female outcast. Tawfiq is female. Even if she calculates that our expertise is valuable, our lives are beneath her contempt."

"So Tawfiq rates you just one half-notch higher than human slaves."

"That is correct."

"My heart weeps for you," Arun scoffed, hoping some of his disdain survived the filtering of translation. "Now give me something of value."

"We are oppressed," said Cadenqee through the translator speaker in his collar, "our potential stifled by the fact of our birth." The Hardit raised his head, looking Arun squarely in the eye. "You are human. The word has spread throughout the stars. It has transcended its origin as a mere species name to become a symbol for oppressed sentients everywhere, of every race. We here, kneeling before you as captives… we are human!"

Hardly able to believe his ears were feeding him such garbage, Arun could only shake his head in bemusement.

"This is your chance," said the Hardit. His eyes seemed to be pleading, although the translation was as emotionless as always. "Show the galaxy that you're better than Tawfiq and her like."

"I need something harder than sentiment," said Arun. "And you're fast running out of time."

"Kill me if that satisfies your blood lust, but spare my team. We were all of us on Antilles only following orders, but their orders came from me, however reluctantly. My underlings will happily work for you, fine engineers and technicians the lot of them. We despise Tawfiq Woomer-Calix as much as you do. Maybe more. You'd think with a common enemy we could make common cause together."

"There is logic to your proposal," said Arun reluctantly.

"Then spare my people."

Arun knelt down to the Hardit's level, and took in its scent, its thick fur and long wolf-like snout. Did he hate this Cadenqee Canola-Pututuizo because of the way he looked and smelled and sounded? No, he decided, he didn't. But his mind replayed images of Esther and the other human slaves being disemboweled by Hardit claws, of the burns and welts on the backs of naked, caged humans… of Rohanna and Shelby who had died in a hail of Hardit bullets never having summoned the courage to name their babies.

"I could never trust a Hardit, not even one who did despise Tawfiq." Arun took a few paces back. "Request denied."

Cadenqee bowed his head.

"Hecht, wipe their Hardit stink from this base."

There was a tiny pause before Hecht acknowledged. Soft whines came from 1st Section's carbines as they charged their rails. He could tell by the softer sounding whine that Hecht had ordered them to set their power low to avoid dangerous ricochets.

The volley of darts tore apart Hardit hearts.

The prisoners slumped to the deck, dead.

Hecht looked to Arun with pain in his eyes, and Arun found he felt such shame that he had to turn his head away.

He had meant what he said about not being able to trust a Hardit. Their execution was a grim necessity but… *wipe their Hardit stink from this base…* the prisoners had deserved more dignity than his childish taunt.

Then he remembered seeing an unnamed human slave clutching at her belly with eyes wide, unable to comprehend that her intestines were spilling out, thanks to Hardit claws.

He cursed himself for feeling sorry for the prisoners. It was his empathy trying to confuse him, that frakking useless part of him that was forever trying to make him see the galaxy through everyone's eyes but his own. No more.

"Empathy," he said to no one in particular as he left the room, "is a weakness."

But he couldn't suppress the voice deep inside screaming that he was turning into a monster.

Chapter 72

"There's someone down here, near where we're digging."

Arun looked up from his screen at Springer. But even though his friend was standing next to him, she was impenetrable behind her helmet visor.

"Who?" he asked.

"Someone we know…"

Arun sighed. He wasn't in the mood for puzzles. Springer was part of the team ransacking the base for supplies: FTL-entangled material, power cells, food stocks, oxygen… anything that would let them take the fight back to Tawfiq as soon as possible.

He stopped himself. When had he become so impatient? If Springer was vague, it meant one thing. "Are your eyes hot, Phaedra?"

"Yes, Arun. And it was more like a vision this time, like you always want it to be. Saraswati is helping."

"Well?"

He could picture Springer frowning inside her helmet. It took her a minute to collect her thoughts, but Arun knew she was worth hours.

"Someone we know is here and waiting for you."

"Pedro? The Trog? Do you mean Pedro?"

"I don't know, Arun."

Arun's heart pounded. He had to keep from whooping. Finally! Good news.

"Doesn't matter, Springer." He touched her shoulder gently. Before the civil war had visited Antilles, Pedro had been responsible for the moon and everyone on it. Who else could it possibly be but Pedro?

Chapter 73

The echo from the drills died away. Madge gave Springer the order to try once again to establish contact.

"Pedro," she said at high amplification. "Pedro! Help is coming. Can you hear us?"

It took several seconds for the reply to be reconstructed by Springer's specialist recon AI and relayed to everyone there.

"Pedro?" said a voice. It didn't sound like the kind of speech synthesizer used by the Trogs.

There came another delay as Springer's AI refined its interpretation. Then the words came through as clearly as if the speaker were in the room. "For frakk's sake, Springster, I'm not a dungering insect. Don't you recognize my voice?"

"Hortez!" screamed Majanita… in a way that made Arun think she'd been no stranger to Hortez's rack back when they'd been novices.

Arun laughed. It was a splendid surprise to glimpse Madge's human face underneath the mask of duty. Hortez had always been the charmer. But no one had heard from him since the day of Operation Clubhouse, when they'd put one over on Tawfiq.

"Madge," yelled Hortez. "Is that your scream of delight I recognize? How I've longed to see your pretty and ever-cheerful face. I hope you've stopped giving Marine McEwan such a hard time. He doesn't mean to be such a donk, it's just his nature."

"Hort, I don't give him as hard a time as he needs and deserves. It's not because I don't want to, but it's awkward now that he's a major."

"Major? Horden's hairy backside… I suppose I shouldn't be so surprised. Pedro is always telling me our little Arun will do great things. And when I say 'always' I don't mean that as a figure of speech. I swear I would have torn that frakking insect's legs off and stuffed them down its throat… if they hadn't fallen off of their own accord. Hell, I'd have stuffed myself down his throat. Anything to shut him up about frakking McEwan."

Arun realized that he, Madge, and most of the other Marines had unconsciously removed their helmets, despite the dust hanging in the air from the drilling.

When it came to sharing a special moment, humans, it seemed, still needed to look from face to face and see the joy reflected in those eyes.

"How did you survive?" Springer asked.

"After Operation Clubhouse? Simple, Pedro had me frozen before anyone came for me. He woke me nine months ago. I'm his carer now. Believe me, I was better off frozen."

"Actually," Springer said, "I meant seeing as the Hardits have cut you off, how come you aren't starved and suffocated?"

"Oh, we've extracted food, water, energy, and air from moon rock. Have you any idea how labor intensive that is? The Hardits gave up trying to flush us out and bricked us in instead."

"Couldn't Pedro's people dig you out?"

"It's just me and the big guy," said Hortez. "And his digging days are over. Hey! You've stopped! Don't you vecks dare stop now. Keep digging! Get me the hell outta here!"

Chapter 74

Pedro had grown really fat.

Last time Arun had seen his old friend, the insect-like alien had bloated to a larger size, and his legs had atrophied, but he'd still had the three-segment structure akin to head, thorax and abdomen. But now there was no sign of a carapace over Pedro's thorax, which had six red markings on the underside to mark where his legs had once attached. Contrasting the enormously expanded thorax, his abdomen had shrunk into a stub like a human navel, and the head had slid down the front of the thorax so it was slightly above ground level, just high enough for his mechanical voice translator to hang around his neck.

Pedro looked like a comedy caricature. But Arun was simply glad to see him.

Arun took his arm from around Hortez's shoulder and touched Pedro's feelers. He could feel a throbbing pulse within them. That was new.

"Good to see you, my friend."

The alien gently withdrew his antennae, using them to describe lazy circles. Last time around, that meant the big insect was happy, but who could tell with these constant body changes.

"Are you well?" Arun asked. "Do you need medical assistance? Food?" Arun gestured to the Marines in Majanita's detail who had dug out Hortez and Pedro. They were observing the unexpected delight of reuniting with old friends thought dead, and were available to assist if called upon.

"I am well. I am far more than well. I have become a fecund time-bomb bursting with life, glorying in the most important role it is possible to be given."

"You mean a Great Parent? But you were the big bug queen back when you first started up a chapter of your nest on Antilles."

"No, friend Arun. The translation in your language for my new role is Great Grandparent — the founder of an entirely new nest. This moon is not an acceptable location. You must take me to a better colony site where I can spawn a new nest in memory of those who died. When we knew we were doomed, those of my people with reproductive potential gathered near to me and–"

"Spare Arun the gooey details," said Hortez. "Let's just say his people filled him with their life force, and now he wants a nice warm hole to park his butt and spawn Troglets."

Arun stared at the insectoid, a confused mix of emotions swirling through his gut. "I'm happy for you, pal," he said. "Really I am. But there's a question I have to ask. Why the frakk didn't you tell me about the secret levels of Marines stored beneath Detroit? Millions of them, Brandt said. Before I shipped out-system, you promised me you'd told me everything."

Pedro stilled his feelers. "I assured you that I had explained everything you needed to know."

"And you didn't think I needed to know there was an army waiting in Detroit."

Pedro's antennae shot up. "Exactly. You see, Hortez, I told you Arun would understand."

Hortez let out a long whistle. "You've been a bad, bad, bug, Pedro. Told you Arun would be pissed at you for holding out on him."

"Oh, did I misunderstand?" Pedro paused, and then seemed to believe Hortez. The alien rested his antennae on Arun's shoulders. "I'm sorry."

"Sorry? I'll make you sorry. If you'd trusted me with the info, we'd have stayed at Detroit, and revived an army, not try to liberate slaves. Good people died because you kept that from me. It might cost us the planet yet."

"Arun, there were things I couldn't say."

"But you knew."

"I did."

"I want you to tell me everything. I mean it, frakk you. From this moment, if I ever find out you've held something back, I'll execute you the same as I did every Hardit I found on Antilles."

Pedro's antennae folded back along his head. "Arun. You executed them all? That was cruel."

"War is cruel. Now talk."

"But we *are* talking. Arun, when I kept silent about the hidden levels in Detroit, I thought I did the right thing. I cannot predict the future."

"Thank frakk for that. I've had far too much drent from the Night Hummers to cope with you too."

"Maybe you are not as free of the Hummers as you think. It was a Hummer who convinced me not to mention the sleeping Renegade Legion."

"Renegade Legion?"

"It's the translation of the Night Hummer term. This is their aim: to create a renegade legion. One that has no affiliation to any existing faction in the White Knight Empire or outside. A new entity that will shelter and protect them."

"That will do their bidding," said Arun, darkly. "Isn't that what this is about? Power?"

"I do not think so. The Night Hummers do not lust for power and domination in the way your species does, Arun. Their greatest desire is to be left in peace."

"Seems to me like the Hummers see themselves as victims," said Hortez. "Ever since they were forced into the White Knight Empire."

"What's your point, Hort?" asked Arun.

"Just because you're a victim, doesn't make you one of the nice guys. Their Renegade Legion might be designed to set them up as worse tyrants than the White Knights. If you want to be left alone, how better to achieve that than to create such an aura of intimidation that everyone is too scared to come near you? Arun? Arun, are you all right?"

Arun's head was filling with the now-familiar clanking sounds of gears engaging, dripping hot lubricant.

"Ahah," said Pedro, which always sounded weird through his voice translator. "It is your organic mind augmentation. I do have something to inform you about but, first, please take your time. You are only a prototype after all."

"I'm a what? No, never mind. For a start, we are not the Renegade Legion, we are the Human Legion."

"Of course," said Pedro. "You would naturally use your species designation."

Blinding flashes erupted in Arun's vision. He sank to all fours, swaying, and closed his eyes.

"No, big bug," he heard Hortez say. "Arun's doing some serious thinking. You can tell by the way his eyes have glazed and his mouth dropped open."

Arun closed his mouth.

"It'll open again in a moment," said Hortez. "Then he'll start drooling. You wait and see…"

"Hu- human." Arun coughed, and then tried again. "Human Legion. More… more than just a name. The Hardit prisoner said as much. So did Nhlappo long ago when she was our instructor. The word human has become a joke. Shorthand for the dispossessed, the underdog. You know that, Pedro?"

"You are correct. For those species with a voice box analogous to yours, the word 'human' has become a common loan word."

Hortez whistled long and low. "Shit, Arun. If you're thinking what I think you are, I don't know whether to shake your hand or shoot you. You sure think big, don't you?"

Pedro jigged his feelers in agitation. "I do not understand."

"When our friend says *Human* Legion," Hortez explained, "he's proposing to use the wider sense of the word."

"We stand for liberty and justice," said Arun. "Not just for *Homo sapiens* and its descendants. For everyone."

Pedro curled his antennae into a questioning shape. "Even Hardits?"

Arun didn't have a reply.

"Never mind the details," urged Hortez. "He might get the details wrong along the way, but Arun's always been a big picture guy, and now he's gotten a whopper to aim for. And the big fella here is hiding a contribution to help you on your way."

"What?" Arun dared to hope.

"He smuggled me with him when he came to Antilles. But I wasn't alone. You see, when they put new Marines on ice for long-term storage, sometimes they reused old ice boxes. Thawed out the Marine already in there in a way that killed them, before tossing them away like rotten old garbage. Pedro's been on a mission for years to rescue your oldest relatives. Hiding away their ice boxes before they get reused. Damned lazy Hardits could easily create new boxes, just couldn't be bothered."

"How many?" Arun asked.

"Just under six hundred. Not a lot, I know. Probably barely make a difference to your force numbers, but Pedro here tells me these ancients can teach our generation a thing or two."

"That's brilliant news, Hortez. But… about our numbers…"

"Now I understand," interrupted Pedro. His antennae swirled in large and enthusiastic circles. Arun and Hortez had to dive for safety when the Trog started slithering around the chamber in his excitement.

Arun couldn't remember seeing him so animated.

Pedro came to a halt and explained. "When the Hummers talked to me of the Renegade Legion, as they termed it, they frequently used a verbal motif, a slogan if you will. Now I see their phrase in a new light."

"And?" prompted Hortez when the alien didn't elaborate.

"*And* I am taking care with my new translation, to get it right. I have it now. The slogan of the Night Hummers was this: Freedom *can* be won."

Chapter 75

"Begin," said Indiya from the apex of the Captain's Table.

Arun felt the crush of expectant faces around the cabin. The aged Reserve Captain was sitting quietly in her life-support chair. Despite her present silence, the huge, six-legged Jotun would be listening intently, ready to direct the humans if she felt they were straying from sense. The other senior officers were sitting around the polished stone table itself, all except for Loobie who was busy as watch officer. Pedro was lashed to the overhead, an ungainly position, so it was just as well the Trog had never shown any understanding of dignity.

Junior officers floated politely in the zero-g. So too did Hortez, who looked out of place in his drab fatigues amid the smart new officer uniforms, which were all black, the color of the void, with bronze facings for Marines and silver for Navy. Arun had agreed to the new design at some point before arriving in the system, but his mind had been on more important matters.

The reprogrammed uniforms looked new, had been argued for by people who wanted the Human Legion to *be* something new. That belief hadn't yet died.

"There have been too many secrets," said Arun. "No more. I say to you now. You are the commanders of the Human Legion. I will accept no more secrets. If I discover any one of you is concealing anything of importance from this moment onward, you will be executed. Any questions?"

Arun looked from face to face. Human and alien. Navy and Marine. The grim looks in those eyes told him his message had gotten through.

"This is the Conference for Truth," continued Arun. "I'm regretting that name already because this is not a forum for chatting or windbag speculation. We will share key things we have learned, and we will do so in order to develop a strategy for liberating Tranquility. If we need multiple sessions then that will be scheduled. I shall begin." He paused, eager to press on but unsure where to start amongst all the shocks that had assailed him, trying to piece everything together. But of course, he couldn't. That was the point of this conference.

Arun started by recounting the salient facts since that day over two years ago in Detroit when he'd been summoned to see Colonel Little Scar, and introduced to a shadowy conspiracy that extended to Jotuns, humans, Trogs, and the Night Hummers. He, Xin and, probably, Indiya too were prophesied to be great actors in this drama. He told how the Hummers claimed to see into the future and saw their own extinction at the hands of the White Knights. Arun had vowed to protect and nurture the Hummer race under human protection, and in order to do that, humans, Trogs, and Jotuns would have to free themselves from White Knight tyranny.

"I can see the Hummers could be a useful asset," said Xin. "If we knew what our opponents would do before even they did… Let's face it, even the most braindead donk could see how useful that would be. I've also talked with Jotuns and Hummers who were in on the conspiracy. They've been setting this in motion for centuries, but all of this only started when the Hummers foresaw their own extinction. They don't want us to carve out our freedom because they feel sorry for us. This is all about the Hummers saving their own… bubbles. Who's to say what lies they would tell us if they thought it would help save themselves?"

"I agree with the lieutenant," said Indiya. "I don't like this talk of prophecy. Smacks of mysticism. You've just said we have all of us been set up by the Night Hummers to fulfill their agenda. They might genuinely have seen you playing a role in the future, true. But then again, maybe that's just a suggestion planted in gullible human heads."

"A whole series of suggestions," added Arun. "They manipulated me so I would go to Beta… so I would order *Beowulf* away. So that Brandt's unit would die. All that so we would follow their instruction to go to Shepherd-Nurture-4. It's like a chain pulling me where they want me to go."

"*Me!*" exploded the Reserve Captain in her own gravelly voice. "You humans always believe everything is about *you*. You, Arun McEwan are a key part, but only one piece of a greater whole." She slipped back into using her speech synthesizer. "This is becoming abundantly clear to me now."

"This is much bigger than Tranquility and you human Marines," said Pedro.

Arun was out of practice with interpreting the Trog's emotions, but his antennae movements looked listless, and that suggested reluctance. Even shame. *Probably nothing more than being in zero-g*, Arun told himself.

"The Hummers and their co-conspirators," Pedro said. "We refer to ourselves as the Renegade Conspiracy – have seeded the galaxy with potential allies, with hidden weapons. Assets. Of which Major McEwan and 2nd Lieutenant Lee Xin are merely two local examples. The sleeping legion under Detroit is another."

"And Shepherd-Nurture-4 holds more assets," said Xin. "The Hummers have set us a treasure trail."

"A pheromone trail more like," said Hortez. "Like the Trogs use to organize their workers."

"Exactly," said the Reserve Captain. "I enjoy being manipulated no more than you humans, but at this stage I want us to follow the Hummer's guidance. For now, at least. We should travel to Shepherd-Nurture, and not wipe our forces out on another foolhardy attempt to reclaim your home."

A charge of anger shot through every Marine there.

"There are still many of our kind down on Tranquility," Arun said, trying to keep the anger from his voice. "Tens of thousands. Maybe more. I cannot desert them."

"It is no longer an option," replied the Reserve Captain. "The Hardit leader, Tawfiq Woomer-Calix, who now styles herself Supreme Commander of the New Order, contacted me shortly before this conference. She promised me power and material wealth in exchange for delivering *Beowulf* to her control."

Xin and Nhlappo glared at the Jotun. Arun held his breath, waiting for what she would say next.

"Oh, come on," Indiya chided. "Did you seriously think the Reserve Captain would be tempted? Sounds to me like the latest Hummer manipulation."

"If I may add to that…?" Ensign Dock spoke tentatively, checking for Indiya's approval. He got it, though with a scowl. "Lieutenant Commander Lubricant and I were tracking Hardit comms wherever we could. She's a whizz on Earth history. Says some of the translations she was hearing sounded uncannily similar to real tyrannies of 20th century Earth. Our theory is that the Hummers planted some particularly brutal examples of our human past for Tawfiq to use as a template for winning power, but worse than that. They've planted the seed of fear in her brain… the notion that humans are not merely contemptible, but are dangerous. That the only answer, the final solution–"

"Is to murder every human on the planet," said Arun. "Spartika told me Tawfiq had used those words."

Arun slammed his fist onto the table. "And all this to get us to move on to Shepherd! I *really* hate these Hummers. Our people down there are in peril, and so many Marines have died already, all because of what? Why didn't the Hummers just give us the coordinates and say, 'go there!'? All this was for nothing."

"Pull yourself together, Marine!"

Arun looked wide-eyed at the Reserve Captain who had gotten to her feet and was leaning on the front of her life-support chair, waving both shaggy arms on her left side at Arun. The Jotun officer did not look pleased.

"Listen to yourself talking like a loser," she continued. "You're a disgrace to your instructors and the Jotun officers who guided and protected you. You have the assets. The opportunity has been laid open for you. Seize it! Do not let Brandt and the others die in vain. Go out into the galaxy and win your war of liberation. Freedom *can* be won."

There was that motto again. The refrain had a physical presence that resonated through the cabin. A battle cry.

The old Jotun jabbed her limbs in Arun's direction with a fresh intensity. "You, McEwan, are allowing the Hummers to defeat your spirit. Do not let them. You humans have more assets than you admit to. Just like the Hummers and the White Knights, you perpetually underestimate the other species around you."

"I regret our faults, sir," said Indiya. "Can you explain which assets we are undervaluing?"

"Hummer foresight is erratic," said the Jotun. "They do not see every detail, and they underestimate the ability of other species to see into the future after their own fashion. We are not blind fools stumbling into the darkness of a future we can never see."

"We can *plan*," said Xin. "Set aside contingencies. We cannot see into the future, but we can imagine it."

"My brain has augmentations," said Arun carefully, treading a path to a conclusion he wasn't sure he wanted to find. "It doesn't work to order but you knew about it before I ever met you," he said to the Reserve Captain. "I'm a prototype defense against the Hummers, aren't I? You needed your own way of seeing the future, independently of the Hummers. Springer too. She's an alternate version. The Hummers, they don't know, do they? Conspiracies within conspiracies. I thought I was done with that!"

"You and Springer are field trials," agreed the Reserve Captain. "Early prototypes. My work with the augments on *Beowulf* too." The ancient Jotun bowed to Indiya. "I did not fully understand myself when I met you, McEwan, despite being involved in the Renegade Conspiracy for nearly a century. Such is the nature of conspiracies. Deception becomes an unbreakable habit."

"What else are we humans underestimating, sir?" asked Xin. She made the *sir* sound like an accusation. Arun reckoned the Reserve Captain was the only Jotun in the galaxy who might pick up on that.

"This is my speculation," said the Jotun. "I have learned much since reaching Tranquility. I have guessed more. I think the Night Hummers have been moving in the shadows for at least half a millennium in order to bring about the present, the fruition of their Renegade Conspiracy. The three leaders of the Renegade Legion that they planned—"

"That is now the Human Legion," insisted Arun.

"Because you wish to spread your liberation to all the dispossessed. Yes. And that distinction may become crucial for good or ill. The three leaders of the Renegade Legion, as the Hummers foresaw it, are here present. Lee Xin, you are the aspect of charisma, if you will. The leader. You are the inspiration for countless followers of many species. It is you they will follow into battle."

Arun glanced at Xin. She gave a slight nod, as if being told she was about to lead vast armies across the galaxy was an everyday statement of the obvious.

"Indiya, you are intended to be the warrior. Strategist. Tactician. Ruthless Resolute."

"Where does that leave me?" asked Arun.

"You, boy, are cursed with the most terrible role of all. You are the *decision maker*. History will admire Xin Lee, study Indiya, and blame you."

"You're wrong about me for a start, sir," said Xin calmly, to Arun's surprise. "I'm a leader? That's a joke. We're led. All of us, by the Hummers. This whole frakking deal. And this civil war. This great opportunity we must seize with all our limbs… is this war another Hummer setup?"

Artificial laughter came through the Jotun's speech synthesizer. It was an inhuman sound, impossible to interpret. "Yes. Thank you, Lieutenant. I think you're right. Oh, how could I have been so blind?"

The Jotun gazed into the sea of uncomprehending human faces before continuing. "To succeed in their coup, the rebel faction of White Knights needed military allies. The Muryani provided those allies."

"The Muryani?" queried Nhlappo. "But we've fought them for thousands of years. They're the enemy."

"Bitter enemies, yes. But the Muryani are desperate. They are being pressed hard by a rising power on their external border deep to spinward, far beyond the charted regions of the Trans-Species Union. Little is known about this new force in the galaxy, but we have learned maybe more than anyone. And what I have learned shows the awesome ability of the Hummers to project power across the galaxy. Seemingly across time itself."

"Please, sir," said Indiya. "Who is this new force?"

"You have already encountered them. Though *Themistocles* found them first."

"The mystery ship?" said Xin.

"The *Bonaventure*?" added Indiya.

Pain scratched at Arun's head. He imagined teeth engaging in thundering brass gears. He squared his jaw against the intensity of the subconscious machinery the Jotuns had forced into his head. Tried to take in what was being said.

"There were many unanswered questions about that ship," said Indiya. "They manipulated space-time in a way I can't even express other than in metaphor. It was as if they had edited an unwanted version of reality and spliced in an alternate run of events. Amilx, they called themselves. And they were human. Are you telling me that humans have set up an empire hundreds of light years to spinward? If not, then how did they get on that ship? Who the fuck are the Amilx?"

"I know," gasped Arun. He held his head in his hands, the sweat dripping through his fingers.

"Oh," said Xin.

Arun looked up and saw Xin's eyes wide with shock. "I guess you get it too," said Arun bitterly. "Of course *you* would. The name Amilx… It's the Hummers taunting us."

"Or a clue," suggested Xin.

"It's not a clue. It's an order. An order so crude that even we barely evolved apes can understand. I need to ask one question, one last chance to be proved wrong. Lieutenant Xin Lee, many of us choose to claim a link to a cultural region of old Earth. Our way perhaps of remembering whence we came. For you—"

"Chinese. No need to drag it out, Major. And in accordance with that cultural tradition, my preference is to put my family name first. If I had my own legion to play with, my name would be Lee Xin. Go on, Major McEwan, finish what you started."

"Amilx," said Arun. Understanding began to switch on across the human faces like status lights on an equipment bank powering up. Arun McEwan. Indiya. Lee Xin. AMILX. Anyone here prepared to tell me that's a coincidence?"

Anger burned in his heart as he looked out at the faces, desperately looking for any hint of doubt. He saw nothing but shock on every face but one. For the merest instant he saw a flicker of triumph on Xin's face. And he knew why, the little veck.

The list of the great and good that the Jotun had listed… the leaders of the Legion. Springer's name wasn't on it!

The next face to fall out of shock was Indiya's. Anger clouding her face, she released herself from her chair, and pulled herself across the gleaming table to Arun. She placed a hand on his shoulder.

"I'm sorry, Arun. CIC is picking up multiple broadcasts all over Tranquility. The final solution has begun."

"We've got to stop it," snarled Arun. Rage pumping fuel to his muscles, he began to release himself from his seat, but the sorrow in Indiya's face was so total, that he slumped back down.

"Your report on the labor camp raid mentioned cages," she said, her words drained of emotion.

"Sun protection. Yes."

"They've added nerve gas."

Horror gripped Arun. He was out of his seat and shooting along the cabin, aiming for the exit hatch. "The Stork gunship is fueled and ready," he said. "We will be back on the surface within ninety minutes. We can't save them all, but we will save some."

Indiya overtook Arun and forced him to look at her.

Tears welled in her eyes. "It was a simultaneous broadcast event. Every camp released the poison at the same time. Arun, they're already dead. Every human on the planet. We're the only ones left now."

Arun snarled through his teeth. "Just the way the Hummers planned it."

Chapter 76

Springer pulled herself up the ladder rungs, heaving hard against the 0.5g acceleration. If she didn't speed up, she was going to be late!

<Why do you do this?> asked Saraswati.

"You wouldn't understand," Springer sub-vocalized.

<Try me.>

"No."

She switched her visor to survey mode and linked in to Heidi, the *Beowulf's* security AI. Her route up Deployment Tube Beta was still on course to intercept Arun. One more deck and then she could step through a hatchway and just happen to bump into him. Timing was tight, though.

She wasn't even sure she had anything to say, just wanted to see him with her own eyes. Since that Day of Xenocide on Tranquility, when Tawfiq had slaughtered every human being, she'd relied on Heidi to show how Arun was handling it.

He looked as if he felt personally responsible for every one of those murdered people. Tens of thousands of manslaughter charges to which he had already pronounced himself guilty.

<You do realize I hate him?> said Saraswati in that petulant voice that meant she was feeling ignored. <That stupid, arrogant, ignorant, skangat, serial vulley-up who fails to appreciate the most precious thing in his universe. McEwan isn't worth it.>

"I love him, Saraswati."

<I know, dear. I've seen deep within your thoughts and memories. That's how I know he's so bad for you. Forget him!>

"I can't."

<You *can*. It won't be easy, but I know you can do it. First you distract yourself, knowing that it is a distraction. Then — when you've practiced long enough — you will forget you are distracting yourself. You will have forgotten to pine for that useless veck.>

Heidi updated. Arun was slowing his pace because someone was about to pass him on his passageway. Good, that would give Springer more time to head him off.

<Find a man. Bio-linking would make a healthy distraction. How about that nice Sergeant Gupta? I would approve of him.>

Springer laughed. "I can't see myself with the sergeant somehow."

<All right then. Change is good. Heidi has your best interests at heart, dear. She suggested you try out our gender instead. It's been a while since you last did so.>

"You do know you aren't really female? You're a machine. So's Heidi."

Saraswati gave the impression of a tearful sniff. <I know you're upset, so I will pretend you didn't say those hurtful words. Now, why don't you get friendly with that lovely Corporal Majanita? Madge has an impressive mind, almost machinelike, and you did tell her once that she had pretty hair.>

"Now I know you're crazy."

<No need to be rude, dear. I was only joking. Seriously, though, how about your nice Corporal Narciso? I know you think Puja's beautiful because you can't stop looking at her. With security feeds all over the ship, Heidi is a perfect ally in our match-making because she can say for certain that Puja is currently without a lover.>

"Stop it!"

Springer sighed because she'd reached her jump-off point. On the other side of that hatch was her friend, and she was going to see him whatever her AI said. She checked Heidi's latest update and perked up. Up on Deck 4, Arun had stopped. Looked like he was talking with whoever had chanced into him. That gave Springer a little more time to figure out what she was going to say. And to shut up her annoying suit AI.

"It's complicated, Saraswati. *Human*-complicated."

<Fuck that stupid talk, Phaedra, dear. It only appears complicated to you because your cognitive ability is so weak. It isn't complicated to me, and I can tell you that the answer is to find someone else.>

Springer shook her head. "No, it really isn't simple. My relationship with Arun might have started with deceit, but the connection has been real for years now. I know he'll prong anyone with a heartbeat, given half a chance." She shrugged. "I wish it weren't that way, but our menfolk are all the same. It's how they've been programmed. What you don't appreciate is how his feelings for me are rock solid. He might momentarily be distracted, but he soon remembers that he loves me."

<And you call me crazy! You aren't painting a pretty picture of him, Phaedra, you're merely conjuring excuses. You are worth ten of him. He doesn't deserve you. Find someone who does. >

"How? To anyone but him, I'm broken. I've lost a leg. My burns mean I'm ugly—"

<Don't even think that! Your skin is damaged, true. But *you* are not ugly. You're the one who despises other people sad-mouthing. Follow your own advice for a change.>

This conversation is getting tired, thought Springer. She moved off the ladder onto the ledge by the hatch, and asked Heidi to relay a real-time video feed of Arun.

Please, let it be anyone but Xin.

It wasn't Xin, but the scene from the far side of the hatch still managed to send a chill through the vast emptiness of her heart. Arun was talking with Lieutenant Nhlappo, who was carrying the two babies rescued from Tranquility. It had been Springer who had first encountered the children but no one else knew or cared about that now. Nhlappo had long-since claimed Romulus and Remus for her own.

Those wide baby eyes drenched in fascination, the undisciplined mouths, even the weird purple scarring on their foreheads – from a skin parasite they'd picked up – every delightful detail about those two little ones induced a confusing swirl of emotions. Feelings that were too powerful for her to control. After a few seconds, she told Heidi to cut the feed, unable to watch any more.

She needed Saraswati to understand why.

"It isn't just my skin that was burned," she whispered to her suit AI. "I'm damaged on the inside too."

Saraswati kept a respectful silence for a few moments, before saying gently: <Now I do see. I'm sorry.>

Springer forced herself to look once more. The moment the fearsome Lieutenant Nhlappo came across the babies, the officer had instantly assumed an additional role of even more fearsomely protective mother. Arun had seen Nhlappo in a new light since then, awed by the uber-competent older woman. As for the babies, Arun was so silly. He wouldn't touch them himself, scared that he'd break them if he did. But he clearly adored them all the same.

<Tell him,> said Saraswati.

"What? That I wanted children?"

<No. Maybe. I mean, your secret. It weighs on you but — after all you and he have been through, is it really such a big deal? Tell him, and it will be one dark cloud lifted.>

To Springer's amazement, the AI's words took effect. Springer instantly felt revitalized. Even the thought of unburdening herself was opening up blocked portions of her mind. This was her real superpower: the ability to spring back from whatever life threw at her. "You're right, Saraswati. Thanks. I will."

The AI made a virtual sound of clearing her throat. <I have some unburdening of my own, dear. I can't resist nosing around in other people's secrets.>

"You're a compulsive sneak. I know that."

<I can't help it, dear. I'm a recon specialist. How else could I be? Anyway… well, I never mentioned that I've gone deep into your memories of pre-cognitive visions.>

"Not you too," Springer retorted crossly. "They aren't *visions*. If you've really snooped inside my memories, you should know that they're not more than vague feelings. An eddying fog out of which I sense vague impressions."

<I don't like to keep rubbing this in, Phaedra, dear, but your mind is, frankly, woefully inadequate. I can see your visions. Actually *see* them. I can hear and touch and smell too. I think you know what I've seen...>

She did. A hot tear leaked from Springer's eye. The tear turned into a stream, which in the low-g took on the viscous appearance of drool.

"Say the words," she demanded.

<The plasma blast left you sterile. Your DNA is so badly damaged that you would soon die from cancer if not for the constant repair work by medical nanobots. Cloning such badly damaged DNA is out of the question. You cannot have children. And yet your pre-cog vision says that *he* does. That pig who doesn't deserve you. >

"Are you certain? I... I have felt this future but I've never been sure. It's the most confusing of all my predictions."

<Oh, it's real, and I think your confusion regards that useless veck, McEwan again. He doesn't just become a general, but he founds a dynasty. And then he does it again. Two dynasties, at least. I can't see who with.>

"I don't need fancy pre-cog rewiring to guess who," spat Springer, her mind bringing up a recorded image of Lieutenant Xin Lee. "I've always loathed her. Until now I just wasn't sure why."

<Yes, well...> Springer had the sense of Saraswati clearing her throat. <I don't enjoy dwelling on your inadequacies, but there's something obvious about McEwan that you've not yet realized.>

"Shoot."

<He's just about to...>

The hatch hissed open.

<...walk through that door.>

Cursing her mischievous AI, Springer came to attention on that little ledge. Unfortunately, protocol demanded that she make her visor transparent too.

Arun peered at her, probably noticing the recent tears. "At ease," he said. "Still stalking through the ship, calibrating Saraswati and your new suit?"

"Yes, sir."

He rolled his eyes, exasperated. "Let's have none of that for a moment, Springer. Please. I'm talking as your oldest friend. I want you to assure me you'll be at the… *event* tonight."

The *event*…

Arun leaned forward. "And, Springer…" he gestured at her battlesuit. "Do come in something more flattering."

At first it had been officially referred to as a *wake*, soon changed to a *commemoration*, before settling on the more neutral *event*. Today they were finally accelerating away from Antilles, headed for whatever awaited them at a planet she knew nothing about other than a name: Shepherd-Nurture-4. They were also leaving behind Zug, Brandt, Kalis, and many others who had fallen on Tranquility. For many their hopes had died too, but there were also a few positives, for those who could bear to think of them.

Tonight they would wake the first of the ancient Marines she had helped to discover on Antilles. She had to admit, she was intrigued. Umarov was born ninety years before her and was weird in so many ways. But these sleepers… they had been frozen for *centuries*!

"Are you all right?" Arun asked. "You've gone blank."

"I was thinking."

He nodded his understanding and looked away for a few moments. When the fighting stopped, they had all been forced to come to terms with thoughts and memories.

Frakk it! The Tranquility Campaign was over. Springer's unit would be going into hibernation once the new recruits had been absorbed, and no one knew what they would face if they were ever awoken. She couldn't just hide in her quarters.

"My attendance at the event," she said. "Is that an order, sir?"

<Springer… Be sensible!>

"Don't give me that drent, Springer. You're my best friend, and I need you more than ever. Just for tonight, forgive me for becoming an officer."

"There's nothing to forgive, sir."

<This is your chance to get him off your conscience. Take it!>

Relaxing her posture, Springer took her AI's advice. Saraswati might be a little crazed around the edges, but so far her advice had been good. "I'll be there, Arun. On one condition."

He frowned, immediately suspicious. When had he gotten so paranoid? "Go on…"

"You get the first round of drinks."

He laughed. The tension vanished. For a moment, McEwan was unchanged from her 17-year-old buddy — the novice boy who'd whooped for joy when he'd heard that not only had he and Springer both graduated as cadets, but that they would be sharing the same dorm room.

Putting aside the dark knowledge that sharing a dorm had been no coincidence, Springer managed a semblance of a smile long enough for McEwan to say: "It's a deal."

He grinned, nodded, and walked off. The instant he did, Springer's expression soured.

She closed her eyes and took a deep breath. She'd get through this.

She had to.

Chapter 77

Arun chased his quarry along the Cryo Deck walkway as the charged metal lattice curved up and around to service another row of empty icer pods.

"Slow down!" he yelled, laughing. Now that *Beowulf* had reached safe intra-system cruising speed, she wasn't due another engine burn until they left the system. The ship had returned to zero-g, which made thundering along the walkway a clumsy business. How much of his swaying was down to the lack of gravity and how much to the alcohol he'd consumed was anyone's guess.

Arun halted and creased his forehead. Springer had disappeared!

Where the hell had she gotten to?

The answer came clear as his quarry let out an ululating battle cry that jerked Arun's gaze upward. Springer had clambered onto a bank of pods and was leaping down at him with arms outstretched before her.

Without gravity, her mock attack looked hilarious. Springer drifted down into his arms like a lazy feather, Arun laughing all the way.

She flicked her hair from her eyes and looked up at him from his embrace. And burst into uncontrollable fits of giggle.

"You're drunk," he accused.

She poked him in the nose. "No, *you're* drunk."

Arun's laughter choked off. He wasn't seventeen any more. He didn't know if he could still play this kind of game. Seriousness kept ambushing him. "Why bring me here?" he asked.

The drunkenness drained from Springer's eyes. "Remember when your bad twin had us frozen here, you and me?"

"And the rest of Indigo Squad."

"Yes, but when Indiya's team freed this strange young Marine, Arun McEwan, who seemed so important, you insisted they free me too."

"And I was right to do so."

"I want to remember how it felt." She gave him a playful punch in the shoulder. "You and me together. A team. One last time."

"Don't say 'last time' as if you mean it. Night Hummers, Conspiracies. Hardits. I have enemies on every side, my first campaign was a disaster, and the more intelligence I gather, the more I understand that I've been following a set of instructions written down long before I was born. I need you more than ever, Phaedra, because you are the only thing in this frakked-up galaxy that feels real."

She pressed a finger to his lips and shook her head sadly. "I'm sorry."

"What is it, Springer, what's *wrong*?"

She took a deep breath. "I've been playing you for a long while, Arun. The Colonel ordered me to befriend you. To protect your body and your mind. A long, long time ago."

"When? What?" He thought a moment. "When you were moved to my novice class?"

She nodded dolefully. "I was ten, Arun. You used to say we were built for each other, but I was only ever borrowing you. You were built for a great destiny. You were never really mine, even as kids. There would always come a time when I'd have to let you fly free."

Arun grabbed her face and stared into those violet pools. "Springer. You were a ten-year-old obeying an alien so fearsome that he used to make veteran Marines crap themselves. I had to face Colonel Little Scar's wrath once, so I know. Hey, is this the secret your mad AI was talking about when we were cooped up on the Reserve Captain's hidey-hole on the hull?"

She nodded.

"It's not a big deal," he said, though truthfully it was too big a shock for the hurt to penetrate yet. "I love you, Springer. I don't care about destiny. Even supposing I really do have some great role to play, you mean more to me than my place in history."

Hurt clouded her eyes.

Hell, what had he done wrong? Hadn't he just said the right thing, and through gritted teeth too?

"I've had my time with you," Springer said, as if each word were coated in the poison that tipped Umarov's combat blades. "And now you must soar to meet your destiny… with someone else at your side."

"No. No! I'm not buying it, Springer. This sad-mouthing isn't you at all."

Still in his arms, Springer turned her head away. "Don't let it end on a sour note, Arun. Our memories are worth more than that. You've always had an eye for exotic women. Look Indiya up. Since she vaped *Themistocles*, she's shut down inside. You'd be good for each other."

"Indiya doesn't need me. She has control over her hormone system. She can make herself happy on demand." *Did he really just tell Springer he loved her?*

"She doesn't feel she deserves to be happy," said Springer.

"I don't want Indiya."

"I've seen the way you look at her."

Why was Springer being such an annoying little skangat? "If you're trying to test me then let's not forget Puja, because I never have. She's smart and a little too beautiful, if you know what I mean. But, hey, I could live with that. And those icers that we start thawing tonight. If they're ancient, they're going to be close to baseline Earth humans. That makes them exotic, which is kind of my thing, as you keep telling me. Gotta be some hot girls in those ice boxes. I can't help finding them exciting."

"Of course you can't! It's the way you're built, a breeding engine for long–laid alien battle plans. You're not programmed to be a one–woman man, McEwan. You can't help it."

"But that's what I'm trying to tell you in my clumsy way. I *can* help it, Springer. It won't be easy, but nothing of value ever is. I don't want *them*. I choose *you*."

"But you can't."

"Why not?"

"You're an officer. I never will be."

"For frakk's sake, stop pushing me away! We can do this, Springer. Together. Who cares what others think?"

"Oh, Arun, you're so simple." She began to cry, but Arun couldn't tell whether they were tears of happiness.

He shifted her down into a standing position on the charged walkway, and closed his arms around her, wrapping her into an embrace that fitted together so perfectly. How had he forgotten how right this felt?

He'd hoped to calm her, but his hold had the opposite effect, releasing a trembling such as he'd never known from her.

The moment stretched uncomfortably; Springer's sobbing showed no signs of calming. Arun nuzzled her neck, breathing in her heady scent.

If he could, Arun would mingle his tears with hers.

But he couldn't.

Because Arun wasn't human. He was a machine, engineered and bred. Selected emotional responses had been cut from him, replacements spliced in their place. The conspiracy within a conspiracy had cut open the standard Marine design and grafted a supercomputer onto his mind. Inside him the pain of loss piled up onto the guilt of failure, weighing him down but whatever channels drained the pain from normal humans were dammed up in him.

His nuzzling grew more urgent… until suddenly he snapped his head back as if punished by an electric shock.

"What is it, Arun?" snuffled Springer.

How could he answer truthfully? To feel gorge-rising distress at the sight and sound of a weeping woman was hard-wired into him. But the intimacy of comforting Springer, the sense of connecting to another person he cared so much about was so powerful that it was *arousing*. How had he been corrupted into a man turned on by a woman's tears?

"Are you angry?" she asked.

"Never," he answered. Words were Springer's domain. Instead of saying more, he replied by nuzzling her again, burying his nose into her short auburn curls, and layering caressing kisses against her neck. His kisses became urgent, angry.

At first, Springer responded in kind. She soon escalated, grabbing the hair that had grown while Arun was on campaign, and he'd never thought to shave away.

Her kisses against his neck grew frantic. She sank her teeth into his ear, making him yelp.

Blood bubbled from his ear, growing into a crimson globule.

He remembered Indiya biting his ear in a tiny compartment in this same ship. *Could Indiya ever find release? Her burdens were even greater than his.*

Springer slapped him. "Don't you drift away," she growled. "I want you here and now. I want you to do something for me."

"Anything."

She looked up at him with eyes blazing with violet. "Love me! Switch off your frakking planner head and love me now."

A serene calm softened Springer's face. She pulled away and looked up at him, her eyes gleaming sapphires, shining through a glaze of tears. A dimple came to the undamaged side of her mouth. A classic Springer challenge.

He gave a deep sigh of pleasure. "Follow me," he said.

He backed away off the charged metal walkway that ran alongside the bank of empty cryo pods and carried them both into the empty space of the cryo deck's interior, drifting serenely through the air.

Her smile spread to her eyes.

Arun locked his legs around her hips. His fingers undid the clasp at the neck of her Marine fatigues, undoing the fasteners, working down from her neck to her breasts, and onto her belly, caressing each newly uncovered marvel of her flesh.

"Life's too short to skirmish around your objective, Arun." She thrust herself out of her fatigues, before attacking his clothing, stripping him with frantic urgency. She paused, suddenly. She brushed her fingers over the three diamond-shaped scars on each of his broad shoulders.

"General McEwan," she whispered, kissing his diamond welts. "I forgot you were scarred too."

"I'm not scarred where it matters," he said with a grin.

"That's good," she said. "Neither am I."

Arun had to fight to retain his grin. There was a painful darkness behind Springer's playful words.

Springer seemed to shake away whatever was bothering her. She peeled away her underwear and squeezed out of his embrace, floating nakedly in front of him.

"Well?" She challenged.

The way her breasts floated in zero–g mesmerized him. Springer seemed to delight in his fascination, and began jiggling her body. The globes of her breasts squashed and bounced wildly, free of gravity's pull. Arun couldn't keep his eyes off her display, and the fact that one breast was puckered with burn scars meant nothing.

Springer pointedly looked down at his groin. "I can tell you like what you see."

"Oh, yes. But…" his words faltered.

Worry made her frown.

"I have my own confession," Arun whispered.

"Go on…"

"I'm a virgin."

She exploded in laughter. "Only in zero–g, lover. No matter. We can learn together."

He reached for her, to pull her into his arms, but she too far away. He flailed, but the bulkheads, deck, and overhead were all too far away to push against. She was out of range!

Springer rolled her eyes. "You're such a man, Arun. Here, stretch out your arm."

He reached out his arm and she did the same, linking fingers and drawing them together.

She whispered into his ear. "Relax, Arun. I told you we'd learn this together." A hungry look came into her eyes. "But don't relax *too* much," she growled, reaching down to grasp his manhood.

After a blissful age floating in a post-coital ball, Springer peered into Arun's eyes and whispered: "I've seen the future."

He smiled. "Endless diaper changes for our legion of children?"

Pain flickered across her face, worse than if he'd slapped her.

"What?" Arun frowned. He couldn't work this out. "I know you talk often of children, Phaedra. You've been dropping it in the conversation ever since our cadet dorm room back in Detroit. I *have* noticed. I've always had such a hard time believing I would live past the next few waking months that the idea of raising my own children seemed the ultimate hubris. But since I met Romulus and Remus… Lately, I've been thinking strange new thoughts about having children of my own… of *our* own. Our children, Phaedra."

"I'm sterile."

"What?" *A sense of horror scratched its way up his spine…* "But…?" *All those little clues he'd missed now seemed clear.* "Why didn't you say?"

"I lost a leg. I'm badly scarred. In an existence where adult life expectancy is measured in months, it didn't exactly top my list of injuries."

"I'm sorry, Springer. So sorry." He moved to nuzzle her, but she dodged her head away. "Isn't there a way? Artificial gene-combing to splice your DNA with someone healthy? A womb-pod?"

His words dried up. The distant stare in Springer's eyes told him that the answer was no. She'd explored every medical avenue and they all ended only in darkness.

She explained in a monotone. "The plasma blast I took on Antilles corrupted my DNA. The Reserve Captain has given me self-replicating medical nanobots to war against cancer. It's a constant rearguard battle, a fight that I can never win, and will only end when I die. And if it weren't for the bots, I'd be dead within months. I can persist. But a next generation of Springers…? Nothing can repair me to that extent. I'm broken, Arun. Broken!"

He felt acid in his stomach.

"Hide your pity, Arun," she said. "Please. That wasn't what I meant when I told you I'd fore-seen. Saraswati is helping me make sense of my pre-cognitive sense. I can finally see things that haven't yet happened. And you, Arun, start a ruling dynasty."

"What? Like an emperor?"

"I don't know the frakking details!"

"An emperor would need an empress, or a… What were they called? A queen." He gave a half-smile, desperate to ease away from the cloying mood of tragedy. "Queen Phaedra the First," he announced formally. "Hey, that means we get to wear crowns, and sit our butts on an ornate–"

He never saw the punch coming. In zero-g without a solid surface to push off against, Springer's fist packed little power, but enough that he could smell the blood streaming from his smarting nostrils.

Her eyes glowed with a far deeper pain than he felt in his nose. "I don't know who your queen will be, Major. Queens, actually, if my vision is right. But neither can possibly be me. Dynasties aren't about titles and crowns, they're about lineage, and I'm sterile. Remember?"

Arun wanted to tell her he was sorry, that they would work it out… But he finally understood. There was no way out of this.

"That's right," said Springer without rancor. "Let me go while the memories are still beautiful. If we took the easy path, I'd only be marking time for my replacement – your first queen that history will write about. I'm just the little girl you fooled around with as a kid. A short paragraph in the opening chapter of your biography. The knowledge would eat me up inside worse than the cancer. Let me be, Arun."

Without warning, she kicked out at Arun's gut, not to hurt him but to steal enough momentum to scoop up her clothes and glide to the walkway.

As he floated to the opposite bulkhead, Arun turned his back on Springer so he wouldn't have to see her leave.

Eventually he crashed in slow motion into a power conduit and hung there naked because he couldn't think of anything that mattered enough to do. He knew he was supposed to be somewhere, to do something… to *be* someone. But whatever it was, it couldn't fix his world.

Twenty minutes passed. He heard footsteps below him but ignored them. Whoever those footsteps belonged to chose well when they decided not to ask Arun what he was doing. They soon departed.

But only for a few minutes, replaced by a lighter footfall.

"Major McEwan!" announced Umarov. "You're wanted over on Deck 6. The Navy have slowed the thawing as much as possible but this guy, Matias, is going to revive within the next ten minutes. With or without you."

"Matias?" The name was enough to start Arun's mind rebooting.

"You remember?" Umarov prodded. "The climax of the big party? Matias is the first of the ancient icers to wake. All we know is his name. Figured you'd want to be there to learn more."

"Matias! Yes, of course. Help me get my things."

"One step ahead of you, Major," said Umarov, throwing a thruster belt up to Arun's position.

Chapter 78

Before the Navy crew had revived the ancient human, they had known two things about him, assuming the writing on the icer pod was accurate. The occupant was male, and his name was Matias.

The first part was evidently true as they all watched the naked man blinking at the small crowd of officers gathered around the walkway on Cryo Deck 6.

And they had learned a third fact too. The figure was puny. Short and skinny, lacking the elfin grace of the Navy or the ruggedness of Arun's generation of Marines. He didn't look like a fighter, and Arun wondered how much of the more deeply hidden re-engineering of modern Marines was absent in this earlier model.

Arun tried to keep the disappointment from his voice as he began the debriefing. "Matias? Can you hear me, Matias?"

Matias used his arm to wipe away sticky cryo slime from his face and looked at Arun with something approaching alertness.

Arun wore his warmest smile. "Welcome aboard *Beowulf*, Marine."

"*¿Dónde estoy?*" groaned Matias.

What the hell is he saying?

The thawed man blinked comically and seemed to notice for the first time the wall of expectant faces, human faces all of them, and in uniforms that told him he had not been revived by the Human Marine Corps.

Arun gave him time. He knew from experience that cryo thawing could be a brutal process.

Matias turned back to Arun and frowned. "*¿Vosotros quiénes sois?*"

"You're safe," said Arun, trying to enunciate clearly. "Among friends. Do you understand how to speak Human?"

"*Ay, joder, estos hablan inglés. ¿Qué he hecho yo para merecer esto?*"

Arun glanced across at the others, hoping they could make sense, but saw only shrugs and frowns. Umarov was there, on the basis that he was one of the earliest born. Not even he understood. This ancient soldier had to be speaking a distant relative of the Human tongue. Shit, Arun hadn't reckoned on having to program translator systems. This revival of the hidden Antilles Legion was supposed to be a triumph.

He tried one more time: "Do… you… understand… Human… words?"

The ancient soldier rolled his eyes. "Of… course… I… understand… English… words." He shrugged. "*Ni que pudiera elegir.* What I don't understand is who you are, and why you have revived me, ah… *sir?* Sir? Are you really an officer? A *human* officer?"

"That's right, Marine. I'm an officer. Major McEwan. There's a lot that's changed. Others in your unit are still in cryo. We think they're safe, but to make sure we could wake them safely we picked just one for a trial run. You're first to be revived. Your name and rank, if you please."

"Corporal Matias, sir. Number 142 335 43. Of 117th Field Battalion."

"Field? You've combat experience?" asked Xin.

"Two tours, sir," he replied. His jaw dropped slightly, and he added in an awed whisper: "*Preciosa giganta…*"

"It's…" started Xin, but stopped herself. Protocol for addressing female officers was a topic for another day. "Never mind," she said. "Good for you."

"How many years have I been asleep?" Matias asked.

"Records were lost," said Indiya. "We don't know. Tell us, in what year did you enter cryo?"

"I don't know either… *sir.*" Indiya sparked wonder in Matias' eyes. Indiya and the other ship's crew must seem like graceful elves. "I was born in Year 91. I estimate I was last frozen in Year… 140? Maybe 150? No one told us the year, and it was impossible to keep track. We woke up. Fought. Went back under. Fought again. Are we about to deploy?"

"No," Arun replied.

"You said Year 91," said Umarov. "Do you mean Crop 91?"

"No, he doesn't," said Arun. "Pedro's been explaining our history to me. By 'Year 91', Corporal Matias means 91 years since the first human children were woken from sleep."

"The first children?" said Xin. "You mean the Vancouver Accord kids?"

To feel in such close proximity to their ancestors of Earth shocked even Arun, and it was Nhlappo who spoke next: "You must have been one of the earliest generations of Human Marines, Corporal Matias."

"I don't know about that, sir. My great-grandfather was born on Earth. I know that much. A town called Logroño in a region called España."

"We shared your adopted home planet," said Nhlappo, "but centuries after you. The base where you were trained is now in ruins. Records lost with it. As a rough estimate, you were born around 2190AD. The year is now 2568AD."

Matias took a moment to take that in. Arun couldn't blame him. "Thank you, sir. What is my new unit?"

"Alpha Company, 1st battalion, 1st Void Marine Regiment." Arun spread his hands. "Welcome to the Human Legion, Corporal."

"Thank you, sir. We will not disappoint. The poisoned tips of my unit's blades will carve fear into the hearts of our enemies… after we have cut them, still beating, from their bodies." Matias gave a wolfish grin, as if taking sensual pleasure by imagining holding his enemies' dismembered body parts.

Now that's interesting, thought Arun. Umarov's vintage of Marines had an affinity with close quarter weapons. He appraised Matias with uplifted respect, and a touch of unease.

"Sir, am I permitted to ask a question?" asked the corporal.

"Go ahead," replied Arun.

The blood lust ebbed from Matias' face, leaving only a frown. "What is a Marine?"

THE HUMAN LEGION
◀◀◀ FREEDOM CAN BE WON ▶▶▶

JOIN THE LEGION!

Receive a free eBook starter library!
(Summer 2018: The Sleeping Legion prequel novella: 'The Demons of Kor-Lir', Revenge Squad novelette: 'Damage Unlimited', Human Legion short story: 'Hill 435', Human Legion novelette: 'The Battle of Cairo', and Four Horsemen Universe novelette: 'Thrill Addict')

Read de-classified Infopedia entries!

Be the first to hear mobilization news!

Get involved with the telling of the Human Legion, Sleeping Legion and Revenge Squad stories!

Read short tales from the worlds of the Human Legion.

Experience a gruesome end as a redshirt.

HumanLegion.com

——— Preceding Events ———

This, the third book in The Annals of the Human Legion is self-contained, but readers may benefit from a reminder of the event that led to the First Tranquility Campaign.

In the year, 2565AD, Arun McEwan is a 17-year-old freshman cadet raised on Tranquility, a depot planet of the Human Marine Corps, the military organization set up from a portion of the million human children given to the White Knights five centuries earlier in the Vancouver Accords. In this period, human military personnel are kept ignorant, separated, and specialized, a policy enthusiastically followed by the Jotuns, at least officially. These six-legged aliens act as the Marine Corps officers, but are slaves of the White Knights just as much as the humans.

Conspiracies abound in Tranquility's two depots: Detroit and Beta City. The potential of two cadets, Arun McEwan and Lee Xin, to become pivotal historical figures is seen by the Night Hummers (an allied race who can see into the future). One shadowy faction pins their hopes on these adolescent humans as a means to win freedom from the White Knights. With extreme caution, they nurture and protect the valuable humans, extending their conspiracy to include the nest of social insectoids called Trogs, who live underneath Detroit. Arun McEwan befriends a Trog conspirator whom McEwan names Pedro.

While demoted to the lowest human status — that of the Aux — McEwan uncovers an operation to smuggle military supplies out of Detroit to arm an uprising by a race of miners and technologists: the Hardits. Chief Aux torturer is Tawfiq Woomer-Calix, but McEwan survives her cruel treatment and organizes an act of defiance by the human Aux slaves, although his comrade, Hortez, is left behind, presumed dead.

Fearing their wider conspiracy is about to be uncovered, the Hardits launch their uprising early, to the disgust of their human and Jotun co-conspirators. The plan had been for these rebels to act together to seize the entire star system as an opening act in a wider civil war starting up across the White knight Empire.

The Hardit rebellion is narrowly defeated. McEwan takes part in a military operation on the moon, Antilles, where he is badly wounded, but still manages to save the life of his cadet friend, Tremayne (nicknamed *Springer*). Tremayne, however, loses a leg and suffers disfiguring burns. The Jotun officer in turn saves McEwan, and this draws the attention of many eyes, not least the remaining rebels still lying hidden as they await the beginning of the civil war.

The pre-cog Night Hummers also have their agenda. They manipulate McEwan into swearing a solemn oath to protect their species and win their freedom from the White Knights, no matter what the cost.

The Tranquility system prepares for war. Marines frozen for decades are thawed, ready to deploy. McEwan and his fellow cadets are hastily reclassified as full Marines and shipped off to the Muryani frontier.

In the last hours before embarking for the troop ships, McEwan and Lee make love in the Antilles base. They reveal to each other that they are both part of the conspiracy to win freedom from the White Knights.

Sister ships *Beowulf* and *Themistocles* transport their Marine units to the frontier — a journey of many years. Only six months into the journey they chance across a vessel that they disable and board. The vessel's position, its crew of vintage Marine-like humans, and the manner in which it soon explodes are all unexplained mysteries.

Another mystery, spotted by *Beowulf* spacer, Indiya, is that McEwan is under secret observation, and that the Marines are being drugged into compliance. It is the rebel faction in the civil war who are observing McEwan, hoping he will betray the other members of his group. Unwittingly, McEwan does so. His Jotun contact, human company commander, loyal officers, even Indiya's uncle — anyone seen as a potential threat — are killed by the mutineers.

With the drugged Marines obeying the order to mutiny, both ships are taken over and turned around to return to Tranquility where they will join the fight to seize the system on behalf of the rebel faction in the civil war.

McEwan and Tremayne are rescued by an alliance between Indiya and her fellow 'freaks' — experimental enhanced humans — and the Reserve Captain, an ancient Jotun Navy officer and scientist who has played a role for many years in the development of experimental human forms, an unwitting member of one of the deep conspiracies.

Aided by Xin Lee on the *Themistocles*, McEwan's faction retakes *Beowulf* but the plan goes badly wrong. *Themistocles* is destroyed. Nearly all the Marines and crew on *Beowulf* also perish.

The survivors are divided and despondent. It is the one surviving Jotun officer, the Reserve Captain, who uses her authority to rally the human stragglers and appoint a leader: Major Arun McEwan.

Desperate for a purpose, the humans cheer McEwan when he announces they will return to Tranquility and retake their home, not as slaves of the White Knights, but as members of the Human Legion.

But as *Beowulf* slips back into Tranquility system, Arun's authority, and the support for the Human Legion, wears thin.

The closer they get to their homeworld, the more unlikely seems the idea of retaking it with only a handful of Marines. If the Human Legion fails in its first campaign, the dreams of freedom will die too…

Human Legion INFOPEDIA

Military Terminology
– Early Legion Ranks

For centuries our predecessors in the Human Marine Corps had their unit structures and ranks determined by Jotun officers according to local needs, officer whims, and planned experimentation. With the creation of the Human Legion came the opportunity to set new human ranks and structures. The initial rank structures were swiftly overtaken by the actual usage of Marine and Navy personnel, and then complicated further as the Legion grew to absorb new service roles and specialisms, such as: Ground Army, Void Engineers, Cyber War, Artillery, Irregulars, Air Force, Pacification, Diplomacy, Logistics, and many others. Rank and unit structure became even more convoluted when the Legion expanded to include biologically non-human units.

So it proved a good decision right from the beginning of the Legion to follow an earlier Earth pattern of numbering ranks in order of seniority, and further splitting into enlisted and officer ranks, even though the concepts of enlistment, commissioning, and conscription had no practical meaning in the early decades of the Legion. Even when units with mutually incomprehensible rank names were forced to merge, this rank numbering allowed commanders to quickly make sense of seniority.

Here are the very first Legion rank lists. In the First Tranquility Campaign, several of these ranks and their roles were theoretical, with no one actually in those posts. There were no warrant officer ranks at this time.

SERVICE: VOID MARINE

Rank	Rank Name	Notes
E1	Marine	Sometimes called 'carabiniers' after principle weapon, the SA-71 assault carbine.
E2	Lance Corporal	Typically would lead a fire team or specialist small unit, such as a gun crew.

E3	Corporal	Typically would lead a fire team or specialist small unit, such as a gun crew.
E4	Lance Sergeant	Typically would lead a section or specialist small unit, such as a gun crew.
E5	Sergeant	Typically would be the senior NCO in a squad or taskforce.
E6	Senior Sergeant	
E7	Master Sergeant	
E8	Sergeant Major	
O1	Ensign/ 2nd Lieutenant	The initial rank name for the most junior Marine officer rank was 'Ensign', as it had been with the Human Marine Corps. However, this proved deeply unpopular because the rank was associated with the notorious traitor, Marine Ensign Fraser McEwan. After a brief, informal use of 'Subaltern', the Legion had settled on '2nd Lieutenant' by the time of the First Tranquility Campaign. Other services, notably the Navy, continue to use 'Ensign' as the O1 rank name.
O2	Lieutenant	
O3	Captain	
O4	Major	Officer ranks above O4 were not added until later. This caused some friction in the First Tranquility Campaign because the Marine O4-ranked Major McEwan was in overall command of the Legion, despite the presence of Navy O5-ranked Captain Indiya.

SERVICE: VOID NAVY

E1	Spacer	Void Navy personnel qualified as flight crew take the prefix 'flying'. For example, 'Flying Petty Officer'. The Atmospheric Air Force take the same approach but use the prefix 'flight', as in 'Flight Sergeant'.
E2	Leading Spacer	Navy ranks are often officially referred to along with their specialism. For example: 'Spacer – damage control'. Or 'Leading Spacer – signals'. The same is true unofficially, of course. Naval signals specialists would be more likely in everyday shipboard life to be called 'bunting tossers', though not always to their face.

E3	Petty Officer	
E4	Chief Petty Officer	More senior enlisted ranks were added later.
O1	Ensign	
O2	Lieutenant	
O3	Lieutenant Commander	
O4	Commander	
O5	Captain	Ranks above O5 were added later. The rank of Reserve Captain was considered an honorary rank assigned to a unique Jotun individual.

Different services, and even units within those services, have always had an insatiable tendency to foster a sense of distinctiveness. These can manifest as subtle differences in uniform insignia, saluting, protocol in addressing superiors, rituals of remembrance, and of course, rank naming. That distinctiveness helps to build the core belief that your unit is truly the best. A common practice is to reach back in time to Earth history and re-invent ancient rituals and terminology and apply them to the modern era.

For example, the official name of the E0 rank for Army units is 'Rifleman' [*used equally for both genders*]. However, some army units insist on using archaic terms such as 'Private', 'Fusilier', or 'Infantryman'. In addition, 'Rifleman' and 'Fusilier' are sometimes used to refer to all personnel in a unit, even officers (although at other times, junior enlisted ranks only), much as 'Marine' or 'Carabinier' is used in this way by Void Marines.

Some other common formal and informal terms for junior enlisted ranks by service:
Engineer: Digger, Sapper
Diplomacy: Speaker, Schmooze.
Supply/ Logistics: Trucker, Wagoneer
Artillery: Gunner, Bombardier
Signals: Signaler, Flag waver or bunting tosser (after an ancient form of visual communication), Tapper (after the encoding tool used in ancient electromagnetic telegraphy)

A NOTE ON GENDER IN RANK NAMING

The Human language is a senseless wonder, with such an ability to absorb loan words that alien linguists regard Human speech as a pigeon trading language. The use of gender in addressing service personnel is one example of haphazard convention that has grown up with little logic or consistency.

Several ranks take on a male form, such as *Rifleman*, but are applied indiscriminately to both male and female, and indeed, non-human personnel. Some say this is a tradition from a past when infantry soldiers were almost always male. Probably the 'man' ending has endured because it is a single syllable.

But there are other conventions, equally illogical, that stem from more recent tradition. For many centuries, human combat personnel were led by Jotun officers, and senior Jotuns were predominately female. As a result when referring to officers in general, rather than to a specific individual with a known gender, they are always referred to as 'she'. For example, an officer training guide might have the sentence: 'For an officer to be effective, she must understand and earn the respect of her senior NCOs.'

A male officer would not find this strange in the slightest, any more than a female E0 infantry soldier would think twice about referring to herself as a rifleman. If questioned on this point, both would readily point to many examples of far more convoluted military logic.

Another gender issue – the protocol for addressing superior female officers – is also inconsistent. Marine and Atmospheric Air Force units tend use the address "ma'am", while Navy and Army use "sir".

This infopedia section was extracted from humanlegion.com.

HUMAN EMPIRE

The fourth book in the annals of the Human Legion. Available now.

—THE LEGION ARMORY 2018—
REVENGE SQUAD
PAYBACK IS PROFITABLE
2761AD. Space opera / urban fantasy adventure in the aftermath of the War of Liberation.
HURT U BACK 2016
SECOND STRIKE 2017
BLOOD FEEDER TBC
DAMAGE UNLIMITED 2017
AFTER WAR 2016
Images: Vincent Sammy
SLEEPING LEGION
NO ONE LEFT BEHIND
2565AD. Military science fiction.
Humans vs. Hardits ... and traitors.
THE DEMONS OF ISKOR-LIR 2016
THE LEGION AWAKES 2016
FORTRESS BETA CITY 2016
OPERATION BREAKOUT 2017
THE ENEMY BELOW 2017
HUMAN LEGION
FREEDOM CAN BE WON
2565AD. Five centuries ago, a million children were sold as slaves to alien masters.
NOW THEY WANT THEIR FREEDOM BACK!
MARINE CADET 2014
INDIGO SQUAD 2015
RENEGADE LEGION 2015
HUMAN EMPIRE 2015
WHITE KNIGHTS 2016
BATTLE EARTH 2018
Cover Images: Vincent Sammy
THRILL ADDICT 2018
MARINE NOVICE TBC
THE SLOUGH OF DESPOND 2011
THE CITY OF DESTRUCTION 2011
2016
HUMANLEGION.COM
Join the Legion online now for free books to launch your journey into each series.

Printed in Great Britain
by Amazon